· THE CANADIAN COMPACT ·

JASON CONNOR

THE
PRODIGAL
SPY

QUAGMIRE
PRESS

The Publisher: Quagmire Press Ltd.
Website: www.quagmirepress.com

Library and Archives Canada Cataloguing in Publication

Connor, Jason, 1977–, author
The prodigal spy / Jason Connor.

ISBN 978-1-926695-19-8 (pbk.)

I. Title.

PS8605.O5647P76 2014   C813'.6   C2013-907110-5

Project Director: Hank Boer
Project Editor: Kathy van Denderen
Cover Images: running spy silhouette © photobank.kiev.ua / Shutterstock;
Canada Place, Vancouver © Volodymyr Kyrylyuk / Photos.com

Produced with the assistance of the Government of
Alberta, Alberta Media Fund.

Alberta

PC: 27

To my family. For everything.

CHAPTER 1

In the midst of the fog, there was water.

He couldn't feel it, couldn't taste it, but he could hear it. He'd heard it on his first day, dripping somewhere behind the cold, stone walls that enclosed him on four sides. He'd even moved the ragged blanket through the dusty floor to lie beside the spot where the dripping was loudest. At his worst, when the drugs wore off, when the pain returned, when the suffocation of isolation felt as if it would choke the life from his soul, he would lie on his blanket, press his ear to the wall and listen, slowly counting.

He did so now as the latest fog began to lift and his senses sharpened. On days like these, days where he was gratefully left to wallow in the dark, musty cell, he counted the drips more obsessively. He knew exactly how many drops fell between meals and between regularly scheduled guard changes. If his captors had been wise to his plan, they would have sought out the source of the drip and stopped it, or at the very least moved him to a different cell. The cardinal rule of interrogation, of solitary confinement, of torture, was to deprive the prisoner of any sense of time, whether it was day or night or how much time had elapsed between visits by guards or interrogators. In a perfect situation, Daniel would have no clue whether the last interrogator had come three minutes or three hours ago. The objective was to render the prisoner so uncomfortable as to make him more pliable, more open to suggestion. Daniel Davis was trained in using such techniques and in holding out against them. That dripping pipe, deep in the recesses of the prison, was his lifeline.

He didn't understand why the *Mabahith* interrogators were drugging him so frequently, but he didn't mind. Daniel puzzled that if the roles were reversed, if his interrogator was in this cell, Daniel would try to aggravate him as much as possible. He'd want the man he dubbed "Skinny" (since his interrogator had not offered a name, Daniel had come up with his own) bouncing off the walls from sheer frustration and discomfort. Instead, after every interrogation session, no matter how casual or painful, a medic appeared from behind a recessed door. For what Daniel judged had been the first few weeks, the bespectacled man would wait until two burly guards wrestled Daniel to the floor and then the medic injected Daniel with a sedative. Within moments, regardless the part of his body that was bleeding or broken,

Daniel would find himself awash in a chemically induced serenity, his memories overshadowed by a hue of euphoria. But if the drug was meant to make Daniel more pliable, it wasn't working.

At first, Daniel thought he had been injected with heroin or some other highly addictive, illegal street drug, given the terrible tremors and cravings he experienced several days after the drug wore off. But when Daniel began to show more compliance and deference to his captors, the medic gave him pills instead. Perhaps the two infections Daniel had developed at the injection site had spooked the spooks into letting their prisoner take drugs himself—God knew the antibiotics were supposed to be taken with food, and they sure weren't giving Daniel enough of that to stave off the nausea, heartburn and diarrhea. Maybe they were trying to offer him some semblance of control over his own body in the hopes he would talk more. Whatever the reason, instead of giving him injections, his captors were now giving Daniel one enormous, oval-shaped white pill, scored in the middle. The medic gave him tea to wash it down, inspected his mouth afterwards, then grunted gruffly to the guards, who escorted Daniel back to his cell and locked the solid iron door behind them.

When he was alone, Daniel would curl up in a corner, drape his disgusting blanket over his head and jam his fingers down his throat. Gagging silently, fighting back the waves of revulsion and acid taste of bile on his tongue, he coughed up the pill. He then used his fingernail to break the partially digested pill in half and swallowed the remainder. He kept the pill segments tucked into a corner of his cell, hiding them under the thick dust and ground mortar. He knew he had to keep up the appearance of being stoned. So he would gather his blanket around him on the floor, curl up against the wall and listen.

He also needed at least half of the pill to stave off withdrawal symptoms and to keep the pulsating pain in his bruised and battered body at a level he could tolerate. Already his fingers were swollen and crooked from being deliberately broken and then poorly set. His thick beard hid the scrapes, bruises and scars from the regular beatings that the skin below his neck could not. His forearms were burned from cigarettes and hot pokers, his fingernails ripped apart and his feet calloused from countless whippings.

He'd even been deliberately sodomized once, without a doubt the absolute worst experience he had ever endured. He hadn't had any clever one-liners for the guard who had used his nightstick in ways the manufacturer probably never intended. Daniel had vomited violently after the ordeal, and in every subsequent interrogation session, Skinny forced him to sit to inflict as much discomfort as possible. And the guard and his stick always stood just to one side. But his interrogators hadn't tortured him in that way since, and Daniel didn't know why, nor did he care. Maybe it had offended their Muslim sensibilities too much, he wondered.

Chalk one up for religiously fanatical homophobia, he noted wryly, letting the drugs obliterate the memory.

Daniel didn't really know how much time had passed because he had no way of measuring the number of drops in a minute, an hour, and so on. He believed he had been imprisoned for about a month and a half, maybe two. He knew from the prison guard uniforms that he was under the control of the *Mabahith,* Saudi Arabia's secret police and home to the kingdom's religious zealots, sadists and psychopaths charged with maintaining the homogenous moral order. Suspected sedition, terrorism, crimes outlined in *sharia* law, all fell under the purview of the *Mabahith* that operated within the Middle East country with total impunity, with the blessing of the King himself.

And the *Mabahith* had imprisoned him, meaning he was being kept in the `Ulaysha Prison in the western part of Riyadh, or as Daniel referred to it in Arabic for his captors, the "hair follicle in the armpit of the universe," an insult that never went over well and always led to more beatings. What he knew of the compound he had learned in his previous life, before being forced to run, before they had found him and locked him away. The prison was modest, but obsolete compared to its Western counterparts—Daniel's cell didn't have a video camera, something that the prisons back home would not have overlooked. The walls were crumbling, and the few glimpses he got of life outside his cell cemented his opinion that `Ulaysha deserved to be retired.

It lacked the security systems and modern equipment of other detention buildings, relying on its architecture to deter any thoughts of escape. Heavy doors, small, cramped spaces and little access to the world outside.

His cell was the last one at the end of a long, tunnel-like hallway. When he was taken from his cell—and lucid—he took in as much as he could of his surroundings without appearing to be overly interested. The carved stone ceiling gave him the impression he was underground. The only set of doors he'd been taken through was at the end of the hall from his cell, to the left. Through those doors was a staircase to the right, and to the left, another door that he'd seen opened exactly once, to allow a service person carrying electrical tools to enter, under guard.

The route to the interrogation and torture rooms for Daniel's meetings with Skinny involved climbing 132 stairs, no small feat in his weakened condition. At the top, a single door led to another hallway that branched out into several directions. He had been down every hallway, but they all led to just another interrogation room where Skinny and his gang were waiting. He noted that Skinny emerged from the recessed doors, beside the two-way mirror. Despite not having access to a window, Daniel knew the outside world was close. Inside the interrogation room, he had seen the mirror wobble and the table tremble, and he heard the faint, passing hum of traffic. The prison's old walls were starting to betray her.

Daniel's captors led him to various interrogation rooms on a regular schedule. Daniel could identify each room by the slight differences in the fluorescent lights and the markings on the tables at which he sat as they peppered him with questions. He paid more attention soon after his capture, when he'd had the strength to fight back or behave defiantly. It was all an act, of course. He dutifully slid into the role of obedient prisoner. Not subservient enough to give up his secrets, but pliable enough not to kick up a fuss.

His captors were acutely aware that if they kept Daniel too long, they'd end up causing more problems for themselves. It was an old trick in the intelligence community called the dead-man's switch or a fail-deadly strategy. The Saudis believed Daniel had information stashed away somewhere, and that if he failed to check in with someone at a certain time or with certain frequency, that information would be released under the assumption that Daniel had been captured or killed.

Daniel planted the suggestion without revealing specifics and was evasive in his answers, even under torture. He'd used the idea to his advantage just two days before, intimating that the time for a check-in was imminent. His tactic gave him access to a computer under heavy guard and allowed him to send a "coded message" from an untraceable email account. The code was not a real fail-deadly strategy because Daniel didn't yet have enough information to create one. However, the code told the receiver he had been captured and set the wheels in motion, ensuring that no matter what happened to Daniel, his son would be protected.

His captors knew, of course. It was only a matter of time before they found out he had a son. As far as Daniel could tell, his captors didn't know where his son was, but it wouldn't take the *Mabahith* long to find out. In his last interrogation, Skinny had asked questions about a son that were so specific, Daniel knew he had to act. The two sides had reached a stalemate—the Saudis were worried that Daniel might have ordered the release of sensitive information if he disappeared, and Daniel feared they had found his son—though both Daniel and his interrogators hid their anxiety.

For now, Daniel stifled his emotions. He needed to rest. Tonight was important. In 1715 drops, the Saudis would learn that in the game of spy versus spy, predictability was the worst offence any person worthy of the title "intelligence operative" could commit.

Sadly, one of the nicest people Daniel knew in this hellhole might have to die before the Saudis would learn the lesson.

CHAPTER 2

1597...1598

The drips came more slowly now as Daniel's appointed time neared. His nerves coalesced in his belly, in his limbs; his whole body trembled with anticipation. He counted the tiny splashes beyond the wall while trying not to let his mind wander.

Predictability would free him tonight, providing all went as planned. But becoming a creature of habit had landed him here in the first place after nine years on the run.

It had not been an easy time, charged with the responsibility of proving something that seemed unbelievable. He had sacrificed much in his pursuit of the facts, including the only family he had. At a critical point in his teenage son's life, Daniel had been forced to disappear, to vanish without a trace, leaving his boy thinking he was gone forever.

Daniel had kept tabs on his son as best he could while travelling through some of the world's most politically inhospitable zones, trying to piece together a large and convoluted puzzle. His sources sent him encrypted emails containing photos, short videos and updates on his now-adult son's status, but Daniel's absence was worse than if his son had died. Receiving regular updates but being unable to speak with him, to touch him, to even pass on some small sign that Daniel was alive and well tortured his soul.

But his boy was flourishing—he knew that much. And Daniel hadn't completely abandoned him—unlike his son's mother who had left shortly after his birth and hadn't been heard from since. Daniel always wired money to his sources to be placed in a trust account that was funnelled to his son in the guise of "life insurance." Daniel was heartened to find out that his son chose hard work instead of a free ride and was excelling in his endeavours. But his son had always wanted more than the world could provide him materially.

The rules were simple—the money was never sent on the same day or at the same time, and never from the same location. Yet Daniel had fallen victim to the complacency of spending nine years in relative safety. Although he had known better, during a brief stay in Iran, he had wired the cash from a bank he had used before.

Despite the safeguards he'd put in place, despite the escape plans he'd rehearsed, despite the disguise he wore, despite all he knew about personal protection, Daniel was no match for a trained squad of counter-espionage agents. He'd been cornered in his hotel room in Tehran as the secret police descended on him. He was beaten, drugged and shipped to

Saudi Arabia, where he was turned over to the *Mabahith* and locked away.

He could have endured this prison for a while longer, to negotiate, to give a little information, until he could find a way to escape. But the mere mention of his son, a trail he had tried so hard to obfuscate, panicked him. When Skinny broached the subject with him the first time, it took all of Daniel's training not to reveal the façade—part smarmy, part acquiescent—he had maintained since his imprisonment. He knew he had to make a move. He'd been stockpiling his medication for weeks, but the revelation that they knew about his son forced him to act. Daniel had to get to his son before they did.

1709...1710...and here he is! Showtime!

Like clockwork, Daniel heard a key scrape in the door lock, and the iron beast groaned open, allowing artificial light to flare in the darkness around him. He covered his eyes while he lay motionless on the ground, gradually spreading his fingers so his eyes could adjust to the light. He would have to move fast.

"Masaa el kheer," a soft voice said in Arabic. Daniel didn't know the name of this guard but called him Ishmael in his own mind. The tall, gaunt, bearded man was his ticket to freedom.

Ishmael had been a constant presence during Daniel's imprisonment. The guard's bearing and attitude were completely different from Daniel's interrogators.

Ishmael appeared at his cell at the same time every night, with a small tray of tea for the two of them to share. Daniel recognized Ishmael for exactly what he was—a "good cop." After Daniel had suffered countless hours of torture and interrogation, Ishmael would always offer tea, kind words and expressions of concern. He was the foil to every other guard Daniel encountered, planted to forge a friendly bond that might somehow make Daniel more pliable.

Daniel enjoyed the tea, especially since they'd stopped lacing it with drugs a few weeks before. And he took pleasure in the conversation, as would any isolated captive.

"*Masaa el kheer,*" Daniel replied haltingly. He was fluent in Arabic—but for the colour of his skin, he could pass as a resident of Riyadh. But no one needed to know more about his language abilities than he wished.

Ishmael had also recently stopped handcuffing Daniel during their tea time, likely another attempt at building Daniel's trust. He was also never searched. After all, he had nothing in his room that he could use to attack anyone.

Ishmael retreated through the door, picked up a tray with a teapot and two glasses, then entered the cell again.

"It is another lovely night in Riyadh," Ishmael said, bending down to place the tray on the floor. "Almost no traffic to speak of. The air smells as if it has been cleaned."

"I'm glad to hear your evening has been pleasant," Daniel replied.

"My wife would not think so," the guard said, straightening up, then turning to his left, towards the corner of the cell nearest the door. He slowly swung the Heckler & Koch G3 battle rifle off his shoulder to stow it, a gesture Daniel believed Ishmael did to demonstrate trust and friendship. "She grows weary of these night shifts. She tires of spending her day alone with our children while I sleep after work..."

As soon as Ishmael turned to the wall, Daniel whipped out his right hand, silently removed the cap from the teapot and dumped in the ground-up medication he had hidden in his left.

"...until these night shifts end," Ishmael finished as he turned towards Daniel. "Perhaps then a getaway is in order." He spread his hands and laughed, then sat down on the floor, cross-legged.

"May I come, too?" Daniel asked. Ishmael laughed again at the suggestion, reaching for the teapot. Ishmael always played host and poured the tea.

Ishmael held his mug aloft. "To our vacation!" he said, toasting Daniel, who returned the gesture. Ishmael drank deeply while Daniel simply blew on his tea to cool it.

Daniel had to keep Ishmael inside the cell for at least five minutes, the time needed for the sedative to kick in.

"It is too hot?" Ishmael asked, noting Daniel's response to the tea. "You North Americans do not know how to handle heat. Weather, or tea or food, you are all soft."

"Remember where I come from," Daniel replied. "In Canada, we don't really have heat. There is snow on the ground eight months of the year in almost every part of the country. And in some places farther north, the snow never melts. The rest of us spend the other four months preparing for the next winter."

Ishmael laughed heartily and took another sip of his tea. "Perhaps that is where my wife and I will go on our trip. We will see Canada! We will see this 'hockey' you all play and all this snow of which you moan. Surely it cannot be as cold as you say."

"It can," Daniel replied and began regaling Ishmael with stories about ferocious blizzards, temperatures so cold that tires froze into squares and snow so deep a man could disappear without his neighbours ever noticing.

He talked for as long as he could, heartened by Ishmael's rapt attention, but more so by his guard's empty mug, which Ishmael filled again. Daniel held his mug to his lips and made a slurping sound, pretending to swallow the tea, then set the mug down.

Daniel had been consuming the drug for several months, so his body had developed some tolerance, but Ishmael succumbed within minutes. His face became flushed, and as Daniel was telling of the great Chinooks that thundered across the western Canadian plains, the guard suddenly toppled forward. Daniel moved quickly, grabbing Ishmael under the arms before he could knock over the tray and make any noise. He silently dragged Ishmael towards the wall farthest from the door.

Daniel checked the guard's vitals; his pulse felt thready and his breathing faint. Daniel frowned. He didn't want to kill the man, but death might be more favourable to Ishmael and his family when the Saudis discovered he had let their most important prisoner escape.

His hands flew over Ishmael's clothes, finding the guard's keys hooked to his belt. Daniel went over to inspect the G3. The clip was full. He jammed it back in and chambered the first round. He then rummaged through Ishmael's pockets, setting his radio transceiver, keys and ID badge into one pile while placing other non-essential items to one side. Working fast but carefully, he stripped Ishmael of his uniform, pushed the man up against the wall and slapped handcuffs on him. He threw the blanket over him, ensuring the guard's hair was hidden. He checked Ishmael's pulse again—he was still alive.

Daniel removed his shabby coveralls and placed them under the blanket. The guard was a full four inches taller than Daniel, but Daniel compensated for the poorly fitting uniform by rolling up the pant legs and shirtsleeves. He put the keys, ID badge and radio into the hip pockets, then bent to the teapot to complete his masquerade.

Disguises. His focus threatened to shatter as memories of his son flooded his brain, but Daniel steeled himself against them; he could indulge later. He thrust his right hand into the teapot and extracted a handful of tea leaves. He squeezed them hard, his fingers still aching from being broken, letting the dark liquid puddle in his cupped left palm. He smeared the tea over his face and hands. His tea-stained skin wouldn't stand up to close inspection, but hopefully the darker colour would fool any casual observers.

His light-brown hair wasn't going to fly, and neither was his beard. Although Ishmael's beret might help, it wouldn't hide everything. Daniel dumped the remnants of the tea on the floor, mixing in the dust and dirt with the sole of one of Ishmael's boots. He then mopped up the mixture with his hands and rubbed it into his hair and beard.

He had no mirror, so he had to assume the camouflage was good enough. He pulled the radio from his pocket and listened. He heard only idle, routine chatter about prisoners being escorted. From what Daniel had divined on his trips to interrogation, none of those guards would be headed anywhere near his cell.

Daniel shouldered the G3 and inhaled deeply. He took a moment to compose himself, adjusting his posture to mimic a guard, his chest full and high, his stance military-like, and even his face was awash with confidence. Passing as another person first required acting like that person, regardless how poor the disguise. And with that Daniel strode out into the hallway.

CHAPTER

The hallway was empty. Daniel quickly scanned the area as he pulled the cell door shut behind him, sliding the bolt quietly into place and locking Ishmael inside. Then he strode down the hallway. He glanced at the ceiling and walls for any sign of a camera or sensor. He saw nothing. His radio continued to buzz with the mundane chatter of prison life.

He approached the two doors at the end of the hallway. Rather than heading left towards the interrogation area, he stopped to examine the door he'd observed the service person enter. A security scanner was mounted on the wall next to the door. He reached into his pocket and pulled out Ishmael's ID card.

I hope he has clearance for this, Daniel prayed. He flashed the card in front of the scanner. The light on the scanner switched from red to green, and the lock clicked open. He shoved the door open and entered the room, closing the door behind him.

The room was dimly lit, but Daniel felt his heart dance in his chest. His inference had been bang on. What other kind of room would a service worker with a trunk load of tools enter if it weren't some kind of mechanical room? And that's exactly where he was now. He walked directly to a big, grey, padlocked box. The universal lightning-bolt sticker on it warned of its contents without anyone having to read Arabic—electricity. *Caution!*

Not wanting to waste time fumbling with Ishmael's key ring, Daniel walked over to a table with an assortment of tools splayed on its surface. Grabbing the heaviest wrench, he returned to the electrical box and hammered at the padlock. After three hard whacks, the hasp shattered, and the door sprang open. Daniel couldn't believe his luck. Not only was he staring at the main electrical junction for the building, but he could tell from the bundle of brightly coloured wires that he had also found the telephone and Internet junctions.

He stepped back, following the lines snaking across the wall and ceiling, looking for something out of place. Along the far wall to his right he found it—a thick cable that led in the opposite direction from the rest. He followed the cable into a small room that resembled a closet. He pulled a flashlight from the wall and shone it inside the room, which stored a huge generator that served as the prison's emergency power source. One sniff told him it was diesel fired.

Time to get to work. Daniel stowed the flashlight on the utility belt he'd taken from Ishmael then selected a screwdriver and set of needle-nose pliers from the table. First, the generator—Daniel walked around it, his keen eyes locating the panel over the fuel tank. One sharp jab with the screwdriver and a few pulls was all it took to puncture the tank and widen the hole. He dropped the screwdriver, ignoring the diesel pooling at his feet, and returned to the electrical box.

He used the needle-nose pliers to grab the telephone wires and yanked hard, tearing them in two. Next, he snipped the main and the back-up fibre-optic in half. Finally, Daniel bent down, his fingers poised over the large switch to the main electrical circuit, ready to throw it.

His borrowed radio crackled suddenly. And Daniel swore silently as he listened.

It was time for prayer.

Despite all the water drops he'd counted during guard changes and between his trips to the interrogation room, he hadn't been able to get a solid handle on when the guards and inmates stopped to pray. Devotees of Islam engaged in *salah* five times a day, stopping their duties to face Mecca and praise Allah.

Daniel doubted that every guard within the facility stopped what they were doing for *salah*, as someone had to keep an eye on the inmates. But those with special dispensation were likely to be few. And a guard walking when he should be praying would attract attention.

The impending blackout, Daniel deduced, should sufficiently interrupt their prayer, adding to the confusion he was trying to create.

Well, that and a little help from my fellow inmates, Daniel thought to himself. And with that, he threw the switch.

The room plunged into darkness. On cue, the emergency generator sputtered and rumbled to life, powering one small light above the electrical panel. The generator then misfired, roared again briefly, then coughed and stuttered to a halt.

Here we go, Daniel thought, opening the door. The guards would check this room first, so he needed to leave fast. He exited and, with the butt of his rifle, smashed the ID badge scanner in a rain of plastic pieces. The act was probably overkill, given that the scanner was no longer powered, but Daniel wasn't taking any chances.

He threw open the door across the hall, grateful he couldn't see a single light anywhere, and ran up the stairs, waiting for a moment on every landing to listen for descending footsteps. So far none. At the first exit, he listened briefly at the door and pushed it open, scanning the hallway. Seeing no one, he continued walking quickly, purposefully. He chose the first interrogation room on his right, entered and, feeling his way along the wall, found the recessed door beside the two-way mirror that he had noticed during one of his interrogation sessions. The door easily gave way, and he walked through.

"Who's there?" called a harsh voice in Arabic.

Daniel squinted and made out the form of a guard approaching him from a long hallway. Daniel swore under his breath for not looking at Ishmael's badge more closely. "Mohammed," he replied curtly, selecting the world's most popular Arabic name, then followed up, in Arabic, with, "What is happening?"

"I do not know," the guard replied, drawing closer. "We have lost all power, all telephones and all computers. During *salah*, no less. I have been sent to investigate. Come with me."

"What about the prisoners?" Daniel asked, moving to one side of the hallway so the guard could pass. The man headed straight for the interrogation room from which Daniel had come.

"We have deployed all guards to the population and cell areas. Some of the jail doors will not seal when there is no electricity," the guard said. "The older cells are lock and key, so they will be fine. Especially that scum in the basement."

The two walked into the interrogation room. As soon as the door clicked behind them, Daniel drove the rifle butt down as hard as he could at the base of the guard's skull. The man slid to the ground, his body twitching before his movements ceased altogether.

Daniel clicked on the flashlight briefly, examining the guard's equipment. He grabbed a collapsible baton and jammed it into one hip pocket. He took three flashbang and two tear gas grenades and placed them in the other pocket.

As he was turning to leave the room, his eye caught a glint in the darkness. Without thinking, he dropped behind the desk in the interrogation room. Sparks erupted against the wall across from him, and the unmistakable roar of a G3 sounded from the door on the other side of the room. When the shooting stopped, Daniel saw the feet of his assailant beneath the table. He was sure the muzzle flashes had blinded his attacker. Daniel rolled onto one knee, thumbing off the safety of his G3 and bringing it to bear. He closed his eyes as he fired a short burst, and when he opened his eyes, his attacker was sprawled out on the floor across the room.

Daniel's radio sprang to life, as did the two others in the room, demanding to know the source of the commotion. Daniel hurtled himself through the recessed door, down the hallway and through a second door, emerging into a darkened rotunda, but his eyes had adjusted to the darkness and he could see pretty well. He heard heavy breathing and saw a few guards milling around. Still no flashlights.

Daniel brought the radio to his lips. "The prisoner in the basement is escaping!" he shouted in Arabic, trying to sound agitated and nervous, loud enough for the guards around him to hear. "He has shot one guard already!"

The guards in the room rushed towards Daniel, who flinched momentarily as they all flew through the doorway behind him. Daniel raced towards the centre of the rotunda and looked around. He made out four separate hallways branching off the rotunda. He quietly approached one and squinted down its length. All he could see in the dim light were the outlines of open jail cell doors, shirtless bodies poised at each cell's entrance and two nervous-looking guards groping their way in the darkness, watching the prisoners who were no longer bound by electronically sealed doors. Exactly the kind of situation Daniel had hoped to create.

He reached into his hip pocket for a flashbang grenade, pulling the pin and rolling the grenade down the hallway. He turned away, shielding his eyes. A heartbeat later, a blinding light flashed in the hallway, coupled with the sharp retort of multiple, tiny explosions as the flashbang detonated. As the flash died, Daniel turned into the hallway and fired a burst from his G3 into the ceiling of the hallway.

"The guards are attacking!" he yelled over the roar of his weapon.

He retreated from the hallway, hearing the first murmurs of dissent rise above the groans of pain the grenade had caused. As he sprinted to the far side of the rotunda he could see prisoners stepping into the corridor and two guards shouting for them to return to their cells. Daniel tossed a flashbang grenade into the hallway. He heard gunshots as the guards tried to defend themselves from the screaming prisoners descending on them.

He looked behind him. Prisoners were spilling out of the two hallways he hadn't yet approached. Realizing he was still dressed as a guard, Daniel sprinted to the door at the end of the rotunda, pulling his radio to his lips.

"The prisoners are rioting!" he shouted. "The prisoners are loose."

He bulldozed his way through the door and clicked on his flashlight, pointing it towards the Plexiglas window of the control room. The room was unmanned, but Daniel's interest lay elsewhere. He reached over and ripped down a small map attached to the wall opposite the control room. The facility was etched in red on the map, showing the location of the emergency exits. The map also indicated he was in the guard's control room area for the northwest section of the building.

He looked up and saw that the control doors around him branched off into separate detention areas, which were divided further into inmate cells. He listened intently to the riot he had instigated. He allowed himself a satisfied smile then headed for the exit door shown on the map. As he moved through the halls, he tossed one of the tear gas grenades into the control room area. Anyone coming out or going in would come face-to-face with a wall of tear gas.

Daniel climbed the stairs in front of him, listening to his radio. The prison population was in an uproar, and guards were reporting to their muster points, demanding flashlights or lanterns—anything to be able to see what was happening. Injured guards overtaken by prisoners cried out for help before their pleas were abruptly cut short.

As far as Daniel could tell, the riot was not taking place near him.

He was sweating now, his body feeling the strain of his actions. His legs trembled as he took the stairs two at a time until he came upon a set of double doors. His brain felt foggy from symptoms of drug withdrawal and starvation. Daniel forced himself to move faster, to get it over with. But rushing when he was so close to freedom would be a recipe for failure. He paused at the doors to take a deep breath.

Daniel entered a large room. To either side were lockers, and benches ran down the centre—the guards' change room. Daniel moved from locker to locker, searching for one that was unlocked. The first open one revealed a set of clothes that were much too small. The second was empty, but the third contained a billowing *thawb*, or robe, sunglasses and *ghutra an iqal*, or headdress. He dug further into the locker and found a set of keys on a fob. He swiftly stripped off Ishmael's uniform, except for the pants, which had sets of pockets for the grenades he'd stolen. He slipped the robe over his head, careful not to let the fabric wipe the tea stain off his face and hair. He reached in and pulled out a small white cap, or *kaffia*, that he put over his head then covered it with the larger, square, checkered *shemagh*, positioning it diagonally. Last came the *agal*, or black cord, which Daniel had to stretch to secure the *shemagh* and *kaffia* in place on his head. He stuffed the rest of Ishmael's uniform in the locker and turned to go.

The lights came on.

Daniel stumbled back onto the bench separating the walls of lockers, blinded. He squeezed his eyes shut and then opened them gradually to adjust to the light. With each passing second, his vision adapted, but his eyes still stung from his time spent in the dark. He again rooted through the locker and sighed in relief as his fingers grasped a pair of aviator sunglasses. They were too big for his slender face, but Daniel put them on.

He had to move fast. Part of his escape plan hinged on executing it in darkness, without guns blazing as if in a scene from some terrible prison-break movie. He inched his way to the locker room's exit and opened the door slowly then closed it quietly after taking in the surroundings in less than a second. Only one small room stood between him and the outside, but one guard was at a desk and the other was roaming the room. Both men were talking animatedly into their radios. Daniel listened in—his disappearance had been noticed. Orders were going out over the airwaves to lock down the prison.

The element of surprise was his last tool. The guards didn't know where he was, but he didn't want to give them the opportunity to find out. He retreated farther into the change room, grabbed the last flashbang and tear gas grenades and stashed them in the pockets beneath his robe. He wrapped the rifle strap around his shoulder then reached into a second open locker. Inside he found another *kaffia*.

This is going to be uncomfortable, Daniel thought, steeling the last of his resolve and pulling the pin on the tear gas grenade. Whispers of gas slowly emerged. He held the *kaffia* to his nose and mouth with one hand, squinted as best he could and, holding the grenade in his other hand, he carefully pushed the door open with his butt. With gas spewing from the grenade, he rolled it through the door where it hit the floor, rolled and came to rest right beside the guard's station, billowing gas. Daniel reached beneath his robe for the flashbang, pulled the pin and tossed it in after the tear gas grenade. He shielded himself behind the closed door.

The hiss of gas was drowned out by the sharp bang of the grenade igniting. Startled cries from the guards beyond dissolved into choking sounds and the splash of vomit hitting the floor as the tear gas took effect.

Holding the *kaffia* as close to his mouth and nose as possible, Daniel pushed the door open. Through eyes already smarting from the gas, he saw a dark shape bent over in front of him, hacking uncontrollably. Wasting no time, Daniel delivered a sharp kick to the guard's stomach, knocking him to the floor. Hopping over the crumpled man, he closed his eyes and sprinted for the exit, when he was sure the gas had incapacitated the guard behind the desk. His eyes began to tear even more, and a growing tingle at the back of his throat told him he didn't have much time.

When he reached the door, he slammed his whole body into it. It gave way, sending Daniel onto sun-drenched concrete, his sunglasses hurled to the side.

And Ishmael said he worked the night shift, Daniel thought, grimacing.

He knew he was not alone. He heard the surprised cry of another voice but dared not open his eyes and expose them to the brilliant sunlight.

"Are you okay?" the voice called in Arabic. Daniel brushed the man's concern away with a wave of one hand as the fingers of his other hand slithered along the concrete, groping for his sunglasses. He coughed, and tears flowed from his eyes, smarting from exposure to the gas. He'd inhaled more than he'd thought.

The guard, however, was suspicious.

"What are you doing?" the voice asked, and Daniel could hear the approaching footsteps. "All guards are supposed to be on duty because of the riot! Where are you going?"

Daniel stopped his frantic search for the sunglasses and stayed as he was, bent over, seemingly on his hands and knees but actually poised on the balls of his feet, his robe concealing his position. His options were limited. The guard would shoot him before he had a chance to use his G3. Daniel heard the man flip the safety off his gun.

But as the man approached Daniel, the sunlight was suddenly less intense, and the Canadian realized the guard was standing between him and the sun. Daniel kept his head bowed as the man came closer, still barking, and Daniel still waving his hand to shoo him away. At last, a complete shadow fell over Daniel as the guard came to stand alongside him, less than a foot away. Daniel slowly opened his eyes—the light hurt, but the man's shadow provided some shade.

"I said, what are you—" the guard started to demand, but he never finished the sentence. Coiled like a snake, Daniel erupted, his left hand shoving the man's weapon away and his right hand exploding into the guard's chin. His would-be captor staggered backwards, dropping his gun, but Daniel kept at him, slamming one foot into the guard's knee and following up with a roundhouse to the temple. The guard screamed as his kneecap shifted but stopped when he fell unconscious to the ground.

As the man fell, Daniel grabbed the sunglasses from the ground and threw them on his face. He took the guard's G3, ejected the clip, threw both it and the stock away and charged through the gate ahead and into the parking lot. He looked furtively around and saw nothing out of the ordinary so he reached into his pocket for the key fob, pressing the "Lock" button and pointing it in all directions until he finally heard a furtive honk. He pressed the fob once more, and a flash of the headlights confirmed his chariot to freedom was a red Toyota Corolla. He pressed the unlock button on the fob and walked towards the car.

Just as Daniel opened the driver's door, he heard a commotion behind him, but he didn't turn around. He flung himself into the sauna-like car that had been baking in the Arab sun and then looked out the window. Two guards had come upon the body of the one Daniel had taken down. He had to get moving.

He started the engine and drove towards the gated exit. Daniel resisted the urge to gun the engine and zip away. He kept his head low and his speed reasonable as he drove past a cluster of guards. He glanced in his rear-view mirror as he passed. Not a single guard bothered to look up.

The beginnings of a smile stopped cold on Daniel's lips as he turned around the south side of the prison to the vehicle exit. It was gated and manned by three guards, all of whom were staring at the Toyota with increasing curiosity as he slowly pulled closer, their weapons tentatively coming up. They were on their guard but appeared hesitant.

Why couldn't you have driven a Mustang? He silently berated the car's owner as he sized up the situation. He had driven Corollas before. Their zero-to-100 speed was far from earth shattering. He needed more torque for a fast approach, so he fought his instincts to gun it.

He stopped the car, put it in neutral and floored the clutch and accelerator at the same time. When the needle on the tachometer inched into the red, he popped the clutch. The Corolla—as much as it could—shot forward on squealing tires, and Daniel ducked behind the steering wheel. The guards each managed to get off a burst of gunfire before two of them scurried out of the way. The third tried but was not so lucky. Daniel felt a lurch as the front fender scooped the guard up and hurled him into the air. Then came a bone-rattling crash as the car tore through the gate. Daniel gunned the engine again and turned hard, slicing between two other cars on the road.

He watched `Ulaysha disappear in his mirrors with no immediate signs of pursuit. Daniel knew that was only temporary. He had to get off the road, ditch this car and keep moving.

The logical choice was to head to the Canadian embassy in the city's diplomatic quarter, to the northwest. But logic and tradecraft weren't always best friends—his captors would expect him to head there. No, Daniel needed specialized help.

He took the next right, onto Al Imam Turki Ibn Abdullah Ibn Muhammad, and then a left on Al Dighithar, heading south. Five minutes later, he found himself in a mix of warehouses and residential homes. To his left he spotted a park with a lot of trees. He eased the car into the parking lot of the park then rooted around in the glove box. He was elated to find a handful of coins. He exited the car into the stifling heat and dropped the keys down the nearest gutter so they would not be found on him if he was stopped. Head low, he crossed the street, away from the park and onto a block dominated by large warehouses.

He crossed two more blocks, all the while the sun beating down on him. His brow was soaked, and he could feel the last of his tea-stain disguise dripping off his face. He had to get out of sight before someone noticed his strange appearance. But first he had to make a call.

Payphones were scarce thanks to the proliferation of cellphones, even in Saudi Arabia, but Daniel hadn't come to this part of Riyadh by accident—he knew exactly where to find a payphone. He jammed a few coins into it and dialled a number from memory.

A soft male voice answered. "Yes?"

"Have you received my package?" Daniel said in Arabic.

"No," a gruff voice replied. "Nothing has arrived today."

"Thank you," Daniel said, returning the handset to its cradle.

He doubled back a block and turned into a narrow alley separating two giant warehouses, hiding himself between a pair of dumpsters. He crouched down out of sight and used the inside of his robe to wipe the remaining tea from his face and hands. Again, Daniel had come to this part of town deliberately—the person meeting him knew where to find him.

The warehouses deflected the sun, but still the heat pounded down on him. His muscles twitching from the exertion of his escape, his brain mushy from lack of sleep, food and water, Daniel fought to stay alert. He prayed his message had gotten through and that he wouldn't have to wait long.

He had no water drops by which to measure time, but he guessed thirty minutes had passed when he finally saw the car scoot past. Daniel calmly stood up, checking his surroundings. The car parked on the street, and the driver pulled down the sun visor on the windshield to indicate he had not been followed. The man got out of the driver's seat, opened the trunk of the vehicle then returned to his place behind the wheel.

Daniel waited a full ten minutes before shuffling across the street, climbing inside the trunk of the car and pulling the lid down. He exhaled loudly as the car drove away.

"There is water for you" the man spoke, just as Daniel felt something cold roll up to his arm. He grabbed the water bottle and drank greedily. The trunk was stiflingly hot, but the water tasted as if it had been carved from an iceberg.

For the first time since he was captured, Daniel felt like he was truly back in the game.

CHAPTER

Gavin Thresher looked up when he heard the knock. The distraction made him forget about the migraine slowly starting to build. The pounding headache came whenever he stared at a computer screen too long.

Why did we ever get rid of plain old paper? Thresher thought, yearning for the ten-thousandth time for the return of the file folder. *Easier on the eyes and harder to steal.*

"Adam. Come in," he beckoned to the tall, thin man standing at the office doorway. Adam Young, barely twenty-four, bobbed his head nervously and shut the door behind him as he strode into Thresher's office.

Interesting, Thresher thought, noting the closed door. Even in this office, a closed door meant a particularly serious discussion. Thresher rummaged in his desk drawer for a bottle of ibuprofen, tossed four pills in his mouth and washed them down with cold coffee.

Adam swallowed, his face flushed red. Going in to speak to Thresher was intimidating for most, let alone someone just fresh out of university. And Adam, dressed in simple bargain-brand khakis and a Costco shirt-and-tie combination, felt almost naked in front of Thresher, who wore his typical tailored suit and shirt with French cuffs.

"Out with it, Young," Thresher said, leaning back in his chair.

Adam exhaled once heavily, his lips spluttering as he did so then he screwed up his courage and blurted out his news.

"Gunsight's gone, sir," he managed. "Gone."

Thresher was not a person given to undue alarm, preferring to approach problems methodically in order to engineer a favourable result given in the worst possible scenario, but Adam's news angered him deeply.

"How long?" Thresher asked, picking at a non-existent lint ball on his shirtsleeve, trying to conceal his concern.

"Twelve hours, sir," Adam gulped.

"Dammit!" Thresher exclaimed, unable to contain his rage any longer and slamming a fist down on his desk and making Young jump. "Twelve hours, and they're just telling us now? What's wrong with them?"

"I don't know, sir," Young stammered.

"That was rhetorical," Thresher snapped, standing abruptly. "Twelve hours. They'll never catch him in Riyadh now. He's probably already out of the country."

"Yes, sir," Adam nodded.

Thresher wished his office had a window. Sometimes he would catch himself pacing and thinking he'd be a lot more productive, solve a lot more problems, if he had a window to stare out of when he was pacing. But windows weren't much use in a basement, especially in a basement office in Burnaby, BC.

"All right," Thresher said. "Get me Gunsight's file for the last six years. And grab anything from the time we know he spent in Saudi Arabia. Contacts, drop points, safe houses both old and new. I don't expect we'll get him on such a clumsy error, not twice."

"Yes, sir," Adam replied before bolting for the door.

"And Adam?"

Young came to an abrupt halt at the door, his shoulders slumping noticeably.

"Do not tell anyone else. Not a soul. Gunsight isn't a team sport."

Adam nodded again and left.

CHAPTER

Two days passed, but Daniel wasn't aware.

Time passed in a tortured, silent scream as he lay on a small cot, huddled in blankets despite the suffocating heat of Riyadh, despite the sweat that drenched his entire body. He shivered, he thrashed, he tried to sleep, but when he closed his eyes, he saw the nightmares of his imprisonment. He would bolt upright and scream, only to be eased back down on his bed by strong hands that held him in place. Hands that brought water to his lips and placed a cool cloth over his brow as his body purged itself of the drugs he had been forced to consume for so long, even the half doses.

Daniel had no idea which drug his jailers had given him. He and his caregiver had discussed the best approach before Daniel had succumbed to the throws of withdrawal and decided against using another drug to quell the symptoms of his withdrawal. He had no time for prolonged detoxification—he had to suffer through the worst to recover in the shortest time possible. His skin crawled, as if tiny ants were wriggling in his veins. At times pain shot through his muscles, followed by icy chills. But every time he thrashed out, tried to run, tried to fight, those same hands soothed him, bundling him back under his blankets.

Eventually, without even noticing, Daniel slept. He knew he had slept only because, slowly as if emerging from under water, he awoke. His head ached, but his mind was clear at last, the delirium that had consumed him little more than a whisper. He threw back the sweat-soaked blanket and sat up, taking in his surroundings.

The room was simple—one door, closed. The walls were white plaster but dirty. The light from the single window was dim as the sun hovered just above the horizon, but Daniel didn't know if it was setting or rising. Dark orange rays lanced through the window, bathing the far wall in shadows. He did not know the day, the month or the time.

Worst...hangover...ever, Daniel mused. *But at least I'm wearing pants.*

He put his right hand on the wall for support and gradually raised himself up, assessing his body for signs of vertigo, but he managed to stand upright without feeling nauseous. His legs trembled from weakness, but he took a deep breath and tentatively stepped forward and opened the door.

Outside the room was a modest home, poor by first-world standards. Threadbare rugs covered the crumbling tile floors in the narrow hallways. Daniel steadied himself with hands on either wall as he worked his way down the hallway. He still heard nothing.

He emerged into a small room lit by oil lamps placed on rickety-looking tables. It was part living room, kitchen and dining room with two chairs—for guests. Everyone who lived here likely sat and also slept on the floor. One person was sitting there now.

"Isaac," Daniel breathed, lowering himself to the floor across from the scrawny man.

"*Sahib*," Isaac replied, nodding his head. "You are well?"

"As well as I can be," Daniel replied. He nodded gratefully as Isaac gestured towards a chipped tea service. Isaac handed his guest a glass of tea then retreated to a table, from which he produced a rudimentary tray of bread and butter. Daniel couldn't help himself and stuffed his mouth.

"How many days?" he asked between bites.

"Two since I found you," Isaac said quietly. "You were not well during that time."

Daniel nodded. "Your family?"

"Gone," Isaac replied. "Visiting friends."

"Unsupervised?" Daniel asked, almost incredulous.

Isaac smiled wanly. "My brother is with them. He believes I am sick. He knows nothing."

Daniel regarded his comrade, someone he had once dubbed his "secretary of Middle Eastern affairs." He had met Isaac three years earlier when his particular occupation had proven beneficial to Daniel. The two had since bonded as Daniel had relied on Isaac for help whenever he was in the country, help Isaac had always been willing to give him.

Isaac was a truck driver, and he and his family of seven subsisted only on his wages, but also with some help from Daniel. It was, in part, an agreed-upon ruse. Daniel's direct assistance was small, but enough to make sure Isaac's family was fed and clothed.

The real payoff for Isaac would come when Daniel no longer needed his services. Daniel had stashed away bonds and mutual funds for Isaac on the condition he moved his family out of Saudi Arabia to the West. When that happened, Isaac would be a rich man.

Daniel still needed Isaac in Saudi Arabia, however, and he didn't want Isaac to arouse suspicion. In a country as well policed as Saudi Arabia, a sudden increase in fortune would alert even the most incompetent police officer.

"You have it?" Daniel asked.

Isaac nodded, reaching for a bag against the far wall and handing it over. Daniel rifled through the contents: passports, currency, toiletries, a change of clothes and other odds and ends, even a handgun. They all came from a drop Daniel had established years earlier and rotated frequently. Daniel gave the items a cursory glance then placed them to one side.

"When can we leave?" Daniel asked.

"Within the hour," Isaac said. "I have some drilling parts to deliver to Jeddah."

"Then let us go." Daniel stood. "Just give me a few moments."

"Of course. Where will you go?"

"Egypt, by Safaga," Daniel replied.

"I feel bad for you, *Sahib*," Isaac said. "First, I place you in the trunk of a car, and now you must ride in a crate."

"I've been stuck in smaller places for a lot longer," Daniel said, laughing.

CHAPTER

Houston, Texas
March 31
9:17 AM

Heavy rain lashed the windows of the high-rise, the dark clouds completely blotting out the sun. Twenty storeys up, the storm was more violent, the wind angrier than on the streets below, suiting the atmosphere of the room.

International calls were not uncommon in this office, especially those from the Middle East. When it came to drilling for oil, American companies had their fingers in every black gold pie they could find across the world. Sometimes their own workers outnumbered the locals on-site. Running a multi-billion-dollar industry, from drilling to shipping to refining, was a complicated business.

But this one phone call had seriously dampened the mood in the room. The three individuals—two men and one woman—that had convened for the conference call were now silent as the conversation wound down.

No one spoke, and the phone line hissed with the static of the ongoing encryption taking place between the secure phone in the room and the one on the other end in Saudi Arabia.

"We have no leads," the voice on the phone said again, trying to prompt a reaction from the three people in the room. Had the caller been able to see their faces, he likely would have also remained silent. Every word jabbed like a painful blow.

"How did this happen?" shouted one of the men, his Texan drawl making his words as accented as those of the caller.

"We underestimated the man," the source said, swallowing audibly. "He is more cunning than we thought. He was able to—"

"We don't need to hear the details again!" a slender, younger man at the head of the table snapped. The voice fell silent. "We need to know what you're going to do about it. Did you get anything at all from him?"

"Not a drop," the source said. "He admitted nothing. He was unlike anyone we have seen before—a stone."

"Even stones can be broken," the younger man said.

"Not this one. We tried everything. He suffered at our hands. But he never once broke. Even when we confronted him with his different aliases, with the mention of a child, he said nothing."

The young man banged the table in frustration. "So what's your next step then?"

"All of our forces have been alerted to his escape, but he has almost certainly left Riyadh, if not the country. He likely has help. Considering how long it took to find him the first time, capturing him again will not be easy."

"What do you need from us?" the paunchy older man drawled.

"At this time, patience," the source said. "Rushing headlong into nothing will only make us more vulnerable. This must be left to the professionals. Bumbling along will only ruin our chances of finding him."

The words hung in the room. "Ruin" was too kind a word for the worst possible outcome.

"Just remember, we all have a hell of a lot to lose," the younger man said, standing and approaching the phone menacingly. "Both sides of this *arrangement* will go down if the truth ever comes to light."

"We all know this. To state the obvious is to waste time. If there is nothing else?"

The younger man looked around the room. The other two shook their heads.

"No," he said. "Nothing else."

"Then I will be in touch when there is more to say. *Ma'a salama.*" And the connection was severed.

"Right," the young man said, stabbing a button to silence the phone. "*Peace be with you*, my ass."

The three in the room looked uncomfortable. No one made eye contact or spoke. It was as if they had all been told their parents had died.

"If they can't handle this, we'll have to make provisions," the older man piped up.

"I think most of us made those years ago, but it might be worth making sure all your contingency plans are intact," his younger associate replied. "But we can't just leave this in their hands. If they fail again, we'll have to deal with it ourselves."

"What choice do we have?" the older man offered. His words cast a gloom over the conference room that matched the weather outside.

"We do have our sources," a middle-aged woman dressed in a dark pant suit said. "We can bring those to bear at any time."

"They have theirs as well," the young man said. "We know we are not alone in this. We're not the only ones with a vested interest in the outcome. If he can't handle it, our other friends can."

"But not without making a lot of noise," the woman countered. "I'm losing confidence we'll be able to end this as quietly as we'd hoped."

The three fell silent, but the rain did not. The staccato hammer pounded at them further.

"For now, we put our faith in our friends," the young man said. "They might just be able to handle the situation."

He surveyed the room, but neither of the faces turned towards him seemed the slightest bit hopeful.

⟨⟩

"Yes?" Adam Young asked, after lifting the phone to his ear.

"It is Jericho."

Young could hear the pauses created by the satellite transmission of the call from Saudi Arabia to Burnaby. "Go ahead," he said curtly.

"I had Gunsight," said the clipped voice over the receiver. "He boarded the ferry at Jeddah for Safaga."

"You're certain?"

"I walked him to the gate myself."

"When?"

"Yesterday. It was not safe for me to call until today."

"Thank you," Young said. "You will be rewarded for your duty." He placed the receiver back in its cradle and paused for a moment.

He looked over his shoulder to the windows into Thresher's office. The big man was reclined in his seat, flipping through a file.

Young tapped a number on his phone. "Sir, do you have a moment? We just had a call in from Jericho."

⟨⟩

"I do love Rome in the spring," Daniel said, craning his head skyward.

A dissatisfied grunt came from behind a newspaper, but Daniel didn't notice. He was lost in the moment, staring at the towering obelisk that loomed over the Fountain of the Four Rivers in the Piazza Navona. Its gurgles and glubs almost washed away any concerns of operational security, threat assessment and tradecraft.

"Bernini was a genius, wasn't he?" Daniel tried again.

"Sorry! I'm not responding because I'm still pissed," said the voice from behind the newspaper.

"About what?"

Craig Milken yanked the newspaper down, crumpling it in the process. "That you spent God knows how long in some Saudi prison, and I'm only hearing about it now," he almost bellowed.

"You're retired," Daniel commented. "How were you supposed to know? And what could you do about it?"

"Something," the "retired" Central Intelligence Agency operations officer fumed. "I might not know right now, but I would have done something. How'd you get out anyway?"

"Jeddah to Port Sudan," Daniel said with a yawn. "A little farther south than I really wanted to go, but I'm a little paranoid now." He gazed at his friend, thinking that the private sector had been good to his long-time friend and nemesis. Despite their different nationalities, they had often worked together, and sometimes against one another, but their friendship had endured two decades.

Craig had once been overweight, balding and pale, but he was now slimmer, his skin was more lively and coloured, and hair plugs replaced the bald patches caused by years of stress. Instead of careening around the world for Uncle Sam, Craig was now a consultant to NATO countries to help ensure their security was robust, or private industry hired him to develop better ways of collecting information. It was all legal and lucrative. Craig, Daniel remembered, had once told him he worked only two months a year.

"Rome is good for you," Daniel said.

"You're not the first person to say that," Craig remarked. "But it has less to do with Rome than you think."

Craig was referring, of course, to his love interest, who Daniel knew quite well. Daniel had worked with Dana al-Yami both officially and unofficially. A liaison with the Canadian Security Intelligence Service (CSIS), she had since left the official world of espionage to be with Craig and worked as a "consultant." She was exquisitely beautiful, intelligent and young. And Craig adored her.

"Not here?" Daniel asked.

"Back home," Craig almost pouted.

"I'll look her up when I get there."

"When do you leave?" Craig asked.

"In a few hours," Daniel replied. "There's something going on. When they were working me over, they mentioned him. Now, I haven't heard anything, but combined with what I learned before they got me…I have concerns."

"No kidding," Craig said. "And us?"

"I need boots on the ground." Daniel shrugged. "You know that, for me, going home won't exactly be a cakewalk. I've burned a few bridges these past few years, and my return, if it's noticed, is going to attract a lot of attention. So if that happens, I need some proxies."

"Dana would insist," Craig said. "I'm not doing anything too important right now anyways."

"Thanks, Craig," Daniel said warmly.

"Besides," Craig said, looking up at the sky. "I've had enough of this amazing Italian weather. It's time for something miserably Canadian."

CHAPTER

"This is your last chance. If there's anything else, I strongly suggest you speak up now."

Ryan Davis looked up from his lectern at the enormous lecture theatre sprawled out before him. The lights over his ever-captive undergraduate audience were dim, but he could still make out the clusters of empty seats, the one or two sleeping bodies and the few dozen students more engrossed with their smartphones than this class.

Ryan sighed. He had tried all semester to bring the message home that what they were doing on their phones was directly correlated to this Linguistics 101 course. No one, it seemed, had made the connection.

Then again, they were all undergraduates, mostly first-years. *Connections*, Ryan thought as he scanned the crowd for a raised hand, *were not their strength. Unless it involved tapping a keg.*

"Nothing?" he asked, more out of habit than any sense of obligation. "Then I wish you all luck on your final exam next week."

Notes and textbooks closed as the thunderous cacophony of 200 bodies organized their belongings.

Ryan flipped off the projector then powered down his MacBook Pro and slapped it shut. When he looked up again, the lecture hall was empty.

"You sure know how to clear a room," a quiet voice echoed from behind him. Ryan turned and smiled. Billy Sexton, his friend and roommate, was standing in the shadows.

"We just do it in different ways," Ryan chided Billy, slipping his laptop into its bag along with a sheaf of notes.

"So how many are you going to fail?" Billy asked as the pair headed for the staircase.

"I'm shocked you would even suggest such a thing," Ryan said in partial sarcasm, climbing the stairs two at a time. "This is an institution of knowledge, of scholarly debate, where the brightest minds gather to challenge the world's way of thinking with their priceless academic pursuits."

The look on Billy's face betrayed his scepticism.

"Probably half," Ryan admitted, shouldering his way through a door and into the brilliant BC sunshine.

"There were a lot of fat girls in your class this term," Billy said as they walked.

Ryan shook his head as he pulled a pair of sunglasses over his eyes. Billy's observations no longer shocked him.

But casual acquaintances weren't quite so accustomed to his friend's outlook on the world.

Billy spoke his mind, but not in an effort to shock or offend. What he said was what he thought, no matter how inappropriate it sounded. This wire-thin computer genius who could compose sonatas on his computer from three different time periods had never been gifted with social graces. Ryan had learned, just like everyone else in his undergraduate year, that Billy was different. But it was only because the two had been mashed together as roommates by the school's computer system in their first year of undergrad that Ryan really understood.

Billy was smart, yes. Gifted, undoubtedly. Ryan had learned one night over a six-pack of cheap beer that somewhere in the history of assessments during this Boy Wonder's youth, a test indicated Billy had a "tendency" towards Asperger syndrome. The test results weren't conclusive. Billy understood the world around him as it functioned. He just didn't get the more complex social part.

"Maybe next year the girls will be skinnier," Billy said as they headed towards their house just off campus. "I mean, how hard can it be?"

"Not everyone is like you, Billy," Ryan reminded his friend. Their relationship was made all the more strange by Ryan's almost parent-like status in Billy's life. Billy could become so consumed in his work that he forgot many of the things others couldn't—eating, for one. Or bathing. And when

Billy did eat, the food was usually deep-fried, covered with extra sugar or smothered in gravy or something else equally unhealthy. And yet because he mostly ate only when Ryan reminded him, he maintained a slender frame.

At first glance, the two roommates had little in common. Billy liked to spend his weekend nights either in front of his array of computers or his PlayStation. Ryan, on the other hand, would rather spend a night talking with a friend over a beer. Where Billy was insulated, Ryan was gregarious. They complemented one another beautifully. And that's why they had been friends for so long.

What they really had in common was intellect—call it gifted, call it genius, both had graduated high school two years early, finding themselves immersed in the university experience before they were even legally allowed to drink. Billy's expertise was in the language of computers; Ryan's was in languages, pure and simple. Ryan could speak fifteen different languages fluently, several with appropriate regional dialect, and was fully literate in nine. Writing Eastern languages gave him the most trouble. Deciphering the intricate characters of the Chinese lexicon or writing backwards in Japanese was where he struggled the most.

But when it came to learning new tongues, Ryan was a sponge and had been since he was five. Like so many Canadians, he had been exposed to the French language early and was fluent by the age of six. It had helped that his father had been multi-lingual, having been a career diplomat for the Canadian Department of Foreign Affairs and International Trade. As a result, Ryan had moved around a lot.

Although he never got the chance to learn exactly what his father's role was in any given country, Ryan did learn the languages, customs and habits of the people. When his father had been posted to Mexico, Ryan added his third language. Less than two years later it was Germany, where Ryan was exposed to not just German culture but also to all of Western Europe as he and his father travelled to France, Poland and the Netherlands. There'd been stops in Saudi Arabia, Russia, China, Egypt and some of the smaller African countries. In each instance, without fail, Ryan had soaked up the local languages and, with increased exposure, the delicate nuance of dialect. His decision to major in languages when he entered university had been a no-brainer. He'd been thoroughly evaluated and judged advanced enough to graduate high school early. That particular school had been in Vancouver, where Ryan and his father had eventually settled, and where Ryan had continued to live since his father's death nine years earlier.

Billy groped in his pants pocket for the keys to their modest bungalow, one that was technically owned by Ryan's Uncle Edward, but to which they had free reign and rent. Ryan just stood back and waited, watching his friend. He could have lived alone but had grown accustomed to Billy's presence. Granted, they did occupy different parts of the house—Billy got the basement and Ryan the main and upper floors—so their activities didn't interfere with one another's lives. They were together, however, more often than not. Billy, after all, was helping Ryan on his doctoral project, even as he worked on his own.

Ryan had tried to introduce Billy to different experiences and lifestyles, but nothing had stuck. From a sweat in the gym, to Ryan's kung fu, boxing or aikido classes, Billy wasn't interested. So Ryan had stopped encouraging his friend to try anything he didn't want to. And their friendship had grown stronger as a result.

"Do you need me to get that?" Ryan finally asked irritably.

"It's here somewhere," Billy grunted as he fumbled through a gigantic chain of keys, searching for the right one. As a doctoral student in computer sciences, Billy maintained the computers and networks for several university departments. He had unrestricted access to all the campus buildings at any time of day or night, yet he insisted on keeping his house key with all the others. Ryan wondered how many of the keys actually worked in locks and how many were just there because they always had been.

"I'm going to get you a string and call you Latchkey," Ryan said, finally fishing out his own key and stabbing it into the lock. "And stop ringing the doorbell when you can't find your house key at night."

"You're always awake," Billy protested, following Ryan into the house.

"Yeah, because the doorbell wakes me up," Ryan replied, offloading his laptop bag on the kitchen table and tossing his keys on the counter. He headed straight to the fridge and grabbed a bottle of water.

Billy was already plunked down in front of their shared computer beside the kitchen table.

"Want to run some code?" Billy asked.

Ryan glanced at his watch. He'd let out his last class early and had some free time. The final exam was already banked, and he'd finished marking some late assignments two nights before. "I think we have some time," Ryan said, pulling up a wooden chair from the table and leaning over his friend.

Between Ryan's expertise in linguistics and Billy's computer coding, they were hoping to finally break through some of the barriers associated with a technology that truly had the potential to help a lot of people in the area of communication—computer-assisted translation (CAT).

Billy's hands flew over the keyboard and mouse, pointing out small coding errors and challenges they had encountered this past week, just as they had done for the previous three weeks. Their Computer-Assisted Translation Lexicon Project, or LexiCAT, had consumed the last two years of their lives. From securing grants to plotting on paper, they had finally moved on to the difficult part—making it work.

At first blush, CAT seemed pretty simple. Just input the words you want the computer to recognize and it will do so. But it was never that easy.

In Ryan's first year of undergrad, his course in cognitive psychology had truly piqued his interest. The professor, Harry Brown, had spoken about his work in the late 1980s. His first attempt at having a computer read out a name—in this case "Harry Brown"—had produced the result, "How are brides owned?" Curious, Ryan had explored CAT on his own. While completing his master's degree in linguistics, he had finally come up with the working concept of a CAT system that could, in effect, learn more effectively and efficiently, across different languages. He had just needed someone as talented with computers as he was with linguistics and languages. And that person had been Billy.

They were trying to create a computer program that could accurately interpret meaning from a specific language. Certain computer programs could already translate languages word-for-word, but they could not interpret the meanings within those words.

The process was pretty complex when you thought about it. With roughly 250,000 words in the English language, there are at least one million word meanings. So the meaning of any word—its lexeme, the basic unit of meaning—depends on the meanings of the words around it. Context, Ryan was always telling his students, was the mother of meaning. The word "bomb," for example," had a totally different meaning in the sentence "That's a bomb," than in the sentence, "That's the bomb"—common slang for describing something as exceptional. The word "the" completely changes the meaning of the word "bomb."

So Ryan and Billy were trying to create a computer program that interpreted meaning, not just individual words. By plotting all the word meanings, the program could look at the meanings of the words around the target word and discern the complete intended meaning. The implications were large—and not just from a scholarly perspective. Translation could be done faster by LexiCAT than by a person in real time. Military and intelligence agencies could use the program to interpret meaning in coded conversations. In commerce and retail, companies could use a similar program to take phone calls from customers and respond to their questions.

But the project was a huge undertaking. It had taken them two years to get this far. And they still had a lot more to do.

———

"Okay, I'm done," Billy announced without warning two hours later, standing up from the table.

Ryan took a couple of steps back, startled. He thought they were on a roll. He'd even stopped paying attention to the clock. Only now did he realize the sun, so high in the sky when they began, was already waning.

"Done what? C'mon, Billy, we're making good time."

Billy shook his head, leaning over and tapping a few keys to save their work. "I have plans. You know that. I always have these plans."

Ryan fought the urge to slap his friend upside the head. Here they were, getting near the cusp of finally completing and submitting their thesis project, something they'd slaved over for two years, and Billy was heading downstairs to play video games online with his anonymous friends.

"There's more to the world than running around on a computer screen pretending you're a wizard," Ryan snapped.

"And there's more to life than just working. You know this is what I do at this time on this day," Billy said, checking his watch.

Ryan made a sound, like a disgusted cough, watching as Billy grabbed a large bottle of Pepsi from the fridge and headed for the door leading to his basement domain.

"You need to learn to relax, Ryan. One day you just might not have the time."

Ryan fought to keep his mouth shut. *Really? The savant is giving me advice on not being so rigid?*

But Ryan had promised himself long ago that no matter the circumstance, no matter what was happening, he would never, ever use Billy's quirkiness against him.

"Go have fun, Bill," Ryan called after his friend. He shook his head, trying to rid himself of the frustration he felt. He looked around for his bag. Just because Billy didn't feel like working didn't mean that Ryan had to stop. But he would have to work somewhere else—Billy's online gaming nights were kind of loud. And annoying.

Ryan was just about to close the door to the house when he heard a loud guffaw echo up from the basement. *Right on cue*, he sighed, closing the door behind him and walking the ten minutes to the Pond Café.

The place was shockingly quiet, but having spent so many years on the university campus, Ryan was familiar with the ebb and flow of student migration.

Today had been the last day of classes, and students—well, undergrads—were doing one of two things: drinking heavily or studying at their parents' house, away from the partiers.

Ryan scanned the room, counting four people and rapidly assessing each person, a habit engrained in him from a young age.

"How many people?" his father asked.

"Six," Ryan replied, staring at the floor. He'd been given two seconds to survey the restaurant and silently count the number of people inside.

His father made a clicking sound, like a tongue on teeth, expressing disapproval.

"There are nine, Ryan. Remember, two seconds is actually a lot of time. Use the time you have to be certain—just don't be obvious."

"Sorry, Dad."

"Don't be sorry. Just do it correctly."

Ryan absently counted again and once more came up with the number four. Small groups weren't difficult.

The larger the group, the longer it took, and that's where the challenge always lay.

He ordered herbal tea and carried the steaming mug to a chair and table near the window. He tossed his bag onto the floor, set down the tea and pulled out his laptop, tapping at the space bar to wake it from slumber. He wanted to keep working while he still felt inspired. He took a sip of his tea, deemed the temperature satisfactory and placed the mug back on the table. He held his fingertips above his keyboard, like Mozart ready to compose a masterpiece.

"Strange choice," a voice remarked humorously.

Ryan checked the exasperated sigh poised on his lips and looked up into a pair of deep-brown eyes. The annoyance he felt at being interrupted suddenly dissipated.

"You mean Mac instead of PC?" Ryan said, trying to be as witty as he could under so unexpected an interruption. *And so welcome,* he thought.

Standing before him was a stranger, but a beautiful stranger. Asian descent, hair more brown than black, wearing a navy blue hoodie and leggings and clutching a stack of textbooks in her arms. She smiled as she looked at Ryan.

"No. Herbal tea," she remarked, pointing to the tea bag wrapper on the table. "Most people on campus tonight are imbibing something stronger."

"And I'm sure they'll be kind enough to leave most of their empties on my lawn tonight," Ryan said. "It's how I afford my tea."

The young woman laughed and, without asking, plopped down on the chair immediately across from Ryan, resting her books on her lap.

"I'm Kara," she said, extending a lithe, smooth hand.

"Ryan," he said, leaning closer. "Gansu?"

"Pardon?" She sounded taken aback.

"Your accent. It's slight, but it's still there. It sounds more northern than traditional Mandarin, so I'm guessing you grew up in the Gansu province of China."

"Very good, Ryan," Kara said knowingly. "But no. A good line, but no."

Ryan smiled big. "It usually works. What brings you here?"

"Same as you," Kara said. "Studying."

"What are you studying?"

"International politics," Kara said.

Ryan listened as well as he could as she described the elements of her master's thesis, trying to focus on her words but unable to ignore the pang of…something…in his gut.

"What do you think?" he asked.

"I don't like it."

"Good. Go with that."

"But I don't know why I don't like it," Ryan said.

"There's time to figure that out later," his father replied. "For now, you go with your instinct. There's something in this situation telling you that what you see isn't the whole story. It could be body language, verbal cues,

the environment, anything. For now, proceed as if what you are seeing is a lie."

Ryan sat back in his chair, more tuned in to the *something* he felt. The answer, frankly, wasn't hard. Ryan came to the Pond Café at least twice a week, more often than not on his own to work or study. He had never, in seven years of schooling to date, been approached by a woman this way. Ryan had approached other women, absolutely, but none had ever just wandered over to flirt with him.

Or is it flirting? Ryan wondered. Kara was also leaning back, as if trying to keep some distance between them. Which Ryan also found strange. A big part of flirting, he had learned, was invading one another's personal space. And that wasn't happening here.

"Sounds interesting," he remarked when she stopped talking.

"Right," Kara said, her eyes narrowing. "Because you were just hanging on my every word."

Ryan felt his face flush. He decided to be honest, which was his unique way of addressing awkward situations. It usually threw the other person off guard and created another opportunity if he had hopelessly messed up the first one.

"I'm sorry," Ryan said. "I've been coming here for a long time, and this has never happened to me."

Kara smiled but didn't miss a beat. "I don't know what you think is happening," she said. "I just came over to introduce myself."

Kara scooped up the books from her lap and abruptly stood.

Ryan also stood. "Why? Will I be seeing you more often?" he asked.

Kara shrugged. "We'll see."

With that she turned and walked out the door, not bothering to look back over her shoulder.

Ryan shook his head and sat back down. On impulse, he glanced around the room. The same four people he had seen when he came in were still bent over their books.

I must be getting rusty with women, he thought to himself, taking one more sip of his tea before returning his attention to his laptop.

———⟨⟩———

It was getting dark by the time Ryan stuffed his laptop into his bag. The last of his herbal tea had long grown cold, and three of the four people had left the café.

Ryan placed his mug on the counter and walked out the door into the cool night air. He walked the length of University Drive before turning onto Marine Drive, heading for home. His mind was done with the world of lexemes and was now occupied with his strange encounter with the woman named Kara.

Who does that? he wondered as he played back their brief conversation. Just walking up to somebody and commenting on their tea. He stopped short, able to answer his own question. *Well, I do...*

Women had always been something of a mystery to Ryan, and he couldn't figure out why, exactly. He did fine for a twenty-four-year-old with a sharp intellect, particularly given his good physical condition. Even describing his PhD thesis, so boring to most he met, could elicit a few laughs. *I'm developing a computer program that decodes the language of women*, he would say. *The biggest problem? It's hard to decode a language that is so often silent.*

Ryan had just assumed most guys got some clue about women from their fathers, but Ryan hadn't had that luxury during his formative teenage years.

He'd loved his father, had looked up to him in ways that sons often stop doing when they reach their double-digit years. Some kids whose dads moved around a lot because of their jobs might be bitter, but Ryan had embraced the experience. His skill with languages came not just from living in different countries but also from immersion in their cultures. He and his dad had concocted a game called "Disguises" in which they did their best to pass themselves off as locals, both in language, dialect, composure and dress. The goal was to make it past the locals in a public place without sticking out. They had both been good at the game. But his dad had been good at a lot of things—his trophies for boxing, marksmanship, running and other events were the proof. Ryan had followed in his father's footsteps, learning the same things his father had learned and expanding on his repertoire. Even after his father died, he had continued taking lessons.

His death had been so tragic, so meaningless. His dad had left Ryan with his Uncle Edward for a weekend to go snowshoeing in the Rockies. He never returned. A week after he'd gone missing, the park rangers found him, but the body had been so ravaged by wild animals that his uncle had strongly urged Ryan not to have a final look. At a small ceremony attended by only a handful of people, his father's ashes were ensconced in a columbarium at a Vancouver cemetery. Since his mother had disappeared when Ryan was a baby, he was effectively orphaned, and his uncle was appointed Ryan's guardian.

Ryan wished he could have asked his father about girls. He hadn't felt comfortable asking his uncle, and Billy, well, Billy didn't offer much insight into the minds or motivations of the fairer sex, as Ryan had witnessed so many times. Ryan had other buddies but none that he could really confide in.

Ryan kicked at a stone on the ground as he crossed Marine Drive. The evening was clear, the air still a bit chilled, even if the spring days were brilliantly warm. He was hunched over as he plodded along, wallowing and self-absorbed. He didn't notice the car that zipped past, then suddenly pulled over. Nor did he notice a second vehicle had stopped behind him. Even the thud of car doors closing didn't penetrate his reverie.

"Can you help us with something?"

Ryan looked up. Two men had exited the car that had parked in front of him. One, sporting a goatee, was clutching a folded map, beckoning Ryan with his other hand. The second man stood to the side, staring at Ryan intensely.

"Sure," Ryan said, instinctively taking a step forward and holding out his hand for the map. But he felt himself tense up, felt his muscles become rigid as his brain began swirling. Something just wasn't...right. Something in the man's tone fired up Ryan's senses.

As he approached the men, he glanced furtively from side to side. His eyes took in the black Chrysler 300 and the small box on the dashboard.

GPS, Ryan realized, his alarm growing. *There's no reason for them to be using a paper map.*

He suddenly picked up the sounds of soft footsteps behind him, pausing briefly. The road was practically deserted. Ryan sensed something foul in the air. His body started to rally. His heart hammered in his chest as it pumped more blood to his muscles. The adrenalin pouring into his veins further honed his senses. He'd experienced the same sensation multiple times in his teens in the boxing ring or before a karate bout.

He slowed his approach towards the men, his hand still out, keeping up a charade as his mind took in as many details as possible. No other vehicles rushed past. Both men were young and of Middle Eastern descent, shorter than Ryan. Both wore jeans; one had on a light jacket and was bald with a full beard; the other man had on a white T-shirt and a large gold chain around his neck, and he had short hair and a thin goatee.

The bald guy had his right shoulder turned towards Ryan while the man in the T-shirt stood with his fists clenched loosely at his sides.

Ryan saw a flash of light. The harsh glow from the streetlight turned the rear window of the Chrysler 300 into a distorted mirror that allowed Ryan to make out the shapes of two more men behind him. The curved glass made the details impossible to discern, but both men were approaching quickly.

Ryan took stock. The real estate around him was getting smaller as he continued forward, but he knew he couldn't lose momentum. He figured he could probably take all four at the same time, but first he needed to get them all in front of him. With them effectively surrounding him, Ryan wasn't confident he could control the situation.

But he did have the element of surprise in his favour. He was moving while the two men facing him were standing still and, from what he could tell, the two behind Ryan were advancing cautiously.

Ryan scanned the skyline to his left and saw the outline of a building under construction.

He had a plan.

First he needed to create separation, just a few seconds would be long enough to take back control over whatever was happening.

Ryan dropped his bag and lunged at goatee guy, one hand reaching for his shoulder, the other for the belt of his pants. As soon as Ryan grabbed his target, he leaned in, transferring his weight to his left leg and striking out at goatee man with his right leg.

Caught off guard, the second man yelped as Ryan drove his right foot into his chest, knocking him to the pavement. Ryan kept up the momentum of the kick, spinning low and pulling with his hands. Goatee guy had no choice but to move with him. Ryan pulled him across his body and to the rear, propelling him towards the feet of the two men coming up behind him, causing them stop in their tracks.

Ryan had no time to think. He had to create an environment where he could deal with his attackers individually. And he couldn't do it here. But he knew where he could.

Before his assailants could react, Ryan turned, grabbed his bag and ran towards the building in the distance framed by spotlights and a massive crane.

At five stories tall and 24,000 square metres, the new UBC Alma Mater Society Student Union Building (SUB) was going to be twice the size of its predecessor. Year one of construction had wrapped up, and the completion date was slated for late next year.

A small part of Ryan was glad the project was taking so long. At $103 million, the unfinished building was, in his opinion, the most expensive playground in BC.

For the last year, ever since the first construction beams went up, Ryan had been using the construction site to help satisfy one of his most recent challenges—free running. He'd taken up the activity, sometimes called parkour, as a new physical challenge after one of his students came to class one day with his arm in a cast. When Ryan asked him what happened, the student showed him YouTube clips of lithe young men leaping over walls, flipping over hedges and using just their strength and agility to navigate a series of difficult obstacles, which were usually parking garages, staircases or in some cases, fountains.

Ryan was intrigued by the freedom parkour seemed to grant. The goal was to find the most efficient way to move through your environment. Ryan saw the sport as an evolution of his skills, which already included karate, judo, boxing and jiu-jitsu, where controlling your body movements was of primary importance, but only within a confined space such as a ring or dojo. With parkour, that space multiplied exponentially.

He started taking lessons twice a week at a parkour gym just off Main Street in Vancouver. Once he felt sufficiently skilled, he had, eight months ago, approached the growing edifice of the new SUB under cover of darkness and launched himself at it, determined to conquer the growing steel monstrosity.

He had promptly sprained his ankle vaulting the staircase.

But once that healed, he had launched himself back at SUB with abandon and conquered the area one way or another. As the construction crew added new elements and layers, Ryan found new ways to manoeuvre. He took risks, and not just in the form of physical harm. More than once a security guard had nearly seen him, but Ryan now knew when to expect company and found places to hide.

As his legs churned, Ryan could sense the four men struggling to keep up. Ryan, however, ran without effort, breathing deeply and luring his attackers into a place where he could deal with them individually, on his own terms.

Ryan dropped his bag behind a pillar and dashed towards the same staircase where he had hurt his ankle back in September. He ignored the spotlights trained on the building to deter vandals and didn't bother looking for the security guard. When he was within three strides of the stairs, he hurled forward, arms outstretched towards the banister. He grabbed the railing firmly and pulled his legs forward. He shot through the yawning door and landed on his feet without missing a step.

He had stepped no more than a few feet inside, but the soaring ceiling of the building's future atrium was already consuming every last twinkle of light. Despite the darkness, Ryan, knew where he was going. He ran towards one of the cement walls of the foundation and headed for the corner. He leapt into the air, and when his right foot felt the solid surface of the wall, he erupted upwards off his right foot to the left, planting his left foot on the wall then shot back onto his right foot. Pushing off for the third time, he reached straight up and grasped the cold steel of the support beam just above his head. He clung to the beam's edge and pulled himself upwards and onto it and paused, breathing as silently and carefully as he could.

He watched the four men as they thundered up the steps and shot into the atrium before coming to an abrupt halt. Ryan didn't move from his perch, his eyes now tuned to the darkness. They conferred in a loose huddle, speaking in low voices Ryan couldn't make out. His attackers split up, each heading in different directions.

Ryan stood and skirted the length of the narrow beam, reaching out for the thick girder at the corner and pulling himself across to the next beam. He took two steps then leapt and grabbed for another beam overhead, pulling himself up higher. The four men scattered beneath him. Ryan honed in on goatee man as he moved gingerly through the darkness. Ryan manoeuvred along the beam until the man crossed beneath him and wandered into an area that had studs in place but was not yet walled in. As he passed directly below, Ryan silently stepped off the beam, his one hand held ready to strike as he rapidly descended. At the same time his feet hit the ground, Ryan slammed his hand into the man's temple. Ryan held onto the man before he could tumble to the ground, carefully lowering his unconscious frame to the floor.

Ryan climbed the walls of the next corner to ascend to the upper level. He heard footsteps to his right and cautiously padded in that direction, stepping as gently as possible.

Bald guy, trying to be clever, was using his smart-phone as a flashlight, but it only made him a target, blinding himself in the process. Ryan hugged the drywall, staying in the shadows as he crept silently towards the man.

"It's impossible. You can't kick the can without the person who's 'it' catching you. Speed isn't always the best tactic," his father had said. *"You can sneak up on a man so closely you can smell his breath before he knows you're nearby."*

Stepping slowly and deliberately, and using the toe of his shoe to detect any debris that could announce his presence, Ryan silently crept up behind his attacker, shifting his position whenever the man changed direction. Without making a sound, Ryan exploded upwards at his attacker's neck, wrapping one hand around his mouth, while clenching his other forearm across his neck in a classic chokehold. Within seconds the man slumped towards the floor, and Ryan softly guided him there.

"Adil?" whispered a voice nearby. Ryan froze and looked behind him. A third man had managed to get up the stairs without Ryan noticing and was only a few metres away. "Adil?"

Ryan remained still. The man was unknowingly walking straight towards him. He would be right on top of Ryan within seconds, and Ryan wanted to take care of these men without facing them all at once.

He reached down to the assailant he had just subdued and tore off three buttons from the man's shirt and threw them on the floor to his left. In the silence of the room, each button striking the concrete detonated like a bomb.

The buttons bounced off the wall and came to rest. The man approaching Ryan stopped briefly before walking quickly in the direction of the sound. Ryan waited a heartbeat then crept after him. When the man reached the wall, he paused, but Ryan didn't. He grabbed the man by the shoulders from behind and rammed his head into the wall then lowered his limp frame to the floor.

"Stop!"

Ryan turned and saw the last bad guy sprinting right for him. Rather than run, Ryan stood to his full height, turned so his left side was facing his final attacker and launched himself towards him, right leg extended. The high kick connected just behind his attacker's ear, sending him to the ground. His head bounced once off the concrete. Then he didn't move.

What did I just do? Ryan surveyed the carnage of the attack. He knew he was capable of defending himself...but this...it wasn't something he had ever expected—that he could be so violent when it really mattered.

It burst upon him out of nowhere, the sudden need to know exactly what had just happened. Unfortunately, none of the men lying on the ground would be talking anytime soon. He couldn't understand it. He couldn't fathom it. He searched his mind for someone he might have recently offended but came up blank. Sure, there were people he didn't like and who didn't like him, but any animosity was academic at best. The only punches Ryan ever threw were at his boxing or karate classes.

He bent down and fumbled through goatee guy's jacket and pants' pockets. He retrieved a wallet, keys, a cellphone and a folded piece of paper. The wallet was useless, carrying only a driver's licence and a few bankcards in the name of Nassib El Koko. But the piece of paper caught his eye immediately. It was a black-and-white image of Ryan walking out of his house.

He knelt there, riveted. These guys hadn't picked a random fight—they had been looking for *him*. He checked both sides of the paper for notes or typing of any kind but there was nothing.

He checked the pockets of the second attacker, who moaned once before falling quiet again, and got the same haul—wallet with a licence in an Arabic name, a cellphone, keys and the same picture of Ryan. The other two prone men carried the same items.

Ryan stood up, barely able to keep his balance from shock, reeling in an awkward circle, his mind unable to grasp what the hell was going on.

He had to move. He would call the police when he got home. If he could get attacked once on the way home, it could happen again. He jammed one of the pictures into his jacket pocket, dropped the wallets, threw the cellphones to the ground and crushed them under his feet. Finally, he threw the keys as far as he could in two separate directions, scooped up his bag and started home, his breathing still ragged.

He fought the urge to run, not wanting to draw attention to himself. Instead he walked quickly, hands in his pockets, eyes constantly scanning his surroundings, listening for any noise.

After a few minutes of walking, he broke into a dead run. He couldn't take it anymore. He needed to be home, where he could sit quietly and think.

———◦◦◦———

A figure stood in the shadows, watching as Ryan hurried away from the scene of the attack, slow at first, then at full speed, his heels kicking up gravel.

She had watched the entire confrontation and was shocked not just that Ryan had defended himself but also by the violence he had used. She frowned. Events had unfolded sooner than she expected and now posed several fundamental problems for herself and the others.

No battle strategy survives first contact with the enemy, she knew, but their plan was in tatters. She had people to alert and other contingencies to set in motion. Ryan had to be intercepted before he got the authorities involved and complicated things further.

She left her silent post and retreated to an old, red Chevy truck. Judging from her experience and Ryan's direction, she assumed he was heading straight for home.

CHAPTER 8

Ryan didn't slow down as he approached his house, but his heart started to beat less rapidly as he caught sight of his home. Nothing seemed out of place—his car was still in the driveway, the porch light was on and the only lights were coming from the basement windows—Billy's sanctuary.

He fumbled for his keys with shaking hands, gulping air as he came to a stop on his porch. The keychain jingled in his hands, but try as he might, he could not steady his hands. Partially from adrenaline, partially from exertion, his arms and legs trembled of their own accord.

Ryan fought with the lock before finally managing to shoulder his way through the open door, stumbling and falling to the floor of the foyer. He stayed there for a second, grateful not to be moving, then stood.

He dropped his bag to the floor and tossed his keys onto the small table he couldn't see but knew was there and kicked off his shoes. He padded into the kitchen, one hand reaching for the phone, the second for the light switch.

But the lights didn't come on.

Ryan scowled, flipping the switch up and down repeatedly as if trying to awake the electrical feed, but there was no change. *Strange*, he thought, *the basement lights were on.*

He held the cordless phone up to his ear, dialled 911 with his thumb and pushed "Talk" as he reached for the switch in the hall. No dial tone?

He looked at the backlit screen of the phone. "Line not connected," it read.

Ryan didn't utter a sound. He simply dropped the phone to the floor and turned, bolting for the front door. He never made it. He heard a snap and felt pinpricks in his chest followed a nanosecond later by the sensation of every muscle in his body contracting as 50,000 volts surged through him. The shock was brief but agonizing. Ryan collapsed to the hallway floor.

He tried to scream for help but couldn't. The hit from the conductive energy device (CED) zapped his entire body, rendering him momentarily paralyzed. Several pairs of hands grabbed at him, turning him over and wrestling his limp arms behind his back. He heard a zipping sound and felt his wrists suddenly immobilized by something flexible but taut. Zip ties? More hands grabbed his shoulders and the back of his shirt and yanked him to his feet.

"Can you walk?" a female voice asked.

Ryan had just enough strength to feebly shake his head.

"So be it," the voice said then barked an order in a foreign language. The language sounded familiar to Ryan, but his brain still felt like mush from the thousands of volts of electricity.

The hands holding him up at his shoulders propelled him forward, forcibly pushing him in the direction they wanted him to go. The hands were efficient, Ryan noted—no hesitation, no tentativeness. He noted three men around him, two grabbing his arms and another his feet as they pulled him from the hallway through the kitchen, down the stairs and out the backdoor. They were walking behind the woman who had spoken earlier. Ryan tried to yell but managed nothing more than a moan.

The men hauled him across the grass in the backyard, through the back gate and into the alley. A large windowless painters' van was parked off to one side, the engine running, another man sitting at the steering wheel.

One man moved towards the back of the van, throwing open the rear doors. The other two men half-pushed, half-threw Ryan into the back, where he landed on his shoulder, and they both climbed in. His muscles were starting to recover, and he was able to shimmy up to a sitting position but felt something underneath his leg. He shoved it away, but it kicked back.

"Watch it!"

Ryan looked up, getting a quick peek at one of his captors, an enormous man with dark skin and short-cropped hair.

Beside him lay another person; a dark black bag covered his head, but there was no mistaking Billy's body for anyone else's. His roommate, too, had his hands secured behind his back.

"Billy!" Ryan said, finally managing to speak as he worked his way up onto his butt.

"Ryan? What the hell is going on?"

"Silence!" a woman's voice shouted. Ryan turned to get a look at her, but because of the silhouette created by the dim streetlamp in the alley, he couldn't make out her features. She was short and had long hair. That was all Ryan glimpsed.

"No talking! If you try to escape, you will die," the woman said matter-of-factly.

"What do you want?" Ryan slurred. The answer was a crack to Ryan's head that left him reeling.

"Right now, I want silence. There will be time for questions and answers later," the woman said, nodding to one of the men. Ryan turned his head just in time to see a black bag, like the one Billy wore, being held up in the air. His entire world plunged into blackness.

Ryan heard a door open and close, and again the woman said something in a language that tickled at Ryan's brain. He recognized the language, but his brain was still rebooting and wasn't quite working properly yet.

Instead of the screeching of tires Ryan expected, the van slipped into gear and crawled down the alley. The road was bumpy, sending Ryan's head caroming into the side of the van, right on the spot the man had just smacked. The pain angered Ryan, but he didn't allow himself to grunt. The last thing he wanted to do was aggravate the situation, one that had already spiralled out of control. First the attack on Marine, now this?

What is going on? Ryan raged internally, feeling the first few tendrils of despair creeping into his gut. He fought to stay calm. For now, he was alive, if sore. These people seemed to want something from him, but Ryan couldn't even begin to fathom what it might be. The woman had said there would be questions later. So they'd just have to wait for later.

*Tension…*the word came to him unbidden. His father's voice emerged from the deep recesses of Ryan's memory. As the van turned out of the alley, throwing Ryan against one of his attackers, he remembered where the word came from. He was eight years old and wanted to put on a magic show. He had mastered some of the basics—sleight of hand, distraction and palming to produce hidden objects and per-form silly card tricks. But he had also wanted to amaze his friends, the kids at school and his dad by escaping from some-thing. Upon hearing his request, his father had produced a rope, and the two had gone to the basement to practice.

"It's all about tension, Ryan," his father told him. "Do me first." Ryan obliged, wrapping the rope as tightly as he could around his father's wrists behind his back and securing it in a tight double knot. Then he watched as his

father got to work. Within two minutes, the rope fell to the floor, the knot still intact and his father's hands free. His dad explained that the key was muscle tension—by flexing his forearm muscles while Ryan was securing the rope, his father had created some room for his arms when he relaxed his muscles, infinitesimally loosening his bonds. That was enough to shimmy his hands free.

When Ryan's captors snapped the flex-cuffs on him, his muscles were still seized from the electrical shock. Now relaxed, his large forearms strained against the plastic biting into his wrists. The van turned, and Ryan fell on his side. As he righted himself, he alternated flexing and relaxing his hands and forearms, but the plastic was tighter than any rope he had ever slipped and wouldn't budge. Still, Ryan pulled as discreetly as he could at his bonds, his wrists becoming increasingly raw and scraped.

"That went well," said a man's voice. At first Ryan paid the remark no heed but suddenly realized the words were not English. They were Arabic, and Ryan's mind, so deft with the nuances of language, had simply heard the conversation and understood without even thinking. The realization set him on edge. He stopped fighting his bonds and concentrated on listening.

"The second time," the woman's voice said. "Who knew those fools were so inept?"

Ryan caught the intonation of the language, and information flooded his brain. *Nadji dialect, most common*

in southern urban areas of Saudi Arabia, primarily centred
around Riyadh.

"What happened to them?" the man asked as the van
made a slight turn and then accelerated smartly. They had
apparently left the residential area near Ryan's house and
were now on a major roadway, but Ryan was so disoriented
that he had no idea which street it was or the direction they
were headed.

"They have been collected," the woman said. "They
will be dealt with."

Ryan assumed they were talking about the men who
had attacked him on Marine Drive. So there had to be a connection between that attack and his present predicament.
He swallowed as a mounting fear enveloped him. Something
larger was going on, but he couldn't figure out what it was.

Their professionalism stood out. Granted, his only
experiences with teams of bad guys had been like most
other civilians—through TV and movies—but Ryan had
absorbed his share of documentary and reality-based pro-
gramming about SWAT teams, Special Forces units and
espionage agencies. Everything that had happened to him
tonight seemed to follow a particular pattern. The first
attack was meant to surprise him, subdue him, but some
sixth sense had spurred him to action, something his captors had not taken into account.

The second attack at his home left no room for error.
A phrase leapt to his mind that he'd heard on a documentary

about hostage rescue—*speed, surprise and violence of action.* He had been attacked within moments of arriving at home, his kidnappers striking from darkness. And they had attacked swiftly and violently with what Ryan only assumed could be a CED. He had been handcuffed as soon as he hit the hall floor and ushered out the backdoor. He was blindfolded, unable to see who his attackers were or where they were going. The abduction had been so clean, so well planned. This wasn't a group of criminals intent on robbing him; this was a well-coordinated snatch operation. They wanted something from him, something that he didn't physically possess. So it must be information.

And Billy? If these guys knew who Ryan was, they also knew he lived with Billy and knew something about his friend. The fact that he had been attacked on the way home from the Pond Café meant someone had been following him. If they had been watching him before this evening, collecting information on his habits and patterns, they would have known he had a roommate. But why had Billy been kidnapped as well? Ryan doubted Billy had anything his attackers needed, beyond his computer skills. And they had come prepared, with two black bags and flex-cuffs. That spoke to advance planning.

All these facts whirled in Ryan's head, stoking his fears. Like any North American living in the aftermath of the attacks of 9/11, he was aware of the potential for terrorism. He knew Canada was not immune, given the heightened attention CSIS and successive governments had received in detaining individuals of Middle Eastern origin for indefinite periods of time, claiming they were linked to some terrorist plot. The prospective attacks on various Canadian sites by a group of Islamic fundamentalists in 2006—that CSIS and the RCMP had disrupted—had pounded that threat home. Yet in all the lectures Ryan had given, he had worked to dispel the myth that all people of Middle Eastern descent were ranting, bomb-toting devotees intent on ratcheting up the body count. In his own world experience as a youth strolling the markets of Tehran, Baghdad and even in the Palestinian territories, shrouded as he was in the dress and disguise of a native as he played Disguises with his father, he had only ever encountered good people going about their daily lives. Their lifestyles were different, undoubtedly, and their adherence to faith was more than the token expressionism seen in 21st-century North America, but they were no different from anyone else in the world. They wanted security, peace and freedom as they perceived it. Islam wasn't inherently violent—the radicals who perverted the faith were the dangerous ones. And Ryan understood that reasoning on a level most of his students and his friends couldn't comprehend.

But now, faced with Arab-speaking individuals who had subdued him and his best friend and were taking them God knows where, the thought of terrorism sprang to Ryan's mind. But even that didn't fully compute in the common lexicon. He had heard no ideological references, no prayer, none of the stereotypical fodder the Tom Clancys and Larry Bonds fed readers through their bestsellers. No one was praising Allah. Of the men he had observed so far on this night, only two had beards, and none wore head coverings. Most significant was the woman—she appeared to be in charge of this crew. She spoke with authority, and the men responded to her commands. And she wore no head covering or *hijab* of any kind. His situation, and Billy's, was incongruent with their abduction being some kind of terrorist act, at least as he understood it.

And besides, what would terrorists want with a languages doctoral student and his quirky friend?

Despite his frustration, Ryan's martial arts training kicked in. He had learned the principles and application of self-defence. When to act was as important as how. His captors had threatened him with death, but they had also gone to great lengths to ensure he had been captured alive. If Billy had been a concern, they simply would have killed him at the house. Despite imposing their will and their way, it was obvious to Ryan that he had leverage. So Ryan had time, and if he could cause some problems, be a nuisance, perhaps he could squeeze a little more information out of them.

He knew he had to keep his guard up. They didn't need to know that he understood their language. So if he was going to be petulant, he was going to do it in English.

"I don't know anything," Ryan moaned.

The guard beside him barely turned but snarled, "Quiet."

"I don't know anything," Ryan moaned again, disregarding the command. "Why are you people doing this? Why are you doing this to us?"

"I said silence," asserted the woman aggressively. Ryan ignored her.

"I don't know what you want with me or my friend. We're just students. We have nothing of value. Please just let us go."

The enormous guard slapped Ryan upside his head, but Ryan shook it off. He could tell from the increased tension in the van that he was annoying them. And irritated people often make poor decisions. Not that Ryan had any great plans for how to use that knowledge to his advantage. He wanted to lay the foundation so he could prepare for whatever situation might present itself.

"Please just let us go," Ryan whined.

"Ryan, what are you doing?" Billy asked softly.

"We need to go home, Billy," Ryan replied. "We don't know anything. They've got the wrong people."

The van suddenly dove to the right as the driver pulled over and screeched to a stop. Ryan fell forward, and the guard beside him grabbed him roughly by the hair, through the bag.

"I said be quiet, or you'll die," the woman threatened.

"Please stop," Ryan continued. "It doesn't have to be like this. We'll never tell anyone. You can trust us. Please just let us go."

Ryan heard a sharp intake of breath to his side, one that he correctly surmised as rage exploding unchecked, and the hand grabbing his hair moved to his neck, where the other hand joined it. Ryan began to choke, drowning in nothing.

"Kamil, stop!" shouted the woman in Arabic.

"You...you are son of spy!" Kamil said in broken English. "You are prisoner! You obey!"

"Kamil!" the woman shrieked. "We need him alive!"

Just as Ryan's world was about to turn black yet again, a violent explosion detonated at the front of the van, jarring its entire length and width. Kamil's hands flew off Ryan's throat as the van momentarily became airborne. Ryan landed hard on the van's steel floor. He felt the van twist and the back end swing around. Over the screams and shouts of his captors, he heard squealing tires and the high revs of a powerful engine. The van bucked again, this time the impact occurring broadside. With a lurch, the van rolled onto its side, sending everyone crashing into the side panels. Ryan braced himself but came down hard on the wheel well with an audible crack from his ribs. Moaning and groaning sounded all around.

Ryan heard a bang behind him as the back doors opened and then closed. A heartbeat later, the interior of the van exploded with light and sound, loud popping noises assailing their ears. The brightness of the flash blinded Ryan even through the bag over his head. The back doors opened again, and someone entered. Ryan heard a whap, like something hard striking flesh, followed by a thud. A cry and another thud, followed by silence, zipping noises and heavy breathing.

*Speed, surprise, violence of action...*Ryan thought suddenly. He couldn't take it anymore. He struggled to his knees, but he doubled over from the excruciating pain in his ribs. Hands touched his face, gently grabbing the bag and yanking it off his head. The face he saw startled him.

Less than an hour ago in the Pond, and now here she was, standing right in front of him in the back of some van after he and Billy had been kidnapped. Ryan felt as though his brain was coming apart.

"Quiet," Kara whispered. "We need to get out of here."

"No, uh-uh," Ryan shook his head, using his feet to scoot backwards. He bumped into something solid and looked around. Kamil was collapsed behind him, his hands restrained with a pair of flex-cuffs. Ryan lost it. The panic he had kept subdued since his first encounter with the kidnappers overwhelmed him.

"Get away from me!" Ryan shouted, in a futile attempt to corral his panicking brain. "I don't know what's going on, but *you* had better tell me, right now! Why should I go with you?"

Kara crouched at the back of the van, her long black hair tied up in a severe bun, her small, lithe hands encased in leather gloves. She held out a reassuring hand to Ryan.

"I promise I'll explain, but if we don't get moving, we're going to die," she said, softly but emphatically.

"You're the second person to suggest my death tonight," Ryan pointed out, finding it hard to keep his mind from seizing on the silliest things. "Why are you any different?"

Kara approached him slowly. Ryan tried to move away, but his restraints and the limp body next to him prevented escape. Kara reached behind Ryan. He heard a snap, and the flex-cuffs fell away. Kara's hand came back into view, holding a pair of wire cutters.

"Let's go," she said, turning.

"Wait," Ryan said suddenly. "Billy!"

"I know," she replied, making her way towards Billy's prone frame. She removed the bag from his head and cut away his restraints. "Are you okay?"

"No," Billy whined.

"I know this is confusing, Billy, but we really need to get moving," Kara said, pulling Billy upright.

"Who *are* you?" Billy asked, as he struggled to his feet.

"My name is Kara, and I'm here to help you both," she said calmly. "Can you walk?"

They both nodded and, on shaky legs, crawled out of the off-kilter van and stepped into the street.

They were in some warehouse district Ryan didn't recognize. It was dark, and as he looked around, he couldn't spot another living soul. As they rounded the back of the van, Ryan saw the cause of their accident—a red Chevy pickup truck was now one with the painters' van, the truck's hood sharply crumpled in from the impact. Black rubber marked the dimly lit street.

Ryan opened his mouth to ask the same question he'd been thinking all night, but Kara spoke first.

"You have questions. I know. But right now we need to get away from here," Kara said.

"Is the truck still running?" Ryan managed to ask.

"We can't risk it," Kara said. "With the damage to the front, if we were stopped, the police would ask questions."

"Whoa, wait just a second!" Billy said, bent over at the waist, sucking in air. "We're not calling the police?"

Kara spoke again, more forcefully. "I told you, I'll explain later, but right now we need to find a ride. I'll go and see what I can come up with." She pointed to a dark alley half a block away. "Wait there, and don't move. I'll come to you."

She reached into a pocket and tossed Ryan an older, flip-style cellphone. "Call your uncle," she said.

My uncle? "How did you...? What the...?" But Kara was already trotting down the street towards a line of parked cars.

Ryan and Billy retreated to the dark alley. A dumpster nearby gave them cover. Both slumped to the ground.

"Who is she? And how does she know you have an uncle?" Billy asked frantically.

"I met her earlier tonight at the Pond. She's a student of international politics. And I have no idea what Uncle Ed has to do with any of this," Ryan replied.

Billy whined again, "I just want to go home."

"I know, bud. We will," Ryan said. "I just gotta make this call, okay?"

Billy nodded, and Ryan flipped open the phone and dialled his uncle's number. But before he brought the phone to his ear, Ryan saw the display on the phone change. The phone number disappeared and was replaced by "Edward." The number had already been programmed into the phone.

Why would she have my uncle's number? Ryan wondered, staring at the blue-lit screen. He was so stunned he scarcely heard his uncle pick up.

"Hello...Hello...Kara, are you there?"

Ryan snapped to and brought the phone up to his ear, unsure of what to say. "Uncle Ed, it's Ryan."

"Ryan? What are you doing with...?"

"Kara gave me this phone and told me to call you. Something happened and..."

"Is Kara with you right now?" His uncle's voice suddenly became urgent and hard.

"She's looking for a car," Ryan said. "Look, some people..."

"Stop," Edward said, his voice so sharp Ryan almost felt chastised. "Stop talking. Are you hurt?"

"A little roughed up, but alive," Ryan replied.

"Okay, listen carefully. You stay with Kara, no matter what."

"But Uncle Ed..."

"Shut up!" his uncle's voice was almost a roar. "No more talking! Just listen! Stay. With. Kara. When she gets back, go with her. Meet me at the stripper's. Now hang up, and smash this phone."

Ryan paused, taken aback by his uncle's reaction—his uncle was normally a pretty easygoing guy. Ryan couldn't remember the last time he heard him yell like that. There were so many questions on the tip of his tongue that they seemed to collide, but he couldn't ignore the urgency in his uncle's voice. For the first time that night, Ryan simply did as he was told. He snapped the phone shut, turned it over and removed the battery and the SIM card. He smashed the pieces into the stone wall behind him over and over until they fell into a mangled mess on the ground and then ground them with his heel.

"What are you doing?" Billy asked, startled.

Ryan sighed, running his hands through his hair, staring down at the asphalt. "Just following orders."

Just then, they heard the sound of an engine gear down at the entrance to the alley. Ryan peered around the corner of the dumpster and saw Kara in the driver's seat of a compact car. She waved them over, and Ryan pulled at Billy. Ryan took the front seat while Billy hopped in the back.

"Really?" Billy suddenly spoke up. "After all that, you steal a Geo for a getaway car?"

CHAPTER

The sudden lurch of the plane's wheels kissing the tarmac at Vancouver International Airport might have upset some, but Daniel welcomed the feeling that sent goose bumps crawling along his skin.

*I'm home...*he thought, staring out of his first-class window into the night.

He was surprised at the dry airstrip. The day he had left Vancouver nine years ago, it had rained a heavy drizzle. The weather had only served to compound the most agonizing day of his life, a day that left him feeling angry and helpless because the choices he had made drastically changed his life, but he felt he had no other course of action.

He had taken a ferry to Vancouver Island then had flown from Victoria to Toronto and from there, on to what had been his life for almost a decade. Since then, Canada had been off limits.

He hadn't watched his own funeral, though he knew a private service had taken place. Instead, he had stood on the deck of the ferry as the wind lashed at his windbreaker and newly cropped hair, hoping the raindrops collecting on his fake eyeglasses hid his tears. He had intentionally and violently separated himself from his son and his friends, charged with a pursuit that would see him scouring the world over, tracking down the proverbial needle in the global haystack, all alone. It had been a hollow, mournful day. A lesser man would have spent it drunk.

Daniel shook himself from his reverie as the plane braked gently to a stop and the call came for first-class passengers to prepare to disembark. Because he had already passed customs at Pierre Elliott Trudeau Airport in Montréal earlier in the day, he was permitted to walk straight through to the baggage claim area. But unlike the other passengers, Daniel simply kept right on walking. He had one carry-on bag and had checked a suitcase for appearance's sake but didn't need the suitcase now. He was in a hurry, and the quicker he got mobile, the sooner his concerns could be mollified. He could make sure his son was okay.

He exited the airport into a night drenched with the scent of the ocean hanging heavy in the air over Sea Island. The smell invigorated his weary body and soul. The last eight days, since he had left Craig in Rome, had been a whirlwind. He'd flown from Rome to Ankara, Turkey, rushed to take a second flight to Warsaw, then travelled by train to Dusseldorf, down to Zurich, Switzerland, where he had recovered another passport and some currency from a lock box belonging to a numbered account, before riding the train to Paris and flying into London's Heathrow. From there it was a long haul across the Atlantic to New York City before boarding another train for Montréal. During his travels, his hours of sleep could be calculated in single digits. He was wary of his surroundings but not outwardly so; he was congenial but did his best to remain in the background. He never complained, and he chatted amiably with people sitting beside him without offering his name. The task was difficult—to remain forgettable without looking like you were trying to—but he'd had a lot of practice.

His legs shivered gleefully as he walked to the parkade. He climbed the stairs to the second level and a few seconds later saw a headlamp flash in the gloom, just once. Daniel glanced casually around him, making sure no one was following then walked towards the car that had flashed its lights. He got into the back seat and pulled the door closed.

"How does it feel?" a light, feminine voice inquired from the driver's seat. Dana al-Yami did not turn around, but Daniel could see the faint trace of a smile in her reflection in the rear-view mirror.

"To be home?" he replied. "Very strange. But it's good to see you."

"How's my man?" Dana asked.

"Like a lost puppy," Daniel chuckled. "But he's on his way here now."

Dana's face registered genuine surprise. "Why the sudden trip?"

"I need his help," Daniel said. "And I need yours, too. What's been happening?"

Dana's gaze shifted. She seemed to be staring through the windshield at nothing. "He's on the move. His friend is with him. They got into some trouble earlier, but they escaped. We're working on tracking them down now."

"But last you heard, he was safe?" Daniel asked.

Dana nodded. "He was then."

Daniel sighed heavily, momentarily feeling the weariness that came with perpetual worry. He brushed the sensation aside, looking up just as Dana began rifling through the briefcase at her side.

"Here's what you asked for," Dana said, handing him a manila envelope.

Daniel peeked inside and saw the cellphone and a fob to a rental car he had asked Dana to arrange for him when he had contacted her the previous day.

"Are you going to look for him?" Dana asked.

"No," Daniel said, pursing his lips and tapping his cheek. "I have something else I need to take care of first. That's what I need you for."

Daniel reached into the envelope and pulled out the iPhone. He quickly logged on to Twitter, the greatest gift to the spy trade since the advent of digital transmissions. With a 140-character limit, messages could be sent as code with little suspicion, especially given the jargon Twitter users had concocted. And with millions of users and a large percentage of spammers or "bot" accounts, a message promising to increase penis size could have more than one meaning.

The account had been created for him shortly after he broke out of prison. He watched the feed load, already prearranged to follow a specific number of random individuals. He checked his Mentions and felt his heart sink. He had several, some sent by "friends" in an effort to keep his account legitimate. But at the top of the LOLs and retweets was a mention from pastie_nose1987, saying he had won an iPad and all he needed to do was click on the link to claim his prize.

The message looked like spam—indeed, it had been distributed to a few thousand other users. But the link was specific to Daniel's iPhone. Everyone else was redirected to a popular porn website, but Daniel's phone opened the web browser and connected to a blank page. In the background, however, a pre-determined algorithm contained within his phone executed a series of commands that verified a match between phone and website, then downloaded a message to a diary application on the iPhone that also had millions of other users. All Daniel had to do was check the "Calendar" for that day.

In red letters were the words, "CONFIRMED MEETING."

Daniel swallowed hard and deleted the message. It confirmed what Dana had just told him. Ryan had been found. And he was in danger. But at least Edward was on his way to meet him.

Daniel gave Dana the information to contact Edward on Twitter.

"Please just keep an eye on them. They might need some help before the night is out," Daniel said. "I'll get there as soon as I can, but in the meantime, please check in with Edward now and then."

Daniel rattled off Edward's Twitter handle to Dana. She didn't write it down, just nodded.

"I'd better go," Daniel said. "Thanks, Dana."

Dana smiled in the mirror again.

Daniel took the envelope and stepped out of the car. As soon as the door closed, Dana backed out of the parking stall and drove away, exiting the parkade. Daniel watched as the brake lights winked and the car slid out of view.

He slid the phone back into the envelope, along with the car keys, turned and casually tossed the envelope onto the ground underneath the car immediately next to him. Daniel left the parkade and walked towards the line of taxis parked outside the arrivals terminal. He chose a taxi well back in the lineup and sat in the back seat, then told the driver to take him to the nearest mall.

CHAPTER

Adam Young rushed through Thresher's doorway, slamming the door behind him.

"What's happening?" Thresher asked, throwing the Gunsight file to one side of his desk. "I thought you headed home hours ago."

"Sir, we just received an alert from the Canadian Border Services Agency," Young said, making his way to the far wall of Thresher's office. Young pressed a concealed button, and one of the panels on the wall slid back, revealing a sixty-inch LED monitor. Once the monitor fired up, he went over to the phone on Thresher's desk, grabbed the handset and punched a button.

"Okay, you can play it," Young said, then put the call on speakerphone and replaced the receiver. He stepped to one side as Thresher turned lazily in his swivel chair to face the monitor.

The screen sprang to life, the first two seconds a chaotic mix of black-and-white frames, but Thresher and Young both stared intently at the images. The feed was obviously from a security camera, overlooking a row of desks. Most of the people standing in front of the desks were carrying bags or suitcases. The people sitting behind the desks all wore dark-coloured uniforms.

"Customs?" Thresher asked.

"Yes, sir," Young nodded energetically.

"Trudeau airport?"

"Not Montréal, sir," Young said, smiling. "Vancouver International."

"Really?" Thresher couldn't keep the shock out of his voice. Given the events that had taken place the last few days, he had a feeling what the video would reveal but was surprised all the same.

"Two hours ago," Young stated confidently, gesturing at the screen. "Stop it there," he said into the speakerphone. The image on the screen froze.

With only a carry-on bag and dressed in casual clothing, there stood Daniel Davis, aka Gunsight. But he looked...exactly like Davis was supposed to. Usually when they found new photos or footage of him, his skin was tinted, his hair was dyed or he wore a fake moustache or beard. But no attempt at concealment was evident now. Daniel just stood there, staring straight ahead. His greying hair was cropped close to his scalp, his face clean-shaven.

"He came in on a flight from Montréal," Young said. "Canadian passport in the name of Herman Wanger."

"Is that important?" Thresher asked, turning away from the screen.

"It might be, sir," Young replied, leaning over his boss to tap a few keys on Thresher's keyboard, then pointing at the monitor. "He's used this passport before, four years ago, when he crossed into Egypt from Israel."

"Interesting," said Thresher. "He's not that stupid. To use a passport he's already used. Not since we caught him so recently."

"I doubt it, sir," Young said.

Thresher tapped his index finger against his lips. "What's the order on this passport?"

"Report only, sir. A detention order was too risky for the Border Services to process properly. Plus, to deal with Davis, we'll want fewer witnesses," Young offered.

Thresher was impressed with Adam Young. So recently a cowering assistant, he was now asserting the analytical chops that had got him recommended to Thresher right out of CSIS training in Ottawa. *There's hope for the future yet,* Thresher thought.

"So what's our play?" Thresher asked Young.

"We watch," Young said. "He's obviously here for a reason, and there's no point in showing our hand until we have a better idea of why he's here. It looks like he wants us to know he's here...I just can't believe he's that foolish. So we just watch him."

Thresher nodded his approval. "Only for so long, though. Ultimately I don't care a lot about why he's here. I just want him gone."

"I'll get the watchers rolling, sir," Young said, leaving the room.

Thresher doubted a tailing group would have much luck, but he let Young go with it. The boy was learning, faster than Thresher had thought, to be sure. He was still green, but showing promise.

He turned to stare at Davis' frozen image. He was up to something, but Thresher realized he didn't care too much about what that was. He just wanted Daniel Davis in a very deep hole somewhere far away.

—⋘⋙—

Detective Susan Bartlett was supposed to be at her West Broadway condo. She was supposed to be in her soft, pink cotton pyjamas, complete with fuzzy bunny slippers, accompanied by a bottle of red wine and a week's worth of recorded TV dramas to catch up on.

Instead, she was back at work, summoned by the second of the two phone lines that ran into her condo, the secure line she hid behind a large vase when company was over, to prevent any unnecessary questions. The voice on the other end had been brusque and to the point—return to work and wait for a message.

So instead of finding out what the gang of doctors at Seattle Grace Hospital were up to this week, she was sitting in her office at Vancouver Police Department headquarters on Cambie Street, just a few blocks from home. She waited while her computer booted up, passing the time by absently clicking her fingernails on the desk.

"Another exciting Friday night, eh?" a voice called from the doorway. She looked up to see her partner, Detective Aly Talwar.

"What were you doing?" she asked as Aly walked in and sat in a chair across from her.

"Canucks tickets. You?"

Susan snorted. "Just trying to relax. Don't know why I bother anymore."

She entered her username and password then waited as the desktop revealed itself. She clicked through a series of folders then opened an obscure email application. A red light on a small box beside her computer flashed as the screen in front of her froze momentarily. She took the card hanging from a lanyard around her neck and swiped it through the card reader. An hourglass whirred then the email program opened.

She turned the swipe card over and chose a row of twelve alphanumeric characters from the list on the back. The list contained ten rows. She had to enter one set of numbers, but only she knew which row contained her exact pass code. The other rows were fakes, just in case her card was ever lost, misplaced or, worse, stolen.

She pressed Enter and a single email appeared in her Inbox. The sender's name was blocked out by a series of Xs. The email contained only three letters, all of them consonants.

"We've got mail," she murmured to Aly. He nodded and stood, walking out with Susan in his wake.

They walked across the length of the large basement their department had been assigned. The environment was a bit depressing—thick walls and no windows, all the better to prevent eavesdropping, electronic or otherwise.

This was the home of the Vancouver Integrated National Security Enforcement Team, otherwise known as INSET for the sake of brevity. INSET was the Heinz 57 of police departments in that its members were recruited from the Vancouver Police Department (VPD), of whom Susan and Aly were most senior, as well as the Canadian Security Intelligence Service (CSIS), Communications Security Establishment (CSE) and Canadian Border Services Agency (CBSA) and even the RCMP. INSET's activities involved mostly counterintelligence, but with a policing element. They were responsible for monitoring issues of national security—counterterrorism, counterintelligence and sedition, as well as organized crime. INSET was the catch-all agency for national security. But with teeth.

CSIS kept an eye on any threats to Canada but couldn't actually arrest anyone. The agency existed to gather

110

and analyze information. The other policing arms had to subsequently investigate, arrest and charge suspected criminals. In order to make the process more seamless and to include as many regional voices as possible, the Canadian government had, shortly after 9/11, set up four INSET teams, one each in Vancouver, Toronto, Ottawa and Montréal. A joint INSET for Alberta, located both in Calgary and Edmonton, had been added a few years earlier.

Although the RCMP were the national police force in Canada and policed activities in most of British Columbia, the VPD was Vancouver's own police force, and the feds wanted INSET in Vancouver because of the city's sheer size. After some intense negotiating, INSET was posted at VPD headquarters, with some RCMP representatives.

These changes had happened years before Susan and Aly had been hired. Susan had risen through the ranks of the VPD and had done some work with its criminal intelligence branch, and was then seconded to the Vancouver INSET. Aly, however, had worked as a CSIS analyst and then jumped into policing, wanting to have the power to act on the wrongs he discovered during his work. His assignment to INSET had been a natural move.

Aly and Susan approached a thick metal and Kevlar door with a pair of scanners on either side, far enough from one another that no one person could ever operate both simultaneously. They each held one thumb against a flat pane of glass that was a part of the scanners on the right.

A reader checked their thumbprints, matching them with an image on file. Both officers then swiped their cards through the reader on the left. A light above each scanner changed from red to green, and with a loud, audible click, the door opened to allow them access.

The room was larger than a typical office but contained INSET's most important piece of equipment—communications devices to ensure messages stayed secure. The room was staffed 24/7.

Neither Susan nor Aly knew the name of the gentleman sitting behind the bulletproof glass to one side of the room, nor did they know which agency he worked for. They only knew that when they received a secure message, they had to go to the basement, walk to the desk and pass their ID cards through a slot in the glass as wide as a slice of bread. The man took both cards, swiped them one at a time through another reader then compared the image on his computer screen to the two individuals in front of him. He then handed back their cards, unlocked a safe set in his desk, removed a USB flash drive and gave it to them.

Pairs-only was the rule to pick up a flash drive. The two then copied the contents of the USB onto a computer in the office that had no outside connections. Both individuals then placed the flash drive into a locked door the size of a mailbox set into the wall. A small conveyer took the USB to an incinerator.

"I wonder how much the government spends on those in a year," Aly mused aloud for about the hundredth time as he watched the flash drive disappear.

Susan said nothing, instead marching over to the computer to look at the contents of the USB. Only two files had been saved to the flash drive. One was a text document and the other a JPEG file. Susan opened the text document first.

"Interesting," Aly remarked as he pulled out a notepad to jot down a few points. Any such notepads were either locked away or burned at the end of every shift, depending on the importance of their contents. The pages were made of flash paper—attempts to photocopy them on a regular photocopier would cause them to catch fire and burn.

"Daniel Davis," Susan murmured. "Sound familiar to you?"

Aly shook his head, still writing.

The text document was a BOLO, or "be on the lookout," request sent from CSIS headquarters in Ottawa. They wanted to find or detain this Daniel Davis, whose name was followed by at least a dozen aliases. Ottawa was to be immediately informed of any sighting. Davis was considered a high-level national security interest, according to the code beside his name.

The JPEG file was a collage of photos of Davis, an original that was a decade old as well as ten photo simulations accounting for changes in hair colour, weight, facial hair and so on. Susan printed the images on the secure printer next to the computer terminal that also required both Aly and Susan to swipe their cards before accepting the print job.

"We could always print off the BOLO too," Susan commented.

Aly shook his head. "If I write down the details, I'm more likely to remember them later."

Photos in hand, the pair returned to Susan's office, and Susan sat down in front of the computer, clicked through a few windows then entered another username and password. The screen that opened was a treasure trove of information—access to numerous CSIS databases, as well as various policing databases such as the Canadian Policing Information Centre.

Susan plugged Daniel's name into a search field and waited. A long list of entries appeared with information on when the file was last used and from which database it originated.

"Whoa," Susan said, clicking on the first entry. It had been entered into the border agency's database only two hours earlier.

"What?" Aly asked, stepping around her desk to get a closer look.

"Davis walked right through the airport here earlier today," Susan said, scanning the report.

"They didn't grab him?" Aly asked, incredulous.

"It was a 'Report-only' tag on the alias." She made a note to request surveillance footage from the border agency, then clicked back into the list and opened up the next entry.

"At least we have somewhere to start," Aly said, scribbling in his notebook.

"Well, that might be the only lead we get," Susan said, frowning at the screen.

Aly looked up. "Why?"

"He's been dead for almost ten years."

CHAPTER

Kara seemed to be driving around aimlessly. And with each new turn, Ryan grew increasingly frustrated.

"What are you doing?" he finally asked tersely.

"Making sure we're not followed," Kara replied for the third time. To be fair, they had been driving in a random pattern for about thirty minutes, but Kara was careful in her craft. Counter-surveillance was one of the trickiest skills of all, and she was bringing everything she knew to bear to ensure they weren't being tailed.

"How do I know you're not kidnapping us as well?" Ryan asked grumpily.

"You have to trust me," Kara said, checking her rearview mirrors before turning again, back down the same road. "Now, tell me again what your uncle said."

Ryan sighed. "He said to meet him at the stripper's. I have no idea what he's talking about."

Ryan had never, not once in his life, been to a strip club. He hadn't attended a single stag party or "boys night out" that involved naked women, mud wrestling or any other kind of common debauchery his gender engaged in to satisfy their hedonistic desires. If Ryan wanted to watch a woman undress, he preferred to be the one helping her get naked.

"Even I've been to a strip club," Kara said, as if still trying to cajole the truth out of him.

Something else was contributing to Ryan's frustration. Kara had yet to explain any part of the evening's events—her sudden appearance and introduction at the Pond, their amazing rescue and why she had *his* uncle's phone number on *her* phone. So although he had no clue as to why everything tonight was happening, he understood Kara's involvement even less.

"Why are you so certain we're talking about someone who takes off their clothes?" Ryan asked.

"Duh. What else could it be?" Billy said, sullenly.

"No, hang on," Kara said, finally pulling over next to a convenience store, putting the Geo Metro in neutral and applying the parking brake. "There are other things that involve stripping. You can strip paint. There's weather stripping. I've also heard it used in reference to some minor surgeries. You can strip upholstery, too."

Ryan shook his head. "I got nothing. Sorry."

"Can't you strip a car?" Billy asked suddenly from the back.

Ryan frowned. Something in his brain was tugging at him now.

"What was that, Bill?"

"I said, can't you strip a car? Like, isn't that what crooks do sometimes? Take parts from cars or something like that?"

The memory was buried so deeply that it took time to surface, but when it did, Ryan was stunned by his uncle's comment. Ryan would never have considered it had Billy not mentioned it.

"If Ryan didn't spend his early adult years in strip clubs, he probably didn't spend them stealing car parts," Kara told Billy.

"No, Billy's right," Ryan said. "I know what he's talking about."

"You did steal cars?" Kara asked, incredulous.

"I didn't. It was just the name for a friend's shop," Ryan said. "I haven't thought of it in years."

"All right then," Kara nodded, shifting into gear and shoulder-checking. "So where are we going?"

"East Hastings," Ryan said without hesitating.

There was silence in the car.

"Oh, good," Billy piped up sardonically. "And I thought this night was going to get less dangerous."

"That's why I remember it," Susan said. She and Aly were driving through Vancouver to check out the first of what could be thousands of potential leads—a former co-worker.

"It was just so strange," she continued. "I mean, people die in the wilderness all the time, and on a slow news day, the media will do a story on it. But with this Davis guy, the coverage was a little heavy. Not over-the-top heavy, like he was some kind of star or saint or something, but the story ran for days longer than you'd expect. It was strange."

Before leaving the office, the pair had done their homework. They had discovered Davis wasn't really dead, even though a death certificate was filed in his name, but that was all they could get out of the CSIS brass. And the answers they got from their INSET colleagues were cryptic and not at all helpful. Davis had worked for the government. His death had been faked for his own protection, and he had since been relocated. CSIS had suggested some leads they could speak with but provided no further details. A plea for more information was rebuffed, despite Susan and Aly's top-secret security clearances.

They had a couple of stills from the airport security footage—nothing earth shattering, but the man in the video resembled the original photo they had of Davis.

That was strange too, Susan remarked to Aly at the time. The man's hair was a little thinner, but he appeared much the same. No facial hair, no hair dye, not even a hat to try to cover his face. It was as if he didn't care or didn't know he was a wanted man.

CSIS had coughed up one small piece of information—the name and address of a former co-worker of Davis', who they thought might be related to him. Susan knew that sometimes co-workers became good friends, but their CSIS contact was insistent that she and Aly should start with this guy.

Before the pair left to check out the co-worker, Aly retreated to his own desk and typed out a BOLO. He'd included Davis' picture and instructions for VPD officers to detain and contact either him or Susan immediately. They had learned as police officers that casting a wide net was often the best way to catch a single, specific fish.

"I guess we know why the news coverage was more than usual," Aly said, watching the scenery fly by. "If you fake someone's death, you want to sell it pretty hard. Even money says only you and a handful of people thought it was overdone."

Susan nodded as she pulled onto a quiet residential street then parked along the curb. They both took a moment to check out the exterior of the house before exiting the car and walking up to the front door. Susan knocked while Aly stood a few feet back from the front steps, looking side to side for anything suspicious. The lights were on in the living room, and the drapes were open, offering a good view of the interior.

No one answered. Susan tried the doorbell, and when no one came, she knocked again. Aly pulled out his cellphone and dialled the number they had been given for Edward Dick. Both heard the phone ringing inside, but no one picked it up.

"Nothing," Aly said, pocketing his phone.

"I think we just missed him," Susan said, peering through the window.

"How so?" Aly said, coming up the steps to stand beside her. Susan pointed to the kitchen table near the back of the room.

"Dinner's still on the table," Susan said. "Didn't eat much of it either."

Aly nodded, walking swiftly towards the detached garage. He pulled up on the handle of the unlocked garage door, revealing a dark chasm.

"Empty," Aly said. They had a description of a Cadillac registered in Edward's name. "BOLO him too?"

Susan shook her head. "What year was the Cadillac?"

"2011."

Susan nodded, then reached for her phone. "Let's try something."

In her INSET work, she found she could be a little more loosey-goosey with her investigative work in the early stages. In normal circumstances she'd need a warrant, but in a case as strange as this, well, there was no harm in asking.

Dead guy not really dead. CSIS won't say why he needs to be arrested. Possible lead disappears right before she and Aly arrive. The sooner they found this Edward guy, the better.

A BOLO would have been the best way to go, but GPS technology now made finding vehicles easier than it used to be. Thanks to security systems like OnStar, locating a specific vehicle was a lot simpler. They just had to ask the company to use their technological magic to locate the car. No fuss, no muss. And if Susan remembered correctly, General Motors offered OnStar as an option at purchase. And most Cadillac owners didn't scrimp on options.

She made her request and waited. Her hunch was right. She snapped her fingers at Aly to get his attention then pointed at his notepad and shouted out an address to him. Aly looked bewildered.

"East Hastings?" he asked incredulously. "Maybe he ran out of crack."

CHAPTER 12

Some called it "Pain and Wastings," indicative of the heartache that seemed to live on every street corner and in every alley in the area of Main and Hastings. Drug addicts, many of them HIV positive, as well as dealers and prostitutes were in abundance. The worst part of Vancouver.

"I hate this place," Billy muttered, staring out the window.

"Me too," Kara said. "I can't imagine why you would ever come down here, Ryan."

As they drove, Ryan explained. Following his father's death, Ryan, then fifteen, had been placed in the care of his Uncle Edward, who had a PhD in languages. To try to get his nephew's mind off the loss of his father, Edward had purchased a 1975 Dodge Charger at an auction for one hundred dollars. It had been so cheap because the car needed a lot of love to make it roadworthy, and his uncle agreed to fund the rebuilding effort if Ryan did the work. Ryan had gladly taken him up on the offer. Because his uncle didn't have enough space in his garage, he had suggested they take the car to a friend of his who could store it and help Ryan with the repairs. That man's shop was located in a warehouse on East Hastings. Ryan's uncle, for reasons Ryan never fully understood, called his friend "the stripper." His real name was Gary.

"And what happened to the car?" Kara asked.

"I sold it for about five grand," Ryan explained. "I was living on campus by then so I really didn't need it."

"Your uncle must have been pissed," Billy said.

"Actually, he was proud of me," Ryan replied with a smile. He pointed out the window and said, "It's that alley up ahead."

Unlike their surroundings, this particular alley was flooded with light. They drove up to a heavy metal gate, two metres high, topped with barbed wire. A pair of surveillance cameras peered down on them from the buildings above. No junkies or hookers here.

"Do you think he's even here?" Kara asked, looking around.

"I guess we're about to find out," Ryan said. He opened his car door and stepped out into the alley, looking directly at one of the cameras. A few seconds later, the gate started to retract. Kara edged through the gate after Ryan climbed back into the car.

"Biometrics," Ryan said. "Always thought it was cool those cameras could figure out who I was."

"Will he mind that we're here?" Kara asked.

"He'll know that we're here," Ryan said. "He has a silent alarm hooked up to the gate. It sends him a text message anytime the gate opens."

"Fancy," Kara murmured.

"Amateur," Billy sputtered.

Ryan directed her to a parking spot beside a large bay door. With the exception of the entryway, the expansive warehouse enveloped them on all sides. All three of them exited the car, and Ryan led them to a door beside the bay door. He turned the knob and pushed it open.

"Unlocked?" Kara asked, suddenly wary.

"Did you see the gate we just came through?" Ryan asked rhetorically. "Gary always said if they can get through that, they deserve whatever's inside."

Motion-sensitive lights suddenly illuminated the cavernous warehouse as they stepped inside. The shop was exactly as he remembered it. Now there were six different cars in varying stages of readiness, and expansive benches gleamed with tools of every description. The bare cement floor had no visible oil or other vehicle fluid stains. It was akin to any man's personal piece of heaven.

"I guess your uncle's not here yet," Kara said, her eyes methodically taking in everything.

"His car would be here if he was," Ryan said. "As for Gary..."

"Right behind you!" a voice bellowed. The trio turned around, startled to see a huge man making their way towards them. He towered at roughly seven-feet tall with thick arms and a barrel chest. His look was further enhanced by a long, grey, bushy beard, a leather biker vest over a black T-shirt and gold chains glistening around his neck. "Yo, Mister Davis!"

"Yo, Gary," Ryan replied, accepting the outstretched hand. Gary's entire hand took his in a viselike grip. "Sorry for just showing up unannounced. I know I finished my car a while ago...."

"Your uncle called. I hear you guys have been in some trouble," Gary said.

Ryan introduced Billy and Kara, but Gary and Kara eyed one another strangely, almost as if they were trying to place the other.

Gary's belt suddenly vibrated. He grabbed the cellphone from his belt and tapped a key. A small video screen popped up, showing a black Cadillac driving through the open gate.

"Looks like your uncle just pulled up," Gary said, heading to the door. "Then maybe someone can explain what the hell is going on."

"I'm hoping for that, too," Ryan muttered to himself.

Moments later, Ryan's uncle entered the garage, his overcoat slightly spattered with rain and his unfortunate comb-over of grey hair askew and flopping across his forehead. Edward was tall, though not as tall as Gary, and very skinny. He had been the one constant besides Billy in Ryan's life, always checking up on him, always making sure Ryan had enough money. Ryan's uncle had been a rock—stoic, gracious and unflappable.

But all that confidence seemed to be coming undone now, right before Ryan's eyes. As he stepped forward to hug his uncle, he could see raindrops on Edward's forehead, except they were actually beads of sweat. His uncle's face was flushed, his focus seemingly scattered. He embraced his nephew more fiercely than usual, and Ryan could feel the rapid rise and fall of his uncle's heavy breathing.

"Thank God you're all right," Edward said, squeezing Ryan even harder.

"We're fine. Just a little scared," Ryan said, pulling back, trying to figure out why his uncle was so perturbed. "And confused."

"Me too," Edward said. He greeted Billy and Gary.

Ryan motioned to Kara, saying, "And you also know Kara since your number was in her phone." Edward nodded at Kara, and they casually shook hands.

Gary motioned all of them over to a grouping of scattered chairs near one corner of the immense garage. There were no tools here—only a fridge and a small table holding a coffeemaker.

"Do you like your caffeine hot or cold?" Gary asked, opening the fridge to reveal a selection of pop. "It looks like you're all going to need it."

Edward took a mug of coffee, raised it to his lips and then set the mug on the table, his hands shaking noticeably. Ryan exchanged a look with Billy, who shrugged his shoulders.

Edward took a deep breath to calm his extremities. He reached for his cup again. "Okay. Tell me everything."

Ryan did most of the talking, with Billy interjecting to explain how he had been snatched from their house—a ring of the doorbell had lured him away from his basement retreat. As soon as he'd opened the door, there'd been a flash and then he was on the floor. He was, like Ryan, hustled into the van outside, cuffed and bagged.

Ryan ran through it all—the initial attack after leaving the café, the assault at home, the van ride and their unexpected rescue. He tried to recall as much as he could, but his uncle had him go over particular moments—what did he hear, feel, see or even smell? Each turn back in time often elicited new details.

"You're sure they were speaking Arabic?" Edward asked, pouring a second cup of coffee.

"Positive," Ryan replied.

Edward's phone beeped, and he took it out and tapped out a message. Ryan caught a look at the screen.

"Really, Uncle Ed? Tweeting? Now?"

"Just one quick message to a friend. Need to look like everything is normal," replied Edward. "And you said the woman appeared to be in charge?"

"She was the one doing all the talking. The rest of the men just did what they were told."

"Dialect?"

"Riyadh, for sure."

Edward nodded, biting his lower lip as if thinking.

Gary's phone beeped, and he excused himself, hustling to the other side of the garage to take the call.

"And she spoke English, but the rest didn't?"

"Yep," Ryan said then stopped abruptly. Something in his brain was trying to get his attention. He closed his eyes, and it came to him. He was surprised he had forgotten—it was the most confusing thing that had happened all night, which was saying a lot.

"No, one of the guards did. I think the woman said his name. Called him Kamil. It was when he was choking me, when I was whining about letting me go..." Ryan said.

"What did he say?" Edward asked.

"He said, 'You are son of spy.'" Ryan glanced up at his uncle.

Edward suddenly turned ashen. He stood up and paced the garage. "Anything else?" he asked Ryan.

"Just that I was a prisoner and needed to listen," Ryan said, watching his uncle. His reaction made Ryan feel increasingly unsettled, but that feeling was the norm tonight. "What did that mean, 'son of spy'? It doesn't make sense," added Ryan. "I mean, I get it's poor English, and he was saying I was the son of a spy, but that doesn't add up either. Dad was a diplomat. I know. I travelled with him."

Edward was facing a wall, tapping a foot restlessly on the gleaming cement floor. He pushed at his comb-over, which just flopped back against his forehead.

Gary returned all of a sudden, putting his phone in the holster on his belt. "I just got off the phone with my guys. The van's still there, but it's empty. Plates are missing, no one in sight."

"You have *guys*?" Billy asked, perplexed.

"Sources," Gary replied, then looked at Edward. "What do you want to do?"

"Why are you asking him?" Billy asked.

"Shut it, Bill," Ryan said.

"No. Look, they're just supposed to be friends," Billy said. "You said Gary was a car freak, and your uncle is retired. Gary has 'guys' he can just call. I mean, even I think that sounds weird," Billy rambled. "So why is he asking your uncle?"

Ryan conceded the point to Billy. "Okay, why are you asking Edward?"

Edward and Gary exchanged a glance. "We've known each other for a long time, Billy," Gary said.

"And that explains everything?" Billy said, almost deadpan.

"No, it doesn't, but it will have to do for now," Edward replied. "First, we need to settle on a course of action, then we can start explaining things."

"That's what everyone's been saying all night. And we still don't know who she really is," Billy replied, poking Kara in the ribs, hard. One of Kara's hands shot out towards Billy's like an uncoiling snake, capturing his finger and bending it backwards.

"Don't touch me," she growled menacingly, throwing Billy's hand to the side.

"You'll get your answers, Billy, but right now, I need something from you," Edward said, crouching in front of him.

"And just what might that be?" Billy asked.

"Your fingers."

CHAPTER 13

"You've got something?" Thresher asked as Adam burst into his office.

"We think so. An old location on East Hastings that seems to be very popular tonight," Adam replied.

"And?" Thresher asked.

"We're still just watching, just to see what's going on. We did intercept a text message from a known phone to an unknown phone. It pinged off a nearby cellphone tower. Something about strippers."

"I doubt Gunsight came all the way here just for a lap dance. Get a team over there. Tell them to keep their distance for now. Just observe, unless something unusual happens."

"Right," Adam said, nodding and ducking out.

Thresher smiled. So many people had come to work here, but few could stomach the actual job. It rubbed their Canadian morality the wrong way. But Adam seemed different.

Thresher's portfolio was very un-Canadian. It went against so many principles held dear by members of the service that finding someone to manage this new department had been incredibly difficult. The task was so awkward that the manager of the newly created Economic Co-operation Information Division (ECID) was paid almost as much as the CSIS director.

But Thresher enjoyed money and making things happen, regardless of how detestable his orders might be, so when he was offered the position of ECID manager, he jumped at the chance. And alone at night, when he thought about it, he could easily convince himself that he was doing important work that helped Canadians from coast to coast to coast.

Really, he helped create jobs. He contributed to Canadians' quality of life. He helped promote his country globally, especially within the G20. Exports were soaring, and imports were staying modest. Money was pouring into the national coffers in ways the federal government had never before seen, and Canada as a whole was benefiting as a result.

ECID's mission, created quietly by an order-in-council in 2011, was to share necessary economic information that would foster more harmonious trade relations between Canada and other countries around the globe. Yet "harmonious" was not the adjective most would use to describe ECID's actual mandate. Basically, Thresher and his staff were fixers. If an issue was holding up a trade deal of some kind, Thresher was brought in to help make that problem disappear.

He had been surprised, at first, to find out that individuals were often the barriers to trade deals. And their positions were often not terribly important either—company CEOs or politicians. In most cases, Thresher and his department dealt with troublesome ex-pats who had long ago left their home countries but were still deemed problematic or dangerous in their native nation. So Thresher's job was to make those individuals go away.

He didn't kill anyone. He'd had that discussion with a few staffers at CSIS over the last few years. He did not have the blood on his hands of any of the twenty-three troublemakers he had since silenced. Canada, after all, didn't commit murder. But with billions of dollars of trade at stake, what was the harm in sending a few men and women—and sometimes their children too—back where they came from?

It was all done quietly and under the table. One day, Tong and Shen Immigrant were living in their apartment in Montréal and the next they were back in Beijing.

That was the extreme outcome. Thresher and his staff most often recorded information about specific persons and their movements in Canada and passed it on to the government. Sometimes those people went away with no CSIS intervention whatsoever.

Occasionally that help went outside Canada's borders. When agitators travelled abroad, the countries they visited might have an interest in knowing about their travels. A few were even Canadian citizens, but no harm ever came to them.

They might be refused entry to a country, or they might encounter hassles or difficulties they hadn't anticipated, but they almost always made it back home safely.

And yet, Thresher thought, twirling lazily in his chair, the "almost always" part concerned him now. Gunsight was one of Thresher's biggest problems and had been since ECID's formation. The Saudis were insistent in requesting Thresher's assistance. And they were dangling a very juicy fish—most favoured nation trade status—in front of Canada in order to make that happen. It meant more Canadian products would make their way to the stores in Riyadh, and precious Saudi oil would come to Canada's borders to supplement the nation's own production. This man—Gunsight—represented hundreds of billions of dollars. With that much money on his head, how could Thresher not hand him over to the Saudis?

But now he was loose. And Thresher knew enough about Gunsight's background to know it would be extraordinarily difficult—if not impossible—to hand him over again.

Thresher also knew he and his staff—and the work they did—could be at risk. Canadians could scarcely tolerate foreign governments treating their own citizens poorly. They wouldn't accept the Canadian government handing over its own people for supposed nefarious purposes.

It was personal too. Thresher and Gunsight had worked together so many years ago and butted heads on more than one occasion. Daniel was a field agent while Thresher was an office man. The two were frequently at loggerheads. Thresher saw Daniel as out of touch with the realities of institutional management, and Daniel accused Thresher of being little more than another paper-shuffling bureaucrat. Daniel was always asking for more resources, and Thresher always refused, citing budget constraints or policy. Just before Daniel had "died," the relationship between the two had eroded to the point where they no longer acknowledged one another's presence if they were in the same room.

So Thresher would get some personal pleasure in tracking down this particular file. Getting him out of the country was best for Canada. And, ultimately, best for Thresher as well.

CHAPTER 14

"Child's play," Billy sniffed.

"Glad to hear it," Edward said, pointing to the well-appointed iMac on Gary's desk. "Get to work."

Gary's office was one floor up from the main garage, the walls covered in posters of sports cars, motorcycles and, naturally, scantily clad women.

"I like it in here," Billy said, easing into the chair and taking in the scenery.

"Just get to it," Edward said. "Time isn't exactly on our side."

The idea had seemed complex, but given Billy's talents, and his access, the task was relatively simple. When Gary had said the van was empty but the licence plate was missing, a thought had occurred to Edward. After the disastrous Stanley Cup riots of 2011 when the Vancouver Canucks had lost hockey's most prized possession to the Boston Bruins, some cities mounted closed-circuit cameras on their streets, especially at known trouble spots. The security measure was even simpler for universities, which commonly ran their own small security forces and had volunteers who escorted female students or staff to their vehicles at night. Universities were, after all, their own little communities. And with the size of the community being that much smaller, fewer cameras were required.

If, as Edward had explained to everyone, a camera was in the vicinity of Ryan and Billy's house or any of the nearby streets, they might be able to get a better physical description of their attackers, if not their licence plate number.

Billy boasted that he could access archived footage from earlier in the evening with relative ease. His skills had little to do with computer hacking—he had programmed the last software update to digitally store the footage off-site in a "cloud."

"It was an easy sell," Billy explained as he woke up the screen on the iMac. "Clouds are enormous servers located in what they call 'farms' thousands of klicks away, usually in California. Whole rows of servers, actually." He sniffed and looked up at Gary. The mechanic leaned in and entered his username and password into the fields to allow Billy access. "You should really change that password," Billy said.

"You were talking about clouds?" Gary said tersely, crossing his enormous arms.

"Yeah, so these server farms, huge buildings, sometimes called data centres, are just rows upon rows of storage devices. Rather than hosting all your archived data in your own server room, which, in the case of security camera videos, eats up gobs of memory, I wrote a program that securely transmits the footage to a cloud. And with the beauty of Wi-Fi, the data can be accessed at any time and watched without downloading," Billy practically bragged. "Less stuff to buy, less money spent—the university only pays for the storage space. Well, that, and they're paying me. It was my idea."

A blue screen lit up with a myriad of icons, the dock at the bottom showing the programs immediately available as well as a smattering of files saved on the desktop.

"Safari is right there." Gary pointed to the compass icon on the dock, indicating Apple's own web browser.

"Pul-lease," Billy snorted, opening the applications folder. "If you want serious work done, you need a serious tool." He tapped a few keys, and a window opened, a status bar slowly filling with a blue line. "A browser I wrote for myself and, well, some friends of mine online," he said. "We call it 'Mage.' You know, like a wizard."

No one said a word. Once the file was downloaded, Billy launched it. His fingers began to fly, tapping in a long, convoluted domain name into the web address bar.

"We're going to have to access this from a different location, just to be safe," Billy said. He typed in some account information, and a long list of hyperlinks, similar to a directory, appeared.

"What's that?" Edward asked.

"Proxy server," Billy explained. "It's fine if I log in to check everything, but if they trace it to an address on East Hastings, they'll think something is weird." He scrolled down the menu, looking for something none of the others in the room could identify. "There she is..." Billy said and clicked on a jumble of letters. "Server for the university's library system. That will be a lot less weird."

Another screen appeared, and Billy again entered a username and password. As an employee of the university, he could use his own information.

His index finger moved like a trigger on the mouse, clicking through a series of links, then he typed in more information. Soon he was hovering over a server located in California that hosted all of the archived digital footage for the UBC campus.

"How many cameras are there?" Kara asked.

"About eighty," Billy replied. A collective sigh was heard as everyone wondered how they were going find footage of one van from eighty different cameras. "Relax, guys, it's easy as pie."

Suddenly the screen displayed a map of the entire campus, with significant buildings denoted and small video camera avatars dotted throughout. "We can limit the field just by clicking on the cameras we want to see and then selecting the hours of recording we want to view."

It turned out that six cameras were in the vicinity of Ryan and Billy's house—Billy just wasn't sure of their

exact positioning. He right-clicked on all of the cameras in
turn, which brought up a small scroll bar menu for each
one. Each menu provided a list of time stamps spanning
sixty-minute intervals. Billy selected footage from an hour
before he and Ryan were snatched and the hour after,
explaining that they could easily fast-forward through the
times they didn't need. Billy clicked open footage for the first
camera then immediately closed it.

"What the hell…?" Ryan said.

"It's facing the wrong direction," Billy said, picking
the next one.

He advanced the footage to the time he thought the
kidnapping took place—around 8:00—then rewound ten
minutes. He clicked on a separate button to increase the
playing speed of the video.

The camera view was at the far east end of their
house, looking out onto a wide parking lot. All of them
watched, almost breathless, as dark figures wandered at an
awkwardly fast speed in and out of the camera's field of
view. But there was no sign of the van.

The next camera, which was across the street from
their house and at the far end of the block, also revealed
nothing of use. The third camera, which faced the opposite
direction, quickly became important.

"There!" Kara pointed, but everyone had already seen
it. The front of a white painters' van passed at the bottom of

the camera's field but didn't come into view again. All they could see was the top of the van.

Billy clicked on the screen to mark the time then opened up the fourth camera. Jackpot. The camera was posted at the opposite end of the alley from the first camera and showed a clear shot of the van turning in then dimming its lights. The van's rear end faced the camera, but the licence plate was too far away to see it clearly.

"Dammit," Kara whispered.

"Relax, baby," Billy chortled. "You ain't seen nothing yet."

He dove back into the applications folder, clicked on "Utilities" and opened a file called Grab. He used his cursor to draw a box around the rear of the van and clicked. A TIFF image of the rear of the van popped up. Billy held down the iMac's Control key and moved the mouse wheel forward to zoom in. The image was blurry, but it was enough. The number on the BC licence plate was clearly visible.

"Genius," Ryan said, clapping his friend on the shoulder.

Gary grabbed a scrap piece of paper and jotted down the number. He pulled his iPhone out. "I'll be right back," he said.

"Going to call your guys?" Billy asked sarcastically.

Gary just kept walking.

Kara pulled a cellphone from her pants pocket.

"Another one?" Ryan asked.

Kara smiled faintly. "I'll be right back," she said and left the room.

Edward, Ryan and Billy kept running through the footage. Unfortunately, the light post at the end of the alley illuminated only the first few metres of the alley. The front three-quarters of the van, and every person that emerged from it, was cloaked in darkness. Billy fiddled with some settings, trying to lighten the black-and-white images, without success. No one could discern a single feature of any of the bodies moving around. Even when they watched as first Billy and then Ryan were brought out to the van, the figures had their backs turned.

Billy switched back to the second camera, wondering why they hadn't noticed anything. At Ryan's instruction, Billy played the footage at regular time. It was no wonder they had missed seeing the van—the headlights had been extinguished as soon as the van turned into the alley. Watching the footage on fast forward, the figures had been visible for only a fraction of a second.

"So what now?" Ryan asked.

"We wait for Gary," Edward said.

"Good, then you can start explaining."

"Ryan…"

"Oh, come on!" Ryan exploded suddenly. Even Billy was taken aback. Rage was not a colour his friend often wore.

"We've been shocked, cuffed, beaten, pursued and freed, all in the space of an hour. There's so much going on right now I don't even know where to begin, but you'd better start talking, goddammit!"

Edward waved his hands in a calming gesture. "Okay, okay. Where do you want me to start?"

Ryan hadn't been ready for his uncle to give in. *Where do I start?* he wondered frantically. Kara miraculously rescuing them? His uncle's name in her phone? The cryptic code word for Gary's shop?

"Son of spy," Ryan sputtered.

"What?" Edward asked.

"I saw your face when I told you what that one guy said to me. Son of spy. It means something. Those bad guys were talking about me. What is it? Some kind of code?"

"Ryan, I really think we should wait and talk about that in private."

"No, not private. Now. Billy's in this, too, so if it means something, if it has something to do with us being where we are tonight, I want to know what it is."

"Fine," Edward said, leaning back against the wall. Ryan and Billy looked on as Edward collected his thoughts. "Ryan, I'm breaking many, many laws by telling you this, so you have to promise that you'll keep it under wraps, okay?"

Ryan nodded curtly, arms crossed, glowering at his uncle.

Edward knew he couldn't drop the bombshell any more softly than to just say it. "Your dad never was a diplomat, Ryan. He worked for CSIS," Edward said with a sigh.

"What?" Billy asked, the acronym strangely foreign to him.

Edward started to speak but was interrupted.

"Canadian Security Intelligence Service," said Ryan, his voice cold. "He's saying my dad was a spy."

CHAPTER 15

Ryan was an avid reader of the news, consuming most of his content online, and had been since the age of fifteen. He knew about CSIS just as well as anyone else in Canada, except for those who worked at the agency.

It was the country's spy agency, though nothing so prolific as the Central Intelligence Agency (CIA) in the U.S. or the Secret Intelligence Service (SIS), known more broadly as MI6, in the United Kingdom. As Ryan understood it, CSIS did most of its work domestically, keeping an eye on threats to Canada internally, as well as hunting down spies from other nations.

He also knew that the agency's history had been somewhat checkered in recent years. Most notably had been the series of warrants issued for foreign nationals, with little tangible proof justifying their detention. Many of those people had since been freed by judges. Ryan knew CSIS had played roles in other infamous Canadian debacles as well, such as the investigation into the Air India bombings in 1985 and the plant of a mole in the leadership of a white supremacy group in the 1990s.

But Ryan's knowledge of CSIS didn't change the fact that his uncle's confession went against everything he had ever believed about his father.

"If he was with CSIS, then why all the travel?" Ryan asked, his mind racing, grasping at mental straws to try to prove his uncle wrong.

"He was a foreign liaison officer," Edward replied, pushing unsuccessfully again at his comb-over. "He worked with intelligence communities in other countries, sometimes for extended periods, to see if they had any information about possible threats to Canada."

"Jesus." Ryan sat down on the edge of the desk. "Why would he lie to me like that? Why didn't he just tell me?"

"Think about it, Ryan," Edward said gently. "Kids watch cartoons and read comic books about spies. When you're young, you think being a spy is the coolest thing in the world, playing with plastic spy cameras and watches. If your dad had told you he worked for CSIS, how would you have reacted as a kid, even a teenager?"

"I don't know," Ryan replied, not sure what his uncle was getting at.

"You would've bragged about it," Edward said. "While your friends talked about how their daddies were doctors or lawyers or something like that, you would've told anyone who would listen that your dad was a spy.

When it comes to intelligence, we take our jobs seriously, and confidentiality and discretion are of utmost importance. We don't hide our job from the people we love, but we don't broadcast it either. We don't want our neighbours telling strangers at the mall, 'Oh yeah, the guy down the street works for CSIS.' So you don't tell your kids, and you don't tell your neighbours or your relatives or friends. You tell your spouse, but you sure as hell don't talk about the day-to-day work of the job. And you don't tell your kids what you really do until they are mature enough to keep it quiet."

Ryan nodded, still in shock, not sure how to respond. It all made sense, but why was this all coming out now?

"What do you mean 'we'?" Billy asked all of a sudden.

"Pardon?" Edward asked, his face suddenly guarded.

"You said, '*we* don't hide our job' and '*we* don't want our neighbours.' What do you mean?"

Edward glanced at Ryan, who was now looking at him with questioning eyes. He couldn't imagine the emotions his nephew was going through right now, losing your father and then finding out that he had lied to you about who he really was.

"Because I worked for CSIS, too," Edward said.

"Hell." Ryan folded his arms across his chest and stared up at the ceiling, unwilling to meet Edward's gaze. "If I didn't already know you weren't my real uncle, I'd wonder if that was even true."

But it was. Ryan had always called Edward his uncle, even though they weren't related by blood. He was a friend of Ryan's father, and as far back as Ryan could remember, Edward had always been there—birthday parties, barbecues, even the occasional Christmas. He understood when his father died that a blood relative wouldn't be looking out for him. Ryan's extended family was small and so scattered that there really never was another option.

"You two worked together?" Ryan asked.

"Yes. We did meet in Ottawa, like we always told you, but it was under different circumstances. I can't go into a lot of detail about our activities, but your father was one of my closest friends. That never changed."

Ryan was sceptical, but he decided to at least take his uncle at his word. Not believing him wouldn't help the situation. He could spend some time thinking about it later, but other questions needed answers.

"And Gary?"

Edward cleared his throat. "Look, Ryan, I've already shared with you more than I should have so don't push it. But, yes, Gary works for CSIS, just not in the same way. He's more of a technical support person, on contract."

"He fixes cars?" Billy asked.

"He fixes up cars," Edward corrected him, declining to go into further detail. "When he's not taking one of his POS cars to a demolition derby, he enhances vehicles on behalf of the agency."

Ryan suddenly thought of Kara, who had left the room without explanation. He was about to ask his uncle about her when Gary burst into the room.

"We got a hit!" Gary said loudly, barrelling in. "And it might be a live one."

"The guys deliver again," Billy muttered.

Gary glared down at the computer whiz, who stared right back, unflinching.

"I told them a bit about us, Gary...including Ryan's dad," Edward explained. "I didn't have much of a choice."

"Us?" Gary asked.

"You, his dad, me," Edward replied.

"Oh," Gary said. "Well then, no need to be keeping secrets. Yes, I have guys. Guys with access to certain directories and registries. Guys who can look up stuff like licence plates and shit."

"Okay," Edward said. "What did they find?"

Gary held up the scrap piece of paper he'd taken with him. "Licence plate doesn't come back to a person. Or a rental, surprisingly. It comes back to a company."

"Stolen," Edward sighed.

"Maybe not." Gary smiled grimly. "The company is called Mansouri Consulting, just off the downtown area. I had my guys," he glared at Billy, "run the corporate title on the company. Turns out it's a holding company with an off-shore address."

"Where is it?"

"South America," Gary replied, looking up with a grin. "But guess who wrote the letter of credit to get Mansouri Consulting in our neck of the woods?"

"Who?" Edward asked.

"Arab National Bank."

The room went silent. Edward was suddenly deep in thought, and Ryan had no idea what they were talking about. Billy decided to whistle ominously.

"Look it up, Billy," Edward said. "Mansouri Consulting. Look it up now."

After showing Billy the paper so he could properly spell the company's name, Gary dropped it into a shredder beside the desk.

"Aren't we going to need that information later?" Ryan asked.

"We know where we got it. We can always find it again," Gary said.

Ryan's head felt like it was about to literally explode, and not just from trying to understand what was going on. It was almost nine o'clock, and all he'd had to eat or drink tonight was a tea and a Pepsi. His throbbing head was telling him that lying down, even for a few minutes, would be welcome.

"Bathroom still in the same place?" he asked. Gary nodded, pointing towards the door leading downstairs to the main floor. Ryan mumbled his thanks and shuffled off, just wanting to splash some water on his face. He passed several workbenches, an engine on a hoist and a disassembled transmission. He momentarily lost his balance and bumped into the wall, his shoulder hitting some kind of black square. A tiny light on the square quietly flickered from green to red. Ryan figured it was a motion sensor, and he'd tell Gary when he returned to the office that he'd accidentally body checked it.

As he approached the door to the washroom, he saw a shadow moving against the far wall. He squinted and saw Kara slouched in a corner, talking on her cellphone. She was whispering, but her tone sounded urgent to Ryan.

She looked up suddenly and saw Ryan. Without a word, she stood and walked to the far side of the room, away from him.

Odd, Ryan thought, but so much about tonight was odd that he had to filter what really required his attention. The bathroom was vintage auto shop. The closet-sized space smelled like oil, with a cement floor, peeling wallpaper and a toilet that looked like it hadn't been cleaned in a very long time. Water dribbled out of the faucet when he turned it, and Ryan sighed, cupping his hands beneath it and splashing the water over his face. The tepid water did nothing to make him feel better. He tried a few more handfuls and then gave up, choosing to dry his face with his sleeve rather than risk one of the towels.

I just want to go home, he whined to himself, throwing open the bathroom door.

He'd taken two steps out of the bathroom when an enormous hand grabbed his shoulder and pushed him back and sideways, a meaty forearm pinning his chest against the wall.

"Don't. Move," a deep voice said.

———

Ryan dared to look at his attacker.

It was Gary.

"What's going on?" Ryan asked. "I'm a little sensitive about being pushed around right now, you know?"

"I said *don't move*," Gary grumbled, more emphatically.

Ryan nodded and froze against the wall. Gary released his grip and reached behind Ryan's back. Ryan inhaled sharply as Gary's hand reappeared, holding not a gun but some sort of...plastic blade?

"I mean it," Gary said, glaring at him. "Don't budge."

Gary leaned closer and brought the plastic blade down towards Ryan's legs. Ryan fought the urge to jump away and watched as Gary stopped, now moving the plastic blade up and down over his pant legs. Ryan squinted at the object in Gary's hand—it looked like one of those wands airport security uses to check passengers for concealed metal objects.

"I'm a real boy, I swear," Ryan said, trying to lighten the mood.

"Turn around."

Ryan obeyed, turning so his back faced Gary. He couldn't hear it, but felt the air moving behind him as Gary waved the wand back and forth. The wand suddenly grumbled as it passed over the rear of his pants. Gary stopped then waved again, this time right over Ryan's right buttock. The grumbling grew louder.

Gary reached into the back pocket of Ryan's jeans, digging around, his fingers reaching for something and not being subtle about it.

"Seriously, Gary," Ryan half-yelled. Then Gary's fingers felt like they pinched together in his pocket.

"You can move now," Gary said ominously as he removed his hand.

Ryan turned. Gary was holding a tiny speck, half the size of a penny, in his fingertips. He flashed the blade over it, and the grumble turned into a distinctive roar.

"What is it?" Ryan asked.

"Tracking dot," Gary said. "Sends signals via GPS to a properly calibrated unit that can plot its location. You passed by one of my alarms here." Gary pointed to the black sensor Ryan had bumped into on his way to the bathroom. "And it picked up the signals from it. Tripped an alarm that went to my cellphone and computer. Do you know how it got in your pocket?"

Ryan looked closely at the grey half-circle in Gary's wiener-sized fingertips. He shook his head.

"They probably planted it on you after they zapped you," Gary said, turning. Billy and Edward emerged from the office, investigating the commotion. "Billy, get over here."

Billy stepped towards Gary, who waved the blade all over him. The wand stayed quiet.

"Clean," Gary said. "They obviously don't care about you that much."

"Hey!" Billy yelled.

"Or they think that Ryan and Billy are going to stay together, so where they find one, they'll find the other," Kara suggested. No one had noticed she had re-joined the group.

"They know where I am?" Ryan asked, feeling incredibly dumb.

"Probably," Gary said, his voice with an added edge. "But we have an even bigger wrinkle."

Ryan said nothing, merely waiting.

"I got a call back from my guys," Gary glowered at Billy as he said the last two words. "The police are looking for the two of you. Your pictures have been circulated to all patrol officers on shift. They're to detain you on sight and hand you over to INSET."

"INSET?" Ryan repeated, perplexed.

"Integrated National Security Enforcement Team," Edward suddenly spoke up. "Hunters. Looking for terrorists, spies, the like."

Ryan felt panic well up inside him. "What could they want with us?"

"No idea," Gary cut back in. "But you can't stay here. With the bad guys trying to grab you, and the police after you, they obviously want you pretty bad. We all need to stay mobile."

"For how long?" Ryan asked.

"Well, I guess that's up to us," Gary said. "We can probably play keep away for a few hours, but once they pick up a scent, it's only a matter of time."

"Or we can find out what they're looking for," Edward said. "If we figure that out, we might be able to come up with a better strategy to get rid of them, or at least stay ahead of them."

"I like it," Kara said.

"Can't we just go to the police and find out what's going on?" Billy half pleaded.

"INSET isn't the normal police, Billy," Edward said gently. "They're basically an action arm of CSIS. That means CSIS wants you for some reason…badly. I don't think you want to just hand yourself over."

"Where would we even start looking?" Billy whined.

"Mansouri Consulting," Ryan said. "It's the only lead we have. I still don't see what any of these people want me for, even if it's about my dad."

A cellphone beeped. Gary reached down and grabbed his iPhone. An image from the camera from the alley outside appeared, showing a Pontiac Grand Prix stopped at the front gate.

"And that's probably them now," Gary said. He double tapped on the phone screen and two other camera feeds came into view. There was no sign of activity from either camera.

"Some day you're going to tell me what this is all about?" Gary asked Edward.

Edward nodded.

"Okay then." Gary slapped his phone back onto his belt.

"You have a plan?" Edward asked.

"Look, we've got two ways to approach this," Gary said, walking towards a cabinet on the other side of the garage. "We can wait for them to come in and then blow them all away—and I've got enough ammo for that—but that's just going to attract a little attention, don't you think? The better option is for you guys to get outta here."

"Yeah," Edward said.

"You take one of my rides, and I'll take another one," Gary said. "I have the tracking dot so they'll follow me. You guys see if you can find out what the hell this Mansouri thing is or if it even means anything. If I can, I'll find you later."

"I'll go with you," Kara said suddenly.

"No way," Gary said, shaking his head. "I'm better off doing this part alone, trust me."

"Trying to get away?" Ryan asked sarcastically, looking at Kara. She turned her back to him.

Gary tossed a set of keys to Edward, who snatched them out of the air.

"They're for that one." Gary pointed to a car covered with a white sheet while he walked to another one. "You take that door out," he said, indicating the overhead door behind them. "It'll take you through the parkade next door."

Edward, Billy, Ryan and Kara pulled the sheet off their ride. They stepped back as their eyes took in a flawless, metallic-brown 1973 Ford Mustang.

"At least we can ride in style this time," Billy whispered.

They looked over to Gary. His vehicle seemed to be a bit of a disappointment compared to theirs. Gary opened the door to a purple 1989 Chrysler Imperial.

"Seriously?" Ryan called out.

"They're the best cars for a derby, with a few improvements I made," Gary said. "Shame most derbies won't let you use them. They're practically indestructible." He smiled and disappeared behind the wheel. The engine roared, much louder than anyone would expect of such a car.

"I don't think that's standard," Billy said.

"Let's go, guys," Edward called from the driver's seat. Kara sat in the back. Ryan took the back seat as well because Billy had already jumped up front.

"So are there lasers and missiles and stuff in here?" Billy asked, poking around in the glove box.

"No, and there's AM-only radio," Edward said as he nudged the car forward. "When was the last time you saw that?"

As the Mustang drew closer to the large retractable door, it keyed a sensor that automatically triggered the door to open. Edward flipped on the headlights and goosed the roaring car into the narrow passageway in front of him, barely wide enough for the car's mirrors.

"Everyone stay quiet, please," Edward said, his eyes fixed ahead.

Suddenly, they came up to another retractable door. Edward eased the Ford through then paused to look around. They were in the bottom level of a parking garage that was, at least for the moment, deserted.

"Let's move," Ryan urged his uncle. But Edward shook his head. Peeling out of there would attract attention they didn't need. He could never understand criminals' need for speed. In most of the stories he heard on the news, three-quarters of the crooks who robbed banks or stole cars were pulled over for driving like morons, whereas if they'd followed the speed limit or obeyed stop signs, they probably never would have attracted the attention of the police.

Edward pulled the Mustang to the garage exit, checked both directions, signalled right and moved out into the night.

CHAPTER 16

Unlike the others, Gary had no reason to be discreet.

As soon as the third garage door opened, he floored the accelerator and burst out onto Hastings, pausing only briefly at the stop sign, then whipped around so he passed the alley entrance where the car seen on his surveillance camera was parked in front of his fence. He lingered for a moment, looking down at the video feed on his phone. He watched as two men inspecting the fence suddenly stopped and piled back into their Pontiac. The car backed out of the alley, right towards him.

The chase is on, Gary thought to himself, punching the accelerator and zipping east on Hastings. The screen he'd installed in the dash showed a feed from an after-market rear-view camera—a pair of headlights emerged from the alley and accelerated, heading right for him.

Gary grinned as he manoeuvred through traffic. He loved the burst of adrenaline surging through his body when behind the wheel of a souped-up car. Granted, this was

no demolition arena, so it probably wasn't in his best interests to turn this little adventure into a derby, even though
he was pretty confident he could easily make short work of
the Pontiac.

The Imperial was no ordinary Chrysler—demolition
derbies were wary of allowing Imperials because demol-
ishing them was difficult—and Gary had enhanced the car as
part of his contract work with different agencies. For starters,
he'd installed armour-reinforced doors, bulletproof wind-
shields and Kevlar-lined tires. Only something slightly
larger than a rocket launcher could put a dent in this puppy.

Gary also installed a turbo-charged V8 motor that
barely fit under the hood. The extra horsepower and torque
not only compensated for the extra ninety kilos of the vehicle but also gave Gary an advantage. A pig on gas, this car
wasn't designed to sip fuel. The Imperial was power, sheer
power. Fortunately, he had gassed it up the previous day.

He saw a red light up ahead and mashed a button on
the dash. Many of his vehicles had transmitters—on the
down-low of course—that were similar to those used by
police forces, fire stations and ambulances. The unit sent
a scrambled message to a receiver mounted on most traffic
lights in the city. If an emergency vehicle was approaching
a red light, all the driver had to do was trigger the unit. The
message from the transmitter, once received, caused
the traffic lights to change sequence. The green light facing
opposing traffic would turn to yellow then red, and the

oncoming emergency vehicle would have a green light. Gary slowed only slightly as he saw the light at Victoria Drive turn yellow and then red. He swerved around a stopped car at the red light just as it turned green and gunned it through the intersection.

His goal was simple—lead the Pontiac away from Ryan, Edward, Billy and Kara—but he wasn't sure how he was going to bring the pursuit to a close. He was confident he could distance himself from the chase car, but he didn't want to give away that his car had only one occupant.

Glad I tinted the rear window, he thought as he switched lanes.

But the longer he drove at this speed, the higher the risk of an accident, or of a police cruiser passing by. Gary had no interest in turning this into a police chase. Plus, from the conversation with Edward and his gang back at the garage, no one wanted the cops involved.

Gary began to form a plan as he motored past Templeton towards Nanaimo Street. He would have to take action before reaching the freeway up ahead. As long as he had the dot, the car behind him would keep following him. So far, he'd stayed well enough in front of the chase car that he doubted they knew the exact make of his car, but he'd have to find another car with a similar contour at least. It was all a matter of timing.

A driver honked as Gary abruptly cut him off. He ignored it and shot through the lights at Kamloops Street, then Penticton. Gary knew he had to act soon. Once he passed Renfrew, there were no turning options to the north, just the shuttered gates of an endless array of attractions of the PNE—the Pacific Forum, the Playland Amusement Park and a fenced fairgrounds. Gary needed more choices in case his plan didn't work.

And then he saw it. He slowed as a distinctive set of rectangular headlights flashed past him. He followed the lights with his eyes and confirmed the vehicle was a dark-coloured K-Car. It was similar enough to the Imperial that it might work.

Gary eased off the gas to close the gap between him and his pursuers then looked all around to ensure he was in the clear. With no vehicles in his immediate vicinity in either direction, Gary cranked the wheel to the left, pressed the accelerator to the floor then hauled on the parking brake. The engine roared and the tires started to skid, yawing the car violently in a screeching half-circle. At the quarter-mark of the rotation, Gary straightened the wheel, released the parking brake and hit the gas.

*Step one…*he thought to himself as the car motored forward in the opposite direction. He could see the chase car slowing as he approached it from the other direction. As the separation between their cars decreased to about fifteen metres, Gary played his next card and flipped on his high beams.

These, however, were no ordinary high beams. Instead of casting a wider glare like traditional headlights, the Imperial's headlights shone directly towards the front centre of the vehicle. The lights, like everything else on the Imperial, were enhanced. The average high beam puts out approximately 20,000 candela (candles) of light, but Gary had modified his to produce four times that amount. It was a defensive weapon to buy time.

Gary looked down as the intensity of the beams exploded into the windshield of the chase car headed towards him. He turned off the beams as he shot past the car so as not to blind any innocent drivers. He glanced in the rear-view mirror as the Pontiac slowed down to make the U-turn to follow him, the occupants temporarily blinded by the brilliant light. Gary watched with bubbling glee as the Pontiac crashed into a parked car on the opposite side of East Hastings Street.

Gary continued to check his rear-view mirror until the accident he had caused was out of view. He exhaled heavily then dug in his vest pocket. He pulled out a pack of gum, shoved a piece into his mouth and chewed vigorously. He spotted the K-Car he had passed earlier and took up a position off its right rear panel. Then he reached into his pants pocket and, after much fiddling, extracted the GPS dot.

He continued driving until his car and the K-Car both stopped at a red light. Gary ripped a small piece of gum from his mouth and affixed it to the GPS dot. He then lowered his window and leaned out as far as he could, using one meaty thumb to press the gummed tracker to the K-car, just above the wheel well. He leaned back, glad the driver of the vehicle hadn't noticed, and closed the window.

When the light turned green, Gary stayed parallel to the K-Car, just off its quarter, making sure the dot held. After three blocks, the gum hadn't budged, so Gary signalled and turned south, leaving the K-Car and its oblivious driver to their evening of adventure.

Gary had every intention of either heading right back to his shop or trying to meet up with the rest. There might have been more than one chase car, and he wanted to make sure he wasn't being tailed. And so he drove smartly down the streets around Pain and Wastings, ignoring the crack dealers and hookers as best he could, doubling back occasionally and dipping into relatively quiet streets. No car followed him, but Gary knew from experience and training that if he was being tailed by a well-trained surveillance crew, he would never know until they closed in on him.

He spotted a fast-food restaurant and used the drive-thru, ordering a burger, fries and pop—the chase had made him hungry. Then he drove around a bit more before pulling into an empty school parking lot to eat. If a whole team was watching him, he wanted to give them every opportunity to come and get him.

His phone beeped. He read the text message and frowned slightly. He could easily accommodate the request. He just had to figure out how to do it without giving too much away.

—◁∘/∘/∘▷—

"Whoa!" Susan exclaimed, trying to shield her eyes with one hand while clutching the steering wheel with the other. She stepped heavily on the brakes, bringing the vehicle to a halt.

Without warning, an intense bright light appeared as if from nowhere, temporarily blinding Susan. She tried to blink away the blotches in front of her eyes, but they stubbornly remained.

"Can you see?" Susan asked Aly.

"I was looking down at my notes so I didn't get it that bad," he said, but he too was blinking furiously. "What *was* that?"

The pair had been tracking down the address that OnStar had provided, where it appeared Edward Dick's Cadillac had been parked. Suddenly a brilliant light filled the night sky, partially blinding Susan and affecting Aly only a bit.

A loud crash made Aly look up just in time to see a car veer across the road and smash into a row of parked cars along the side of the street. Aly looked around to see if any VPD cars were nearby and, seeing none, alerted dispatch and requested a squad car to the scene.

"I'll go check on the people in the wreck. Once patrol gets here, we can go," Aly said. Susan nodded. Aly left the car and jogged towards the crash site. Just as he neared the scene, the doors on either side of the crashed car popped open and two men emerged. Both sprinted away from the collision.

Aly stopped. They had at least a two-block head start, so he had no chance of catching them. Besides, he and Susan had another task at hand. He turned and jogged back to the car.

Aly reached into the car to get the mic for the radio and paused, noticing Susan was talking on her cellphone. Aly stepped outside the car with the mic and reported the two runners to the officers headed to the scene. As he leaned in to replace the mic, Susan ended her call.

"We've got a hit," she said. "He just used one of his known credit cards at Pacific Centre Mall—Tip Top Tailors and New York Fries."

Aly heard a siren wail and waved to the arriving patrol car. He didn't see the black sedan pulling away from the curb a block behind the accident scene.

"Fashionable and hungry," he said. "With any luck he's sitting in the food court right now."

CHAPTER 17

$\mathcal{E}$dward had taken the same approach as Gary but opted for vigilance over speed. He, too, meandered through the city making random, sudden turns and doubling back every so often. Their predicament might be dire if a dedicated team was following them, but he was sure they were in the clear. Gary, after all, had taken the tracking dot with him. It would have taken a large, organized and well-prepared crew to cover all possible exits from that massive garage. And a crew like that would have been difficult to assemble without standing out like a sore thumb solely on account of its size.

Ryan and Billy's abduction appeared at first glance to be related to a drug debt or turf war, which were not uncommon in Vancouver. But Edward knew Ryan as well as anybody, so neither scenario was even a remote possibility. The same went for Billy. Ryan's attack on Marine Drive, the snatch at the house and the GPS dot all smacked of professionalism, albeit somewhat flawed. The culprits weren't part of some stupid Vancouver-based organized gang. This was serious business. This was a trained intelligence unit.

And Edward had an idea of exactly who was involved, but he didn't want to jump to conclusions. He'd seen too many strange collaborations during his decades with CSIS to discount any possibility. But when all elements were equally weighted, the most obvious answer, even in the intelligence community, was usually the right one.

"What are we doing?" Billy asked from the front seat. He had been remarkably quiet since getting in the car compared to the more talkative side he had displayed back at Gary's garage, where a lot of the attention had been focused on him. Having known Billy for almost nine years, Ryan recognized what was happening. Billy was tired, and when he was tired or hungry, or both, he just shut down, and worst, he whined.

"Hang in there, Bill," Ryan said, clapping his friend on the shoulder. "We'll grab something to eat in a bit."

"Tradecraft, Billy," Edward explained, checking the car's mirrors. He had instructed his three passengers to do nothing unusual, like craning their necks around to check if they were being followed. The last thing they wanted was to tip-off an observer or have a cop pull them over for driving erratically. Edward wasn't even sure the registration for the Mustang was in the glove box, but he definitely wasn't the registered owner. Explaining that would be tricky.

And he had to control for the possibility that the police, even unwittingly, were looking for them too. Intelligence agencies used many tactics to find the people they wanted, and one of them involved exploiting the local police, usually duplicitously—someone calls 911 and says their house has been broken into or that three guys and a woman in a Mustang have robbed and beaten them. The next thing you knew, every officer in the Vancouver area is keeping an extra eye out for a metallic-brown Mustang.

Ryan knew exactly what his uncle was doing because he'd done it too, though he hadn't recognized it at the time. Shortly after Ryan had finished rebuilding his first car so many years ago, he and Edward had spent some evenings "chasing" each other through Vancouver; one tried to find the other driver, while the other tried to lose the follower. Ryan learned to be discreet, keep a low profile, take long drives and essentially motor around in circles. On weekends, his uncle took him to an enormous parking lot at an abandoned shopping centre and taught him "offensive driving," how to make the sharpest possible U-turn and how to weave through traffic. Ryan had at one point accomplished the feat of cornering on two tires.

Just like everything else he had done with his father, such as playing Disguises, Ryan was beginning to realize that the lessons of his youth had served a deeper purpose. He didn't yet know the reason, but parts of it—from his martial arts training to watching his uncle drive—were coming together.

The AM-only radio, though at first a curiosity, provided some entertainment as the quartet tuned into the last period of the Vancouver Canucks hockey game, followed by the post-game show. Edward tried to keep the mood in the car relatively relaxed. After thirty minutes of driving, he stopped at a convenience store and instructed Kara to go in and buy snacks, the sweeter the better. She returned with a case of pop, several bags of chips and a few chocolate bars. They scarfed down the food as Edward eased the Mustang back into traffic. His meandering was actually headed in a specific direction, though he was taking a circuitous route. Once everyone had filled up on simple carbs, Edward broached their next step.

"You missed out on some information when you went to the washroom back at the garage, Ryan," Edward said, his eyes fixed on the road. "You too, Kara."

Ryan nodded. Billy and Edward had been searching the Internet when Ryan had gone downstairs. In the excitement that followed, Ryan hadn't thought to ask what they had found out.

"Mansouri Consulting?" Ryan asked.

"Yep," Edward said. "They appear to be a legitimate business, based on their corporate website. The source of their funding makes them a little suspicious, but the front they put up is passable."

"And what's that?"

"Jobs," Edward said. "It's a company that helps people from the Middle East—mostly Saudi Arabians—find job opportunities in Canada."

"That's it?" Ryan asked.

"Well, they're not offering jobs at restaurants or gas stations. More executive-level positions, mostly corporate, some manufacturing," Edward said, absently scratching at his chin. "Their offices are located in the right place, just on the outskirts of downtown. They have their own small building, nothing much to look at. Almost a shack, really."

Edward's tone told Ryan something was giving his uncle pause. "What else?"

"Well, when Gary's friends checked into the corporate title, besides finding out where their money was coming from and the address and so on, it also revealed the date they opened up shop."

"And that was?" Ryan said.

"Two months ago," Edward said.

"How is that suspicious?" Ryan asked.

"I don't really know yet. But it seems strange. These people—who you say spoke Arabic—were driving a van with a licence plate registered to a company funded by an Arab bank that set up shop only two months ago to help people from Saudi Arabia find jobs?" Edward strung it all together. "Sounds a little quirky to me."

"What about the people working there?" Ryan asked. Often, companies listed names of employees or the board of directors on their websites.

"All Arab names," Edward said.

"Well, I guess that makes sense," Ryan said. "If you open a business that helps people from Saudi Arabia find jobs here, you're probably going to hire staff that understand the language and culture."

"True," Edward nodded. "It's just..."

"What?"

"It's not uncommon for foreign intelligence agencies to operate that way in foreign countries," Edward explained. "Typically, most larger intelligence agencies work out of an embassy or consulate. They usually staff it with a few espionage agents with fabricated titles, like Press Attaché or Military Consultant or something like that."

Edward decided it was time to pull over to free up more of his brain to think. They were in a residential area, so he pulled to the curb. During the time they had been driving, he hadn't noticed any vehicles attempting to follow them, nor had he seen the same make, model or colour of vehicle more than once. He was reasonably sure they were safe. He only hoped Gary was, too. He knew his friend would make contact when he could.

"The advantage to working from an embassy or consular ground is diplomatic immunity," Edward continued, putting the car in park. "If you get caught playing spy, you can't be arrested or prosecuted in the foreign country—the worst that happens is the government kicks you out of the country and sends you back home.

"But embassy grounds are monitored regularly by counter-intelligence units," Edward said. "At CSIS, we always knew who staffed the embassy or consulate, and we fleshed out as much background as possible so we knew who we were dealing with and which people demanded the most surveillance. It's a natural hunting ground, a focal point in the espionage community. So if you want to run something a bit more clandestine, you set up a business. Some of them get checked out, but with more foreign investment in all parts of the world, following up on each business gets increasingly difficult."

"Isn't it difficult for non-Canadians to set up business in Canada?" Ryan asked.

"Not as hard as you'd think," Edward said, scratching his chin again. "It depends on the nature of the business—foreign ownership of major industry is completely off limits, which is why we've been witnessing such growth in economic espionage. It's not companies stealing secrets from one another—they have more to lose if they get caught. It's less-developed or industrialized countries that want to learn more so they can create their own product and compete globally. And a lot of focus can be easily applied to military development, weapons research, that kind of thing."

Ryan remembered reading some newspaper stories about China's heightened interest in North American manufacturing and technology. With the growth of high-tech industry, much of it closely watched by government, countries like China were continually searching for technical innovations on anything from microchips to computers. The information wasn't necessarily military in and of itself, but the advancements made in one country could be adopted in another to make it so. Manufacturing smaller microchips meant smaller computers, which could be adapted to computers in fighter jets, submarines or any other piece of military equipment.

"But in terms of something like Mansouri Consulting, the government has no national interest in finding workers from a specific country to come and work here. It welcomes immigration, but it's not going to just throw open the doors. The government even offers programs where Canadian companies can bring in foreign workers and pay them less than Canadian employees. It typically leaves the process up to private business, and in this case, the best people to find jobs for Saudi Arabians are Saudi Arabians," Edward said, shrugging.

"If we looked deeper into the CEO or founder of this business, we'd probably learn that he's not a recent immigrant. He might be a permanent resident, a new Canadian citizen or a naturalized citizen that still has ties to his home country. But we might also find something more."

"Spies?" Billy asked, more alert now that he had eaten.

"Sleepers, we call them," Edward explained. "Agents inserted into the country long ago, under forged identities, who set up shop, go about life as any other person in Canada might and try not to make trouble or stand out. Or it might be a family that has been here for a generation or two but keeps close touch with their roots through local community groups or friends. It's easy to tap into that kind of resource—someone who still harbours patriotic feelings for their home country and will do what you ask. So, let's say Person A, who was born in Canada, is asked by Person B in his home country if Person A can help set up a business here. Names of people to hire are suggested to Person A, who might even hire recent landed immigrants or people from out-of-country, say, Saudi Arabia, to come and work for them through Canada's temporary foreign worker program. That way, Person B gets the people he wants in-country, where he wants them, with fewer eyes watching. On its face, the procedure looks totally legit. But underneath, well, there might be more to it."

"A spy shop," Kara said matter-of-factly.

"More or less," Edward said. "There's a chance Mansouri, like many businesses in Canada, is owned by upstanding, respectable people, and this is all just a coincidence."

"But...?" Ryan urged his uncle on.

"I don't believe in coincidences," Edward said flatly. "It's the nature of the business. When too many things line up too perfectly, it begs questions."

"So how do we answer those questions?" Kara asked.

"That's what we decide right now," Edward replied.

CHAPTER

Although it was late, he wasn't sleeping. The beautiful, naked blonde in his bed was wrapped in black silk sheets. She helped pass the time, which he desperately needed on a night like this. But even she had her limits and was now dozing, unaware of the tension that filled the entire penthouse apartment.

Christian Wright waited in his office, reading his email then checking out various websites, trying to find another suitable distraction, without success. He stared at one of the two phones on his oak office desk, willing it to ring. The call should have come hours ago, but the phone remained silent.

I don't like where this is heading, he thought to himself, scrolling through the CNN website. More rallies, in both the United States and Canada, against the Crescent Pipeline, the one project in which he and his fellow businessmen had invested so much political and financial capital, yet were unable to move forward.

The pipeline was a simple concept—a big conduit that could easily carry Alberta's bitumen to refineries and points of export in the United States. Bringing it to life, however, was proving more difficult than either country had imagined. It was a bid to tap into a resource the United States could not realize by itself, a resource so vast it dwarfed America's own oil supplies and potentially surpassed the reserves of most Middle East states of the Organization of the Petroleum Exporting Countries, called OPEC. The Canadian oil sands was located in the northern tip of the province of Alberta where winter was harsh but business was booming. And the United States wanted some of that business.

Those oil sands, once thought too expensive to mine, were now the key to ensuring the United States' dependence on oil came from a closer neighbour, not a fleet of super tankers that take weeks to deliver their cargo. The very earth in northern Alberta was saturated with oil. That earth was mined and the oil extracted and transformed into petroleum products. The goal of the Crescent Pipeline was to deliver the base of those products, bitumen, to the United States in an efficient and cost-effective way. The pipeline would, of course, pass through thousands of kilometres of territory in both countries, some of it ecologically sensitive and some of it claimed by other landowners, companies or lands occupied by the First Nations in Canada or by Native Americans. But the investment would reap thousands of jobs for both countries and billions of dollars for owners of the pipeline.

But the public didn't seem to understand. And although the sitting Canadian prime minister did, America's own president didn't. He had just rejected the permit that would have allowed the first phases of construction, angering state governors and legislators, as well as many members of Congress. In response, the Canadian government was holding a symposium in Edmonton later in the month to try to turn the tide of the narrative being spun. And Christian planned on attending.

But he was waiting for something else.

He heard a warble, and his eyes snapped to the second phone on his desk—the encrypted line was ringing. He picked up the receiver and listened to a series of tones as the scrambled transmission matched that of the incoming call. After a few seconds, the line cleared.

"Hello?"

"Good evening, sir," said a man's voice. It was the same voice he and the rest of the conglomerate had heard only weeks ago, telling them the bad news. He had since spoken privately with the man, which had led up to this call.

"And?"

"There have been…complications, I'm afraid," the voice informed him. "It seems we underestimated the resources our friend had available."

"You mean you don't have him?!" Wright thundered, erupting from his chair. "How could you possibly have screwed this up as well?"

"You do not understand, my friend. We can only control for what we can anticipate, what we know," said the man angrily. "The events that have transpired this evening, as I am told, were unpredictable. There is some sort of protective web in place we did not know about."

Wright forced himself to breathe. He heard a sound at the office door and turned around. His angry shouts had awoken his companion, and she was standing in the doorway. He simply walked over and pushed the door closed in her face, locking it.

"So what now?" Wright asked, anger giving way to panic.

"All is not lost," the voice said. "There is no need to take any drastic action. So far our pursuit has been quiet—nothing has occurred that has required any investigation on the part of the local authorities. We still have many pieces in play. We will find them."

"Well, you'd better," Wright spat out. "I want hourly updates."

"I will update you when I have something worthy of saying," the voice replied. "To call and report nothing is just a waste of my time when I could be doing what you have asked. When we have him, I will let you know."

And the line went dead.

Wright paced for a few moments then headed to the shelf behind his desk and poured a taller-than-usual glass of bourbon, but even that couldn't calm him. He doubted the assurances of this person, who twice now had failed to complete tasks that seemed so simple. But Wright had no choice. They had voted to leave it in their friend's hands for now. Not one of them could take action otherwise—they'd all agreed on that point.

He tossed back his drink and killed the lights in the office. If his companion was still awake, he might as well pass the time with her in more pleasurable ways.

A few people in the food court were lingering over their fast food, but none of them matched the description of this Davis character. Susan and Aly had gone to the Tip Top store and obtained a copy of the receipt for the clothing Davis had bought. They'd even looked at the kinds of clothes he had purchased, trying to burn the images into their memories. If he was trying to evade detection, a new set of clothes might be one way of walking around incognito.

"Still," Aly said as they left the store. "Doesn't it seem weird to you? If he did buy the clothes to try to alter his appearance, why use plastic? If he's smart enough to think about ditching his clothes, he should be smart enough not to use his credit card."

Susan grunted as they made their way towards the mall security office. "You're assuming he's that smart.

Remember, just because CSIS wants him doesn't mean he's that bright. Wonder why we're the only two working on this right now? We're not exactly looking for some mastermind here."

The security guards were helpful, cueing up the mall's surveillance footage to the time stamps on the receipts they'd obtained. Sure enough, the videos showed someone matching Davis' description arriving at a mall entrance by taxi, buying clothes at Tip Top, eating a hot dog and drinking a pop in the food court, then leaving in another taxi.

Susan's phone rang as the pair left the security office. She spoke a few curt words and then hung up.

"He just bought a ticket at Tsawwassen for the next ferry to Nanaimo," she said. "It leaves in ten minutes. He's a walk-on."

"Lights and sirens, we won't make it," Aly said. "What's your plan?"

Susan exhaled heavily through closed lips, making a sputtering sound. "I guess we need to find a fast boat to Nanaimo."

CHAPTER 19

Thresher wasn't going anywhere, even though he'd been at work for more than twelve hours already. And so long as he was staying at work, Young was staying with him.

It wasn't his first overnight—he kept another suit and a set of toiletries in the closet for nights like this. In a way, he kind of relished the change— ordering take-out, the adrenaline of working on an exciting case. It reminded him of his first few years in the agency when spending a night at work happened more frequently.

I was younger then, Thresher reminded himself, reaching for another antacid tablet. Chinese food didn't sit as well as it used to.

"Sir?" Young was at the door again.

"Yes," Thresher said, belching awkwardly.

"Something strange is happening on East Hastings."

"Such as?" Thresher said impatiently. He didn't like suspense.

"Well, the two teams we have stationed near the address we discussed earlier reported a car chase that might involve the people we're looking for."

"A chase?" Thresher asked, momentarily perplexed.

"Yes, sir. It seems one car came flying out of the garage, and a car parked nearby took off after it. One of our cars followed, and there was a crash. The first car is missing. There were two men in the car that crashed, and they left the scene on foot. No descriptions. The plate on the crashed vehicle came back to a rental agency and...the plate of the first car came back to a John Smith."

"Really?" Thresher asked sarcastically.

"There's no John Smith registered that lives in the area. In fact, the address on the registration doesn't even exist."

Thresher thought for a moment. "One of ours?" he offered.

"Perhaps. Or an outside contractor. Those guys can be a little paranoid. But I don't have clearance to search contractor, safe house or black site addresses," Young said, shrugging his shoulders.

Thresher mulled over what Young had told him. Paging his way through a database wasn't how he liked to spend his time. That's why he hired people like Young.

"Here," Thresher said, pulling a sticky note from a nearby pad and scribbling a jumbled sequence of letters and numbers. "Use this. Don't tell anyone I gave it to you. Find out what we need, and then log out."

"Yes, sir." Young nodded. "Thank you." He left the office.

Thresher belched again and reached for the bottle of antacids. It was just as well he was at his office. It didn't look like he'd be getting any sleep anyways.

———⟨0/0/0⟩———

Gary knew it was a bad idea, but the demand had come from a pretty important individual. As much as he was a stickler for operational security, some requests couldn't be ignored.

He parked his car out on the street and walked down the alley to his garage, his head swivelling, eyes flicking from side-to-side. He didn't see anyone. When he stepped inside his garage, he checked the alarm system. None of the sensors had been triggered, meaning no one had broken in.

Still, he was cautious. He descended the stairs and entered the bathroom, but for a different purpose. The cracked mirror over the sink pulled away easily, as intended, and Gary reached in to extract a small case. Then he went back to the street to move the Imperial inside, covered the car and hopped into a Dodge. He drove out of the garage and took a wandering route down to the park, which was for the most part abandoned at this late hour.

A horn sounded in the distance, repeatedly, like someone had pressed the panic alarm on a key fob. Gary waited five minutes as instructed, then grabbed the case from the passenger's seat and exited the car, locking it behind him.

A set of headlamps flicked on and off. Gary forced himself to walk slowly, his nerves jangling like his gold chains, his beard soaked with the rain that was falling incessantly. His hands shook as he opened the passenger door of a Toyota Corolla and slid inside.

CHAPTER 20

"You think you can do that?" Edward asked as the four sat in the Mustang, still parked on the side of a residential road.

Billy didn't respond. Edward was about to repeat his question, but Ryan waved his hand side-to-side, cutting off his uncle. He knew Billy. He was just thinking, even though the question was relatively simple.

"Of course I can," Billy said. "I mean, it depends on the type of set-up they have, but it shouldn't be a problem."

Their plan was slowly taking shape, although at face value, it seemed somewhat bold. Billy had protested early, begging for time, even a night's sleep before they made their next move. But Edward had pointed out that time wasn't exactly on their side. Three times tonight Ryan and Billy had been followed, in rapid succession. They had a break now, but their luck might only last so long. They needed to take the offensive, for lack of a better phrase in Ryan's mind, while they could. Their efforts might yield nothing, but his uncle explained that it was better to eliminate a possibility than leave the option unexplored.

The plan meant splitting up the group, but it couldn't be helped. Edward and Billy would work as one team while Kara and Ryan were out in the field. Four people together would attract unnecessary attention, plus they needed a physical presence near their target.

In between sending a couple of Tweets, Edward had also used his phone to locate an Internet café near the downtown core. He'd come up with several and, against Billy and Ryan's joint intuition, had chosen the larger, more popular one.

"More people means more witnesses!" Ryan had objected.

"But it's also less conspicuous," Edward had replied. With so many people in one place, two individuals were less likely to stand out. Sometimes it paid to hide in plain sight.

Billy was tasked with the fundamental part of the plan—hacking into the Mansouri Consulting network. Leaving a trail didn't matter—he'd enter from an independent location after all. Edward would be in the café as well, watching Billy's back and communicating with Ryan and Kara, whose job was simpler but not without risk.

They would drive the Mustang around the office building, checking for activity inside and seeing whether Ryan recognized the faces of anyone in the area. The fewer people in the building, the less likely Billy's hack might be detected and shut down, although Billy was confident he could get in and out without anyone being the wiser.

But Billy continued to reveal his quirks. He *could* hack as well as anyone else, but he had standards. In the parlance of the hacking community, Billy was known as a "white hat," or an ethical hacker. It was a strange dichotomy to some, almost an oxymoron, but Billy engaged only in ethical hacking. He wasn't out for personal gain or ambition or to make a name for himself in the hacking community. Billy contracted his services as a freelance hacker to companies that wanted to test the security of their networks. He brought his computer skills to bear by penetrating the network so that the company could then fix any vulnerabilities he found.

Billy could have used his substantial skills in more deceptive, manipulative ways, but all those behaviour camps he had attended as a kid and teenager had ingrained in him some fundamental basics about the rule of law. In a nutshell, it was "do good, not bad." The "black hats," on the other hand, subscribed to only what benefitted them, whether it was personal glory, fame or riches.

"Wait," Kara said. "I've studied some basics in computer security myself and...I mean, do we have time for this? Hacking into an unknown target can take hours, days or even weeks, I think. Plus, if Mansouri does something more than just consulting, we could be up against a pretty powerful network."

Ryan and Edward were grinning.

"You're right, Kara," Billy said in a tone akin to veiled contempt. "It *can* take a long time. But it won't."

"Why?" Kara asked.

Billy shook his head and sighed, as if he was stooping to a lower level by explaining himself. "Normally, yes, hackers, even the good ones, have to spend a lot of time on their projects," he said. "It's really funny, actually. Hacking is supposed to be so cool and so non-conformist that you have to learn it yourself, make a name for yourself. It's supposed to be so different from the rest of the world.

"And yet they have a specific way of going about their hacks. They even have a list of steps they have to take—and they give them names!" Billy laughed. "So, yes, you have to start off with 'targeting' in deciding who you want to go after. And then there's 'collecting information and research.'" Billy enclosed the terms in air quotes as he said them. "Then you have to 'evaluate' the network for its overall strength, then 'analyze' its flaws and finally 'exploit' the network."

Ryan tried not to laugh harder. Billy was in a zone seldom on public display; he was comfortable expressing himself on subjects he knew a lot about. The air quotes, though, were getting to be a bit much.

"But don't we need all those steps?" Kara asked, wondering why they were laughing.

"Of course not," Billy harrumphed. "Think about it, Kara. Computers are fundamentally identical the world over—some may run slightly faster, or maybe they're newer or bigger, but commercial computers all use similar equipment. They also, for the most part, all speak the same languages—C++, Java, Pascal, whatever. So if computers are all the same, and they all know how to talk to each other, do you think there's much of a difference in security?"

Kara didn't even prompt him.

"No," Billy continued. "Look at it this way—cars are all the same. Even though they may look different and have different options, they all use the same, really old I might add, technology. So, what did you do earlier tonight after you rescued us?"

"Stole...a...car?" Kara said, unsure of Billy's train of thought.

"Right." Billy was getting increasingly excited, so much so he that he was talking faster than Ryan had ever seen. But he had never held a woman's attention for so long. "What kind of car was it?"

"A Geo Metro?"

"Did you have to learn how to steal a Geo Metro? Specifically?"

"No."

"Did you have to learn how to steal every car ever made according to its make, model and year?"

"No."

"Why not?"

"Because cars are the same. You only need a few tricks to steal one."

"Thank you," Billy said, pumping his fist. "Computers are no different, especially when it comes to security. Once you figure out the language they use, all you have to do is apply the 'right tricks,'" he said, using the air quotes again.

Kara shook her head. "But doesn't that take time too? I mean, how do you do that?"

"With this," Billy said, pulling a USB flash drive from his pocket. Ryan recognized the keychain it was on. Billy never left the house without it.

"I don't get it," Kara said.

Billy was kind enough to elaborate. For every system he had successfully hacked in his work—which meant all of them—Billy wrote scripts that automatically executed the actions he had taken in each instance to successfully hack into a network. So now, whenever he was testing a new security set-up, he simply plugged in his flash drive, picked a script and clicked on "Run." He hardly even had to touch his keyboard to complete a job. And the jobs all paid well.

What Billy wouldn't say—which only Ryan knew—was that he had designs on his scripts. Billy knew that, besides his white cap status on the Internet, his way of hacking was considered fairly "inelegant." There was even a derogatory term, "script kiddies," for people who used programs to hack, but Billy didn't believe he qualified. Most script kiddies downloaded hacking software readily available on the Internet and followed a set of instructions. Billy created new scripts and refined them as he went. Each script meant Billy spent another day or two locked in his room, working on what he considered his life's work—the ultimate commercial security system. If he could incorporate the most common vulnerabilities in networks into his program, he could make life even more difficult for the black hats he despised so much. And the money would be nice too.

"So all you have to do is plug that in, and away we go?" Kara asked.

"Essentially." Billy shrugged. "I mean, it depends on what I'm up against. If it's your run-of-the-mill security system, well, I can't think of a commercial one in the Lower Mainland that I haven't broken, helped repair, then broken again."

"What if it's military?" Kara challenged.

"That would take longer," Billy acknowledged. "Probably too long for us. But I doubt it. Hackers often talk about the stuff they find on the boards. And I talk with a lot of local guys. If something was hanging around, one of *my* guys would have found it by now, and one of them would be trying to take it down. And I haven't seen anything to suggest such a network in the last couple of weeks."

But Ryan had a question. He had no doubt in his friend's abilities—that was clear. But in every discussion they'd ever had about whether or not hacking served a true purpose, Billy had never expressed any interest in committing an illegal act.

"But why are you doing it, Bill?" Ryan spoke up. He was asking more out of curiosity. His friend hadn't objected to the plan, even though what they were doing was clearly unlawful.

Billy shrugged. "They started it," he said simply.

Ryan chuckled. His friend never ceased to amaze him. He could take something as complex as a possible international intelligence plot and boil it down to three words.

"Sounds like a plan," Edward said. "But we have one more stop to make."

"What now?" Kara asked.

"We need some supplies," he said, looking at Kara.

She smiled and nodded in agreement.

CHAPTER 21

The store windows were dark—it was past ten in the evening, after all. But the foursome just sat there in the Mustang, waiting.

"I'd heard places like this existed, but I've never been in one," Ryan said. "I've always thought stuff like this was for people who stalk their exes or for that guy in *Silence of the Lambs.*"

"I love that movie," Billy said.

Ryan didn't respond. He was trying to keep a straight face as his uncle and Kara spoke.

"Pinhole?" Edward asked.

"For sure. What do you think about audio surveillance?" Kara asked seriously.

"Sticky microphones?" Edward suggested.

"Can we get close enough?" Kara wondered.

"Ryan's got a good arm. He can do it."

"Oh, and don't forget night-vision goggles!" Ryan snorted.

Both Edward and Kara looked at him as if he was stupid.

"Commercial models drain their batteries too fast," Edward said, looking at Ryan seriously.

"How foolish of me," Ryan murmured.

The four were parked a block down from Spy Stuff, one of the few stores that sold so-called spy gear to the general public. Ryan had looked over his uncle's shoulder as he'd browsed the store's website on his phone—it sold night-vision goggles but also plastic flowers with hidden microphones and cameras, GPS tracking units like the dot Gary found on Ryan earlier and expensive police scanners.

"People actually buy this stuff?" Ryan had asked.

"Shane's done quite well for himself," Edward replied. He looked down as his phone beeped. "That's us. Let's go."

They walked casually to the front door. It was locked, the store still dark. They didn't see anyone inside.

"Up there, guys." Edward pointed. Ryan looked up to see a security camera pointed directly at them. Edward waved. The door clicked open, and they walked in.

"That's trust right there," Billy remarked.

"I helped Shane start this store," Edward said. "He gave CSIS a try but kind of washed out. The rules in training were a little too strict for him. Genius, but as you can see, he supports certain causes an intelligence agency might frown upon." He pointed to the wall. An old poster with a red background screamed "4/20" at them, listing an address for a local park.

"This is Vancouver," Billy piped up. "What else would you expect?"

"It's still illegal," Edward commented, reaching for a nearby light switch.

The store was not neat as it turned out. The shelves were blocks of white metal wire that formed individual cubes. Little of what this Shane guy sold was on display—almost everything was in boxes, but every other box was empty.

"Sorry about the mess. It's been a crazy week," a voice suddenly boomed from above.

Ryan and Billy stared at each other then looked at Edward and Kara.

"Speakers," Edward said pointing up at the ceiling.

Ryan couldn't think of what to say. "Four-Twenty, right?" he managed, feeling lame.

"Totally," the response came.

"Everything going well?" Edward asked.

"For sure," the response came. "Busy as ever. Lots of new product that's in high demand. The smartphone has been awesome for us."

"I bet," Kara said, poking through a few boxes.

"Nice to hear your voice again, my lady," Shane said politely. "So whose credit card is this going on?"

"Mine," said Edward, raising his hand. He then reached inside a box and extracted a few items.

"Anything in particular you're looking for?" Shane asked.

"Sticky microphones?" Kara said.

"Up near the counter. Too easy to steal," Shane replied. "Doing a little surveillance, I guess."

"I guess," Edward said evasively.

"If you need an extra pair of eyes, I have an excellent recommendation."

"Go on," Edward said, looking at the ceiling.

"Towards the back. Large blue boxes stacked against the wall. Just came in last week. Works with most smartphones." Shane laughed for no reason Ryan could discern. "They've been super popular."

Kara lifted one up from the box and smiled.

Ryan went over to see for himself. "Really? A toy?" he asked incredulously.

"This isn't just a toy, Ryan," Kara said with a wicked grin.

The front of the box showed a remote-controlled helicopter. A small icon on the bottom of the box indicated it was made for iPhone.

"This is basically a store-bought surveillance drone," Kara said. "I mean, they only last a few minutes with a charge, and the resolution isn't high, but you can use it to have a look at an area from the air. And with what we're going to be up to, we could use a little surveillance to help us make better decisions. Besides, I've worked with drones before. I'm one of the best pilots around."

"And people call *me* a nerd," Billy said, shivering involuntarily.

CHAPTER  22

Ryan and Kara had been watching the building for thirty minutes, having dropped Billy and Edward at the Internet café earlier. So far there had been nothing worth watching.

Kara leaned back in the driver's seat of the Mustang and sighed. They'd had eyes on the three-storey building the entire time, even driving by a few times to see if someone could get by without them noticing. They hadn't seen anyone. The building was about twenty years old but looked like it had been built fifty years ago. There was a restaurant on the ground floor and offices on the upper two floors. The restaurant was dark, and since the two had arrived, not a single light on either office floor had flickered on.

"Ready?" Kara asked, an enormous smile on her face.

"I want to drive," Ryan said, almost petulantly.

"No way," Kara said. She exited the car and placed the small remote-control helicopter on the pavement. She had one more look at the sleek-looking black model to make sure it was on, then closed the car door, pulled out her smartphone and gritted her teeth in anticipation.

Ryan stepped out of the car to stand beside Kara, watching as the helicopter's two small lights came on and the rotors slowly started to turn. "Looks good."

"Okay, here we go," Kara said, her thumbs dancing over her phone. Slowly, the helicopter, whisper quiet, ascended.

The phone screen began to flicker as a small camera under the belly of the helicopter began transmitting.

"Not bad," Ryan said, looking over Kara's shoulder. "Might be hard to really see anything though."

"Just wait," Kara said, her thumb skipping to a button icon on her iPhone. The image being transmitted to her phone from the helicopter flicked green, more detail now visible.

"And I thought we weren't doing night vision," Ryan sighed.

Kara didn't pay any attention to his pouting. She focused on the controls as she navigated the helicopter over the office building. The two watched the tiny screen but, besides the occasional passing car, they didn't see any movement near the building.

"Okay," Kara said. "Just let me bring this baby back home. Why don't you go test your accuracy?"

Ryan nodded and retrieved a small bag from the car. He looked around him but didn't see anyone.

No one in his life right now—not his friends, not his family, not even himself—was who they had claimed to be a few hours ago. Internally, Ryan was now some hand-to-hand-combat expert who could drive cars fast and aggressively, interpret threatening body language and God only knew what else. Everything he had learned in his life seemed to be coalescing into someone he hardly recognized—the things he had enjoyed doing, such as kung fu or playing Disguises, were no longer fragmented activities. They had served a purpose, and only now was Ryan starting to understand that purpose. The problem was, he couldn't remember even half the things he had learned over the course of his life or how he'd learned them. He was fearful of what else he might discover he could do.

I even like to shoot guns, he realized with horror, recalling that one of his favourite ways to blow off steam was to head down to the closest firing range, pay the exorbitant fee for the special permit and empty a few clips. He could fire an entire 9 mm magazine into the centre mass of a human-shaped target with fractions of a millimetre separating the bullet holes.

Jesus, he thought, then shook his head. *Focus.*

As he approached the building, he dipped his hand into the bag and came up with a small black square, about four centimetres wide. After peeling off the thin plastic film, he stared up at the windows three metres above him, raised his arm and threw the sticky microphone as hard as he could. It arced in the air, smacked the window and stuck in place.

Ryan exhaled and did a quick lap around the building, throwing five more sticky microphones, only three of which stuck to the windows. With the last window done, he returned to the car, where Kara was sitting in the driver's seat and holding a receiver in her hand, listening intently to an earpiece.

"Anything?" Ryan asked, taking his spot in the passenger seat. Kara shook her head, her thumb clicking through the three different channels to listen to each individual sticky microphone. Not a single sound remotely human emanated from inside the building.

"Nope. I think we're good," Kara said, removing the earpiece.

CHAPTER 23

Billy didn't drink coffee. It tasted gross and made him pee a lot, but Ryan's uncle had insisted that most people, when they go to a café, even an Internet café, ordered coffee, so Billy bought an enormous cup of black java when all he really wanted was a Pepsi and a ham sandwich. He turned to look back at Edward but stopped himself, remembering one of Edward's many rules. *Don't look at me. If you need to talk to me, cough*, Edward had said. *I'll come to you.*

And Billy had already coughed twice. But not to get Edward's attention—he had a tickle in the back of his throat. Both times, Edward had approached him, and each time, Billy had been forced to apologize. Now he felt like the boy who cried wolf.

The rules were thorough and difficult to understand at times. *Don't look around too much. Talk to people if you have to, but keep it short and simple. Try not to stand out. Order a coffee, drink it for fifteen minutes then move to the terminal you want. Don't use your flash drive right away—check the*

weather or hockey scores or something. Wait until the per-
son beside you leaves and I'm sitting across from you before
you start. Don't acknowledge my presence when I sit down.
If you find something, cough. If anyone asks you what you're
doing, just say you're working on your doctoral project.
Talk a lot about it. It'll drive them off in no time.

Billy stared out the window, as Edward had instructed, in a cheap faux-leather chair, leaving his coffee untouched. The café was four blocks away from their target, and he was wondering what he might run up against once he got to work. Before the four of them had split up, they had driven around the block of the consulting building with Billy using Edward's iPhone to scan for available wireless networks in the area. A half-dozen had appeared, but one—Mansour—had broadcast a strong signal. Given the location and name, Billy was fairly confident they had found the correct network. The network was secure, but as Billy knew, security was only as strong as the customer believed it to be.

Most wireless networks were designed for home use and small businesses, clients who didn't require any extravagant or heavy security. Their main concern was blocking neighbours from using their signal and bandwidth for free and, to some measure, protecting their own computers.

Billy snorted to himself. It was fallacy, really. The two most common security protocols for wireless networks—Wired Equivalent Privacy (WEP) and Wi-Fi Protect Access (WPA/WPA2)—might protect the typical family or small business from a novice hacker, but the most common breach doesn't come from an outside attack. Worms and viruses were the biggest culprit.

Billy fingered the flash drive in his pocket, sniffing absently. He had captured a few viruses and worms, just to spend time going through the script to see how they worked. He knew he didn't have the time to use any of them this evening. The more quickly he could get in and out, the sooner they could figure out what was going on.

And that was Billy's only concern. The length of time he spent getting into the network and how long he stayed there was only the first part of their plan. He had no idea what they were looking for. And the process might be complicated by the number of computers connected to the network and the number of servers and files they found. So he would have to be selective. Burying information inside a network was easy, and individual files could be encrypted to varying degrees. It wasn't quite the proverbial needle in the haystack but damn close enough.

While pretending to sip his coffee, Billy scanned the layout of the computers scattered throughout the café. He had his eye on one tucked away in a corner of the room, far from either the bathroom or the café bar, and it was finally free. He took his coffee, now cold, and sauntered over to the computer table, plunking himself down in the hard-backed chair. He hid a look of disgust—an off-the-shelf Acer, typically underpowered and cluttered with useless software that hogged up RAM. Still, Billy was confident it would serve his purposes.

He had already signed in at the bar, so he waved abruptly to the barista, who pressed a button near his cash register. The screen flickered to life, displaying a Windows 7 desktop. Billy mindlessly scrolled to the bottom of the screen explaining the terms of use and clicked "Accept." He opened Internet Explorer and spent a few minutes doing exactly what Edward had told him to do, looking up the score from the Canucks' game, even though he didn't really care, and checking a couple of news websites. Finally, he closed Explorer and got down to work. In less than a minute, using a flurry of keystrokes, Billy disabled the terminal's monitoring software and inserted his flash drive into one of the USB ports on the CPU located at his feet.

As soon as the small red light on the flash drive stopped blinking, Billy opened the Windows command screen reminiscent of DOS. He typed in a series of commands to access his flash drive and scrolled through the series of folders that popped up. He called up five and paused, scanning the room as discretely as he could. No one was watching him, and the barista was busy behind the bar. He typed in "DIVINR" and then "Run."

A second window popped up on his screen that looked slightly different from the command menu. It was a short program Billy had developed himself that let him quickly target specific networks. He used it in his white hat work instead of the paths his clients gave him. Why should he follow their instructions? They would just see him coming. This way they never knew how he was going to get at them. He'd named the program "DIVINR," for "diviner"—or the people that wielded the mystical wands that can supposedly locate underground water sources. Billy smiled—he thought the name was pretty clever.

A line of text prompted him to enter the name of the network he was looking for. Under normal circumstances, Billy would jump through a series of different networks to disguise his location, but time was of the essence, not subtlety. Billy typed "mansour" into the prompt and hit Enter. The screen churned briefly as the program used the computer's Internet connection to search out any networks containing the same name. A total of four came back, each with different spellings and different "ping" numbers—the amount of time it had taken a "packet," or small package of information, to reach to Billy's computer. The Mansour network he had located earlier had the smallest ping number, meaning the signal had been returned in the shortest possible time of the four. He quickly cleared the other three from his screen, typed another sequence of code into the command monitor and typed "Run."

A second program from his flash drive popped up, this one more of a diagnostic tool than a locator. HRTBT, opened up in a third window. Billy keyed in the location information for the network Mansour. HRTBT scanned the network and reported back on its characteristics and set-up. It took less than a few seconds, but the third terminal now lit up with an orderly series of rows and columns of the information the program had read from its initial scan, essentially a light probe, to see what came back.

Billy ran through the information almost as fast as the computer provided it. The IP address, the type of network Mansour was and the most available access point (AP), or channel anyone accessing the network from the outside—legitimately or not—were all displayed. He skipped past that to two other columns of code that were the most important. Under the WN heading (wireless network), the screen showed an "O" for "other," which told Billy that the network was WPA/WPA2. Although more complicated than a WEP network, the programs on Billy's flash drive were designed to defeat WPA networks. The second column showed how many users were on the network. In this case, there was just one.

Billy's plan was relatively straightforward—he was simply going to disrupt the user's connection and force them to log on again. Once they logged on again, Billy would collect their information, kick them off the network again then log in himself using that person's data.

No fuss, no muss, Billy, thought, watching.

Billy tapped in a few more commands. It happened quickly. In a mere moment, the user was booted off the network. Billy watched as the sequence went out to disable the managed access point. After a pause, another window lit up. The access point was down, and the new "virtual" point was off and running. A cursor blinked, waiting for the user to pop back up. Seconds in the computer world, where data flashed around in a millisecond, felt like hours.

But soon the monitor erupted in code, and Billy fought to conceal his elation. The user was back. Another string of commands appeared as the virtual access point captured the data needed for the client's computer to successfully match the network's. Billy smiled.

Billy had no idea how long the client would stay engaged with the network. He thought for a moment and decided on a drastic course of action. He needed time, and he didn't want to be virtually looking over his shoulder the entire time. He scanned the information on the packet and rooted out the user's IP address. Then he sent out the command again to knock the user off the network. Now Billy was the only one on the network.

He clicked over to his DIVINR screen and punched in the data he had recovered from the previous user during the first attack. Billy's smile turned into one of wonder as he continued examining the code as it flashed past. He guffawed inwardly—he had access to everything, which meant that the person he had knocked off the network had been a super-user or an administrator.

I better get cracking, Billy thought, clicking open a new window. It showed all of the devices connected to the network.

He was in.

Billy turned his head slightly and coughed. This time he meant it.

———

Kara's smartphone warbled. She read the one-word message.

Contact.

The pre-arranged signal indicated that Billy had successfully hacked into the network of Mansouri Consulting. Both Kara and Ryan breathed a quiet sigh of relief. Kara started up the Mustang, flipped on the headlights and pulled into traffic. She drove around the block and around the building. Ryan watched for any sign of activity inside.

No lights. The streets and alleyways around the office building were empty and dark, and not a single person was in sight. Whatever Billy had done didn't appear to have captured anyone's attention.

Kara parked the Mustang half a block over from their previous location, so as not to draw too much attention to their presence. She turned off the car engine and sent a text message.

Clear.

CHAPTER 24

Edward looked up from his terminal, which was so close to Billy's that the two could have mumbled back and forth to one another. Instead, Edward added Billy's address to his Skype contacts, so they could chat as Billy searched. Only if he really needed help would Billy call Edward over by coughing.

Clear, the Skype message read. Billy nodded, replied with a simple *OK* then started his search.

The Mansour network itself was fairly simple, typical of a small business. The peripherals consisted of two computers, one printer, one printer/photocopier, a server and an external hard drive that Billy guessed was used as a backup.

He dove into the first computer's hard drive. A scan of its contents revealed hundreds of files, all with regular, innocuous names. Billy didn't really know what they were looking for, so opening every document and scanning it for information would be incredibly time-consuming.

Suggestions? Billy tapped into the Skype window then hit Send.

For what? came the reply.

Billy frowned, tempted to kick Edward under the table out of irritation. He refrained, simply explaining the scope of the problem.

I need keywords, Billy wrote. *I can narrow this down if I have a set of keywords to search for.*

Billy clicked over to the DIVINR window while he waited for Edward to reply. The user Billy had kicked off the network still hadn't reappeared.

Movement at the bottom of the Skype window showed that Edward was typing.

Try Billy, Ryan, Davis, Edward, General Intelligence Presidency, Al Mukhabarat Al A'amah, came the reply.

Billy copied and pasted *General Intelligence Presidency* and *Al Mukhabarat Al A'amah* into his message window and added several questions marks after each term.

Saudi Arabian foreign intelligence, came Edward's reply.

Billy's eyes widened, but he kept the screen visible as he went back to check the first computer on the Mansour network. He tried the suggested key words one by one. "Davis," "Presidency" and "Al" returned several dozen files. Billy re-entered the two names of the intelligence agency, this time enclosed within quotation marks to search for the two words together. Both came back with zero results. Billy checked the "Davis" results. All three hits pointed to a Microsoft Excel file, which, upon closer inspection, listed the potential employers the consulting firm had assembled. Billy opened the spreadsheet and searched for "Davis." The only mention was an Eileen Davis, the president of a graphic design company in Abbotsford, BC.

Billy cruised around a few more of the directories, but the mundane nature of the file names, such as Address, Client List and Schedule, made it clear this particular computer was predominately clerical in nature.

No dice, Billy wrote. *Time for number two.*

He engaged the second computer. Another look at his array of windows showed the user was still nowhere on the network.

This second computer contained similar names to those found on the first computer, but some names were different. A few had file extensions denoting some sort of accounting software—Billy didn't recognize it but guessed from the other files that this was the boss' computer where all of the real action happened. He opened up the search window again. He tried the search terms for the intelligence agency, both with and without quotes, and again came up with nothing. "Billy," "Edward" and "Davis" all returned a similar lack of results.

But "Ryan" returned one search result.

Billy leaned forward, looking at the path for the file. It was an image file, specifically a TIFF file, in the computer's Recycle Bin.

Billy dragged the file back to his desktop. When he opened up the image, his jaw dropped.

He forgot about coughing and kicked Edward as hard as he could under the table.

CHAPTER 25

"Cheese and rice," Billy breathed as he and Edward stared at the screen together.

Billy had picked up on the common Twitter expression because any references to the Christian Lord and Saviour typically resulted in a bombardment of religious-themed spam messages. The Twitterverse had come up with its own set of expressions to avoid provoking the attention of the spam world.

Edward got up from his desk after Billy kicked him and stood at Billy's terminal with an expression of rage on his face. But as soon as Edward saw the computer screen, his anger fell away. He moved to Billy's side and crouched, obscuring the screen from any prying eyes.

It was Ryan.

The file was called RYAN045.tiff. In the picture, Ryan had a bag over his shoulder, hair slightly damp with sweat and sunglasses over his eyes. He wore a UBC track-and-field

jacket and shorts. He did not seem to be aware that someone was taking his picture.

Billy right-clicked on the image to get more information about it. The information box that popped up showed
the photo had been taken approximately three weeks before
by a Canon 5D Mark II camera. No changes appeared to
have been made to the file because there were no further
entries after the creation date. That didn't mean the image
file hadn't been reproduced or distributed, just that it hadn't
been modified.

At Edward's prompting, Billy searched for file names
similar to the one containing Ryan's picture but with different numbers, thinking it might be part of a string of photos.
If it was, those other photos had long since been deleted.
RYAN045.tiff was the only one left.

Billy copied the file to his flash drive and continued
searching Mansouri's second computer but found nothing
of value. The only curious find was the picture of Ryan.

"It at least links the company to the attack on you
and Ryan," Edward whispered. "But there must be something else."

"I'm not done yet," Billy whispered in turn. "There's
still the hard drive to look through, and the server."

"All right, go ahead," Edward said. He didn't move.

Billy hovered his mouse over the external hard
drive connected to the Mansour network. He was pleasantly
surprised—a five-terabyte system, apparently. He read the

manufacturer's key and didn't recognize it. He mentioned that to Edward.

"A lot of this stuff around the intelligence world is custom," Edward whispered. "Developed in-house. It's no surprise you've never heard of it."

Billy shrugged, and he expanded all of the folders so he and Edward could get a better look at the contents of the hard drive. For a five-terabyte backup, only about two Gigs of memory was occupied.

"They're not backing up everything," Billy whispered. "I saw at least 300 Gigs of data on the two computers alone."

"Maybe they use more than one device as backup," Edward offered. "Or it's not actually meant to back up anything."

Only six folders were on the hard drive. On a hunch, Billy typed in the file name for the photo they had found of Ryan. It came up in the search window. Billy traced the path to a folder called "Hare." He double-clicked on the folder to expand it.

And then his screen went nuts.

There was a blur, almost as if the screen briefly warped, and a window appeared, superimposed over the folder name.

"ENTER KEY" flashed on the screen.

Billy looked at the window and swallowed hard.

"What?" Edward asked, quietly but urgently.

Billy had toyed with this before but had never in real life come across a file or folder like it. He knew exactly what it was. And he also knew he wouldn't be able to open it.

"What?" Edward implored.

"It's AES," Billy said.

"Huh?" Edward said, sounding perplexed.

"Advanced Encryption Standard," Billy explained. "It's the highest standard of encryption available. This folder is locked."

Edward felt as if he'd been struck. He knew exactly what AES was. He had just been hoping that Billy had meant something else.

"How strong?"

Billy looked over the number of spaces in the field in front of him.

"If I had to guess, I'd say it's either 192-bit or 256-bit encryption," Billy breathed. "I mean, theoretically there's a way to get through it, but I…I…"

Billy was stammering now. Edward clapped him on the shoulder.

"You can't do it here, now. I know," Edward said. "Just drag the folder over to your flash drive, and we can deal with it somewhere else when we have some time."

Billy shook his head. "But I can't. When I said it's locked, it's locked! Even if I could go back in and try to copy it using my super-user privileges, it would probably be a big pile of scrambled code or a corrupt file. It'd be even more worthless than if I just typed in random numbers and letters for the daily key."

"Daily?" Edward asked.

Billy nodded. "Look at the screen."

Edward did. Just below the entry field for the decryption key was a small digital clock read-out, counting down until midnight.

"When this rolls over to midnight, the key to access this hard drive will change. This is serious stuff, Edward," Billy huffed. "This is intelligence or military grade."

Edward's mind was spinning. "Isn't that something you can capture?"

Billy shook his head. "I don't know how they get the key. I mean, the key is the most critical component of any encryption. If you turn it over to someone else, you are seriously screwed."

Edward nodded, his brain finally catching up with Billy's. He had dealt with encryption all his working life, just not at this level. That was for the boys at Communications Security Establishment to worry about. AES was the strongest, highest-level encryption available. It was a substitution-permutation network that took letters, broke them down into subkeys, mixed them up using a mathematical algorithm and then flipped them around according to column orders and block sizes. It was practically unbreakable.

"What do you need, Billy? Tell me."

"We need the hard drive itself," Billy said. "It will stop the countdown, for starters. And we need to somehow recover the key. I can do a lot better if I can hook up the hard drive directly to a computer, but when that key rolls over at midnight and we don't have it, there is no way in hell we're getting in."

"What makes you so sure we can find it?"

"Because this key is measured in bits. It has to be generated randomly and contain enough disparity between its elements that it would be completely un-guessable. It's not something you can memorize—it's complex and has to be written down somewhere."

Edward thought. It was almost eleven o'clock. They had less than an hour to get to the hard drive before the day rolled over and the key changed.

"You're sure about this, Billy?"

"As sure as anything," Billy breathed.

"Okay," Edward said. He hit a button on his phone. It was a desperate plan, and those types of plans seldom worked, but their options were limited. Whatever was in that hard drive was vital to what was happening.

"Uh, Ed?" Billy said. "We might have another problem."

Edward turned just as the line picked up. Billy's shaking finger was pointing to one of his command screens.

The user that Billy had kicked off the Mansour network was back.

CHAPTER

The Vancouver Police Department had two helicopters for patrol purposes, and because the night had been relatively quiet, Air One was able to fly Susan and Aly to Nanaimo.

The ferry had a head start of almost thirty minutes, but the helicopter covered the thirty-eight nautical miles between the two ports in less than half-an-hour, easily dispatching both officers in Nanaimo with plenty of time to meet the ferry. Susan and Aly took along two RCMP members who had radioed ahead to the ferry crew, telling them to dock at their port but not to let anyone leave. The officers had a photo of Davis and a description of the new clothes he had.

They worked in pairs, searching the length of the ferry; Susan and Aly checked the walk-on passengers while the two Mounties checked every vehicle, asking drivers to pop their trunks to look for stowaways.

Aly had just finished checking the ID of a man visiting Canada from Germany when he saw another man walk away from the group.

Why is that guy stumbling? Aly thought.

He handed the German back his ID, and ignoring the rest of the people in line, Aly advanced on the man. The height was right. And he was wearing what looked like a yellow golf shirt and dark khakis, exactly the same clothes Davis had bought at Tip Top.

Aly motioned to Susan, who walked over, took one look at the man, then nodded at Aly. The man was lurching his way towards the stern of the ship, reaching out to the railing for support.

Drunk? Susan mouthed to Aly. He shrugged in return and brought one hand to his waist, unclipping the holster to his sidearm and drew it.

"You against the railing in the yellow shirt! Don't move!" Susan yelled loudly, also drawing her gun. There were audible gasps from the passengers as both officers slowly worked their way closer to the man, who began to turn around.

"Don't move!" Aly screamed, shaking his gun to emphasize his point. The man froze in place. "Put your hands on your head, and lay down on your stomach."

The man put his hands on his head and lowered himself to the ground but lost his balance part way and simply fell over. Susan rushed over to him and forced his hands down to the small of his back and then cuffed him.

Susan recoiled instantly at the smell—even with her years of experience, she had never gotten used to the intense aroma surrounding a drunk, especially one that hadn't bathed in some time. The body odour and alcohol created a fume so nauseating that Susan thought the scent could be used as a chemical weapon in warfare.

Her intuition gnawed at her. Something about this situation, the smell, wasn't right.

Aly approached and holstered his gun. Susan followed suit. Both reached down and grabbed an arm, then hauled the man to his feet.

"Dammit," Aly almost shouted. Susan could feel his frustration but chose to keep it to herself.

The face they were looking at was old, wrinkled, gaunt and jaundiced, likely brought on by a lifetime of drinking.

It wasn't Davis.

CHAPTER 27

Kara said only a few words into the phone.

"I understand," she said curtly, then hung up. She turned to Ryan.

"We're going in."

They had discussed the possibility earlier in the evening, but it had been considered the least viable and a last resort. Billy was relatively confident he could find anything they were looking for when he hacked into the network. Ryan and Kara had been stationed outside the office building to watch for any activity in case they needed to get inside quickly.

Kara explained the situation to Ryan as they got out of the car. They had to find a hard drive unit connected to the office's local network, and disconnect it within the hour. They also needed to retrieve any file or piece of paper that might contain a long, complicated password. Only when they disconnected the hard drive could they concentrate on a more intense search.

"And you know how to do this?" Ryan asked, his knees trembling. His muscles were feeling the effects of adrenaline overload, with another wave mounting on top of the countless others he had experienced this evening.

"It's not my first break-in," Kara said, walking to the back of the car and popping the trunk. She fished around inside and sorted through its contents. She gave Ryan a flashlight and a case that looked like an emergency vehicle repair kit.

"Good thing Gary always keeps his cars stocked," Kara said. She also handed a small cloth bag to Ryan then closed the trunk. "Come on."

Kara talked to him as they crossed the street. She told him to walk at a normal pace and went so far as to reach down and hold his hand. They didn't want to stand out to anyone in the vicinity. Still, Ryan found Kara's closeness and the touch of her hand reassuring. Her calm, measured voice was soothing against the roar of apprehension welling up inside him.

"We're going in, grabbing what we need and getting out. It's that simple. Edward and Billy will be here in a few minutes," Kara whispered.

"Strength in numbers," Ryan said, managing a smile.

"You've got more people looking out for you than you think," Kara replied.

Once they reached the corner, Kara led Ryan farther down the sidewalk, toward the back of the building, before crossing the street again. She was deliberately trying to keep them out of the pale wash of streetlights. Another reason for approaching the building from the rear was the long wooden staircase that led to a door on the second floor.

Kara pulled up alongside the building, looking around nonchalantly.

Ryan froze and suddenly pushed her back against the wall.

"What are you doing?" she hissed.

Ryan jerked his head up towards the roof. A single security camera was staring down at them.

Kara pushed him away gently. "Do you think someone is sitting in a room, actively watching this one camera?"

Ryan shrugged.

Kara shook her head. "You can buy dummy cameras that look real in order to scare away potential thieves. Even if it's real, cameras are a passive form of surveillance. They act as a deterrent for people *like you*," she said, "and also to simply record what's happening. When they realize they've been burgled, they'll check the tapes, and yes, they'll see our faces. But they already know what we look like. And I doubt they'd contact the police anyway."

Ryan nodded and stepped back. He hadn't thought about it that way.

Instead of using the stairs, Kara continued around to the rear of the building. She held out an open hand, gesturing for the flashlight, then turned it on. The beam danced along the lower part of the wall until it came to rest on a panel. Ryan recognized it as a telephone switching panel.

"What are you doing?" he asked, as Kara took the kit from him and walked towards the panel.

"Most security systems run off telephone lines," Kara said, placing the kit on the ground and leaning over it. "Hold this." She passed Ryan the flashlight. He kept it fixed on the case as she cracked it open.

The kit's contents were like no car repair kit Ryan had ever seen. It held the usual tools—Phillips screwdriver, pliers and an adjustable wrench—but also a pair of wire cutters, a box cutting knife and what looked like a set of dentist tools.

"If we cut the telephone line, it will kill the alarm system," Kara said, reaching for the box cutter. She extended the blade and tore into the thick rubber sheath at the base of the panel.

"What if it's a cable phone line?" Ryan asked.

"Then we'll cut that, too," Kara replied.

Ryan moved the beam up to the conduit Kara was ripping open vertically. In less than thirty seconds she had exposed a thick network of wires, all bundled up and leading to the panel above.

"Pliers, please," Kara said. Ryan handed them over. Kara reached into the cables, opening the pliers as wide as they would go. She cut the thinnest wire first then moved on to a thicker cable. The pliers easily severed both.

Kara sat back and waited. Ryan looked around and listened. He didn't hear anything.

"Okay," she said. "Let's go."

She packed up the tools and carried the kit towards the stairs. Ryan extinguished the flashlight and followed. Both took their time mounting the slick steps, Kara leading. When they reached the landing, Kara stooped and held out her hand. Ryan passed her the small bag. Kara fished out the pinhole camera and small monitor, flicking the screen to life. When it was set, she threaded the thin camera wand under the door, slowly passing the wand back and forth. Even with a night-vision camera, she couldn't see any kind of movement inside. She passed the camera back to Ryan and reached inside the kit, this time choosing the small set of picks and mirrors.

Kara motioned to the doorknob, which Ryan illuminated with the flashlight. Using her left hand, she inserted a tension wrench into the lock on the doorknob then inserted a small pick, working by feel to correctly orient the pins inside. After a few seconds of finessing, she turned the wrench. The door sprang open. Ryan held the door while she packed up the tools.

"Here we go," she said and walked in.

Ryan saw blinking red lights beaming from the walls. As he cast the flashlight over the walls, he also saw a series of motion sensors.

"They're inoperative," Kara whispered, guiding Ryan into a short hallway.

Given the less-than-pleasant exterior of the building, the interior was surprisingly modern. Dark wood baseboards and trim accentuated the walls, which appeared to be a dirty-yellow colour. The hardwood floor was also dark in colour and gleamed in the scant light.

They passed one door as the hallway opened up into a small reception area with a desk and workstation. There were a few plants, a Saudi Arabian flag hung on one wall, as well as a portrait of the Saudi Arabian king, Abdulla bin Abdul-Aziz Al Saud, fixed above a door at the far end of the room. The door led to another office.

"Let's start in there and work our way down. Remember, the hard drive first," Kara said.

Ryan nodded.

The door opened easily, and Kara and Ryan stepped into the room. Ryan moved towards the light switch, but Kara waved him off.

"If someone outside saw that, they might call the police," she said.

Ryan nodded, scanning the office with the flashlight.

The room was well appointed with a wooden desk, leather chair and desktop computer. Another, smaller, portrait of the king was displayed on a bookshelf that held numerous books. A file cabinet sat to one side of the desk;

the blinds on the windows behind it were closed. Ryan swung the beam around more, but he didn't see anything resembling an external hard drive.

"I'll start with the desk, you take the shelves," Kara said.

"But we only have one flashlight," Ryan whispered.

"I'm sure wherever this hard drive is, it has a light that glows," Kara replied.

Ryan nodded and rifled through the books on the shelf. He pulled back on each one to see if anything was concealed behind the titles but came up empty. He looked over at Kara. She stood still, shaking her head.

"Nothing," she said. "Let's go back and check reception."

CHAPTER 28

"How did that happen?" Edward asked Billy as they marched outside, Edward having flung a bunch of money down on the barista's counter to pay for their Internet time. They had left quickly.

"He probably changed locations or terminals," Billy said as they power-walked down the street, heading in the direction of Ryan and Kara's location. "He just went to another computer, I think."

Edward nodded. This was a problem.

"It's a big problem," Billy said, as if reading Edward's mind. "He logged in using his usual information and couldn't, so he used another ID and now he suspects something is going on."

Edward wanted desperately to break into a run—they were only four blocks from the Mansouri building, but he didn't want to draw any attention. Besides, for a skinny guy, Billy didn't move that fast. Edward thought about leaving him behind but decided against it. If the people who wanted

Ryan got their hands on Billy, they might be able to extract information from him.

Edward was worried. If the user was back on, couldn't he erase the hard drive or change the key temporarily? Billy had shaken his head no. The user had signed on as a network member without super-user privileges, meaning he wasn't allowed to perform certain actions. Plus, before leaving the café, Billy had changed the super-user login name and password to an unguessable jumble of keyboard-mashed letters, numbers and characters. It was as random as random got, effectively locking the user out of that account for the short term.

"He could still raise an alarm," Billy panted as he struggled to keep up to Edward. "He knows two things: he couldn't log in earlier because he was already logged in—I mean, we were logged in as him. And he knows the terminal he was using is under attack. So, at the least, he suspects a hack."

Edward nodded, careening across the street and cutting through an alley. His head turning as if on a swivel, he looked for signs they were being followed. In retrospect, giving Ryan and Kara the car had been stupid in case he and Billy needed to act fast. Edward had only one real play left—he slowed his pace slightly and pulled out his phone.

"Seriously? You're tweeting now?" Billy asked. "Are you telling the bad guys we're coming or something?"

Edward hit "Post" on the Twitter app and locked his phone, pocketing it. "You have to trust me, Billy," he said, picking up the pace again.

"Why does everyone keep saying that?"

CHAPTER 29

Susan and Aly's captive was spilling his guts in the interrogation room at the Nanaimo police station.

About everything, not just about how he got his clothes. Perhaps fortified by the coffee Susan and Aly were pouring into him, the man was recalling almost every arrest he'd ever had, which turned out to be many. He confessed to shoplifting and some outstanding warrants for violating conditions of his probation on older theft charges. He also had a few citations for loitering and being intoxicated in public.

Susan had to interrupt him to get his name—Joseph St. Armand.

They had easily found the credit card after they searched him for weapons. They'd also found a bunch of random items—cigarettes, loose change, old food wrappers—in his pockets, which they bagged as evidence. They found a receipt for a liquor store date-stamped for shortly before the ferry left. Joseph explained that he'd bought a bottle of rye with the credit card.

"He just stopped and picked me up," Joseph said. "I'd just finished my mickey of rye, and he stepped out of a cab and offered me a quick job. Gave me these nice clothes, bought me a ticket for the ferry and said he needed me to deliver something to some people in Nanaimo."

Joseph was wearing a blue prisoner's jumpsuit courtesy of the RCMP detachment. The yellow golf shirt and khakis were technically evidence.

"After he bought the ticket, he gave me the credit card and said, 'Thank you.' I bought some rye and got on the boat. That's about it."

"What did he give you to deliver?" Susan asked.

"Well, that's the funny part," Joseph said. "Nothing. He didn't actually give me anything."

"You didn't think that was strange?" Aly asked.

"I didn't really care. I got some clothes and liquor out of the deal. I guess it was strange. Not as strange as the message he gave me, mind you."

"Message?" Susan asked. "What was that message?"

Joseph slurped his coffee then looked at Susan. "Said to tell the police that he had eaten at New York Fries. Isn't that strange? Like the police care where you eat."

Aly and Susan stared blankly at each other.

"So he knows we're watching him?" Aly asked.

"I guess," Susan said, shrugging. "Probably not us specifically, but just that the police are watching him."

"Wait," Aly said, heading to the corner of the interrogation room to check a box of paper bags containing the evidence. After putting on gloves, he unfolded the top of one bag and pulled out the fast food wrapper they'd taken from Joseph's pocket, then held it out so Susan could see.

"New York Fries," he said, pointing to the black checkers on the wax paper wrapper.

"Give it to me," Susan said, forgetting about Joseph and snapping on a pair of latex gloves. She grabbed the wrapper, which she noted had only a couple of grease stains, and held it up to the light, passing her eyes over every inch of it.

"Anything?" Aly asked.

Susan shook her head. "The light in here sucks," she commented, holding the wrapper up closer to the fluorescent bulbs overhead. She noticed a scratch in the wax paper. Then another.

"Write this down!" she yelled at Aly, barking off a sequence of numbers that had been scratched into the wax paper.

"It's a phone number," Susan breathed. "Local, too."

She picked up the phone on the desk and asked the officer on the other end to run the number. He called back moments later, just as Susan was returning the wrapper to the bag.

"Prepaid cellphone," she said to Aly. Untraceable. All they could hope for was to get a ping off a nearby tower.

"What do you want to do?" Aly asked, perplexed.

Susan frowned. This chase had changed abruptly.

"We call it," she said, walking out to the squad room. She asked a Mountie to take Joseph back to cells then strode across the workspace to an open desk. The desk phone had a digital voice recorder connected to a "bug" that recorded all conversations on that line.

She turned the recorder on, then picked up the phone and dialled.

Aly walked to another unoccupied desk and selected the line Susan was using. He pressed the mute button on the phone and put the handset up to his ear.

A voice answered after only one ring.

"Daniel Davis," a man's voice spoke.

Susan was caught off guard. She had not expected him to answer using his actual name.

"This is Detective Susan Bartlett with the Vancouver Police Department," Susan said, momentarily flustered. "Who is this?"

Susan rolled her eyes upon hearing her own question and breathed deeply, trying to calm herself.

Davis chuckled on the other end. "A pleasure, detective. A question if I may before you start asking. Are you really just a detective with the Vancouver Police Department?"

Susan swallowed, unsure of how to answer. *Why not the truth?* she figured.

"No," she said. "My partner and I are with the Vancouver INSET, and we're interested in speaking with you."

"Why?"

Susan faltered again. "We've been ordered to detain you for questioning."

"That's not an answer," Davis almost laughed. "You don't know, do you?"

Susan couldn't imagine what she was supposed to say.

"Detective, I'm afraid I'm not available at the moment, but I did want to pass something on to you, one intelligence operative to another. There's a lot happening tonight that you don't understand and that those who cut your marching orders don't want you to understand."

"What I understand," Susan growled, "is that we need to talk to you. It would be in your best interests to come in on your own terms."

"Not right now, detective," Davis replied. There was a mumbling noise on the other end of the phone, like someone was talking to Davis. Davis' voice dropped as he said "Yes" to the person, then his voice came back on the line more clearly.

"But I'll give you a lead into this evening's activities. Come by this address, and I think you'll find something very interesting."

He rattled off an address near downtown Vancouver. Aly scribbled it down.

Susan blustered her way back into the conversation. "We will track you down!" she said forcefully.

"I'm afraid all you'll find is my phone," Davis said. "I'll even leave it here for you."

Then the line went dead.

CHAPTER 30

"Nadda," Ryan said from the darkness, using the flashlight to search underneath the receptionist's desk. A computer tower was on a shelf mounted below the desk, and besides the monitor and the connection to the printer/copier in the opposite corner, there were no other peripherals. No glowing boxes. No external hard drive.

Kara sputtered, blowing a few stray hairs away from her face. They had gone over the first office thoroughly with no success. She had searched the reception area while Ryan had groped around the desk, lightly knocking on the walls to check for false panels. He also looked under chairs and behind the assorted flags and art pieces on the wall—all with no luck.

With the right equipment, this search would have been a cinch. A thermal scope would have led them straight to any device giving off heat. At the moment, the two computers were silent, so they would have appeared negligible. The scope sensed heat through walls and would have detected the hard drive if it was sequestered out of sight.

But Ryan didn't believe the hard drive was tucked behind a wall.

"It needs a power source," he told Kara, drawing on everything he had learned from Billy over the course of their friendship. "If it's hard-wired into the LAN, there has to be cables running from the server or modem to it. If it's wireless, it needs to be in a relatively unobstructed area. The more walls you put between your wireless access point and your peripheral, the weaker the signal."

Ryan knew this from hard experience when he had tried to set up a new Mac Time Capsule and an Apple TV unit while Billy was at work. Ryan had spent four hours trying to reconfigure the home network without success. Billy had done it in less than fifteen minutes.

"So you think it's out in the open?" Kara asked, her eyes searching the dark floor for cables that seemed out of place. She walked over to the desk and examined the cable bundles behind it. She traced the ones that ran to the peripherals, and sighed. No extra cord.

"Wait a minute," Ryan said. "I haven't seen that either."

"Seen what?"

"The Internet source," Ryan replied. "I haven't seen a modem or router or repeater or anything that would indicate this office even has Internet access."

"But Billy was able to hack in," Kara argued.

"Right," Ryan said. "So where is it?"

"Off site?" Kara volunteered, crestfallen. If the modem was somewhere else in the building, it would take longer to find it. It was already eleven-thirty, and she felt pressured.

Ryan shook his head. "I've seen where Billy works. The modems, the servers, they're all locked up in big rooms. So the hard drive has to be here."

Kara pointed down the hallway to the door they had passed when they came in but hadn't yet tried. Ryan nodded. They took the half-dozen steps towards it, and Kara turned the doorknob. Locked. She retreated to the reception area to retrieve their kit, but she stopped as Ryan raised his right leg and propelled his foot at the door lock. The doorframe cracked and splintered but didn't give. A second kick sent the door careening open. The resounding crash reverberated off the walls like thunder. Kara winced.

"Quick access," Ryan said simply.

"But loud," Kara replied, waiting for a moment, listening, but she heard nothing out of the ordinary.

"Well, we're in," Ryan reasoned, stepping through the frame and casting the beam from the flashlight around the room.

The room was big and empty. It looked like it had once been a lunchroom or small kitchen, with shelves, drawers and kitchen cabinets higher up. The rough-ins for a sink stuck out of one wall. But there wasn't a kettle, a coffeemaker or even a microwave in sight. Kara haphaz-ardly pulled open a few drawers and cabinet doors but found nothing.

"Maybe they don't use this room," Ryan suggested. "Maybe when they leased the space, they just locked this place up because they didn't need it."

"Maybe," Kara said.

Both of them heard it—a thud above them, slight but still audible. They waited a few seconds, Ryan instinctively raising the flashlight to the ceiling and waving it back and forth, as if he could see through the ceiling to the source of the sound. He shook his head in disbelief. He was getting jumpy.

There was no more noise. Ryan was about to join Kara in her search of cabinetry when the cone of light from the flashlight caught something high, in a corner of the ceil-ing. He moved the beam back to the spot and walked closer.

"Jackpot," he whispered, nudging Kara with his elbow and gesturing with the light. Tucked into the farthest corner, in between the wall and a cabinet mounted flush with the ceiling, was a bundle of cable, exiting the wall and entering the cabinet through a small hole drilled in its side.

Ryan reached up and threw the cabinet doors open wide. One shelf held the modem, the server and the wireless router. But one shelf lower was a black, plastic box, perched vertically, with a small green light occasionally winking.

"There it is," Ryan said. He reached in to grab the drive but felt resistance. He chanced a jump up to get a better look.

"It's screwed into the cabinet," Ryan said. "I don't suppose you have a normal screwdriver in that car kit of yours?" he asked.

"Stop," a voice spoke simply.

Ryan waved the flashlight around in shock. Kara was right beside him, her hands in the air. Four men were standing inside the room, between him and the door. The gleam from the flashlight washed out their features, but he couldn't mistake the small handgun the largest of the men was pointing in their direction.

"Turn off the flashlight and drop it," the man with the gun said, gesturing at Ryan.

Ryan noticed that the men were squinting. The bright flare of the flashlight was interfering with their eyes' ability to adjust to the darkness. Ryan thought about keeping them blinded for a few seconds and then attacking, but the distance between him and the group was too great. He wouldn't reach them before that gun went off.

His arms shaking as fear clenched at his muscles, Ryan thumbed the beam of the flashlight off, plunging the room into darkness. Only the soft street light from the room's window to Ryan and Kara's right offered any kind of illumination. He bent over and placed the flashlight on the floor.

"Now kick it to me," the man ordered.

Ryan's hopes faded—the flashlight was the only weapon he had. Reluctantly, he snaked a toe underneath the flashlight and sent it tumbling towards the man.

"Good," the gunman said.

As Ryan's eyes adjusted to the dark, he could make out features. The men were all of Arab descent and looked big and tough. He didn't recognize them, save one.

"Hey, Kamil," Ryan said to the man who had choked him in the back of the van earlier that evening. "Had a fun night?"

Kamil didn't respond, his arms folded across his chest.

"What are you doing?" Kara whispered to Ryan, but he ignored her.

"My neck's right here if you want to choke me again," Ryan called, trying to bait him.

Kamil grumbled but didn't speak or move.

"What are you *doing*?" Kara whispered out of the side of her mouth.

"Quiet," the gunman said. "You have had enough liberty for one evening, Mister Davis. Now you are going to come with us. Fight back, and I will let Kamil finish what he started."

"I bet you tell all the ladies that," Ryan quipped. He felt a sharp pain in his ankle as Kara kicked him to be quiet.

"I will not tolerate cheeky behaviour, Mister Davis. You can shut your mouth and come with us voluntarily and quietly, or I can zap you again and drag you away," the man said, frustration evident in his voice. "Now turn around and face the wall."

Ryan turned deliberately to his right, around Kara, facing the window. He caught sight of her eyes in the faint reflection. She looked defeated.

Time, Ryan thought, *buy time.* He knew that whoever these guys were, they were trying their hardest not to kill him. He knew Edward and Billy were on their way and might be able to help them. Well, Uncle Ed might…

Out of the corner of his eye, Ryan saw the gunman reach behind his back. When his hand emerged, the gun was missing, replaced with two pairs of flex-cuffs. With his free hand, the man motioned to the three men closest to Ryan, all of whom advanced on him.

Oh boy, Ryan thought to himself. He looked up, caught Kara's eye and winked, steeling himself.

He watched their reflection in the window as the men descended on him. The image was reversed, but it was enough for Ryan to at least judge the distance. When the trio closed to within a half-metre of him, Ryan pumped with his legs, propelling himself into the air and onto the lip of the countertop in front of him. He pumped again, launching himself backwards at a diagonal angle and twisting in the air as his body approached his attackers.

Ryan heard a trifecta of grunts as he crashed into the men, his arms and fingers extended, looking for soft spots, trying to inflict as much damage as possible. Two of the men fell to the floor with Ryan, while the third stepped backwards, struggling to keep his balance. Ryan fell to the ground, too, but landed on his hands and feet, crouched. He stuck out his left leg and drove it in a wide circle along the floor, taking the third man's legs out from under him.

Ryan focused on the gunman, who would hopefully be so shocked he wouldn't immediately reach for his gun. In his last glimpse of the reflection in the window, Ryan saw that the gunman was to Ryan's left, slightly behind the three other men. Now facing the room, the gunman should be to Ryan's right. Ignoring the two men he'd taken down, Ryan tucked his left leg back in, looked to the right and saw the gunman, reaching behind his back while stepping away. Ryan drove off his left leg, propelling a solid, straight-leg side kick into the gunman's shoulder, knocking him off balance and forcing him to use his hands to keep himself upright. Ryan dropped his left foot to the floor in front of him, transferred his weight to it and stepped forward, using the momentum to power his right fist into the gunman's temple. The gunman fell to the ground like a stone, the pistol visible in his waistband.

Ryan had no designs on getting the gun, but he needed to make sure no one else could get their hands on it. But as he turned, a familiar powerful pair of hands grabbed his throat and squeezed. Ryan didn't resist but snapped his arms up to shoulder height and craned his forearms up at the elbows. He torqued his body around at the waist, his feet following him in the turn, and rammed his bent arms into Kamil's wrists. The force of Ryan's turn was too much for Kamil, who was forced to let go of Ryan's throat. Ryan kept turning, bringing his right foot up high in an arc, bowling Kamil over to the ground.

Ryan still didn't like his odds. The three men he'd knocked down were back on their feet and spread out, pinning Ryan against a wall. He looked up and his heart sank. Kara just stood there, stock still, a look of horrified surprise on her face.

He pushed Kara out of his mind and focused on the three attackers in front of him but still between himself and the gunman. One man lashed out suddenly with a solid right hand that connected with Ryan's collarbone. The hit stunned him momentarily, but he was able to capture the arm. In his confined space, Ryan knew he didn't have enough room to execute any kind of throw. So he turned, using his attacker's momentum against him, pulling him around, headfirst into the wall.

Ryan's attention snapped back to the other two men, just as a heavy boot collided with his knee, causing his leg to buckle. He fell to the side and tried to roll away, but four hands reached for him. He scissored his legs, knocking one man down and away, but the other man grabbed Ryan and rained blows down on him. Ryan kept his hands over his face, protecting his head from most of them, but the same foot that had kicked him in the knee stomped down on his ribs, and Ryan instinctively protected his chest. Two shots caught the top of his head, and he tried to roll again, but he was surrounded. When he tried to pull his arms up to cover his face, strong hands intercepted them and forced him to his feet. Another punch collided with his nose, and Ryan felt the blood flow.

The beating stopped. Ryan stood, one man holding back his arms. When Ryan looked up, he saw the gunman facing him, his eyes fired with unbridled rage. He was holding the barrel of the gun in his hand, over Ryan's head.

"When we are done," the gunman panted, "Kamil gets to finish you." And his hand came down, the butt of the gun aimed squarely for Ryan's head.

Suddenly the entire room exploded in light. Everything happened at once as every person in the room reached to shield their eyes, but the damage was done. Accustomed to the dark confines of the room, their pupils had expanded to allow in as much as light as possible. With the explosion of brilliance, their pupils screwed up as tight as the tip of a needle, effectively blinding everyone.

The man released his grip on Ryan, who fell forward, blinded and off balance. The incoming pistol whip had glanced off the backside of his neck, causing spasms of shooting pain. The gunman fell too, screaming and clawing at his eyes. Uncontrolled in his fall, Ryan's head bounced off the tile floor, dazing him.

A bunch of feet sped past Ryan's head, but he couldn't tell who it was. He kept his eyes shut tight and held his head as if trying to massage the pain away. The sounds in the room echoed around him. He heard thuds that he guessed were well-aimed blows, as well as screams and shouts. Then the noise receded, until there was silence.

Someone muttered, and Ryan heard footsteps approaching. The voice spoke in English, good English, not accented. Ryan tried to get to his knees, but a pair of hands grabbed him by both shoulders.

Ryan stopped, his skin afire, his heart frozen. A finger traced a path along his forehead, pushing sweat-soaked hair away and Ryan leaned into the sensation. A scent reached Ryan's nose, one that he had never been able to forget. His mind and his heart erupted. He opened his eyes, but all he saw was darkness. He blinked desperately, trying to clear his vision, but the hands that were so shockingly familiar him held firm. The scent lingered. There was a faint murmur, and he couldn't make out the words, but the timbre jarred something deep inside Ryan that made his whole body shake. He prayed for his eyes to start working, but they refused. He tried to speak, but his soul was so choked with emotion that Ryan found he couldn't make a sound.

Then a second pair of hands grabbed at his shoulders. The first pair lingered, squeezed his arms gently then disappeared.

"No!" Ryan cried, scrambling forward, his shuffle as desperate as an uncoordinated flailing infant, but there was nothing. He lunged forward, his hands extended to grab the person he thought should be there but instead collided with a counter.

"Come back!" he yelled as tears fell and his lips began to quiver. He thought maybe he had been too quiet, and he cried in a voice loud and tormented. "Come back! Don't... don't go!"

But the second pair of hands caught him by the arms again, pulling him close. He heard his uncle mumble in his ear but couldn't understand the words. And Ryan collapsed in his Uncle Edward's arms, curling up his legs and sobbing enormous tears as old wounds long since healed tore open, and a storm of sorrow enveloped him.

CHAPTER 31

In an effort to better understand how the human brain processes language, Ryan had taken undergraduate-level classes in cognitive psychology. Although language had been only a peripheral topic of discussion, he had learned a lot about memory, the theories on how the brain stores information and how our senses can evoke a psychological or even physiological response.

The senses, he'd learned, play an astonishing role in association with memory. The sense of smell is the most widely associated with memories, either good or bad, but each of the five senses—taste, sight, touch, smell and hearing—can trigger memory recall if paired with a particularly strong sensation. The response can occur consciously or unconsciously—Ryan had been shocked to learn that a high percentage of intravenous drug addicts overdosed when they shot up in a new environment from where they typically got high, even when using the same quantity of the drug. The passive cues from their surroundings played a role in how their body responded to the drug. When the surroundings changed, so too did the effects of the drug.

Ryan had once joked with a girlfriend that, if he was placed blindfolded in a room with 100 different women, and they all took turns kissing him, he could pick her kiss out of all the rest. He had meant it romantically, saying he knew her kiss so well that he would know it even while blindfolded. The same went, he added, with her natural scent. She had accused him of wanting to kiss 99 other women.

But any sensation could be familiar. Smell was the most potent sense because people often paired the aroma of specific foods with a feeling, such as comfort. And when Ryan had felt that pair of hands on his shoulders and smelled a vivid musk he had not encountered in almost nine years—and had thought he would never again—he was absolutely certain he had experienced the sensation before.

And the sense of hearing was equally powerful. He hadn't been able to make out any words, but the sound, the mellow hiss of a certain voice speaking softly, had been undeniably familiar.

Ryan sat in the back seat of the Mustang, pinching the top of his nose to stop the bleeding. His head was swimming in a sea of painful, long-forgotten memories of touch and times and places. Falling off his bike. Getting dumped by his first girlfriend. Losing the provincial kung-fu championship when he was twelve. Dozens, scores, hundreds of instances all rushed back at once, throttling him with an intensity that overwhelmed him.

He'd been a mess at the office, after he and Kara had been liberated. When Ryan's vision returned and the violent sobs became soft whimpers, he took in the scene around him—the four men seated on the floor, hands cuffed; his uncle cradling him in his arms, much like he had done almost a decade ago; Kara cramming gauze up his nose, unwilling or unable to meet his gaze; and Billy, staring quizzically at him.

Gary was there too, holding some sort of bazooka that was later revealed to be a "stun light." It burned at the strength of 100,000 candela, enough to temporarily blind anyone caught in its path, an effect only amplified in darkness. He had burst into the room, blinding everyone, giving Edward and Billy the opportunity to move in and mop up their assailants. Kara had, luckily enough, been looking away when Gary had stepped in, so she had disconnected the hard drive and switched it off with less than two minutes to spare. She checked Ryan over, making sure his ribs weren't cracked, and gave him another surprise from the "emergency car kit"—a Percocet for the pain.

While Billy helped Ryan out to the car, Gary, Edward and Kara grabbed both computer towers, the server, as well as a bag of documents resembling a "burn bag." They carried the items down to the Mustang, leaving the bad guys behind, and made a hasty retreat with the gang split between the Mustang and the car Gary was now driving—a Toyota Corolla.

Ryan was silent. Overcome with emotion and his mind clouded with opioid, he didn't have the energy to speak. He'd been running on reserves the whole evening—his experience at the Mansouri offices had taken the last of his strength.

No one said anything. Edward wouldn't look at Ryan, focusing on driving the car. Kara draped an arm around Ryan's shoulders and stared out the back window. Billy was riding with Gary.

Ryan was convinced another person had been in that room, someone who had held him, if only briefly. Someone whose touch Ryan's body had memorized in every inch of his skin, a memory that lay dormant for years until it was unleashed this evening.

But he didn't ask. His mind was too foggy, his soul desperate. All night he'd been begging for answers about who was after them, what was going on and who everybody was—he doubted he was going to get a straight answer now.

Ryan drowsily raised his head, looking around. They were on Lagoon Drive, snaking their way through one of Vancouver's most celebrated pieces of land—Stanley Park.

He sat upright, trying to get a better view of where they were headed. The Stanley Park Pitch and Putt, which Ryan had played more than a few times in his life, flashed by on the right. Lagoon Drive came to an end at a T-intersection with Stanley Park Drive. Edward slowed the car and then turned right onto a side road.

"Where are we going?" Ryan asked.

"To a meeting," Edward said softly. He stopped the car a few hundred metres after turning. "You okay to walk?" he asked Ryan.

Ryan stepped out of the car gingerly. His legs felt warm and relaxed from the Percocet, but he had no problem keeping his balance. His pounding head was down to nothing more than a dull roar.

"I think I'm good," Ryan said. He turned as a pair of lights came up behind them. He could see the faces of Gary and Billy through the windshield of the Corolla.

"Okay," Edward said, opening his window but making no move to get out of the car. "You're going that way." He pointed down a slope that ran towards a small playground. "Air India Memorial. We'll watch you from here."

"What? You're not coming with me?" Ryan was feeling a little slow on the uptake.

"This is just for you, Ryan," his uncle said, a faint smile creasing his face. "Get going."

Ryan stumbled across the road, almost slipping as he descended the slope next to the bike path that ran beneath Stanley Park Drive. The grass was moist and slick. He probed his way through the dark, his head casting about as he wondered who could possibly be waiting for him in this place, so late at night.

He crossed the basketball court and picked his way though the Ceperley Playground, towards the memorial wall. It was a monument that contained the names of all 331 people who had lost their lives in 1985 when misguided fundamentalists, seeking a separate home for their people in India, had placed bombs on two Air India flights that took off from Canada. One bomb detonated at Tokyo Narita Airport, killing two baggage handlers. The second exploded in mid-flight, off the coast of Ireland, raining down the bodies of men, women and children into the Atlantic Ocean. The bombings had always been a strange event in Canada's history—it was seen as an Indian tragedy even though the majority of those on board, many of Indian descent, were Canadian citizens.

Ryan looked around and saw no one at first. He listened to the distant waters stir off the park's coast and felt the salt-tinged wind course over his sweaty scalp.

And then Ryan saw him, sitting on a bench, just fifty metres away.

Ryan didn't run. He stumbled, his legs unsteady with raw emotion and shock. The man stood and walked towards him. As the two neared, Ryan could see the same familiar features, the same slim build, aged a decade perhaps, but still the same look in his eyes.

The power of the moment overcame Ryan, and he stopped despite his will to keep walking forward. He slipped and began to fall, but arms caught him, strong, wiry arms, and Ryan felt the same touch that less than an hour ago had sent his entire body into shock. The arms held him close, and for the second time that evening, Ryan began to sob as he held the other man in a stranglehold.

"Oh, my son," Daniel Davis whispered, cradling Ryan in his arms for the first time in what he now believed was too long. "I've missed you."

—⟨·/·/·⟩—

"Well, son of a bitch," Aly breathed, pocketing his cellphone.

He was standing in a room inside Mansouri Consulting at the address Daniel Davis had given them earlier. Aly and Susan had decided against calling any backup to the address, just in case it was a trap. They also didn't want to draw attention to the situation.

They had searched the building and happened upon a collection of men in one room, all cuffed, a few sporting bumps and bruises. All were having trouble seeing, complaining of spots in front of their eyes.

"A popular ailment this evening," Susan had said, remembering the brilliant light that had blinded them on the road earlier that night.

Aly was just getting off the phone with the duty officer at the INSET unit back at headquarters. They ran the names of the men they had found and discovered two were on a CSIS "watch" list for possible espionage activities. The rest were in the country on work visas.

"Saudis," Aly said.

Susan had helped pull each man, one by one, upright so she could search their pockets for any weapons or other paraphernalia. As her hands worked their way across the fourth man in the room, who was enormous, her hands brushed against a bulge in a shirt pocket. She felt something almost crinkle under her fingers. She pulled out a pair of latex gloves from her coat pocket and snapped them on, then reached in to fish out the item.

"What is it?" Aly asked, his eyes still locked on the other three men.

Susan felt her heart beginning to race as she smoothed out the balled-up fast food wrapper.

"New York Fries," she said triumphantly.

She didn't have to hold the wrapper up to the light. A message had been scrawled across it in black felt pen.

"STAY IN TOUCH." Underneath the message was a generic Gmail address that Susan was almost certain would turn out to be untraceable.

"What's that supposed to mean?" Aly asked.

Susan shrugged, placing the wrapper on the counter. She used her police radio to call for some patrol units to help transport all four men to cells downtown. Aly and Susan, of course, would have to go with them. These weren't run-of-the-mill bad guys. They were the kind of guys Aly and Susan hunted for a living.

"Maybe he's going to turn himself in," she said wistfully.

Aly just laughed.

CHAPTER 32

Ryan couldn't remember the last time he had held his father's hand. It had probably been back when he was a child, still too young to cross the street safely by himself or during some other time when he needed reassurance. Ryan never remembered missing the contact because fathers and sons, after a certain age, don't hold hands.

But now the two stood against the Air India Memorial in Stanley Park, their hands interlocked as both struggled for words. Ryan was deliriously happy, however awkward their reunion might have looked to outsiders. His father's hand, though more worn than he remembered, felt just right. The touch that so electrified him earlier was proof against the disbelief in his mind that, after more than nine years of wondering and grieving, this was in fact, his father standing next to him.

"Why didn't you just wait for me?" Ryan asked in a quavering voice.

"At the office?" Daniel shrugged. "The last thing I wanted was to have this happen in front of a bunch of other people. Plus I needed to get away and make sure we weren't being followed. I had to give our cars a quick sweep, in case anyone had put tracking units on them—sure enough they tried, so I got rid of those quick. I didn't want to drop this on you—on us—in the middle of a fight like that."

Ryan nodded, grasping his father's hand tighter. He knew he had to ask. "Why?"

Daniel released Ryan's hand, turning to look him in the eyes. They were red from tears. Both men had cried mightily upon their reunion, but Daniel had pulled himself together first. On the outside at least. Inside, his heart was bouncing all over his chest with joy, pride, sorrow and love.

"Ryan, I want to tell you everything, I really do. The decision I made wasn't fair. And I will tell you everything, once I'm sure we're all safe."

"Just like everyone else has been saying tonight," Ryan sighed.

"There is a lot at stake, son, and I'm sorry you're caught up in this mess," Daniel said, reaching out to grasp Ryan's shoulder. "I can give you the Coles' notes version, but you need to be patient. When I know we're safe, I'll explain everything to you. Fair?"

Ryan nodded, waiting.

Daniel exhaled heavily. "Uncle Ed said he already told you what I did for a living. So yeah, I worked as an intelligence officer for CSIS. When you and I travelled, it was because I was working in other countries, trying to figure out if anyone was out to harm our country. All that travelling came later in my career, of course, shortly after you were born. Before that, well, this was one of my first cases." He pointed to the memorial.

Ryan remembered the news stories in recent years, about how CSIS had wiretap intelligence potentially implicating the Air India bombers but had fallen behind in its translations because the agency couldn't find enough interpreters who spoke the proper dialect. CSIS had eventually erased the tapes because it viewed itself not as a police agency that preserved evidence but as an intelligence body that kept secrets.

"It wasn't pretty," Daniel acknowledged. "But somehow I came out of that with my career intact, and you and I travelled the world. After a few years, I decided it was time for us to settle down here for a bit, so you could make some friends and get to know your country, and I could work behind a desk somewhere." Daniel frowned. "But 9/11 changed all that."

Ryan remembered that day clearly. His father had pulled him out of class, sent him to Uncle Edward's saying he was needed in Ottawa. He was gone for almost a month.

"About a year after the towers fell, someone came to me with information. It was explosive, and if true, would put a lot of people, especially you and me, at risk. But there were larger international implications. It didn't matter whether or not the information was true—I became the target of some powerful people."

Daniel leaned back against the memorial, crossing his arms and looking at Ryan.

"No one could guarantee my safety. So I had two choices—I could sit back and live with it and hope they never caught on and never found me. Or I could just leave. And there was only one way to do that and protect you."

Ryan sniffed, trying to hold back an unexpected wave of anger at his father.

"No one teaches you this stuff in life—how to really protect your kids. And you never think that keeping them safe means one day giving them up. At the time, Ryan, I felt I had no choice. Maybe it'll turn out I was wrong. But we need to find out."

"What do you mean?" Ryan asked.

"Son, I've spent the last nine years on my own, flying all over the world, talking to some of the worst people in the world in the shittiest slums of society trying to figure out what it is I have that they want. I've got an idea what it is. But I don't have solid proof. And the whole time it's been a big game of hide-and-seek, trying to stay one step ahead of the people trying to stop me.

"A few months ago they caught me. My captors started asking about a son, and I knew I had to get out, just in case this," he spread his arms out wide, "happened. In case they tried to get to me by going after you."

Daniel grabbed Ryan's arm fiercely. "Because, Ryan, you have to understand that I'd do anything to protect you."

Ryan nodded, emotions bouncing around every part of his body. He believed his father, but that didn't make the situation any easier. There was ferocious truth, and fatigue, in Daniel's words.

"So I came here, they found you and you've done a good job of getting away. And in doing so, you might have led us to something important."

Ryan tried to take it all in. He was sure that with more specifics it'd be easier to make sense of his father's decision to fake his own death. But he'd agreed to his dad's terms. Just the basics; more information to come later.

"So it's over now, right?" Ryan asked. "We can go to CSIS with the information we have and let them figure it out, right?"

Daniel stared at the ground, unsure of how to respond. "No, Ryan, we can't." His voice sounded hollow.

"Why?"

"Because I don't really work for CSIS anymore," Daniel said. "I haven't since before I left. I mean, I guess technically I do because I'm paid through their budget, but only a handful of people know about me. It's all backchannel stuff—some help when I need it and so on—but for the most part, it's only been me, my friends and the people I've met all over the world."

"But," Ryan said, staring at his father, "we can still give it to them. They can take care of it, right?"

Daniel shook his head defiantly. "That place is leakier than a rusty barge. The minute we take the information there, it disappears, and then we're all in even more danger."

"How do you know?"

"Ryan," Daniel said sharply, his head snapping up to look at his son. "How do you think those guys found you?"

Ryan's mind went blank at the question. He hadn't considered it, but then again, given that up until now he had no idea of what was really happening, he hadn't thought about the "how."

"Look, we're going somewhere safe, and we'll be able to sit down and hash out what we know and what we don't, but for now, we—all of us—need to get moving. The longer we stay in Vancouver, the easier it is for them to find us."

Ryan nodded dumbly. There was so much to say, so much to feel, so much still to figure out that he felt as if his brain had finally just gone flat. If Daniel had told him to wait here for the Mothership to arrive to take both of them back to their home planet, he probably would have done so obediently.

Daniel hugged his son again, then put an arm around Ryan's shoulders and guided him towards the two cars parked back up on the road.

Gary and Edward were waiting outside on the street for them, smiling broadly. Kara's eyes glistened with tears at the sight of the two Davis men together.

And Billy lay in the back seat of the Corolla, snoring loudly.

CHAPTER 33

He wanted to smash the phone into the wall.

Instead, he replaced the phone ever so gently into its charging station and leaned back in his office chair, contemplating the recent news.

Christian Wright had been on edge all night, despite the companion in his bed who he had hoped would soothe his frayed nerves and provide some measure of distraction from the events unfolding thousands of kilometres away. But for the first time in his life, what was happening outside of his world had intruded on his vigour in bed. For now she was sleeping, likely unsatisfied, but his own dissatisfaction went far deeper.

Everything they had put in place to protect themselves had proven to be nothing more than a stall tactic. And putting their faith in the hands of a man they had never met, even though both parties had mutual interests, had been a gamble that was turning into a mistake. The phone call had confirmed it. Their last best chance had been a disastrous failure—not only had their quarry escaped, leaving four men hogtied, but everything he and his business partners had worked for more than ten years to keep secret might also come undone.

Wright chewed at a manicured fingernail as he weighed his options. It would have been so easy, in retrospect, to have simply arranged a meeting a decade ago and explained away the events. They would have been annihilated in the public eye to be sure, but they would likely have emerged relatively unblemished even though they may have lost their positions with their respective companies. In the world of big business, such losses were nominal—another big company was always looking for leadership, regardless of past mistakes, even a mistake as critical as the one they'd made.

But they had convened in a room on that fateful day and, perhaps in part as a result of shock and haste, had sworn each other to silence. When they met again a year later, having heard the news that someone might have knowledge of their actions, they had agreed again to keep matters under wraps and trust their international friends to take care of the "problem." For the better part of a decade, they had operated as usual but always with the spectre of disaster lingering in the shadows. Now those looming shadows were the closest they had ever been to being exposed, and their efforts to suppress it had resulted in a string of failures.

No one in the group was supposed to make decisions on their own—they had all agreed. But it was three in the morning, and getting everyone together at this hour would take time. This couldn't wait until morning. They had one final play, and as hesitant as they had been to use it before, Wright could see no other option.

He woke his computer and opened up a program buried deep inside the recesses of the hard drive. A screen with a window for text appeared. A second window for a secret email account opened up beside it. He began typing into the text window, watching out of the corner of his eye as his words were converted into a seemingly random string of characters, numbers and symbols in the email document. His message was only two lines long, but that was all he needed. He closed the text window, clicked on the email document and hit Send.

His associates would be unhappy with the email, but there was nothing they could do about it now. If they didn't see the desperation in the situation, well, they were almost duplicitous in their lack of foresight. The stakes had never been higher, and the potential loss, at both a personal and business level, could be devastating.

He would notify them in the morning. For now he needed rest.

——⊰⊹⊱——

There was no casket for the memorial service because there was no body.

A simple urn sat on display on a table at the funeral home as a priest who never knew his father led the few mourners through a brief service to commemorate the life of Daniel Davis.

Ryan was out of tears. He'd spent the last week crying non-stop, in addition to the five days before when he'd experienced an hourly tornado of despair and hope as he waited for news of his father.

Daniel had gone snowshoeing in the foothills of the Rockies, as he did a few times each winter when he had the time. When Ryan was younger, his father had even pulled Ryan out of school a couple of times to take the trip with him.

But on his last trip, his father never came home. Daniel's cellphone went straight to voicemail, and the police and park officers couldn't triangulate a position based on the location of his cellphone. His dad had either turned it off, or the battery had died. Beyond the usual route he had planned to take, no one could say with any certainty where his father might be. They told him his experience in the wild and survival skills gave him an excellent chance at survival. But the first half-dozen search attempts were delayed as blizzard after blizzard descended on the area.

Ryan wanted to join the search parties, but his uncle refused. Uncle Ed kept him confined to his home, under perpetual watch as they waited. Ryan seldom slept except for when his uncle forced him to take half of a little blue pill, and even then he slept for only four or five hours at a time. He stared at his uncle's phone and at his own cellphone, willing them to ring. Too often the calls were for his uncle, who would retreat to his office. Ryan dialled his dad's cell-phone again and again, just to hear the recorded voice on the other end of the line. "It's Daniel. I'm not available..."

Ryan found it strange when men in suits came to his uncle's door one afternoon. Ryan came up from the basement too late to hear the men explain who they were, but his uncle just looked at him with an expression so muted Ryan couldn't tell what the men had said. They all sat down in the living room, Uncle Ed's arm around Ryan's shoulders as the men explained they had found his father's body.

Ryan demanded to see his father, to prove them wrong, but the men shook their heads. Apparently a blizzard had caught his dad off guard, and in the blinding snow, he had tumbled off an embankment and broken his leg. There was no cell service in the area, and even though they found empty packets of food and his sleeping bag, the mercury two nights later had plunged near the $-45°C$ mark. Unable to move, his sleeping bag not warm enough, his father simply froze to death. When Ryan again demanded to see him, they explained why he couldn't—the animals in the mountains had gotten to his body before the search team. The forensics team was forced to use dental records to identify him.

His father's will designated Edward as executor of the estate and, after a brief discussion with Ryan, the decision was made to cremate Daniel's remains before the service. His uncle took him to buy his first suit—black—and arranged for a limousine to take him to the funeral home *and to the cemetery afterward. During the service, Ryan only felt hollow inside.*

Only Edward spoke to the gathered few at the funeral home, at one point addressing Ryan directly and saying there were more people than he knew looking out for his best interests now, but in a room of less than a dozen people, Ryan couldn't understand how that was possible.

Despite his uncle's protests, Ryan was adamant that he alone would take the urn to the cemetery where he could spend the last few moments with his father before he was locked away forever.

Ryan left immediately after the service. With the cold urn in his arms, he left through a back door, into the waiting limo.

The snow that falls in Vancouver never sticks around, but as if intuiting the morbid aftertaste of the day, white flakes had fallen during the night and clung stubbornly to the ground. The sky was as grey as the urn on his lap, and Ryan spent the entire trip to the cemetery staring at it, not daring to open it.

Thankfully, the columbarium was free of visitors. Ryan sat down on a stone bench so wet it soaked his pants, and he stared at the urn in his hands. And after a day of no tears, Ryan broke down, cradling the urn close to his chest, as if trying to ignite a last spark from which he could resurrect his father's memory. He felt only cold steel. And that just made him cry harder.

Hours blended; more snow fell, stopped and fell again. His hands were fiery red from exposure by the time Ryan had cried himself out; the grey sky had turned to black. In spite of the force inside of him that compelled him to sit still, to never let go of the urn, Ryan managed to find the strength to stumble towards the columbarium. He kissed the urn to try to let his dad know how much he loved him, how much he would be missed, how Ryan's life would be forever lonely. Then Ryan placed the urn inside the niche and stepped away, sitting back on the bench and staring down at the stone floor.

He felt a hand on his shoulder and knew it was his uncle. They stood silent for perhaps another hour, Uncle Ed alternating between manly squeezes of his hand and gentle murmurs of reassurance.

Finally, Edward gently pulled at his hand, and Ryan rose to follow him to the car. Ryan noticed three men standing on a nearby rise, as if paying respects. He wondered how long they had been there because they seemed so out of place.

When they returned to his uncle's home, Ryan took half of a blue pill. In his room that night, Ryan finally came to understand how truly alone he was—his mother gone, his father dead.

There was no resolve in knowing that to some degree, you were the last of your kind.

With that solitary thought, Ryan finally slept.

CHAPTER 34

"They can't just be gone!" Thresher yelled.

"They appear to be, sir," Adam replied as calmly as he could. "We just heard from our team in the field. The son and the woman went into that building, a Saudi employment services office. A group of individuals went in after them. Then Gunsight arrived."

"You're sure it was him?" Thresher demanded.

"Our team is certain," Adam replied, shifting in the chair opposite Thresher. "Gunsight and the rest came out, got into two vehicles and left, but our team noticed the other group of men didn't leave. The team elected to go inside and found four men cuffed and dazed. In so doing, they lost Gunsight and the others."

"They didn't put a tracer on any of the cars?" Thresher asked.

Young shook his head. "They tried, but they're not showing up."

Thresher snorted. Gunsight was too smart, too skilled for them to simply put a tracking unit on the car. He would have known immediately and promptly disappeared again.

"What else do we know?" Thresher asked.

"I was able to dig up some information on that address on East Hastings. Belongs to a contractor we apparently use for technical consulting," Young said. "Code name is Stripper?"

Thresher chuckled. He'd forgotten about the Stripper. It had been years since they'd needed his services. "Guy who soups up agency vehicles for fieldwork," he said. "Interesting choice there. Not sure how he fits into this."

"There's no mention of him specifically in Gunsight's file, which I have to say, is pretty extensive," Young said. "You've been watching him for a long time."

"Longer than even the file indicates," Thresher said.

"What'd this guy do anyway?"

Thresher leaned his elbows on his desk and steepled his fingers in front of his mouth, smiling faintly. "Nothing you're cleared to know about. What's our next move?"

Adam swallowed, suddenly nervous, like he had committed some sort of mistake by asking about Gunsight. "We have the team looking for the two vehicles they were travelling in, and we're keeping an eye on those cellphones we caught earlier, the known and unknown ones that traded

Tweets about the Stripper, but the known one has been silent. We think it might be off. It looks like the unknown is pre-paid. No way to track it."

Thresher sighed. He had no better ideas, mostly because he'd never encountered a situation like this since he had taken over the Economic Co-operation Information Division. Most of their cases were relatively straightforward: they'd get names from a government, build the case against them, then grab them and ship them out of town. The cases usually didn't run like this.

"Sir? Are you listening?"

Thresher shook his head.

"The four men we found, sir, they claim they work at the office building where they were found," Young said, handing Thresher a sheet of paper.

Thresher looked it over, then swung around and typed the name of the company into his computer.

"Maybe they do." Thresher smiled and looked up at Young. "Keep looking. I'll handle this list."

Young seemed perplexed but merely nodded and walked out of the room.

Thresher clicked through several screens until he found the name and phone number he was looking for. He turned to his secure phone line, punched in the number and then a code permitting him to dial long distance.

CHAPTER  35

Ryan sat upright as his instant recollection of the previous night's events crashed down on him, filling in that momentary gap of amnesia upon waking. He looked frantically around the vehicle until his eyes fell upon the one person he still didn't expect to be there. Ryan relaxed, rubbing at his eyes.

His father, Daniel Davis, was behind the wheel of the van.

Ryan leaned back against the bench seat, waiting for the cloud of sleep to evaporate from his brain. He looked at the clock on the dash. He knew he hadn't slept long enough, but sleep hadn't been his idea. He'd wanted more than anything to take the seat next to his father in the van and spend the night talking. But no sooner had the vehicles pulled out of Vancouver's interior than Ryan had found himself in the back, fighting to stay awake.

"Just sleep, son," Daniel had said. "I'll be here when you wake up."

Billy was in the bench seat beside Ryan, still sleeping. Kara was in the front seat beside Daniel, staring out the window. Gary and Edward were in a second vehicle, somewhere, headed for the same destination. Ryan didn't yet know where they were going and hadn't bothered to ask. His father had promised them safety and, as a precaution against the highly unlikely scenario they were being followed or the van was somehow bugged, had implored them to refrain from talking about the night's events or the trip they were on.

After Ryan's reunion with his father at Stanley Park, Gary, Edward and Daniel had huddled near the Corolla while Kara stood beside Ryan. They needed new vehicles for the next leg of their journey if they were going to get themselves somewhere safe. They couldn't go back to Gary's. They'd already tapped that well once, so there was a good chance the garage was being watched, possibly even infiltrated. Gary might have been able to return alone, but for all of them to do so would have been foolish.

So Daniel and the rest had followed Gary to another workshop, this one in Burnaby, run, he explained, by one of his "guys." They had ditched the Mustang and Corolla, trading them for a Dodge Caravan and a Ford F-150 truck. While they waited at the workshop, Daniel sent Kara to a nearby all-night pharmacy for hair dye, and she returned with a mix of shades for everyone. Only Gary refused to dye his hair; his only concession to altering his appearance was to trim his beard, making him appear significantly less menacing. Edward and Daniel's grey hair was now dark brown, Ryan's was black as night and Billy decided to go blonde. Kara had simply cut her long, straight black hair and added a few blonde highlights. All changed into clothes that Gary had retrieved from his workshop—Daniel even convinced Gary to trade his biker gear and gold chains for more subdued business attire. Bouncing between exhaustion and exultation, Ryan felt practically giddy as he and his father stared at each other's hair, compared their clothes and giggled like little girls. It was like his youth all over again, and they were playing Disguises in the markets of Bangkok.

The group had split up into two vehicles and had started off on the Trans-Canada Highway, but Gary and Edward had peeled off north in their truck when they reached Abbotsford, headed for the Lougheed Highway. Only Daniel, Gary and Edward knew their destination, and by that time Ryan, Billy and Kara were asleep.

Now, as Ryan looked around him, all he could see in the daylight were endless expanses of evergreen trees, interspersed with large tracts of green and yellow fields. They had left the highway and were now travelling on a well-worn dirt road that jostled the van in every direction. Ryan caught a sign as they flashed past a turn-off onto a rural road.

Turtle Valley Road? Where the hell are we? He searched his memory but couldn't think of one instance in which he'd ever come across the road before. He opened his mouth to ask but then stopped, remembering his father's earlier reproach.

"Almost there," Daniel whispered.

Ryan nodded, watching the beautiful scenery unfold around him. He heard the clicking of the van's signal lights as they turned left across Turtle Valley Road onto Skimikin Road.

This road wasn't even packed dirt—it was more like two slightly overgrown grooves through tall grass, but the van hopped along. One particularly large depression bounced the vehicle so hard that it propelled Billy's head into the passenger's window and woke him up.

"Hey! Where are we?" Billy practically yelled, holding his skull. Ryan looked over at his friend and shook his head. It took a few moments for him to clue in. "Oh, right," Billy said. "No talking."

"Here we are," Daniel said. He slowed the van to a stop in front of a locked gate. He exited the van, unlocked the gate with a key, then hopped back in and kept driving.

Ryan hadn't spent much time on farms, but knew he was looking at one, or a place that once had been a farm. The fields around him, thick with waist-high grasses seemed to go on for miles and were surrounded by a barbed-wire fence. He turned his gaze to the windshield and watched as they approached a cluster of buildings—a silo, a barn and a large house. Ryan shook his head—he'd always thought farmers lived in trailers or tiny houses, but this was a new two-storey with a walkout deck.

Daniel parked the van on a concrete pad and got out, leaving the engine running. He opened the barn door and waved at Ryan, who shimmied his way to the front seat, took the wheel and drove the vehicle inside. The barn was large, sturdier on the inside than it appeared from the outside. Ryan was surprised to find the barn smelled nothing like he had expected—no animals, no hay or straw. It smelled…clean.

"Appearances," Daniel replied to Ryan's querying look. "It has to look like a farm, even though it's really not."

"What is it then?" Ryan asked, climbing out of the van along with Billy and Kara.

"Safe house I set up years back," Daniel said. "It's owned by a company that runs through so many shell companies, it would take several forensic accountants months to figure out who actually pays the taxes. Eighty acres of fenced land practically in the middle of nowhere. Not another soul around for a good twenty klicks in either direction."

Daniel slid and bolted the barn door shut, and the four of them walked towards the farmhouse.

"An electrified fence runs around the outer perimeter," Daniel explained. "And there's a pressure plate under the ground in front of the fence. If someone or something tries to get in, we'll know about it."

They took the steps up to the red-bricked home and stood in front of a plain white door. Daniel removed the mailbox to reveal a keypad. After he typed in a code, the door whirred as several locks released. Daniel pushed open the door and led them inside.

The house was chilly, all the lights were off and the windows covered with thick curtains. Upon entering the foyer, they were greeted by a spiral staircase that swept both up to the next level and down to the basement. Daniel led them to the expansive kitchen that opened onto a balcony outside. He turned up the thermostat, and immediately warm air began circulating throughout the house. On the wall next to a large refrigerator was a glass panel. Daniel tapped at the screen, examining it closely.

"Besides a few curious animals, looks like no one has been here for some time," he said, tapping the screen twice before it went dark. "I think we'll be fine."

He turned to his guests. "Coffee, anyone?" he asked, making his way to a coffeemaker on a granite countertop. Within ten minutes they were all sipping from giant mugs around a quaint oak kitchen table. No one spoke. Daniel looked at his son, Billy and Kara in turn—they were all dazed from fatigue and panic. They'd had one hell of a night.

But in that he was surprised. When he'd first heard the news about the trouble, he had expected the worst-case scenario—having to confront his son's attackers openly. But this trio had proved more resourceful than he could have hoped. They had evaded capture, tracked down reliable resources and put together a large piece of the puzzle, entirely on their own initiative. He wasn't surprised that Kara or Edward had done so, but for his son and Billy, well, he was proud.

CHAPTER 36

Thresher raised his hand, signalling to the young waitress for more coffee. It was disgusting sludge, but he needed the caffeine.

He was at IHOP, supposedly meeting a friend for breakfast. He'd managed barely two hours of sleep and felt dreadful. Although the caffeine helped, the taste of the coffee made him shiver. He was used to making his own coffee—in a French press, one splendid cup at a time, not choking down pre-prepared swill left on the burner for who knows how long.

He looked down to make sure his signal was in place. The newspaper, a copy of the *Vancouver Sun*, was folded in half and placed perpendicular to the edge of the table. His eyes flicked around the room, but nothing gave him reason to suspect he was being watched.

"The waffles here are particularly tasty," a voice said beside him.

Thresher stood up and held out his hand. The man standing beside him was not familiar, but both gave the appearance of being friends. He was dressed entirely in black—black jeans, a black turtleneck and a black leather jacket.

"Faisal," the man said.

"Thresher," he nodded, motioning for Faisal to take a seat.

"So what looks good today?" Faisal asked, grabbing the laminated menu and looking it over.

"I'd be wary of any of the breakfast meats," Thresher said. "Ninety percent of the menu is pork."

"Indeed," Faisal nodded. "Just some toast and fruit, I think." He set his menu down and looked at Thresher. "My commander has authorized me to speak with you. I will answer the questions I can. Any I cannot answer, I will have to take back to my superiors for answers. What are your concerns?"

Thresher was blunt. "You guys are running an op in my country."

Faisal didn't speak.

"Against several citizens. Using agents with false passports. They've broken several laws. I can't even begin to describe the number of reasons why that isn't okay," Thresher practically hissed.

"If that is your contention, why not have them arrested?" Faisal responded, with a hint of conceit. "If you could prove it, you could have us arrested as well for running this operation."

"Because from what I can tell, we have common goals," Thresher said, reaching for his smartphone. He pulled up a picture of Gunsight and passed the phone across the table.

Faisal glanced at it, nodded and gave the phone back to Thresher.

"We both want the same thing. I don't understand why we have to trip over one another to get it," Thresher said, pocketing the phone.

"I have been told my country wishes to avoid some form of embarrassment, the details of which they have not shared. Apparently that man, and some others, are some-how involved," Faisal said.

Both men paused as the waitress came over. Thresher opted for an egg-white omelette, hoping it would suit his stomach better than last night's Chinese food.

"But I am told we have had more success than your own people in finding this man," Faisal said, smirking as the waitress left. "So why should we bother discussing this? What help could you possibly offer?"

Thresher reached in his pocket again, pulled out a folded piece of paper and placed it on the table. Faisal took the paper, unfolded it and looked. The smirk on his face fell instantly.

"If I hand those four guys over to the RCMP or Vancouver Police, this goes public. Not just my government will know about it, but the Canadian people will know about it, too. Every person associated with Mansouri Consulting will be booted from the country and barred from ever returning," Thresher said.

Faisal offered the paper back with a nod, but Thresher motioned for him to keep it. "Our people are well?"

"They look like they got the tar beat out of them, but they're fine," Thresher said. "You can have them back, quietly, if we can come to a mutually beneficial arrangement."

"Such as?" Faisal asked.

"We can work together," Thresher said. "You've done a remarkable job so far, but you need extra eyes and ears. I can give you that."

"We have a pretty good idea of what to do next," Faisal said. "And we have an asset that we can still use."

"I can help you make sure it actually gets done," Thresher replied, a little more forcefully. "For all the information your people have, you just can't seem to seal the deal without making a bunch of noise. I can help...turn down some of that noise."

Faisal nodded. "I will have to take your proposal to my people, but I do not foresee any problems, if we can get our people back quietly."

"Splendid," Thresher said. "Now let's enjoy our breakfast."

CHAPTER 37

Billy and Ryan stayed up to talk. Billy wanted to know how Ryan was feeling about his dad coming back. But mostly, Billy wanted to discuss the hard drive.

"This is tough shit, Ryan. I mean, that folder I found in the hard drive? We're talking near-to-highest possible encryption. If we don't have the key, we can't get in. I mean, even with the most powerful computer trying to brute-force it, running every possible combination in a 128- or 196-bit encryption scheme, it would take millions of years to eventually get it, theoretically."

"What do you mean?" Ryan asked.

"Okay, so the advanced encryption standard, or AES, came out sometime in the late 1990s. It's called a substitution-permutation network, where every letter or value in a message gets changed into something else. Say you want to encrypt the letter 'A.' Within AES, let's say the 'A' gets substituted with an 'R.' Then within that 'R,' there are other possible subcategories or subbytes for each piece or bit of information, such as R zero, zero, R zero, one and so on. Then all the new subbytes get scattered around to make it even more complicated. The only way to unscramble it is to have the key or the piece of information that turns it from cipher text into plain text."

"So if it's 128-bits..." Ryan started then stopped. He'd never been good with math.

"It's actually represented as a one followed by thirty-eight zeroes. That's the number of possible values it is to guess just one value in the key. The longer the key gets, the longer it takes. So if you have a computer that, let's say, can guess one trillion keys a second—in their full length—it would still take you...well...two million, million, million years to crack the whole thing."

"Eighteen zeros?" Ryan asked.

Billy nodded.

"Is there a computer on earth that can do that?"

Billy shook his head. "Not even close."

They needed the key. But Ryan had a feeling his dad had something in mind that would solve the problem. And with that they went to bed.

When Ryan got to the kitchen later, he found Billy and Kara tucking into a meal of eggs, hash browns and ham. Ryan took a seat and filled his plate. It had been almost twenty-four hours since he'd had anything resembling a proper meal.

"Where's Dad?" he asked, the name sounding strange on his lips.

"Downstairs with Gary and Edward," Kara said in between bites.

"Who whipped this up?" Ryan asked.

"Me," Kara mumbled meekly through a mouth full of hash browns. "I have a feeling we're going to need our energy."

There was noise from the foyer as Daniel, Gary and Edward, each looking worn out, came up the stairs and into the kitchen. Daniel clapped his son on the shoulder as he passed by, heading straight for the coffeemaker. The three older men each poured themselves a cup.

"What's going on?" Ryan asked.

Billy burped audibly. No one paid attention.

"Just setting up," Daniel said. "We've got the hard drive and computers here. Just trying to figure out our next step."

"Goody," Billy said. "Any chance I can go home?"

"No, Billy," Daniel said softly. "Not yet."

Billy shrugged and dove back into his eggs.

"Once you're done eating, come downstairs," Daniel said. "It's time I explained everything."

"I'm done," Billy responded instantly, pushing his half-full plate away. Kara and Ryan both immediately stood.

"All right then," Daniel said and headed for the basement with the rest trailing him.

Daniel turned left at the bottom of the stairs and led them into the well-appointed media room. Brown leather couches formed a "U" just off to one side of an electric fireplace that was turned on. A flat-screen TV in the corner was blank.

Daniel hadn't bothered with the lights—the fading sun was shining directly through the windows above them, providing ample light.

Everyone took a seat, Ryan, Billy and Kara all on one couch, Gary and Edward taking a second. Daniel set himself down on a stool next to the fireplace so that he faced all of them. He stared at the floor, sipping his coffee. For the first time since Ryan had seen him again, his dad looked truly nervous.

"A lot of this is personal," Daniel said to start. "A lot of it is why I disappeared from Ryan's life. We've been telling you all night that any questions would have to wait until later. Well, later is now."

Daniel set his coffee cup on the fireplace mantle and leaned forward to look at them, his hands clasped on his lap, his posture stooped.

"Ryan and Billy, you already know I wasn't a diplomat," Daniel said. "I was a senior officer with the Canadian Security Intelligence Service. I've been with the agency since 1985. The first part of my story begins with 9/11.

"As soon as we got the first reports—from the media, no less—I was called back to Ottawa. I told Ryan I'd be gone only a few days, but I was actually gone for a month.

"The reason I was called was simple—it was still early in the morning, the first plane had hit the first tower, and no one had a clue what was going on. When you consider how close ties are between the U.S. and Canada, especially in the intelligence world, the effects on one country have a ripple effect on the other. And no one on either side had seen anything like this. We didn't know what was happening, how it was happening or if there would be other events. Would there be more strikes? Were any of the people involved from Canada? Were we next? Was a plane going to smack into the CN Tower in Toronto or into the Parliament buildings? We just didn't know, so every CSIS employee was called in.

"I was lucky enough to catch a government jet to Ottawa before airspace was shut down. I followed the reports on the subsequent crashes as I flew east. I was on the phone and on my computer constantly. It was a terrible time because no one had any answers, and people were hollering for them."

Daniel sniffed. "By the time I landed in Ottawa, the towers were down. We were essentially on the cusp of a war, trying to figure it out. Accusations were already flying around that the hijackers had passed through Canada, and we were trying, with the help of the RCMP, to nail that down. We were reasonably confident, after the first couple of days, that none of the hijackers had crossed our border into the U.S.

"But it didn't end there for me," Daniel said, looking at Ryan. "I wasn't in Ottawa for the whole month. By the end of the week, I was on a plane to the Middle East. My job was to get in touch with people I had met during my time overseas and look for answers, connections. We knew

Osama Bin Laden and al-Qaida were behind 9/11, but we didn't know if a second wave was coming at a later time. We still didn't know much about the hijackers themselves, and we were looking for the source of the money.

"These guys hadn't given up their lives for free—they needed money to carry out the plot, and they would've made sure their families were well taken care of. The money had to come from somewhere. From Osama Bin Laden? Probably. But the entire Western world needed to know for sure."

Daniel shifted in his seat, his voice growing increasingly monotone as he rattled off his story. "The contacts I made in the Middle East didn't amount to much at the time, or so I thought. I went everywhere—Israel, to get into the Palestine territory, Iraq, Saudi Arabia, even spent some time creeping around Afghanistan, just before the first Special Forces troops from the States got there," Daniel said. "I was handed a lot of speculation and supposition, but none of it mattered. Guys from the CIA and I got together and threw ideas around, but we didn't really have anything. Most of the information was coming out through work that had been done stateside. For the most part, we knew that Canada's involvement had been zero." Daniel held up his hand, his finger and thumb formed into a zero as if to drive home his point. "So I was finally called back home."

Daniel reached for his coffee, took another sip and stared at his hands again. "So six months later, around

February 2002, I think, the war in Afghanistan got under-
way, the U.S. was making noise about heading into Iraq, and
I was working in my office at the station in Vancouver.
That's when I got a letter that changed everything."

Daniel shrugged. "The letter didn't contain information, just instructions to meet someone at the beluga whale
show at the Vancouver Aquarium on a certain day. We sent
in an advance team to make sure it wasn't some kind of set-
up. It was routine stuff…people often reach out like that if
they know who I am. And if they have something to share,
I'm always willing to listen. Most of the time they're carrying
a sack of lies they think they can trade for cash or citizenship.
Occasionally one or two are legitimate. So I went.

"I'll never forget it," Daniel said. "I was sitting there,
watching these beautiful whales go through their motions,
when a man sat down next to me. I didn't look because I was
trying to act natural, as if I was enjoying the show. He didn't
say anything to me, but then the guy stood up and left.
I caught a glimpse of him as he walked away—dark skin,
dark hair, wearing a suit. I didn't bother chasing him because
I wasn't sure if he was the one I was waiting for. Then I checked
my pockets, and I found this." Daniel reached into his pants
pocket and pulled out a worn-looking flash drive, holding
it up for everyone to see.

"Trust me, it hadn't been there before," Daniel said.
"I got the guys back at the office to examine it first to make sure
it wasn't a virus or some sort of explosive device—standard

practice—and then plugged it into my computer. One file was a picture, and the other was a document."

Daniel turned and picked up a remote sitting on the floor and pointed it at the TV. After a few seconds, a black-and-white image appeared. The man in the photo was obviously of Arab descent, complete with *kaffia,* long beard and a flowing robe. He wore sunglasses that only drew more attention to his enormous nose.

"Meet Prince Suleiman Al-Salah, one of the many members of the Saudi royal family," Daniel said. "I didn't recognize him right away, but after running the photo through some facial recognition software, his name popped up.

"What you have to understand about the Saudi royal family is that they have approximately 30,000 members," Daniel said, spreading his hands apart. "Of that total, maybe 2000 exert some power or influence. Prince Al-Salah, at the time, was in an interesting position. He was too far removed from the throne to be considered a government player, but he was close enough that a significant amount of the family's wealth flowed in his direction. Just so you have an idea, last I saw, the estimated wealth of the entire royal family was about 1.5 trillion dollars. So it's not uncommon for the most extended members of the royal family to be multi-millionaires. They have lots of money to throw around. Some are good with their money, and some aren't. Well, Al-Salah wasn't."

Daniel coughed. "The prince, besides having four wives, preferred to spend time with women of a different persuasion. In a country where drug trafficking is a capital offence, Al-Salah was moving a lot of dope from Afghanistan through the rest of the Middle East. And he also enjoyed some of his own product. It was an unspoken fact—the family knew but kept it quiet because Al-Salah, for the most part, wasn't drawing any unnecessary attention to the family.

"The other file was a simple text document containing just a few words. It said Al-Salah was responsible for 9/11, and if I wanted to know how, I was to arrange a new meeting by placing a chalk mark on a light post on Knight Street, which I did. A few days later I received another letter in the mail, again no return address, with instructions to be in the food court at Pacific Centre mall the following day. We had enough time to get a few operatives together to back me up, placed out in the crowd with cameras, in case this was another drop. And it was. A guy walked up to me, dropped another flash drive into my pocket and took off. Fortunately, we had someone with a camera watching, and he got a few pictures of the guy who made the drop. Nice enough looking guy, but I didn't recognize him."

Daniel hit a button on the remote control, and another image appeared, in colour, taken at a strange angle. The camera seemed to be facing up, towards an ornate ceiling. Prominent in the middle of the photo was Al-Salah, apparently seated with his hands steepled, his head cocked to one side as if listening. There were three faces besides Al-Salah's in the picture, all of which were distinctly white—two men, one woman. One of the men was older, the other quite young. The woman appeared to be middle-aged.

"There was no text file this time on the flash drive. Just this picture. But the time stamp on the photo—the date it was taken, the camera name and so on—showed the picture was taken in early 2000. And the quality of the photo, with it being crooked and shot at an upward angle, indicated that it was taken surreptitiously," Daniel said.

"We ran the faces through recognition software and got a couple of hits." Daniel pushed another button, and individual photos of the three Caucasian people in the picture appeared on the TV. "The woman is Anna Strongback. The older man is Samuel Smith, and the younger guy is Christian Wright. It turned out they were bigwigs in Texas oil—big Texas oil." Daniel nodded at the screen. "Old man Smith has an estimated personal fortune in excess of five billion dollars."

Billy whistled. Ryan ignored him, trying to piece together the story his dad was telling them.

"So we did a little digging around the Internet and came back with something. A small item, buried in a U.S. oil-and-gas trade journal, announced that Tri-State Oil, a newly formed joint venture in the Texas oil market, had obtained lease rights to several thousand acres of land in northeast Saudi Arabia." Daniel shifted on his stool. "And, of course,

Strongback, Smith and Wright were the new partners in Tri-State. They had to pay royalties to the royal family, as all companies do, but initial estimates put the scope of the reserves in that area at full output at about three million barrels of oil per day for approximately seventy-five years. That's second only to the Ghawar Field farther south and east, which pumps out five million."

"When did the journal article appear?" Ryan asked.

"March 2000," Daniel replied, turning back to the screen. "So you have to wonder—what's the connection? In the meantime, our agents who had watched my last meeting with the source ran their photos of our new friend through their computers, and we got a name—Shahid Issah Ali."

Another photo popped up on the TV screen, this one of a clean-cut, nervous-looking man with dark skin, short hair and a dark tailored suit. "Turns out he had been in Canada for about a year, attached to the Saudi Arabian Embassy as a cultural attaché and had set up shop in Vancouver to connect with the local population." Daniel swallowed. "We found out he was actually looking for information on expatriates, at the behest of his government. He just happened to be an accredited member of the General Intelligence Presidency. In other words, a spy."

Ryan nodded. The basement was getting darker, Daniel's shadow grew longer and larger as if his story was reaching out and touching them all.

"So, the next step? All he did was pass out hints, obscure hints. But here's a professional intelligence agent handing us cryptic clues on his own behalf. Why? Usually it's for the same few reasons—money, power, looking for Canadian citizenship, ego and so on. All we could do was sit back and wait. And sure enough, two days later, my phone rang—the number came up as a payphone. A male voice asked me if I enjoyed the pictures. When I said yes and was wanting more, he told me to go to Tojo's Restaurant that afternoon and wait for contact. It was a little suspicious—he hadn't given us any time to prepare, so it could be that he was trying to hurt me somehow. On the other hand, requesting such a quick meeting ensured that only a few people were going to know about it because we didn't have time to update everyone in the office. And of course, I hate sushi." Daniel made a face. "But I went over there, barely making it in time. I followed my instructions and took a seat at a table in the middle of the restaurant and ordered something for lunch. About five minutes later, a man walked out of the bathroom and sat at the table behind me, with his back to me. Sure enough, it was Shahid."

Daniel's voice grew increasingly hollow and rough as the story progressed. Ryan began to wonder if they were coming to the tipping point.

"He had already eaten—I'd noticed on my way in that the dishes at his table were dirty and the bill was there. All he did was lean back and whisper, 'The money went to *Hajj*.'

Then he dropped his napkin by my chair as he stood up and walked out."

Daniel's gaze drifted to the floor, as if the napkin was right in front of him.

"After he left, I reached down and grabbed the napkin. No flash drive this time, just a ball of paper that I pocketed. I was just about to try to like green tea again when all hell broke loose outside." Daniel's eyes grew distant. "Tires squealing, an engine accelerating and a bang. Then the engine accelerated again. I ran to the window, and there, lying in the street, was Shahid."

Daniel swallowed, fighting back emotion. "I stayed inside the restaurant out of some instinct of self-preservation, but I told the waitress to call 911. From what I heard through the window from passersby, a car had come barrelling around a corner and slammed into Shahid. By the time the ambulance arrived, he was dead."

Daniel paused, reaching for his coffee, which was by now cold.

"So I called in the cavalry, so to speak. The RCMP showed up, as a well as a surveillance team in plainclothes, just to make sure there wasn't someone waiting to take me out, too. They got me out a back door and to the office. We looked at the crumpled napkin and found a piece of paper.... It was a transfer drawn on an offshore account of a numbered company and sent to another offshore account. We were able to dig deep enough through the shitload of shell companies on either side to drill down to the meat of what had happened. We found out that on February 12, 2000, an offshore account held by the three partners of Tri-State Oil transferred 1.2 billion dollars to an account held for none other than Prince Suleiman Al-Salah," Daniel said. "The actual legitimate transaction that was detailed in the journal story was somewhere in the neighbourhood of nine billion dollars to the Saudi crown."

"A bribe," Ryan said reflexively.

His father tapped the tip of his own nose. "A bribe," Daniel confirmed. "A hefty bribe to get their hands on those oil lease rights. But that kind of money was just pissing in the wind with oil prices tickling almost ninety dollars a barrel around then and seventy-five years of it in the ground just waiting to be extracted. Those three will be buying their own islands when they retire.

"It was something, but so what? Why should we care that an American company gave a billion-dollar gift to a Saudi prince on the outside looking in? Then Shahid's last remark hit me. *The money went to Hajj.* I'd been wearing a small microphone, so we knew I'd heard that part correctly. But what did it mean?" Daniel shrugged. "If we assumed it was Arabic, *Hajj* could mean only one thing."

"The pilgrimage," Ryan said.

"Yes," Daniel nodded. "The great trip to Mecca that every Muslim is expected to make once in their lifetime if they can afford it. It takes place in Saudi Arabia, where Mecca

is located. *Hajj* is a display of solidarity within the religion
and also another form of submission to Allah. Hundreds of
thousands of people make the pilgrimage every year."

"Don't a lot of people die?" Billy piped up suddenly.

"Yes. It seems that from year to year, stampedes or
fires cause some fatalities," Daniel said. "But the message was
cryptic—was Shahid telling me that the money the three
Americans allegedly gave to a washed-out Saudi royal was
given to the pilgrimage? It made no sense. Muslims have
been making the pilgrimage since the seventh century.

"So we had two photos, two documents and one
statement. We figured out the identities of everyone in the
photos. The documents, especially the banking stuff, gave
us a reasonable idea of what actually happened. But the
statement was confusing.

"But," Daniel said, suddenly with renewed energy as
he flipped back to one of the first images, the document on
the first flash drive. "We had this, which said that Al-Salah
was responsible for 9/11. And we now had a Saudi Arabian
intelligence agent who had made, no doubt, unapproved
contact with a domestic intelligence agency and got run
down in the street in broad daylight in Vancouver. No one
was ever arrested. They didn't even find the car."

"It was a hit," Kara said.

"Sure looked that way," Daniel nodded. "But why?
What was Shahid really trying to tell us? How could this
loser prince possibly be responsible for the worst terrorist

attack of all time on North American soil when we know it was Bin Laden and al-Qaida that were responsible?"

Daniel shook his head, half-laughing. "I never used to believe in fate," he said. "I always thought that everything in my life happened for my reasons, that it was all a matter of choice. Whether those were good choices or not, my life, my future, were the result of my decisions. But as soon as Shahid sent that first letter and I chose to meet him, I might as well have given up right there and then."

"Why?" Ryan asked, leaning forward.

"Because none of the rest was my choice," Daniel replied. "My only decision was to meet with him at the aquarium. Looking back, had I known the bigger picture, I would have refused further contact. I would have passed it on to someone else. I never would have given up on my son."

Daniel sniffed and sat silently for a few seconds. Everyone else waited for him to continue.

"So," Daniel's voice warbled with emotion, "that same night, I tried to thread this all together. The most important question—what is *Hajj* besides a pilgrimage? I tapped away on my computer, looking for possible connections, something to do with 9/11 and with the keyword '*Hajj*.' It didn't take long to find something."

Daniel paused, as if for effect. "There was one person of Saudi Arabian origin tied closely to 9/11 who, it turned out, went by the nickname '*Hajj*.' He also went by the nicknames 'Emir' or 'Prince,' 'Sheik' and 'Sheik al-Mujahid' or 'Jihadist Sheik.' The most recent name attributed to him was 'Geronimo.'"

The TV screen flashed again, and an unmistakable face popped up on the screen, a face known to the entire Western world as a heartless monster and to his believers as a true warrior of Islam.

"So what Shahid was implying, as far as I could tell, was that Prince Al-Salah gave all or part of the bribe money he received from Tri-State to Osama Bin Laden, which Bin Laden then used to help finance the 9/11 attacks."

Billy, Ryan and Kara all sat back on the couch, stunned expressions on their faces.

"God," Ryan whispered. "What you're saying is that Americans were responsible for the attack on their own country, on their own people."

Daniel nodded, but Ryan was still talking. "Tri-State's role in 9/11 sent the U.S., Canada and the other allies to war in Afghanistan...even to Iraq. That's 158 dead Canadian soldiers and almost 2200 American soldiers in Afghanistan alone."

"Yup," Daniel said. "Of course it was all well and good for Shahid to say it—by now everyone was putting forward their own radical ideas about who was ultimately responsible. Pretty much all of it was horseshit. But this..." Daniel shook his head. "If this is true, it blows everything wide open. Bin Laden planned 9/11 and executed it, there's no question about that. But if American money helped finance the attacks, it changes the larger picture. It changes the view of the wars overseas. It throws the entire intelligence community, friendly U.S. relations with Saudi Arabia, the U.S. military and the entire government under the bus. It transforms the entire narrative of everything from the moment the money was paid to the present day.

"But how to prove it?" Daniel shrugged. "I tried to figure that out, but we didn't have any solid information. We had our resources, but so much of it was internal, within our own borders. Float it to the CIA?" Daniel practically spat the last words. "I've got one or two people in that entire organization that I trust, but not with this information. Chances of anything happening were zero. The CIA had already been dragged through the dirt by Congress over its failure to predict 9/11. They weren't going to subject themselves to that kind of scrutiny again.

"So I decided to keep this close—but not too close. I called in Edward, who was my supervisor." Edward nodded. "We talked it over, and he decided we needed more guidance from higher up—right to the director of CSIS. Ed disappeared into his office to call him. I was sitting at my desk wondering how the hell I was going to pull all this together when all of a sudden my phone rang."

"The director?" Billy asked.

"Nope." Daniel shook his head. "Important people don't provide the impetus to make radical changes to your life. The phone call usually comes from someone lower down the totem pole who is simply doing their job. In this case, it was the security supervisor for the building. He was doing one of his walk-arounds and saw some activity in the parking lot. He told me that a motorcycle had come up and stopped behind my car and that the driver disappeared briefly behind it and then took off again. Being the curious type and in charge of our safety, he went over and checked out my car, just to be safe. And he found this." Daniel clicked on the remote, and Bin Laden's face on the TV screen was replaced by a grainy still image, obviously from a video file. It showed the underside of a car, and beside the exhaust manifold was a one-foot-wide, circular plate with a green light.

"It was a mine with a magnetic plate," Daniel said softly. "It turned out to be pressure-triggered. Just setting my foot in the car would have applied enough force to the mine to detonate it. And I would have been dead."

Ryan felt his nerves jangling.

"The security chief checked the surveillance video. The person on the motorcycle was wearing a helmet, so we couldn't get a good view of his face or even the plate on the bike. The driver honed in specifically on my car and then zipped off. I was obviously the target."

Daniel stood. "So we now had one source dead and an attempt on the life of the person that source made contact with, all in the same day. And it was all very professional. I called Edward to tell him, and he called on one of our surveillance teams to make sure you were okay," Daniel said, looking at Ryan.

"But we had a problem. If we detonated the bomb, they might think I was dead. If we didn't, their people watching would know something went wrong. But something had to happen to me because we now were fairly certain of a connection between Shahid's death, the information he had passed on and the attempt on my life.

"Enough activity had occurred within that twenty-four-hour period to prove that whoever killed Shahid, whoever put that bomb on my car, wanted their secret to remain just that. And we had no idea who it could be. American? Al-Qaida? Saudi? Who knew? We had to take action, but sharing the information would put more people at risk. It would also put you at risk." Daniel pointed at Ryan. "We could have assumed new identities. But because we couldn't nail down who was responsible for the attempt on my life, we weren't certain that our identities would remain safe." Daniel's voice changed again, his emotions visible.

"So Edward, the director and I got on a secure video conference call. It was obvious what had to be done...it was just a matter of doing it the right way. The first and most important step was to remove me, then we could worry about the rest. So we came up with a plan. We put together what I needed to get out of the country—a passport under a different name, currency and so on. Then we had to get me out of the building but make it believable. Our plan was simple but grisly. We 'snatched' an unclaimed body from the city morgue of a recently deceased homeless person and put it in a van and," Daniel shuddered, "dressed the body like me. It was about five in the morning. I'd put on a show of working all night, and a team watched the house to make sure Ryan was okay. So I walked out of the building just as the van pulled up. It paused briefly by my car to make sure my approach was shielded from view, and I hopped in. They tossed out the body with a small explosive charge attached to it, making sure that it was on the ground, kind of out of sight. As soon as the van pulled away, a techie inside the van hit the remote for the charge." Daniel paused. "Boom! The charge went off, the force of that explosion detonated the mine on my car, and it went up like a Roman candle. And I was officially dead.

"Of course, we didn't get off totally unscathed. To make it believable and less suspicious, the van had to take some of the blast, but it was more like an armoured car than a regular van, courtesy of someone in this room." Daniel gestured to Gary, who nodded. "The van got tossed around, and the driver and I ended up a little banged and bruised but otherwise okay. The driver got out and played along with his little fire extinguisher, screaming and making a scene. Fire units were called in, and all hell broke loose. And I spent three hours inside that van, waiting for it to be towed away. During that time, I called you," Daniel said, looking at Ryan, "and told you I was going snowshoeing."

Daniel opened his mouth, like he was going to say something else, but he stopped, shaking his head. "The story was easy to sell. Given the witnesses on scene who said it was me that had died in that car, no questions were asked at the autopsy. Plus, whoever was watching knew *someone* had died, and since everyone was saying and believing it was me...." Daniel shrugged. "The announcement was put out on the media, but you were really the only person who was ever told directly that I had died snowshoeing," Daniel said, looking at Ryan. "That's why there was so few people at the funeral. CSIS held its own service. But Uncle Ed arranged it so that you never knew otherwise, and the announcements in the paper about my death were kept out of your sight."

"So I got shipped out," Daniel said, pointing around him, indicating the house they were sitting in, "with Gary by my side. Along with one other CSIS trainer and one person from the CSE, we were trained for going after this secret. On the day of my 'funeral,' I was actually on a ferry to Vancouver Island. By the end of the day, I was on my way out of the country under a fake name. And that was that."

No one spoke. Ryan was sniffing, trying to hold back tears. Hearing his father speak so matter-of-factly about his own faked death, the worst moment in Ryan's entire life, made him angrier. It was like his father didn't seem to care, as if it was just another job.

Who is this person? Ryan wondered.

"My only job for the next nine years was trying to prove or disprove the information I was given. And it was hard. I basically spent the whole time on every continent on Earth, except for Antarctica." Daniel smiled in an attempt at humour. "I followed up leads, trailed the prince, worked with Special Forces in Afghanistan and Pakistan, looking for Bin Laden. Early on I was able to verify a few pieces of the puzzle—first that the prince and Osama Bin Laden had both been enrolled at King Abdulaziz University in 1979. It turned out they had even attended a few classes together. Second, one of the prince's first wives was one of Bin Laden's cousins through his third wife, Khairiah Sabar, who he married in 1985. The connections were distant, but there was a good likelihood that the two men knew each other personally, if not from school then through their marriages.

"But half of this game I was in also involved hiding," Daniel said, staring at the fire. "For every month I spent actively pursuing a lead, I spent another two lying low, covering my tracks. I spent most of my time in the Middle East, operating out of safe houses and working with contacts I had cultivated over the years, including new ones that were fed to me. The first two years I did low-level surveillance and information gathering, looking for instances in which these two men met. That work turned out to be relatively fruitful. I found documented proof that the good prince, for a period of time, had thrown off his royal ways and travelled to Afghanistan to become one of the *mujahedeen*, the resistance fighters combating the invasion of the Soviet Union dating back to 1979. I was able to dig this up from an ex-servant to the prince."

Daniel flicked the remote again and the picture changed, this one in black and white, showing a young man wearing a *kaffia*, sporting a long beard and pointing a long metal tube at the sky as a thinner man in a robe holds his shoulders, as if instructing him.

"The man holding the Stinger mobile anti-aircraft missile launcher is the good prince himself, and the man behind him was one of Bin Laden's top lieutenants during the insurgency. Again, this meant a better-than-average chance that the prince and Bin Laden had met. So? What if they had met? A lot of people met Osama Bin Laden. Even members of Canada's own Khadr family had met him," Daniel said, referring to the "terrorist family" that was widely believed to have helped al-Qaida overseas. The youngest son, Omar, had become a fixture of the "war on terror" when he was arrested during a raid in Afghanistan at the age of fifteen and imprisoned at the notorious Guantanamo Bay prison for "enemy combatants."

"That didn't mean anything. It was the money that mattered and finding out where it went. So, like the guy from the Watergate scandal always said, 'Follow the money.' That became my job for the next few years—trying to find out if and how that money got to Bin Laden—because a terrorist mastermind isn't going to have a chequing account.

If you want to send money to him, it has to be in the form of cash, drugs, weapons...some sort of consumable. In this case, the inference was that the cash went to support the 9/11 attacks. So the chances it was shipped as bricks of heroin or AK-47s wasn't particularly high. The key was that Bin Laden had enough money to support the hijackers' training, flight lessons and cover identities in the U.S., which the 9/11 commission estimated at about half a million dollars, and also enough to ensure that the families of all involved were well compensated for their loss."

Daniel leaned back against his stool, his hands between his legs. "I think it was in the fifth or sixth year—it all blurs together—that I finally got a solid lead in that direction. I'd wasted the better part of 2006 chasing down a phantom arms shipment someone had told me was definitely the key to establishing the relationship. I was a little wary of that lead. I was working in the Palestine territories when a friend got in touch with me, saying he had someone who wanted to talk to me. Now this is rare," Daniel said, spreading his hands to explain. "Palestine has always had a strong anti-Israeli as well as anti-Western philosophy, so to find someone in that area willing to divulge information that could hurt Palestine's pursuit of sovereignty was almost unheard of. But I managed to get in touch with a disgruntled member of *Hamas*. *Mossad*, Israeli intelligence, was already using him, but a friend connected us. It turned out he had been

working in the prince's estate when 'the Americans' came."
Daniel swallowed. "He told me that about a month after the
prince received his money from Tri-State, the prince called
in a former member of the *Mabahith* for a meeting. That
man left the meeting with a large briefcase and was never
seen again. When my source asked the prince what had
happened, he said, 'This will strike the Americans hard,' but
he would say nothing else.

"So I turned my attention back to the prince, looking
for signs of this former *Mabahith* agent. Using some connections with former members of the Northern Alliance,
who were fighting the Taliban for control of Afghanistan
around 9/11, I discovered that the man with the briefcase
had been killed in a skirmish between the two sides about
four months after the prince met with him. Meanwhile, the
prince was getting extremely dodgy and paranoid. In early
2008, he hid out in his palace and never left his compound,
not even when those higher up in power wanted to meet
with him. In late 2010, he began getting visitors, and I mean
important visitors—heads of internal and external security,
military, even the Crown Prince dropped by for a chat. For
some reason, our beloved prince was now quite popular
with the establishment.

"Within a month, I was back on the run," Daniel
said. "And that's how I've spent the better part of the last
year and a bit. Whatever was happening with the prince had

a direct effect on me. I spent more time sleeping and hiding out in shitholes, caves and basements than I ever care to again. And a couple of months ago, I got caught."

The words hung in the air, but no one was surprised. The story was so fantastic, so bizarre, so twisted that nothing was surprising.

"When Edward found out I'd been captured, we needed to keep an eye on Ryan because Edward knew that if he was ever at risk, I would sing like a canary. We needed someone discreet, and we found Kara, who had spent a couple of years with CSIS before being discharged. She had field experience and training, so Edward asked her if she would join our loose little group and act as your bodyguard. Once Edward got word I had escaped, we figured people would start looking for me even harder, so we sent Kara in to meet you at the café."

Ryan couldn't be shocked anymore. He didn't look at Kara. He just put his hands over his face and shook his head.

"Sure came in handy," Billy piped up.

"So where does that leave us now?" Daniel said, rising and pacing the room. "We know that money changed hands between Tri-State and the prince. We know the prince dispatched a courier with a briefcase to Afghanistan sometime well before 9/11, and we know that people are very interested in the prince and in the work I've been doing," Daniel said. "And now we know they're equally interested in all of you...because of me."

"That's it?" Billy asked.

"I don't think so," Daniel said. "We still have these computers and hard drives. I'm confident that if they've set up an operation in Vancouver to search for me and for Ryan, someone knows part of, if not the whole story. And if they do, that means there could be more information on one of those units. The level of encryption means that at least one of those folders was not intended to be seen by others in that office building."

"But we still have a problem," Billy said. "Even if your good buddies at CSE got their best computer working on it, it would take…"

"Millions of millions of millions of years to crack the key, yes, I know," Daniel said. "Fortunately, there's another, simpler, more elegant way of cracking that folder."

Billy snorted in contempt. "The only way to do that would be if you had the algorithm that generated the key. Then we might be able to deduce the key by the end of the year."

"It's not the only way, Billy," Daniel said softly.

Billy looked annoyed, but he sat silently, waiting for Daniel to explain.

"We can always use the key itself."

CHAPTER 38

$\mathcal{D}$aniel led the entire group into the office on the opposite side of the spiral staircase.

"How is that even possible?" Billy asked.

"The Communications Security Establishment, Billy," Daniel explained. "Although CSIS tends to get most of the press in Canada when it comes to intelligence matters, the CSE does the bulk of the work. They collect foreign intelligence, especially anything aimed at our country, monitoring electronic communications of various kinds. They're the country's code breakers."

"I know that," Billy sputtered, following Daniel into the office. "But how do we get the daily key to access this file?"

"I'm not sure on the exact specifics," Daniel said, moving to one of the office chairs. He motioned Billy to take the other one. Everyone else crowded around them. "But I imagine at some point, either by the CSE's own computing resources or through a human source that passed on the relevant information, it cracked the code that the Saudis use to communicate encrypted messages. My personal guess?" Daniel shrugged. "They intercept the daily code and use it to suit the country's purposes. How they knew the code or its uses, I don't know exactly."

Daniel woke up one of the four computer monitors in front of him and double-clicked on a file. "Two days ago, shortly after midnight, the CSE captured the daily code that locks this particular folder we're trying to get into. They detected a burst transmission, and it was pointed right at the City of Vancouver. So my guess is this is what we're looking for."

The document opened on one screen, and Daniel suddenly reached out, turning the screen away from Billy so he couldn't see it.

"Now, Billy, this is as serious as it gets. You're about to see top-secret material. In Canada, clearances are classified as confidential, secret or top secret, so this document is as important as you're ever going to see with your own eyes. I'm not lying when I say I could go to jail for showing you this material, especially if you were to blab about it to anyone outside this room. Do you understand?" Daniel asked.

Billy nodded his head up and down vigorously. Daniel paused for a moment, as if weighing how sincere Billy was, then turned the screen back.

Any doubts the group had that Daniel was lying evaporated as soon as they saw the document on the screen. Emblazoned across the top in enormous letters were the words "TOP SECRET EYES ONLY."

The rest of the message contained mostly numbers, interspersed with the words "INTERCEPT," "SOURCE" and "CAPTURED" typed along the top left-hand side of the page.

Underneath the words was a two-line-long uninterrupted sequence of letters, characters and numbers, scrambled as if by random. Daniel used his mouse to highlight the entire sequence. "There's the key," he said.

"That's nobody's birthday in reverse, that's for sure," Gary muttered.

"The hard drive is already hooked up," Daniel said, pointing to the unit now poised on the desktop. "Get to work, Billy."

Billy's hands were trembling as he shook the mouse, and two more screens lit up. Daniel dragged the document over to Billy's screen and sat back to watch. Billy located the port to which the hard drive was connected, and clicked. A window opened, listing the files contained on the hard drive. He clicked through until he found the folder he had tried to access previously—HARE—and double-clicked. He was greeted by the same prompt he had received at the Internet café the previous day.

"ENTER KEY."

Billy minimized the screen, clicked on the document Daniel had dragged over, highlighted the entire key and copied and pasted it into the field.

"Here we go," Billy breathed, moving his cursor over and clicking Enter.

The field into which Billy pasted the key disappeared. A tone sounded twice, and the HARE folder suddenly expanded, showing its contents.

"Copy it all over first, Billy. Just to be safe," Daniel said.

Billy nodded and dragged the HARE folder to the desktop. A small window appeared, showing how many files were being copied. There weren't many, about a dozen. But they were different kinds of media. Ryan caught a few file extensions as they flashed by—avi, wma, mp3. Some of the files were video or audio.

The window disappeared as the file transfer finished. Billy reflexively reached over, disconnected the hard drive and powered it down.

"Okay, let's have a look. Start with the text files," Daniel instructed.

Billy clicked on all of the text files and opened them. Not surprisingly, they were in Arabic. Billy frowned. Ryan stepped forward to read over Billy's shoulder.

"This is some kind of report," Ryan said, scanning the document, "on somebody's movements, like they're watching someone." Ryan paused for a moment. "Oh. It's about me."

The contents illustrated that someone or some people had been surreptitiously watching Ryan for at least a week prior to his attempted kidnapping.

"Move on," Daniel said.

Billy clicked the file away and brought up another.

Ryan read it again. Another surveillance file. "This one's about you, Bill."

"Sweet," came the response.

"Next," Daniel commanded.

Ryan read only a few lines before he tapped his father on the shoulder.

"Yup, I see it too," his dad said. Daniel pointed to a section of text on the screen for the rest to see and read aloud.

"'The actions of the prince, if discovered and made public, would cause irreparable harm to the kingdom and its status globally, particularly with our allies in the United States,'" Daniel read, pausing briefly in between words to ensure he was translating them correctly. "'Taking the Americans' money was foolish, but not unconscionable. However, if its purpose was discerned, it could lead to conflict between the kingdom and the United States.'"

"These are marching orders," Daniel concluded, noting the March date and the language in the document. "It's basically a memo to the staff that were working here in Vancouver, explaining why they needed to find Ryan. It's good but...damn." He sat back, frowning. Then he tapped on a large audio file. "Right there. Let's see it."

Billy opened the media player, and they all leaned towards the screen. Surprisingly, the conversation was in English. There seemed to be four participants; three voices on one end—two male, one female—spoke in distinctly

Texan drawls, and the other one spoke English with a harsh Middle Eastern accent. Judging by the quality of the recording, the Middle Eastern man had recorded the call, unbeknownst to those on the other end.

"We don't need to hear the details again! We need to know what you're going to do about it. Did you get anything from him?"

"Not a drop. He admitted nothing. He was unlike anyone we have seen before—a stone."

Daniel cocked his head in interest.

"Even stones can be broken."

"Not this one. We tried everything. He suffered at our hands. But he never once broke. Even when we confronted him with his different aliases, with the mention of a child, he said nothing."

Daniel waited for the recording to finish. "That's about me, shortly after my escape," he said. "Time stamp, Billy?"

Billy double-clicked on the file. The date popped up—March 29.

"That sounds about right," Daniel said. "I was told I broke out on about March 28, so that fits with the timeline."

"You were told?" Ryan asked.

"It's a long story," Daniel said. "I'll fill you in later." He turned and looked up at the group. "Anyone have any doubt as to who those three other voices belong to?"

Everyone shook their heads.

Daniel poked at another file, a video. "Play it, Bill."

Billy clicked on the file, and a new media player window opened. The initial frame was that of Prince Al-Salah, seated at a table. Billy clicked play, and two men came into view. They began speaking in Arabic, and because Ryan and Daniel were fluent, they leaned forward intently as everyone else watched.

The video was only twelve minutes long but was torturous to watch, even for the four in the room that didn't understand the language. What began as normal conversation escalated into shouting, first the prince standing up and pointing at the two men in the room with him and making like he was going to leave. One of the men stood, blocking the prince's path and shouted back. As the prince raised a finger in defiance, the man on one side struck him with a backhand across the face, sending Al-Salah to the floor in a tangled heap of robes. The second man stood, and the pair descended on the prince with a flurry of kicks. The second man hauled Al-Salah to his feet as the first man continued to slap him, shouting the whole time.

By the end of the clip, Al-Salah was a bleeding, sobbing mess that the second man simply dropped to the floor as both left the room.

Daniel and Ryan leaned back, both looking at each other with wild eyes.

"I knew it'd be here," Daniel whispered.

"What?" Edward asked loudly.

"Back it up, Bill," Daniel said.

Billy rolled the cue back to the beginning of the clip when the two men walk in.

"These two guys are *Mabahith*; they identify themselves right away," Daniel explained. "They tell the prince they are concerned about some money he received from an American oil company and want to discuss it with him. Al-Salah tells them it's none of their business. When they insist, he gets up."

Billy fast-forwarded to the frame where Al-Salah stands up and starts pointing.

"He's trying to use his title and connections to make them leave him alone, telling them they have no business questioning him. This guy here," Daniel pointed to the first man on the screen's left, "says their authority overrules his. When the prince asks who that could be, they say 'the king.'" Daniel's voice was practically a whisper. "Take it to about the eight-minute mark, Bill."

The screen moved again, offering a fast-forward version of the prince's beating. "Stop there," Daniel said. Al-Salah was bent over the table, the second man holding him in place, the first grinding the prince's face into the tabletop. "Let it run."

Billy pressed Play. The first man steps away, and the prince suddenly begins to sob, nodding his head then wailing in Arabic.

"Right there, the *Mabahith* guy is asking, 'You did it, didn't you? You gave Osama the money?' And that's where the prince sobs. He goes on to say he sent one billion dollars in unmarked bills by courier to Afghanistan, and right here… slow it down, Bill, and play it."

Billy clicked on a menu above the screen, selecting a slow-play setting and hit Play.

Daniel reached over to a speaker by the monitor, twisting the volume knob all the way up, holding a finger to his lips.

They all heard it. It was unmistakable.

"Osama Bin Laden…" the prince wailed.

Billy stopped the video. They all looked around, exchanging glances.

"Jesus," Edward remarked, scratching at his face.

"Copy that file into a new folder, Billy," Daniel said. But it was all he could bring himself to say. He looked at the screen and tried his best to maintain a façade of control. The last nine years of his life had finally been confirmed—his purpose, the truth Shahid had wanted him to find encapsulated right there, courtesy of the brutality of nations that did not place a high regard for human rights, even for those who were supposed to rule.

Daniel swallowed. They needed one more piece of information. "What's the time stamp on the video file, Bill?" he asked.

Billy clicked on the "Get Info" option from a drop-down menu, and the date appeared.

"2004," Daniel muttered to himself. "They've known about this for so many years and haven't done anything.

Well, they haven't done anything about him." Daniel gestured to the prince's sobbing face.

"So it's over, right?" Billy said. "We can turn this over to the RCMP or to CSIS and they can take it from there, right?"

"Not quite, Billy," Daniel said.

"But we've got it all, Dad," Ryan said in frustration. "We've got Al-Salah on tape saying he gave the money to Bin Laden, and we've got the Americans on tape basically saying they want you taken care of."

"*Basically saying*," Daniel quoted his son. "We believe that, but we can't say for certain, and I don't have any voice samples to match them to for confirmation.

"Look, this nine-year hunt has finally come to its end game, just like when they killed Bin Laden in 2011," Daniel said. "I am so fucking tired right now that I don't know what the next step is, but it's not as simple as calling in the Mounties. It's the United States that will want to know about this, that needs to know, but..."

"You can't trust them to just take it and act on it," Gary said. "You said it earlier, and we know it. If you hand that video over to the CIA and walk away, it'll just disappear."

"What about the press?" Kara asked.

"That would probably get someone killed," Edward chimed in. "You don't go to the media to reveal something this explosive. Plus, we don't have any one thing we could turn over that documents every step. Someone would have to explain it to them, and none of us is really in a position to do that."

"So what, then?" Billy asked. "Because this is all fun, but I really just want to go home."

"Well, we're expecting visitors," Daniel said. "I have a couple of friends I trust who will be here tomorrow. They've been waiting for me to tell them what I've been chasing for years, and I guess it's finally time. At least we'll have home-ice advantage, doing it here. It's not like they can just run off with it."

"And you still trust them?" Gary asked.

"As much as I trust anyone," Daniel said wanly.

The office was silent.

"All right then," Gary said to no one in particular.

"There's nothing left to do tonight," Daniel said. "We'll get into it more tomorrow." He turned and looked at Ryan. "You and I need to take a walk."

CHAPTER 39

Thresher was back in his office. He'd stopped at home after breakfast for a quick power nap, a shower, shave and a fresh suit. He felt reborn. He punched his intercom and asked Adam to come in.

"Is it done?" Thresher asked.

Adam nodded. "We handed them over about an hour ago."

"Good," Thresher said. "What else do you have for me?"

"Not much," Adam said, flipping through the stack of paper in his hands. "We checked the security footage from Mansouri, but someone cut the lines before they went in. We have fingerprints, but that doesn't tell us any-thing beyond who might have been in the room. That cell-phone still hasn't shown up."

Adam looked up, his expression grim. "I guess we just keep beating the bushes."

Thresher grunted in acknowledgement. "We need to get them contained to Canada at least," he said. "Contact Border Services. Release Gunsight's photo to every airport, ferry terminal and border crossing. Put a detention request out along with it. We need to make sure he can't leave the country."

Adam scribbled himself a note, nodding. "Done. And until then?"

Thresher shrugged. "Wait."

CHAPTER 40

"I have to admit, Dad, even with everything that's been going on, that's a little unnerving."

Ryan was sheltered from the crisp night air by a hoodie he'd found in one of the closets, watching his father tuck a large handgun into a holster on his hip.

"Do you really think it's necessary?" Ryan asked.

"I'm not worried about anyone finding us out here," Daniel said as they strode off into the darkness, away from the house. "The bigger concern is predators—bears, wolves, coyotes, mountain lions. In the dark, we make pretty good prey."

Ryan nodded, shoving his hands inside the pockets of his hoodie. Their pace slowed as both struggled to say something.

"Ryan," Daniel started. "I never wished for this, not even for a second. I never thought in my entire life I'd have to do something so drastic. Faking my own death was supposed to serve a higher purpose, and it will, even if I don't know exactly how it will play out. But I did it in part to keep you safe."

"I still think you could've done something else," Ryan snapped back.

"I know you're angry, son," Daniel said. "I would be, too. But honestly, from everything I've told you, what alternative did I have that would keep us both safe?"

"I don't know if you've told me everything," Ryan said, his voice hard. He knew he should be overjoyed his father was alive, and he was, but all his pent-up emotions came spilling out. "You never told me your real job. You lied about dying, of all things. How do I know this is it?"

"Son, you know why..."

"I'm not saying my feelings make sense, Dad," Ryan shouted inadvertently, turning to face Daniel. "It's just how I feel right now. And listening to you talk about it, like it was some sort of mission, even the last phone call we had...I mean, it all sounds like it was just a part of the job."

"Ryan," Daniel said, half in shock, half in agony. "Do you have any idea how difficult that phone conversation was for me? Do you know how badly I wanted to tell you something, something secret, to let you know that all of what was about to happen wasn't going to be for real? When I hung up from talking to you and after the car bomb went off, I was devastated because I knew I was abandoning you."

He reached out and grabbed Ryan by the shoulders. "Son, if I could have taken you with me, I would have, in a heartbeat. But you needed to be here. You needed to live your life, to follow your path, even if I wasn't here to watch. And you needed to be safe to do that. Of all the things I was able to offer you, the one thing I couldn't do was keep you safe! There was no way that could happen if I stuck around!"

"My path?" Ryan said, ignoring his father's last sentence. "My life?"

"What do you mean?"

"Am I a spy?" Ryan asked.

"Pardon?"

"Am I a spy? Was I supposed to be a spy, follow in your footsteps?" Ryan demanded. "Why did I learn all those things? Why did I learn karate, kung fu and boxing? Why did I learn to shoot rifles and pistols? Why did we play Disguises in all those cities? Why do I know fifteen languages fluently? Were you training me to follow in your footsteps? To be some kind of secret agent?"

Daniel stumbled over his words. "I guess…I…I wasn't doing it to make you want to follow me in life. I did it to give you the opportunity to do whatever you wanted," he said. "I looked back on what I had to learn when I was in my thirties, when I went into intelligence and realized what people really need to know. And one of the biggest lessons I wanted you to learn was how to protect yourself, how to adapt, how to improvise, how to talk your way and occasionally fight your way out of certain situations. I did it because I wanted you to be able to look after yourself, in case, one day down the road, I guess, I wasn't around."

"Well, you planned that perfectly, didn't you?" Ryan retorted, overcome by emotion. Daniel couldn't see Ryan's tears in the darkness, but he could hear his son's voice, that beautiful voice he'd heard only on audio files and grainy videos for the last nine years. He knew Ryan was having a tough time and was expressing part of how he was feeling, but Daniel wasn't sure how to respond.

Where in the parent manual does it tell you how to explain to your kid why you faked your own death and encouraged him to learn spy tradecraft? Daniel wondered.

"You never complained," Daniel pointed out. "There were some activities you tried and didn't like. Hockey? Fine. Soccer? Fine. Guitar? Fine. I never made you do anything you didn't want to do, but you had talent for the others, Ryan. From a really young age we both knew you were an exceptional kid. I was doing my best to nurture that. I wasn't trying to brainwash you or train you. I was trying to give you opportunities."

Ryan stood in silence then collapsed against his father, sobbing.

"I'm sorry, Dad, I just...I just wish you hadn't left," he mumbled through Daniel's jacket.

"I know. It's okay. This is rough for both of us," Daniel said, gently pushing Ryan away and looking him in the eye.

"But for every day that's passed since I left, you've thought about me less because you thought I was gone forever. Imagine what it was like for me. Your uncle sent me tapes, short videos and pictures and other stuff, and I'd end up crying every time I looked at them because I knew you were alive and becoming everything I knew you could be, but I wasn't a part of your life! You buried me once. I never got to bury you. You were always out there, but I couldn't be with you."

Ryan nodded his head, finally understanding. "That must have been awful."

"It was," Daniel said, embracing him again. "But it's over. We have a few things to get through first, but when it's over, we'll find our way back. I can't do anything stupid and cliché like make up for lost time, but I can make sure whatever time we have going forward, if you want, is the best we can make it."

Ryan nodded into his father's shoulder, then pulled back, wiping at his eyes. "You realize you have a problem, though." He sniffed.

"What's that?" Daniel said.

"The next time you die, I'm probably not going to believe you."

Daniel laughed, hugging Ryan again then throwing his arm around his son's shoulders as they resumed walking.

"What about Kara, Dad?" Ryan asked suddenly.

"What about her?" Daniel asked quizzically. "A little crush?"

"No, Dad," Ryan admonished him. "What's her story?"

"I don't know that it's mine to tell, but I will tell you this—Kara's had her own battles, quite a few actually. But as a result, she's incredibly talented and resourceful. She is a little closed off and mysterious, but that's why we recruited her. We didn't want someone who really stood out." Daniel shrugged.

"Then you should have picked a less attractive body-guard," Ryan laughed.

CHAPTER 41

Ryan and Daniel finally wandered back to the house, chuckling together as if they were old friends. Ryan didn't know if it was the fresh inland air or the joy of having his father back in his life, but his soul felt invigorated. Despite the strange situation in which he found himself, Ryan felt better than he had in a long time.

The exhaustion finally hit him; he was ready to drop on the spot. He hugged his father goodnight then climbed the stairs to his room. He stopped at the top and looked longingly at the door to the bathroom, the thought of a hot shower almost orgasmic. But that would mean standing, and Ryan's muscles cried out for rest.

I guess it's sleep and stink, Ryan decided as he opened the door to his room. He stopped on the threshold. The lights were on. He had a visitor.

"Sorry, I thought I'd wait for you here," Kara said. She was seated on Ryan's bed.

"No problem," Ryan replied, closing the door behind him. After his conversation with his father, he was a little on edge.

"I thought...well...how are you doing?" Kara laughed nervously. "I'm sorry, this is all so weird, even for me."

"Tell me about it," Ryan chuckled. "I'm good. Tired as hell, but the world is a happier place than it was yesterday."

"I bet," Kara said, shifting uncomfortably on his bed. "Are you okay with me or at least the job I was sent to do? You're probably feeling strange about what's been happening."

Ryan shrugged, sitting down next to her on the bed. "Well, I'm still...confused. Everything I thought I knew yesterday is completely different today, and you are one of those things. Yesterday you were just a girl at the Pond, right?"

"Right," Kara nodded with a laugh, staring at her toes. "I don't want things to be awkward. Because of who I was supposed to be. You know, your bodyguard."

"I know what you mean," said Ryan. "To be fair, I've never had a bodyguard before so I'm not sure how it's suppose to work. What would it have been like?"

"I don't really know," Kara said, still not looking up. "I was supposed to make contact and then forge some kind of friendship, so that if I ran into you while I was tailing you or something, it wouldn't seem out of the ordinary. I mean, it wouldn't have gone too far or anything but..." she trailed off.

"Of course not," Ryan said.

"But I have to say, and I think this is really why I came to your room tonight," Kara said, standing and finally making eye contact. "I did a lot of research on you before I met you at the Pond, and I think, well, I think being your friend would have been really cool."

"Yeah?" Ryan said, taken aback.

"Yeah," Kara said, laughing again nervously.

"We can still be friends?" Ryan said.

"I hope so," Kara said, turning to go. "Maybe once you've worked through all this crazy stuff you're feeling, maybe then."

She took a few steps then stopped and turned slightly, looking over her shoulder.

"You were right by the way," she smiled. "About Gansu. My family came from Gansu."

Ryan was surprised. In all that had happened, he had forgotten his poor attempt at a pick-up line. "Where are they now?"

Ryan almost missed it, but a wave of unmistakable sadness passed over Kara's face, for barely a second. Then it vanished.

"They went back," she said softly.

CHAPTER 42

"Sir, you have a call," Young said through the intercom.

Thresher grabbed the handset.

"We have a location," the voice on the other end said. It was Faisal.

"Do you need anything?" Thresher asked.

"Not at this time. We are bringing our resources into the area and should be able to move within the next twenty-four hours," Faisal said. "I thought I would alert you as a courtesy."

"I appreciate that," Thresher said. "Understand though, if something goes wrong, I cannot come running to your aid."

"It will be taken care of," Faisal said. "I will be in contact."

Thresher replaced the handset and leaned back in his chair. He loved having others do his work for him. It kept his hands squeaky clean.

CHAPTER 43

When Ryan went downstairs after he'd woken up, he found everyone else seated in the living room, joined by two new people. Daniel introduced Ryan to Craig and his partner Dana al-Yami, both former colleagues of Daniel's. Craig was ex-CIA, while Dana worked as a liaison between the CIA and CSIS. The couple looked tired, nervous and genuinely troubled.

"They got in about three hours ago," Daniel said to Ryan, sipping his morning coffee. "They've seen what we have."

"Okay," Ryan said, taking a seat and stifling a yawn.

"Why did you wait so long?" Craig asked Daniel, almost in an accusatory tone.

"Hey!" Ryan objected.

"It's okay, Ryan," Daniel said. "I had to be certain, Craig. I wasn't sure how you'd respond if I dumped a bunch of suspicions in your lap. Maybe you'd go running to your old bosses and ruin everything I was working on. I had to know for sure before I took the next step."

"And what's that?" Craig said.

"Well, telling you, for starters," Daniel said. "After that, I don't really know. Did you look up those names I gave you?"

"I had to beg a little, given I'm no longer a U.S. government employee, but I got it." Craig rifled through his briefcase and pulled out a thin file. "I ran all three names. They're all clean. No records except for a few traffic violations. Their net worth is considerable, and they do their part in the charitable world, too. Millions of dollars to community groups in Houston, Texas, across the U.S., even overseas."

"How is that interesting?" Gary asked.

"Oh, that isn't, but this is," Dana replied. She pulled out a wad of papers from her own bag. "According to this printout from the Transportation Security Administration, all three arrived in Edmonton yesterday. They're there for four days."

Now it was Daniel's turn to be surprised. "Why would they come to Canada?"

Dana examined her paperwork more closely. "They've booked several suites at the hotel at that giant mall. Apparently some sort of big symposium is taking place there—has to do with the Crescent Pipeline. Even your Minister of Natural Resources is dropping in for a visit, I guess. They've been asked to take part in one of the panel discussions, give their two cents on whether or not the pipeline is in the U.S.'s interests. Basically act as experts."

Daniel shook his head. "Someone's going to have to fill me in. I don't really know about that pipeline."

Kara spoke up. "It's a proposed pipeline from the Alberta oil sands in the northern part of the province to refineries in the southern States. It was supposed to be a joint energy venture between several companies in both countries, but about two months ago, the U.S. president ordered a moratorium on all work until the proposal could be studied further. The prime minister wants the jobs the pipeline construction and operation would bring, and American oil companies want the raw product to refine. But the president is concerned about some parts of the route the pipeline would take, so he's asked for more time."

Edward nodded. "The Alberta government announced the symposium about a month ago, sort of a pressure tactic on the U.S. administration. All the key players in the energy sector from both countries are in town to attend a series of meetings about how wonderful the pipeline would be for both nations."

"Convenient," Daniel remarked. "So they're in Canada."

"Let's get them," Billy said.

"We don't have a reason to, Billy," Daniel reminded him. "Under Canadian law, they've done nothing wrong."

"But under American law they have," Craig piped up. "There's a whole host of terrorism charges they could face."

"So send the RCMP to get them," Gary said. "If Craig can get a grand jury convened in the U.S., a warrant would be issued that would be international in scope. Mounties can pick them up."

"There's a problem with that, though. A big problem," Daniel said. "If we arrest them here, they'd have to be extradited and would face capital changes in the United States. They'd be looking at the death penalty."

"Several times over," Craig muttered darkly.

"Under Canadian law, the government is not allowed to extradite anyone to a country where that person would face the death penalty," Daniel said. "Even if that person isn't Canadian. Even if that person has killed thousands of people. Unless the U.S. promises it won't use the death penalty, we can't hand them over. Even if our government wanted to try to change that law, it has been affirmed by the Supreme Court of Canada on several occasions. It would take years to approve the extradition. That would upset the American people and would really sour the relationship between the two countries."

"You're saying the death penalty is okay?" Billy asked, incredulous.

"No," Daniel shook his head. "I'm not saying that at all. I'm saying if we arrest them here, we'd create an international situation. If the crime was less serious, I'd say let the politicians sort it out. But if we provide refuge to three mass murderers, things will no doubt get ugly. We need to get them back to the States without anyone knowing."

"How do you propose to do that?" Dana asked, looking intrigued. "Have a grab team waiting for them when they leave their hotel? It won't just be the three of them."

"I know," Daniel said. "But all we need to do is detain them and return them to the States. If they've taken their own charter flight, that gives us some possibilities."

"Careful, Daniel," Edward said. "I know you want this to be over, but is this really the right way?"

"I don't know, guys. I don't know," Daniel said. "Maybe we've done enough, right? Maybe after everything I've had to do, maybe after everything you've all been through the last few days, maybe it's time to leave it up to the legitimate authorities."

"That sounds strangely reasonable," Craig said. "Are you feeling okay?"

Daniel smiled at the joke.

"There's another problem though," Dana said. "They're not flying back to the United States after the symposium. They have a flight plan booked already—they're all heading to Venezuela."

"What?" Ryan asked. "Why?"

"Based on some information on their website, it looks like their company has holdings there," Dana said, checking her notes.

"Return flight?" Daniel asked.

"Not booked," Dana said, looking up.

"Is that a problem?" Ryan asked.

"It's a big problem," Daniel said. "Venezuela is as anti-American as you can get in the Western Hemisphere. There's no extradition treaty. And with no return flight plan filed, that makes me nervous. They may never return to the U.S. if they've been tipped off."

The room was quiet. Over the last few days, through all that had happened, Daniel had never appeared so indecisive.

"Let me sleep on it. You guys are welcome to stay while I do that," Daniel said.

"I will, but Dana has to get back," Craig said.

"Just a couple of meetings I need to keep," Dana smiled. "But if you decide to go after them, let me know. I'd love to help."

————

Ryan awoke thrashing but didn't know why at first. He felt pressure on his face and tried to recoil from it, but whatever it was held firm. He opened his mouth to bite down hard.

"It's Kara," a voice whispered urgently in his ear. "Quiet. We need to go."

Ryan nodded that he had heard her, and Kara retracted her hand.

"Get down and stay low," she whispered, disappearing to one side of the bed. Ryan slid from beneath the blankets, obediently following while his mind struggled to wake up fully.

"Get dressed and make your way to the kitchen. Your dad's there. Stay low and away from the windows."

Ryan nodded again, threw on his clothes and crept as softly as he could towards the hallway. A faint cry and a thump came from the room beside his.

"*You* 'sssshhhhh!'" Ryan heard Billy rumble, guessing that Kara had awoken him, too.

The lights were off, and Ryan thought it best not to change that as he crouched low and tiptoed down the hallway towards the stairs, which he descended on all fours. His head cleared as the familiar rush of fear and heightened attention scrubbed his mind of sleep, and adrenaline once more flowed into his bloodstream.

He saw his dad standing in the kitchen in front of the security panel he had checked when they first arrived. Ryan stood and peered over Daniel's shoulder. The screen was a dark green hue, punctuated with a few bright, moving flickers of light.

"Thermal cameras mounted on the perimeter," Daniel said, watching the screen intently. "We have company."

Ryan looked more closely. The flickers of light were moving towards the house, which was a softer hue in the distance.

"They're coming fast," Ryan murmured.

Daniel nodded. "I think these guys are pros. No dumb goons this time. We need to act if we're going to get ahead of them."

Ryan heard shuffling behind him and noticed the rest of the crew was awake and standing in the kitchen.

"We can't make a stand here and fight them off," Daniel said, glancing at the screen. "We need to scatter, get mobile. They're operating under the assumption they'll find us here unawares. We need to surprise *them*."

"They'll have someone watching the doors, snipers probably," Craig said. "What do we do?"

"There are two tunnels out of here," Daniel said. "Both are in the basement. One takes you to the barn, the other to a rock outcropping a few hundred metres away."

Daniel pointed to Gary, Edward and Billy. "You guys take the trip to the rocks. Entrance is through the office we were in last night. I'll show you."

"Weapons?" Edward asked.

Daniel shook his head, moving towards the basement stairs. "No time. Stay in the tunnel. If you have to move, move north and stay low. Just keep moving. Do not come back to the house."

Daniel pointed to Craig, Ryan and Kara. "You guys take the tunnel to the barn. There's an arms locker there with radios. Grab a weapon and turn the radio to channel three. Check in with me when you're set."

"What about you?" Edward asked as Daniel motioned them into the office. Daniel pulled back a filing cabinet that was snug against the wall, revealing a waist-level door. He opened the door and motioned for them to get moving.

"I need to draw their attention away," Daniel said. "I'll find you when it's all dealt with."

Gary was the last person through. Daniel closed the door behind them and pushed the filing cabinet back into place, then motioned for Craig, Kara and Ryan to follow him.

"We're not going to shoot it out with these guys, okay? Just get to the barn and radio in, channel three."

Daniel opened a door that led into what appeared to be a cold storage room. He walked the group to the far end of the room, where he moved a couple of light boxes out of the way revealing another door.

"Dad," Ryan tried, but was cut off by light creaks from upstairs. *Likely the attackers getting ready to come inside*, he thought.

"Just go, Ryan," Daniel said, half-shoving them in. "Get in contact as soon as you can."

Ryan wanted to say more but he nodded and plunged head first into the darkness of the tunnel. He heard the door shut behind them but didn't bother looking back, instead reaching forward to make sure Kara and Craig were still close. His hand touched a distinctly feminine backside.

"Sorry," he whispered.

"Now's not really the time to worry about apologies," Kara whispered back. Ryan swore he could hear the smile on her face.

There were more creaks as Daniel shot up the stairs. He knew what was likely happening outside—the bricks assaulting the house would have split up to cover all the entrances they could find. The assailants were now "stacking up" or lining up behind the door, preparing to breach it by either kicking it down or blowing it open.

Daniel dashed into the kitchen, back to the panel. He assumed the people assaulting the house were wearing night-vision goggles. He had one easy trick that could buy some time. He jabbed a button on the touch screen.

Every light inside and outside the house instantly flared to life. Cries of pain came from the front of the house. The goggles were designed to amplify low levels of light, so the onslaught of light would have blinded the person wearing them.

Daniel reached into a cupboard below the panel and felt around, then pulled out four canisters of tear gas. He jabbed the screen once more, extinguishing all the lights, then made his way back to the basement stairs. He pulled the tabs on two canisters and tossed one towards the front door, then took a few steps the other direction and lobbed the second at the back entrance. Daniel heard the telltale hiss as gas seeped into the air.

He descended the stairs and dropped the last two canisters in the basement before heading to the office. He yanked open the gun safe and took out a pistol, an extra magazine and a radio, which he tuned to channel three. There was a crackle of static but no communication from Ryan, Kara and Craig yet.

Daniel closed the safe and walked to a third exit he hadn't mentioned to the others—he wanted to stay mobile and independent of the group, and that was easier if they didn't know he had his own way out. Otherwise someone would try to follow along and slow him down. The third tunnel would pop him up through a camouflaged hatch about fifty metres west of the house.

He pushed a second filing cabinet to the side and crawled into the small entrance behind, turning to pull the filing cabinet back in place. As he did, he heard a thunderous bang as the front and back doors were blown in, one right after the other. The blast of the breaching charges was replaced by a torrent of coughing as the assaulters ran head-long into a cloud of tear gas.

———

The tunnel seemed to stretch on into the very night sky itself, but Ryan soon felt Craig and Kara come to a stop in front of him.

"It's latched from the inside," Craig whispered to them.

All three of them quietly crawled out of the tunnel, with Ryan closing the door behind him. The barn was dark, but less dark than the tunnel had been, so they were able to see. The van was still parked inside from earlier, and there were no signs that anyone had been inside since.

"Over here," Kara said. Both Ryan and Craig walked over to the sound of her voice. She was standing in front of a wooden footlocker that she had already opened. Inside was a small arsenal of Tasers, handguns and other weapons.

Kara spied radios inside and handed one to Ryan and Craig, then switched hers on and found channel three.

"Okay, we're up," she whispered into the radio.

There was a moment of silence and then Daniel's voice came over the radio. "I'm out of the house now, on the perimeter. I've got a good view of the house. It looks like about five guys in the house and two outside."

"What's our play?" Kara asked. She reached into the locker with her free hand and passed weapons back. Craig and Ryan each took a Taser, a handgun and a collapsible baton. Kara reached more deeply in and drew out a rifle. Craig stepped forward to take it.

"Containment for now, while I think about this," Daniel said. "I managed to gas the people inside, but I don't know if that's going to be enough. We need eyes on the house. Have Craig get up to the loft in the barn with the rifle and scope to check out the scene. Make sure he has a radio."

Craig nodded and walked to the far wall of the barn and climbed the ladder.

"What about me and Ryan?" Kara asked.

"That's what I'm trying to figure out," Daniel said. "I don't want to expose you to anymore risk than necessary and end up shooting it out with these guys—they look like they know what they're doing. But I don't want them chasing us around either."

"We've got Tasers," Ryan said. "Can't we just take them out that way?"

"You'd have to get too close to them, and I don't think they're as risk-averse as we are," Daniel said, huffing slightly. It sounded like he was on the move.

"What if we try to separate them?" Kara suggested. "Get them moving after different targets. Or if we can lure some of them in here, maybe that will help."

"Maybe," Daniel said, puffing a bit more. "I'm moving around towards the back of the house to see if I can get a better look at what they're up to. Craig, you up yet?"

"Just about," Craig's voice broke in.

"Okay, once you are, let's—"

Daniel's radio abruptly cut out.

"Say your last again?" Kara said.

There was nothing. She tried again but still the radio was silent.

"Craig, can you get your eye on where he said he was? Towards the back of the house?" Kara said into the radio.

"You bet. Wait one sec." There was a shuffling noise from above Ryan and Kara as Craig worked his way into place.

"Shit, they've got him," Craig's voice came urgently over the radio.

Ryan felt an electrical jolt of fear run through his body.

"What do you mean?" Kara asked.

"I've got about two people moving around...hard to tell because it's still too dark. But I can just make out Daniel on the ground."

"Is he…?" Kara asked, but Craig replied quickly.

"No. He's twitching. Looks like they Tasered him," Craig said. "I've got clear shots on the bad guys."

"No," Kara said.

"What do you mean no?" Ryan erupted in fury. "Shoot them now!"

"A rifle makes a hell of a lot of noise, Ryan. If Craig pulls that trigger, the rest of that team is going to come looking for us here."

"Then I'm going," Ryan said, making his way for the door.

"Don't be stupid," Kara snapped, trying to keep her voice a whisper. "It's you against at least six guys, and they have guns. Your dad's alive. We need to think, not just react."

Ryan stood locked in place, torn between the wisdom of Kara's words and the need to get to his father immediately. He didn't nod, but he didn't move any closer to the door either.

"What's happening, Craig?" Kara whispered back into the radio.

"They've picked him up and they're…wait…. There's a van moving out there. Lights are off, but it's moving really slowly. Headed for the guys that have Daniel."

"Come on, Kara," Ryan pleaded.

"Stop it!" she hissed back. She held the antenna of the radio to her forehead, as if thinking. "What's happening at the house?"

"Four bodies moving, all falling back to the gate," Craig said, his voice robotic. "Looks like they think they've got what they came for."

"Can Craig take out the van?" Ryan asked.

Kara shook her head. "It's a .30-30. It's good against a human target, but it's not going to crack an engine block. And I don't think Craig can shoot out the tires in the dark. Besides, then we become the target."

"Then we need to go after them," Ryan said, heading for the van parked in the barn.

"Yeah," Kara said. "Craig, can you cover us as we go, then loop over and pick up the rest of the crew? We'll keep you informed of our position, and we can figure something out."

"Okay. Just don't do anything stupid," Craig said over the radio.

"Roger that," Kara said, opening the passenger's door of the van as Ryan went for the driver's door. He reached out for the door handle and pulled.

Without warning, a tremendous bang and a wave of pressure blasted from inside the van, tearing free the door, sending it smashing into Ryan and knocking him back against the wooden wall of the barn. His entire body exploded in pain from the impact of the door and from slamming into the wall, and he fell to the ground in a heap.

The roar in his ears was deafening, and everything around him seemed to be moving in slow motion, his head

THE PRODIGAL SPY

354

fuzzy from the impact. But he saw smoke spewing from the driver's seat and the first few tendrils of flame licking at the wheel well. Despite the haze that was locked over his brain from the explosion, he knew he'd better get moving before the flames got any bigger.

Strong hands grabbed him under his arms and dragged him towards the exit as the flames grew larger, spreading from the wheel well to the driver's and passenger's compartments inside the van. From behind the inferno, through the smoke, Ryan saw Kara, one arm hanging at her side, limping towards him. And behind her the flames kept growing.

He felt earth beneath him and grass as he was dragged along the ground. Kara was moving faster now. She was shouting, waving her free arm frantically, as if trying to tell whoever was pulling Ryan to pick up the pace.

Then Ryan saw the flames and smoke mushroom, expanding rapidly out and up, consuming the van and threatening to swallow the rest of the barn. Kara suddenly jolted forward, as if swatted from behind by a giant hand, and as she soared towards Ryan, he felt an unbearable wave of heat wash over him. Then he was no longer being pulled. Just as quickly the world went black.

———

When Ryan came to, more people were crouched around him.

Edward, Billy and Gary were there, along with Kara and Craig. The barn was completely engulfed.

"You okay?" Edward asked.

"What happened?" Ryan grumbled, shaking his head.

"We saw the fire and came running," Gary said while he tended to Kara's injured shoulder. "Found you two scattered over the ground here. We had to get you away from the fire."

"Where's your dad?" Billy asked.

"Gone," Ryan managed, struggling to sit upright. His head, his ribs and his back hurt mightily. "They managed to get him and take him. They were about to put him in a car when the van exploded."

"Exploded?" Edward asked.

"Looks like they got to the barn and booby-trapped the van before they hit the house," Craig said. "Didn't do a very good job. That bomb should have killed us. Whatever explosive they used must have malfunctioned for the bang to be so small."

"Says you," Ryan said, shaking his head. "That door didn't feel too good when it hit me in the ribs. Kara, you okay?"

"I got tossed into the wall. Just hurt my shoulder and twisted my ankle, I think," Kara smiled wanly. "I'll live."

"So we have no wheels?" Billy asked, his voice sounding hopeless. "And Daniel is gone?"

"Wheels aren't that big a deal, Billy," Craig huffed. "The biggest problem we have is finding Daniel."

"How did they know where to find us?" Billy asked.

"That's not important right now," Edward said. "Our first priority is finding Daniel. But I'm not sure how we're going to do that."

"I do," Gary said. "When I first met up with Daniel in Vancouver, he asked me to bring him a couple of things. One of those was a batch of GPS microdots. And the first thing he did was to stick one in his shoe."

"Seriously?" Billy asked.

"Yep," Gary said. "I'm sure he's been stashing them elsewhere. Hell, he's probably been swallowing one a day. I've known some guys who do that."

"So how do we check?" Edward asked.

"I need to get back into the house. I can use one of the computers in there, or my phone. Either one."

"Is it safe?" Edward asked, looking at Craig.

"Should be," Craig said. "They were hustling Daniel into a car, and the brick that hit the house was withdrawing to the road when I came down from the loft to take care of Ryan. Besides, if they were still here, we'd all be dead or captured by now."

"Can you walk?" Kara asked Ryan, holding out a hand. Ryan nodded, using Kara's hand to get to his feet before they set off for the house.

Ryan was surprised by how unafraid he was for his father. Although he had reacted with some shock when Craig had radioed down that Daniel had once again been captured, he now felt more composed, less fearful. Maybe it was the head trauma, but he didn't feel as scared for his dad as he had been earlier.

It was probably because he had seen everything his dad could do, knew what his dad had endured and that he had already freed himself from some dicey situations. Ryan still felt a sense of urgency, but it was somewhat muted. The bad guys had gone to great lengths to ensure his dad was taken away alive. Ryan was sure he would be alive for a while longer.

"Try not to breathe too deeply," Craig said as they approached the door. "Daniel said he gassed the place before he left. Should be gone, but be careful."

The acrid stench of tear gas still hung in the air, but it didn't affect the ragtag, weary group as they stumbled through the front door. Craig took the lead, cautiously checking every room before declaring them all clear.

"Bring your phone downstairs," Edward said to Gary. "We should be able to get a good read on where he is once we capture the signal."

Ryan collapsed in a chair, his body protesting loudly as he felt aches and pains everywhere. Kara sat on the floor, waving off Ryan's offer for her to take his chair.

Gary stood to one side, waiting for an application on his phone to start up. "Okay, here we go," he said, staring intently at the screen. He tapped it a few times, then grunted. "They're not too far off," he said. "I've got a strong signal coming from about thirty kilometres away. It's still moving."

"We have to get moving," Ryan gasped, standing slowly, painfully.

"We do, but we need to think first," Kara said, her voice weary. "The first thing we absolutely need is transportation, given our van and the truck were just blown up in the barn explosion."

Edward spoke up. "Not entirely. The place Daniel sent us when we evacuated the house had a small outbuilding nearby. I saw an old truck inside. Kind of a farm truck. It's not much, but it will get us started."

"Okay," Kara said. "We're all going to pile in the truck for now. Next farm we see, we'll help ourselves to a vehicle so we can at least split up."

"I'll run back and bring the farm truck around. Gary, I'll need you to hot-wire it," Edward said, heading for the stairs.

"Right. Daniel is still moving," Gary said, staring at his phone.

"We're falling behind," Ryan said.

"We're doing the best we can," Kara said. "Besides, this is your dad. He's going to buy us as much time as he can."

———

Daniel had been Tasered before. He'd never had cared for the experience.

The worst part was when his limbs and his brain finally started working again—it felt like a fire radiating through his body.

A voice muttered in the distance as Daniel rolled into a sitting position and leaned back against what he believed to be a van, given the straight, cold edges of the wall behind him. He could see at least three different forms inside the dark van.

He was face down, and his hands flex-cuffed behind him. He tested the area around him by moving his feet, but felt no one nearby. He lifted his head to take a quick look but saw no feet.

"Don't move," someone grumbled from the other side. Daniel could see the shape of a submachine gun pointed at him. He nodded his understanding.

"Where are we going?" Daniel asked. No response.

Daniel remembered the professionalism this group had displayed when they rushed the house—they had by no means been perfect, but they knew how to handle themselves in combat. So Daniel wasn't surprised that his question went unanswered.

Daniel knew the area well from when he had first explored and then began upgrading the farm. He knew there were few ways in and out, and although he didn't have a watch with him, he knew they had not been travelling for long. There was really only one major road in and out. Head one direction and the road took you straight through town.

But go the other way...Daniel knew it led to a good place if you had the right friends and were looking for some help getting something out of the country.

"Funny," Daniel said out loud. "You guys don't strike me as big drug users."

———⟨∘∕∘⟩———

"What?" Kara said, perplexed.

Ryan looked over at her, but Kara shook her head.

Kara, Craig and Ryan had dropped off Edward, Billy and Gary outside the nearest farmhouse. Even in the early morning twilight, they had easily seen two vehicles sitting out in the open.

"Given this is a farm, they're probably not locked," Kara had suggested.

"Given this is a farm, the owner probably owns several guns," Edward had groused as he'd stepped out of the truck with the others.

"Satellite imagery shows an airstrip where Daniel's signal stopped moving," Gary said.

He had placed another call to his phantom "guys," who were apparently well connected enough to access the most recent satellite imagery of the area, at least more recent than Google had. The "guys" also had another tidbit of information about the airstrip.

"This area is associated with major marijuana trafficking," Gary said. "Which explains the airstrip in the middle of nowhere. It's not even on local maps."

"I don't get it," Ryan said.

"Good ol' BC Bud, young one," Gary said. "Highly coveted across western Canada and the western United States.

The airstrip is clandestine, used for shipping product, nationally and over the border. Might even be a grow-op nearby."

"So my dad was abducted by drug dealers?" Ryan asked incredulously.

"I doubt it," Kara chimed in. "Whoever took your dad—and I think we can hazard a guess as to who is responsible based on what he told us—probably thought the airstrip would be a quick escape. So I'm sure they're dangling something in front of the owners of the airstrip to make use of it—weapons, cash, international markets for their product—that kind of thing."

"If they have access to a plane, we might not make it in time," Ryan said, his voice rising in panic. "We need to move faster."

"I think I have an idea," Kara said to Ryan.

"Calling the cops?" Ryan asked.

"No," Kara said. "Just sowing a little dissension in the ranks."

⟞◦/◦/◦⟝

When the van stopped, the man seated across from Daniel stood and pulled Daniel roughly to his feet and propelled him out the open back door of the van.

A second man came around from the passenger's side of the van, hoisting a submachine gun in front of him, and stood at Daniel's side. The driver of the van looked at the two standing on either side of Daniel and nodded his head towards a group of five men clustered about twenty metres away.

The men standing beside Daniel pushed him firmly forward, holding their weapons in their free hands. The driver walked about a metre in front of them but came to a sudden halt.

Daniel craned his neck around the driver to see why he had stopped so abruptly. The five large men that made up the welcoming committee were all brandishing guns, and none of them looked happy.

"What the fuck?!" the driver suddenly exclaimed, holding his hands out wide to show he wasn't holding anything.

"Drop 'em," the tallest of the five men yelled to the two men escorting Daniel. Both dropped their guns to the ground, but they didn't ease their grip on Daniel.

"Seems we have a little problem," the man continued angrily. He was almost seven feet tall, had a shaved head and looked like he tipped the scales at 400 pounds. Daniel assumed he was the dealer. "Just got a phone call saying you guys aren't who you say you are."

"Who made this call?" the driver asked indignantly. "What'd they say?"

"Don't know who it was, but they say you guys are cops," the dealer said, his voice growing increasingly angry. "Said this was all a ruse to get in here and take some pics, plant some stuff around here to try to take us down."

"You've been well compensated," the driver said, trying to remain calm.

"They said the guns are all traced, the money's all marked," the dealer said, stepping even closer to the driver. The dealer's men didn't budge, their guns still trained on Daniel's captors.

"That's a lie!" the driver said, his voice sounding desperate.

Daniel's eyes took in as much information as he could. He didn't know what was going on, but his instincts told him this was not going to end well. He and his captors were at a decided disadvantage, and Daniel wasn't sure what he was going to do. All he could really do was watch and try to keep the driver in front of him, as a kind of shield.

"Maybe it is," the dealer moved even closer. "How am I supposed to know? You guys contact us out of the blue, saying you need our strip to move something quietly. Then you show up with just some guy? And before you get here, we get a call saying you guys are trying to fuck us over?"

"Don't you think that's a little suspicious?" the driver asked. "Everything is fine until all of a sudden you get a phone call from some unknown person saying we're the cops?"

"The whole thing is suspicious," the dealer said, gesturing with his gun. "So until you can convince us otherwise, you aren't going anywhere."

"That's not an option," the driver snapped. "We're on a schedule. We get here; we leave. That was the deal."

"I'm afraid the deal has been renegotiated for now," the towering gang leader said.

Daniel tensed as the man guarding his right side slowly moved from Daniel's side to stand behind him. Daniel kept his head facing forward, but he could hear the guard rustling around a bit, as if reaching for something. Daniel guessed he had a concealed a weapon and was using Daniel for cover as he drew it.

"Start walking!" the dealer suddenly shouted, pointing towards a large barn-like structure roughly 500 metres away. "Move!"

Daniel glanced from side to side, searching for some sort of escape, but all he could think to do was run once the shooting started. The nearest cover—a small stand of bushes—was fifteen metres away.

He was hoping the driver would just go with the angry hulk, buy him some time, but the driver was standing ramrod straight, anchored by indecision.

The hulk suddenly strode up and jammed the barrel of his gun under the driver's jaw.

"I said move."

Without warning, an intense beam of piercing white light cut through the night, enveloping the dealer and his posse, all of whom dropped to the ground, their guns discarded, covering their eyes as they writhed and screamed in pain. Daniel averted his eyes as the light swept towards his captors, but the two guards were already moving, dragging Daniel with them as they charged in the opposite direction of the light source. Daniel tried to lean forward to knock them off balance, but both guards had a good grip, pulling him backwards, so he could nothing except dig in his heels. Still they kept moving.

Suddenly, the guard to Daniel's left disappeared. Daniel couldn't hold himself upright and fell away from the other guard and onto his back. He rolled over onto his knees and brought up one leg, getting ready to run, when something he saw stopped him.

The guard collapsed on the ground beside him, convulsing. Daniel looked up.

Ryan was standing over him, holding a Taser. Daniel watched as his son pulled on the Taser's trigger, shocking the guard one more time.

"Can't be too careful, right?" Ryan asked his dad.

"The other one?" Daniel asked.

"Taken care of," Ryan said. He leaned down and removed his father's cuffs. "Let's get moving."

———⟡⟡⟡———

The second guard looked over his shoulder as he ran. He had felt Daniel jerk and tumble away, and he saw his partner fall to the ground. He didn't stop running. No longer having to pull someone along with him, the guard pumped his legs harder, trying to get away as fast as he could. He angled his path towards their van.

He heard a sudden snap in front of him and felt a tiny prick in his right arm. He looked down and saw a barb embedded in his arm with a thin wire running from the barb.

Someone had tried to fire a Taser at him but only one of the two barbs required to complete the circuit actually hit him. He reached across with his free hand and tore out the barb.

A flash of motion to his right stopped the guard, and he turned to face whatever was coming, bringing his arms up in a defensive posture, but he was too late. Something hard hit him along his right side, knocking him off balance and sending him careening into the dirt. He rolled as he fell and sprang back to his feet, looking for his attacker.

The guard was shocked to find himself facing a slender, young Asian woman, whom he guessed couldn't weigh more than 100 pounds.

And she came right at him.

He quickly blocked her left foot as it came snapping towards him, but she yanked it back, and then flicked her foot at him again with blinding speed. The hit caught him high in the shoulder, knocking him backwards. He tried to roll with the impact, but she attacked again. She reached forward and snared his left arm, pulling it across his body, throwing off the angle of his roll and sending him plummeting to the ground on his right shoulder. He tried to scissor his legs as he fell to knock her over too, but she skipped out of the way, still pushing him around by his left arm until he had no choice but to turn and fall face down on the ground.

No sooner had he landed, the air rushing out of his lungs, than she was on him from behind, her arm wrapped around his neck in a classic chokehold. He tried to buck her off, but she was straddling him, her inner knees holding him in place. He flailed back with one arm as he started to pass out, but he couldn't reach her, and he lost consciousness.

Both Daniel and Ryan ran upon Kara as she stepped off the limp body of the guard she had choked out. Ryan whistled aloud as he came to a halt. The man Kara had subdued was at least a foot taller than her and probably weighed 250 pounds.

"You choked him out?" Ryan asked, incredulous. "He's three times your size!"

"I think Kara's going to continue to surprise you," Daniel said, grabbing the zip tie Ryan offered. He bent down and ran it around the guard's wrists. Ryan grabbed the unconscious guard under his arms and dragged him towards the barn-like building.

"Just drop him over by the barn. We don't have time to dawdle. We need to get moving. Where's everyone else?" Daniel asked.

"Uncle Ed, Billy and Gary are taking care of the guys they zapped with the light. Craig is somewhere nearby with a rifle," Ryan said. "He was our cover. But we figured we'd try to go non-lethal first. Didn't think you wanted us shooting a bunch of people if we didn't have to."

"Thank you for that. Who made the call?"

"That would be me," Kara said. "Gary got the number through his contacts. I just called and hinted that everything wasn't on the up-and-up. In my experience, drug dealers tend to get pretty paranoid about cops. I figured that would buy us some time to get to you."

"Things got a little hairy, but it worked," Daniel said.

"Where are we going?" Ryan asked.

"I'm not sure right now, but we need to get somewhere we can talk. This changes things dramatically."

"The house?" Ryan suggested.

"Not safe, now that they've hit it. And especially since I have no idea how they found us," Daniel said.

Kara pointed to a small trail for them to follow behind the barn. "It leads back to the road," she said. "Craig will be watching us to make sure we're covered."

"We still need new wheels," Daniel said, eyeing the barn. "And I don't think these guys will call the cops if we borrow a vehicle or two."

———<o/o/o>———

Two hours later they were gathered at a small picnic site well back from any of the main roads in the area, some fifty kilometres from the airfield. In that time they had borrowed the van in which the attackers had transported Daniel, as well as one truck from the illicit airstrip. Daniel, Craig and Gary had returned to the farmhouse briefly to collect what they could while the rest had been responsible for zip-tying and securing both Daniel's captors and their drug-growing "buddies."

Now they sat huddled together trying to figure out what to do next.

"I think that decides it," Daniel said, his voice hard with anger.

"I think you need to calm down a bit first, Daniel," Craig offered, but Daniel just shook his head.

"I'm calm enough, Craig," Daniel said. "I'm calm enough to realize that this will never end if I don't deal with it myself. Even if the RCMP or your guys go after them while they are in Canada, this will never end. They'll keep coming after me. They'll keep coming after Ryan. And they'll probably keep coming after the rest of you too because I'm pretty sure they know who you are. I think there are people in this very country that would try to get to us, to me especially."

Daniel looked up at all of them. "This won't end until we end it."

No one spoke for a good minute, digesting Daniel's words.

"What happened at the farm was an escalation," Edward said. "They didn't just try to kidnap you. They tried to take out the rest of us with that bomb in the barn. They didn't know about the tunnels we used, but still, if that bomb had gone off like it was supposed to, Kara, Craig and Ryan would be dead. Until now they haven't really tried to kill anyone. They've just tried to capture. We can't ignore this."

Daniel nodded. He looked up and saw Ryan and Kara staring at him, slowly nodding their agreement.

"I just want this to be over," Billy suddenly wailed, burying his face in his hands.

"Bill," Ryan said.

"I want to sleep. I want to eat. I want to be at home. I don't want to be running around all BC being chased by people with guns. I just want to go home!"

"Billy, do you understand that if we don't do this, you'll never get to go home. You'll never be able to live your life without looking over your shoulder?" Daniel replied. "Your best bet for ever getting back to the life you were living is to come with us and finish this."

Billy whimpered, his face still in his hands, but he nodded.

"I don't expect anything more from the rest of you," Daniel said, looking at Kara, Edward, Gary and Craig. "You've done so much already. You've taken care of my son and helped bring us back together. I think we can take care of it from here."

"You have got to be joking," Kara said.

"We're all here to help you, you old fart," Craig said. Gary and Edward nodded in agreement. "And I think I can safely say that Dana will also help in any way she can."

Daniel smiled. He knew his friends well. He had known they would want to help, but he hadn't felt right asking for so much more.

"Then I guess we're headed to Edmonton," Daniel said.

CHAPTER 44

Billy was alone in the hotel room, but he could see people everywhere he looked.

His small desk inside the hotel suite was crammed with gear. He had two keyboards at his disposal and six computer screens, each split into four different viewing windows. A seventh screen, connected to his laptop, was his actual computer monitor. The screens showed people walking through various parts of the hotel.

Billy was nervous, a feeling he didn't often experience and didn't particularly enjoy. The events over the past week hadn't exactly been positive…well, besides Ryan finding his dad; that was cool. Billy had been ripped from a life he had distilled down to his own level of comfort, and all of this uncertainty, suspense and spycraft was infinitely more potent than anything he was used to.

The only place he felt comfortable was behind a computer screen. But one look out the hotel window was a cold reminder of where he was, souring his mood further. It was the middle of April, and it was snowing, for God's sake. In all his life, Billy had never left Vancouver's boundaries. He preferred dealing with the familiar in everything he did. Now he was in an unfamiliar city—province even—with a weird group of people, going after some international criminals, all on the down low.

Billy rocked back and forth in the chair, keeping his eyes focused on the monitors in front of him, waiting for the appointed time, about twenty minutes away.

The last twenty-four hours had been a whirlwind of activity. The group had ditched the vehicles they had stolen from the drug airstrip when they had reached Chase and rented new vans. Daniel and Billy shopped for about an hour, picking up enough computer equipment and other supplies to fill the back of one of the vans.

The symposium was being hosted at, of all places, the Fantasyland Hotel in Edmonton, which was connected to West Edmonton Mall, the largest shopping mall in North America. Not only was the hotel booked solid for the symposium, but roughly 100,000 people daily also came by to shop or play at the indoor water park or amusement park. So en route to Edmonton, Billy had hacked his way into the hotel's reservation system, scrambled some of the entries, deleted another and made reservations for all of them.

He registered the group under aliases, of course. Daniel and Craig would be going in as oil and gas executives, having managed to snap up a couple of spots at the symposium.

Dana had flown out to meet the group in Edmonton and would act as the public relations officer for Daniel and Craig's company. She had left for Edmonton earlier than the others, tasked with ensuring everything was in place before the rest of the team arrived. Ryan was going as a journalist, with a forged Canadian Press pass. And Billy and Kara were registered as guests in the hotel. Edward and Gary would be their eyes outside the hotel just in case anything went wrong.

There hadn't been time to sleep on the drive because Daniel had given everyone lessons on how to disguise themselves and how to escape from the hotel if they needed to. He had even given Billy a rudimentary demonstration of how to operate a handgun.

Two hours from Edmonton, Daniel had received an email containing some blueprints of the hotel, as well as the itinerary for the symposium and the sessions their three targets would be attending. Now they had to figure out how to grab them quietly, away from public view, and get them back to the U.S. They thought about taking them in the night in their hotel rooms, but Billy discovered through the hotel's booking system that the three had booked a boardroom for five o'clock that evening for a private working dinner.

Daniel and Craig had been initially suspicious of the convenience of this meeting, popping up right when the team was planning to grab them, but when they reached the hotel later, Dana had gone out to snoop a bit and reported back that the three had a meeting with the Minister of Natural

Resources the next day and wanted some time to strategize, away from the noise of the symposium. She confirmed that the hotel's kitchen had been asked to prepare an elegant meal for three in the boardroom at that same time. Daniel and Craig concluded that, although seemingly convenient, the meeting appeared to be legitimate, and it was probably their best opportunity to grab them.

When they reached the city limits, the vans had pulled over, and Daniel and Craig took one van and the others had piled into the other. Craig was going to rustle up some CIA resources that operated in the city, including a pilot who could fly them out when they were ready. Billy wondered what the CIA was doing in Edmonton and had asked Craig, who had simply replied that the CIA had resources in most major cities worldwide. Daniel had rented another couple of vehicles and stashed them somewhere south of the city limits in case their initial plan didn't work out. They finalized their plan once they all reconvened at the hotel.

Billy set up in one of the hotel suites and hacked into the hotel's security system so he could monitor the cameras. Everyone was equipped with small wireless radios so Billy could communicate with them at any given time. If Billy saw anything suspicious, he would contact the team. After their targets were in custody, they would be moved to a rented van parked at the mall parkade. From there, they would be taken to the Edmonton International Airport where Craig's pilot friend would be waiting. Then Craig,

Dana and Daniel would escort the trio to the United States. The rest of the team would pile into the rented van and head back to BC.

Simple, really, Billy thought as he checked the monitors again. His job at the moment was to watch out for any suspicious activity, such as any or all of the targets leaving the hotel when they were supposed to be in session. The Minister of Natural Resources wasn't arriving until the next day, but his RCMP security team had an advance squad in place, so Daniel and his team had to be careful about attracting too much attention. The presence of the RCMP added an extra wrinkle to their plan, but as long as they worked quickly and efficiently, they should be able to pull off their plan right under the Mounties' noses.

So now, here they were, at the Fantasyland Hotel, waiting for their prey. And the Tri-State members were behaving exactly as expected. They had so far attended all of their sessions, and Billy watched from his video monitor as staff trickled in and out of the boardroom the trio had reserved, preparing it for the scheduled dinner meeting. The team's frequent radio checks confirmed that nothing was out of order. Everything was still green.

Billy sighed and tapped a few keys, switching between camera views. Nothing of importance was happening right now.

CHAPTER 45

Ryan was trying not to fall asleep.

He was sure real journalists didn't yawn so much, but he wasn't there to report on anything, regardless of the phony credentials hanging from the lanyard around his neck. He was seated near the back of the conference room keeping an eye on his three targets—Strongback, Smith and Wright, all of whom were seated at a large table, debating with their Canadian counterparts about the need to ensure proper ecological protocols were followed in the pipeline corridor. Ryan occasionally leaned over and scribbled in his notepad as if taking notes, but he really just made erratic zigzags, occasionally turning the page.

He spied his father, seated at the other side of the room, arms folded, looking dapper in a three-piece suit. Daniel wasn't so bold as to take part in the discussion, telling anyone who asked that he was simply "auditing" the session.

Ryan remembered his father's advice about not look-ing too much at him during the symposium, so Ryan tried to concentrate on the discussion. The room was full, and he was getting hot. He pulled at his tie to loosen it; he was sweating underneath the cheap white shirt his dad had insisted he purchase as part of his disguise. His tie at least matched the scratchy polyester pants.

It was almost half past four, and Ryan was getting nervous. The session would be wrapping up in about ten minutes, and then…all he could think was, "It's go time." All their preparations boiled down to the next half-hour.

Billy had patched into the hotel's security system with relative ease, and the group had spent hours watching the comings and goings of staff, security and random guests, looking for familiar patterns or any signs of an increased alert level. But everything had looked normal. The team moved as casually as possible while eyeballing their targets in person, keeping Daniel away from the trio as an extra degree of caution.

Dana was dressed to the nines, chatting amicably with the symposium guests and handing out phony business cards. Kara was dressed almost as casually as Ryan, but she was attending another session. Only Billy was still dressed as himself, but he'd barely left his hotel room since they'd arrived and, knowing Billy, that's the way he liked it, Ryan thought.

Ryan's eyes were sweeping the room again when he felt a shock of adrenaline hit him. Anna Strongback seemed to be staring directly at him. He remembered his father's advice about avoiding accidental contact of any kind—*just be natural, be quiet and move on.* Ryan flashed a smile then feigned a yawn. Strongback seemed to giggle, then returned her gaze to the discussion.

Ryan shuddered inwardly then looked at his watch, 4:40. He looked around the room discreetly, then rose to leave, before the session ended. They had been instructed to leave one minute apart, starting with Ryan and Kara. Kara would be responsible for opening the door to the boardroom if it was locked, and also shepherding out any staff still inside. All had different routes to the boardroom, with Kara and Ryan taking the elevator and the rest taking separate staircases. Dana was set to arrive last, a kind of reserve in case of trouble, though Daniel didn't foresee any. The boardroom was on the third floor and wouldn't take long to reach.

The key to their plan, as Daniel had underscored, was timeliness and discretion. "Be on time, but don't make a big deal about it," he'd told them all.

Ryan exited the back doors and stood in front of the elevator. Kara soon joined him. They paid no attention to one another as they entered the elevator. Kara stabbed the number three button and waited for the doors to close. No one else had entered the elevator with them.

"Stay calm," Kara said, meeting his gaze. Ryan stared back and exhaled sharply, comically shaking his head back and forth vigorously.

The elevator chimed, and the doors opened. They took a quick left, heading for the boardroom. Kara verified it was the correct room by reading the plate mounted to the door, then reached out and tested the knob.

"Open," she said. Ryan skirted a quick gaze down the hallway and saw Daniel and Craig moving towards them.

"Let's go," Daniel said when he reached the door.

CHAPTER

Billy was looking at his monitor, waiting for the action to start. He had stopped rocking in his chair, instead bouncing his right leg to work out his nervous energy.

He saw a light flicker in the frame of the monitor showing the interior of the target boardroom. From the looks of the hallways outside the kitchen, a lot of food was being moved around the building right now, so maybe the cooks were running a little late.

*A bit early, but okay...*Billy thought, watching the boardroom door open all the way. A form stepped into the darkness, and the room was suddenly flooded in light.

At first Billy was confused—Daniel and the rest of the group must've gotten their timing wrong. But his confusion instantly turned to horror as he watched the scene unfold in front of him. He found himself counting instinctively, collecting information, like Ryan's dad had told him to. *If anything goes wrong, the biggest thing we need from you is information. Try to get as much detail as you can.*

Billy reached for his mic, jamming in the earpiece and making sure the transmitter was on.

"Guys," he said. "You need to abort the operation immediately! Abort! Abort! Abort!"

The response to the abort code was supposed to be the word "Green" from everyone. Billy waited, cranking the volume knob on his transmitter to make sure it was loud enough. He couldn't hear anything.

He desperately called out names. "Ryan! Daniel! Kara! Anyone! This is Billy! I said, Abort! Abort! Abort!"

He listened intently, but no one responded. He double-checked his transmitter, only to find that the battery had somehow died. He'd sworn he'd given it to Dana to charge last night.

His eyes flew back to the screen, in time to see the lights go back out again. A heartbeat later, the door cracked again, and he saw Kara step inside.

They're walking into a trap! Billy raged, scooting back from his desk and reaching into the soft suitcase underneath. *Why do I have to be the one to play hero?*

Billy found what he was looking for, grabbed his room key and made a beeline for the door, throwing it open and praying he had enough time.

But someone was standing in the doorway.

—⋙⋘—

Kara pushed the boardroom door all the way open and stopped, frowning.

"The lights are out," she whispered over her shoulder as she stepped inside. She reached out for the wall, fumbling for the light switch.

From out of nowhere, a hand grabbed hers, yanking her into the darkness. Before her team had a chance to act, a swarm of hands shot out and grabbed them, too. Ryan tried to fight against the hands that had grasped his arms, but another pair of hands immediately seized him, pulling his arms behind his back.

The lights came on. Kara squinted against the onslaught.

Ryan, Craig and Daniel, who were being held in place by large men, visibly Arabic, were conscious and alert, and their eyes were riveted at a spot to Kara's right. Kara turned her head to see what they were looking at, and her heart dropped like a stone.

"Jesus," Daniel muttered in shock.

They'd been had.

——————

Billy tumbled backward into the suite, unable to keep his footing against the strong shove that had sent him flying to the floor. He rolled onto his back and came to a stop, struggling to get to his feet.

The man standing in the doorway had been waiting for Billy to emerge. As Billy got to his knees, breathing hard, a name came to mind for the guy now approaching him menacingly.

"Kamil!" Billy said, half in surprise, half in shock, almost as if in greeting. It was the same oversized Arab that had twice tried to choke Ryan back in Vancouver.

"You and your friends are finished," Kamil breathed heavily. He kicked Billy's leg hard, and Billy went down with a loud yelp, clutching his knee. Kamil then turned away from Billy and attacked the desk. He ripped the computer monitors from their ports and dropped them on the floor, the screens shattering one after the other.

Billy wasn't prone to anger, but after so much disruption in his previously well-ordered life, he'd finally reached his tipping point. He felt like he was in elementary school again, being teased because of the way he talked or behaved. In those days, in a blind rage, he was just as quick to attack someone who made fun of him as he was to apologize afterwards. Billy had learned to control the instinct to lash out, but he knew of many others with Asperger syndrome, either farther down the spectrum or further up, who erupted in anger at the slightest provocation or when overly frustrated. Billy had been taught, in all those camps he had attended, to understand his feelings and find better ways to channel them into proper behaviour, and by the time he was in Grade Three, he had stopped throwing fits altogether.

But now, sprawled on the thick carpeting of a fancy hotel room 1000 kilometres from home, Billy felt anger rise up in him. He'd felt out of place since he had first been attacked at home and had managed to keep his emotions in check only by telling himself that it would soon all be over and he could go back to his life.

Kamil's attack and the destruction of the computer monitors while Ryan and the others stood helpless in that boardroom pushed Billy over the edge. If Kamil didn't stop, if Billy couldn't get to his friends, then these Tri-State people would escape, and he might never be able to return home.

Billy screamed as he rolled to one side, grabbing a lamp from a nearby end table. He watched as Kamil turned, his smug, arrogant expression changing to one of shock when he saw the lamp coming at his head. The next thing Billy knew, he was standing over Kamil's unconscious body, holding a broken lamp.

Breathing heavily, Billy clued back into his surroundings and dropped the lamp. He stole one last glance at the two remaining computer monitors, grabbed the item he'd dropped when Kamil pushed him and ran as fast as he could out the door and to the stairs.

⸻

None of them could believe it. There, perched on a low table with a handgun trained on them, was Dana.

"Goddammit!" Daniel thundered, trying in vain to fight free from his guard's grasp. "You traitor!"

"Quiet," Dana replied, gesturing with her gun. "If you want this to end peacefully, I suggest you cooperate."

"I don't believe it," Craig said, as he was being frisked by the man holding him. Craig's face was ashen. "What are you doing?"

"What does it look like?" Dana replied. "Sorry your little plan isn't going to work. All three execs are on their way to the airport. Too bad."

"Why?" Daniel was sputtering, lost between rage and confusion. "How?"

"The why is not important," Dana said sharply. "Just do as you're told."

"Stop this!" Ryan shouted.

"Why?" Dana smirked, her voice suddenly dropping, mimicking Ryan's own. "Because you don't know anything?"

Ryan stared at her in shock. "That was you in the van!" he said, suddenly recognizing her. "You were the woman in charge. You were the one who helped kidnap me."

"That's right, little Davis," Dana said, watching the wave of realization wash over him. "You obviously did not inherit your father's smarts, or you would have picked up on it sooner."

Ryan's head dropped in disbelief and shock.

"Why, Dana?" Craig asked, tears forming in his eyes.

"I think that has been the worst part this whole time, especially this last year," Dana said. "Pretending to love you. Giving myself to you. I would pass the time you rolled around on top of me counting down the days until I was off on another 'consulting trip.'"

"But this is your country," Daniel tried, appealing to her patriotism. "You're as Canadian as the rest of us. I don't understand."

"There are some things you and I share, Davis. Nationality might be one of them, but if you knew the other, you would understand." Her grip on the handgun tightened.

"You must have been deeply hurt to do something like this." Ryan couldn't believe the words came from his mouth, but they had. He wasn't sure why he'd spoken them.

"Whatever you feel is probably true," his father had once said. "Instinct is, perhaps, the most powerful weapon of all."

Dana leapt off the table, walking briskly towards Ryan with the gun extended. "Quiet," she said, her voice menacing.

Ryan's mind slowly caught up with his own words. Something in her choice of words, the tone, and the way she was acting, her body language, told him that this moment was agonizing for her.

"This can't be your only choice," Ryan said plaintively.

Dana's eyes glistened. "Unfortunately, it is," she replied.

The door to the boardroom suddenly banged open. Billy entered the room, holding out the handgun Daniel had given him in case of emergency. He yelled at the top of his lungs as he barrelled in, firing rounds wildly, one right after the other, as fast as the semi-automatic weapon could chamber a new round. But the bullets he fired, every one, hit the ceiling, a window, the walls or the floor. He was still screaming when his gun finally clicked empty.

But the surprise factor worked. As stupefied as they were by Billy's entry, Ryan, Daniel, Craig and Kara realized the opportunity the distraction offered, and they acted. Their respective captors had crouched or flinched as Billy fired, and the four freed themselves.

As their captors cringed and dove in response to Billy's surprise entrance, the team attacked. Ryan drove an elbow up into the temple of his captor, grabbed the man's free arm and flipped him to the ground, then stomped on his head. Kara rammed an open hand into the nose of the man holding her. Daniel drove his own head back against his captor's, breaking his nose, then grabbed the man's arm and threw him to the floor. Craig jammed an elbow into the solar plexus of his attacker, winding him, then turned and knocked him out with a sharp punch to the temple.

After quickly disposing of his guard, Ryan was already up and surveying the room. His eyes flashed instantly to Dana who was standing in the middle of the boardroom, her face etched with despair and confusion as her would-be prisoners easily freed themselves. Then her face suddenly hardened, and she brought her gun up to point it straight at Daniel. Ryan watched as his father reached for the floor to retrieve his gun. Ryan could tell Daniel wouldn't get it in time. Ryan instinctively understood Dana's plan: Daniel knew everything about Tri-State, about the prince and the money transfer. If she killed him, she also killed their best chance of making sure the people responsible faced justice.

As soon as Dana's gaze shifted to Daniel, Ryan sprang. She was about a metre away, her free hand sweeping up to grasp the gun with both hands before firing. Facing her left side now, but with his weight on his back left foot, Ryan spied the location of the gun in the air then took a leaping step towards her. As his right foot landed on the floor in front of him, slightly closing the distance between them, Ryan pivoted on his foot and swept his left leg upwards in a reverse kick. As his leg came around, he propelled the heel of his left foot into her clenched hands. His foot slammed into its target at the same moment the gun barked, and Ryan felt his foot kick back from the force of the gun blast after making contact. The gun inched slightly off its mark, and Ryan watched from the corner of his eye as his father fell backwards and the bullet slammed harmlessly into the wall above Daniel's head. The rest of the group scattered. Ryan saw a flash in the distance as Kara came bounding towards the spot where he was fighting Dana, but she was still too far away to help him.

Ryan's kick hadn't dislodged the gun from Dana's hands, and Ryan knew he had to separate it from her before he could deal with her alone. As his left foot touched the ground, Ryan shifted his weight and resorted to the elementary attack any white-belt karate or tae-kwon-do student learns first. He raised his right foot straight up in front of him with all the force he could muster, his thigh muscles straining as he lifted his leg above his hip. Dana was bringing the gun back down when Ryan's second kick connected

389

with her wrists. The force of the kick broke Dana's grip, and the gun tumbled to the floor. Kara dove in and grabbed the gun, spinning around to train it on Dana.

"No!" Dana screamed. As Ryan's leg fell back, he leaned forward, and in a move he'd learned from watching professional wrestling, swept his left arm across his body, cocked slightly at the elbow and made contact with Dana's neck in a classic "clothesline," unceremoniously dumping her to the floor.

"Don't even breathe," Daniel said menacingly, as he suddenly appeared at Ryan's side, his gun pointed at Dana's head. Behind him he heard the zip of flex-cuffs as Kara bound the other men's wrists.

"Well done, Billy!" Daniel shouted in triumph.

"God, that was loud," Billy said. He was cowering in a corner of the room still covering his ears. He had dropped his gun on the floor, its open slide revealing the empty clip.

"Ryan, my God," said Daniel, turning to his son. "You are really good in a tight spot."

Ryan was panting from the exertion and adrenaline, his hands on his hips, looming over Dana. Her gaze was frightened and anxious, her eyes locked on Daniel's gun barrel.

"What are we going to do with her?" Ryan gasped.

"Not sure yet," Daniel replied.

"We could just leave her here," Craig said, his voice filled with disdain. "Let her and these guys try to get out of here before the police arrive."

Ryan clued into what Craig was saying. In general, a lot of different noises resemble gunfire, but people know the sound when they hear it, and Billy had fired a weapon several times, and there was Dana's shot as well. Someone was certainly coming to check on the noise or likely calling the police. And given the presence of the advance RCMP team sent to secure the hotel for the Minister of Natural Resource's arrival the next day, the police were probably on their way.

"We take her," Daniel said. "Maybe she talks. If not, she goes down with the rest of them."

"She's a Canadian citizen, though," Kara called out.

"We'll figure out exactly what to do with her on the way. For now, she comes with us," Daniel replied.

Dana's face turned to stone, but her eyes broadcast unspeakable grief.

Ryan cocked his head, and for a moment they made eye contact. He was hit with a weird feeling...

"We need to get moving. Now!" Craig called out.

"Where to?" Kara countered.

"I saw them," Billy gasped, coming up beside Ryan and Daniel. "I got a look at them on the monitor before I came down here. Them...the three Tri-State people! They were in a stairwell, headed down to the mall parkade. At least that's what it looked like."

"Did you see anything else?" Daniel asked.

Billy shook his head. "I only had two working monitors left."

Everyone looked at him quizzically.

"Kamil dropped in for a visit." Billy shrugged. "He's having a nap right now."

"They're on their way to the airport, remember," Craig remarked, pointing at Dana. "She said so. And if she's right, they've probably filed a flight plan that takes them somewhere well over the ocean, then on to Venezuela. They'll never come back."

"What time is it?" Daniel asked.

"Almost five o'clock," Ryan replied.

"So, they have about a ten-minute head start," Ryan said.

"Not necessarily. We have Gary and Edward watching them," Daniel said. He raised his radio to his lips.

———◁◦/◦/◦▷———

"Do you have them?"

"Affirmative," Edward's voice came back. "We're right behind them. Southbound, Anthony Henday Drive," he said, watching Gary expertly steer the van through traffic, following a small convoy holding their prey. "We've got three Lincoln Town Cars. One target in each, along with personal staff, assistants, that kind of thing. Guess they like to have a little room in the back on long drives to the airport."

"Roger," Daniel replied. "Standby."

"Billy, punch the fire alarm," Daniel said, pointing with his radio to the red handle on the wall.

For once, Billy didn't ask why; he threw the switch. A klaxon instantly blared to life, and a pre-recorded voice instructed guests to go to the nearest exit. The ceiling lights began to flash on and off.

"We need chaos to get out of here undetected," Daniel said, turning to face Dana. "You're coming along. I'm going to have this gun in your back the whole time. If you even make eye contact with anyone, I'll pull the trigger. Got it?"

Dana didn't react as Daniel hauled her to her feet.

"Wait," Ryan said, holding out one hand. He turned Dana so her back faced him, pushed her gently against the wall and frisked her.

"Something is not right about this," Ryan said, his hands reaching for her ankles.

"I know, Ryan, but we don't really have a lot of time to sort it out now," Daniel said.

"It'll just take a second," Ryan said. His hands moved up her legs, past her hips and stomach…

"Sorry about this," Ryan whispered. His hands moved over her chest, where he felt something crumple under his palm. His right hand darted into the top of Dana's shirt and extracted a folded piece of photo paper from her bra.

"Stop," Dana said, trying to get away, but Ryan held her in place.

Daniel came over as Ryan unfolded the creased paper. The image was faded, but it was clearly a young girl, maybe four years old, with brown skin, dark hair and eyes, smiling for the camera.

It looks like one of those school pictures parents give to… "Who is this?" Ryan demanded sharply, shoving the picture in Dana's face. She said nothing but disintegrated into tears.

"We need to go! Now, Ryan!" Daniel shouted.

"These guys?" Kara shouted over the blaring siren, gesturing to the men corralled in the corner of the boardroom.

"Leave them," Daniel said. "We'll lock the door behind us. They're not going to talk to the police, and the police won't know what to do with them."

The hallway was empty. The lights were flashing on and off, the fire alarm blaring, the pre-recorded voice urging everyone to remain calm. They didn't run but walked as quickly as they could. As they rounded a corner, they saw a porter checking rooms. He looked at them and pointed to the exit sign. They all nodded and continued on. When they reached the exit door, Kara threw it open, and they all rushed down the stairs, at times stepping on one another's ankles.

The group entered the parkade on the south side of the mall, bolting for their van.

"Can't you ask Gary and Edward to stop them?" Ryan puffed at his father.

"They're chasing three Town Cars in a van," Daniel said. "I don't think they can stop all three. They could stop maybe one, but then they would lose the rest. I'd rather keep them in the chase position. They could always try to get them at the airport."

"They know what's happening, Daniel," Craig said. "Even money says one or more of the people in each of those cars has a gun. They wouldn't stand a chance. If we were all there, the odds would be better."

"What if they get to the airport in the meantime?" Billy asked, breathing hard.

Daniel felt frustration welling up inside him. "We should get there around the same time if we ignore most of the civilized world's traffic laws. But it'll be close."

Ryan suddenly screeched to a halt in the middle of the parkade, his eyes searching the sky.

"What are you looking for?" Daniel asked, still moving, pushing Dana ahead of him.

"An alternative," Ryan said, pointing a finger upward.

Daniel and Billy looked up. They could see a sequence of lights, red and green, flashing in the east, and the throbbing of rotating blades churning their way through thick, moist air also reached their ears. From what they could see, the lights were descending towards a tall building about three blocks away. That building had a sign on the side of it with a large white "H" emblazoned on a green background.

"It's probably an air ambulance," Daniel said, dumb-founded at first. Then a realization dawned on him.

"What other option do we have?" Daniel said, throwing the van into gear and peeling out of the mall parkade after everyone had piled into the van. Fortunately, both the mall and the hospital were on the same avenue.

"Wait a minute," Kara exclaimed in disbelief. "We're going to hijack an air ambulance?"

"I like it," Billy said.

"We need a fast ride," Ryan shrugged. "It's the fastest one around."

"It's not even remotely inconspicuous," Kara practically thundered. "The police are going to know pretty quickly that an air ambulance has been hijacked. They'll be able to track us."

"Kara, one step at a time," Daniel said as he roared through a major intersection against a red light, almost hitting three cars. He pulled the van over to the far left lane and turned into the parking lot that ran behind the hospital.

"Can any of us actually fly a helicopter?" Kara asked.

"I'm sure we can convince the pilot to take us for a ride," Daniel replied.

Daniel sped by the sign "Misericordia Community Hospital," bounced over the curb and headed in the direction he'd seen the helicopter disappear behind the hospital. This particular helipad was on ground level, which worked to their advantage. Fewer people to get in the way.

Daniel guided the van around a left-hand curve then saw the helicopter lit up by a circle of lights that ran the circumference of the helipad.

The helicopter was a brilliant red, with "STARS," standing for Shock Trauma Air Rescue Society, emblazoned in white on the side. Its rotors were still turning. Off to the left of the helicopter, a group of hospital staff with several more people wearing helmets and flight suits were walking a stretcher through a door marked "Emergency."

Daniel looked at the helicopter. One pilot sat in the front right seat, but there didn't seem to be anyone in the back, although Daniel's view was obscured as they were parked behind the helicopter. Its clamshell rear doors were flung open.

"We're going to rush it," Daniel said. He grabbed the handle of a large plastic case wedged between the two front seats of the van, pulling it onto his lap. He reached into his jacket and removed his handgun, passing it to Ryan. "Ryan and Kara go in through the front doors and take care of the pilot; Billy, Craig and I take the back. Go."

Ryan hazarded a glance back in the van at Dana, who was not looking at anyone. Her eyes were cast down and tears stained her cheeks. Her mouth moved repeatedly in a barely audible whisper.

"*Roohi*," Ryan murmured as he divined the word she was mouthing.

"My soul," Daniel translated and shook his head. "Children are every parent's soft spot. I wish she had said something. But she stays here. Strap her in so she can't get away."

The five of them scrambled out of the van and thundered across the space to the helicopter, heads bowed low against the whirling blades and hurricane-like rotor wash. Ryan saw in his peripheral vision Daniel, Craig and Billy clamber through the rear doors. As his hand reached for the pilot's door handle, Ryan could see the pilot looking over his shoulder at the three intruders.

Ryan yanked the door open.

"What the...?" the pilot said, but he was cut off as Ryan jammed the barrel of the gun into the side of his neck. The pilot froze in place. Ryan glanced down at his nametag.

"Steve, we need you to fly us somewhere. If you do, you'll get out of this just fine." Kara slid into the co-pilot's seat. Steve tried to turn to look at Ryan, but Ryan smacked the side of his flight helmet with the gun. "You just do what we say."

Steve nodded reluctantly.

"Everybody in?" Ryan called and jumped in behind the pilot.

"In," Daniel said. Ryan pulled the door shut.

Daniel leaned forward and spoke to Steve. "Turn off the IFF now. I know the codes. If you use the emergency code, we'll shoot you," he said.

Steve reached down and flicked a switch, turning off his IFF box—Identification Friend or Foe—that broadcast a special code or signal that told radar stations the type of aircraft it was. If not for boxes like this on both military and civilian aircraft, a radar operator would only see a series of identical blips without knowing what they were.

Now they were just one blip on the screen that would hopefully fade into the background in among all the other air traffic above and around the city.

"Anthony Henday Drive southbound," Daniel said to Steve. "Best possible speed. Now." The Eurocopter BK117 shot straight up into the air. When the altimeter reached 1000 metres, Steve pushed forward on the cyclical and eased off on the collective to slow the helicopter's ascent, and began flying southwest.

"Where on Anthony Henday?" Steve asked.

Daniel shouted into his radio and held it close to his ear, struggling to hear over the loud *thwomp-thwomp* of the rotors beating the air only a few feet above their heads. He tapped Kara on the shoulder and shouted to her "Callingwood Road."

Steve nodded and the helicopter started accelerating forwards. In moments, the craft was slicing through the air at 225 kilometres per hour.

Ryan saw what he deduced was Anthony Henday Drive ahead of him and watched as Steve brought the helicopter parallel to the road, following it.

"You're doing great, Steve. Doing great," Ryan shouted to him.

"What are we looking for?" Steve asked.

"A convoy of three Lincoln Town Cars," Daniel said. "Gary is going to flash his high beams for us!"

Ryan saw a steady pulse of light to his right that grew then faded repeatedly. He pointed to the car beams about 500 metres ahead. Steve nodded.

"I see it," the pilot said.

"Get in front of them, then turn around and hold steady. Face the side of the helicopter towards them!" Daniel yelled.

Steve nodded.

Daniel dove for the case he had brought with him, pulling out one long tube, which he placed on his shoulder and aimed at the helicopter.

"Stand back!" he yelled, shifting his body towards the helicopter's side door. "And brace yourself!"

Billy nodded, understanding Daniel's plan and grabbed the back of Daniel's pants, belt and all.

Steve flew to the next overpass then put the chopper into a straight hover, rotating the helicopter perpendicular to southbound traffic so that Daniel's door immediately faced the oncoming traffic. At Ryan's urging, Steve descended to seventy metres.

Daniel slid the door open, the downdraft from the rotors washing over him. He eased forward, pushing his legs out the door until they dangled over the edge. He shouldered the rocket launcher and pointed it at the oncoming convoy of Town Cars that were approaching at a steady clip.

"Hold it steady, Ryan!" Daniel shouted, sighting the light antitank weapon. "Here we go. Hang on!"

When the distance between the helicopter and the convoy of cars closed to about ten metres, Daniel pulled the trigger mounted on the tube. A small charge inside kicked the small rocket inside free of its housing and out of the casing. Daniel threw himself back inside as the rocket's motor ignited, barely escaping being singed. The rocket slammed into the freeway just in front of the first Town Car, sending up a shower of asphalt in a fiery flash. The first Town Car swerved left, caromed off a concrete guardrail that separated the two directions of traffic, then spun, ending up sideways across the highway. The second and third cars bounced off the crater that had now formed in the centre of the freeway, skidding left and right and smacking into other nearby vehicles. Several cars behind the Lincolns, their drivers stunned by what had happened in front of them, started to fishtail around the busy road as well, adding to the chaos. Finally, all three Town Cars, including several other vehicles, came to a smoking, dented rest.

"Put it down, Steve!" Daniel called, passing the light back to Billy.

Steve nodded and looked down. Traffic behind the convoy had rolled to a stop, but the cars in front had continued on, leaving an open area directly in front of the crash site. He carefully pushed forward on the collective, setting the BK117 down gently on the road.

"We need to grab them and go!" Daniel shouted, reaching again for the plastic case. He grabbed three handguns, kept one and passed the others to Kara and Craig. "Be careful! Grab your target and get back here."

Daniel picked up his radio. "Gary, Edward, get up to the crash site with your weapons to cover us if we need it."

Gary and Edward, who had been trailing the convoy, ran from their van behind the crash and spread out, bringing their guns up to cover the three cars. They watched as Daniel, Kara and Craig each ran up to one car, glanced quickly inside, then extracted one person and pushed them towards the helicopter.

"Will they all fit?" Kara shouted.

"We can get up to ten people in there," Craig yelled back. "We'll be fine."

Daniel motioned to Gary and Edward, who came running. "Meet us at the stash point. We need to get moving fast."

Gary and Edward nodded and headed back to their van.

Daniel pushed Smith forward through the side door of the helicopter while Craig and Kara took their captives around to the back doors. Daniel barked an order to Kara, who jogged back to the three cars and then returned to the helicopter with three briefcases.

As he and Craig closed the doors, Daniel hollered, "Go!" The helicopter shot back into the air.

CHAPTER

"Sir!"

Thresher couldn't ignore the loud, energetic shout, even though his sashimi lunch was beckoning him. He placed his napkin on top of his desk and sighed, walking to his door.

Adam was staring at his computer monitor. He looked over his shoulder, saw Thresher and pointed at the screen.

"That cellphone we were watching? The one that went dead? It just lit up again," Young said, reaching for a scrap piece of paper and scribbling. "It pinged off a tower in southern Alberta an hour ago with a text message. The message lists a series of coordinates."

"Find it," Thresher snapped.

Adam nodded, pulled up a screen that gave him access to recent satellite imagery and typed in the GPS coordinates from the text message. The screen blinked for a moment then a dot appeared on a nation-wide map of

Canada, close to the BC–U.S. border. Several screens flipped past as the image zoomed in to the location.

"So that's it," Thresher said, standing back.

"I'll get a team to that location, sir," Young, reaching for his phone.

"No," Thresher said, placing a hand on Young's shoulder. Both men were quiet as Thresher stared at the image on the computer screen for several moments. "I think we've had enough outside intervention for now," he said. "We need to handle this ourselves. Just you and me."

CHAPTER

Near Lindell Beach, British Colombia

April 17

2:30 AM

No matter the outcome, Ryan was convinced he never wanted to drive anywhere ever again.

He wasn't actually driving at the moment, just sitting behind the wheel of a van, waiting and listening. There wasn't much life in the middle of the night near this sleepy lakefront village, which, Ryan supposed, explained why Daniel had brought them here.

He looked over his shoulder to the rear of the van. Billy was stretched out on one of the bench seats, snoring loudly, while Kara stared out the window. The end was in sight, at least that was the hope. Every minute that ticked past was another sixty seconds of watching, waiting and worrying.

After bundling their captives into the helicopter, Ryan had directed Steve to fly northwest of Edmonton and land in a farmer's field. This was where Daniel had stashed two rented vans as a contingency if their original plan to fly the Tri-State execs out of Edmonton fell through. Everyone agreed it would be easier to just hop in the vans and drive rather than try to fly a stolen air ambulance back into Edmonton and meet up with their CIA pilot. Once everyone had been loaded into the vans, Daniel told Steve to wait ten minutes before taking off, then radio in.

"Sorry about that, Steve," Daniel had said as they were leaving. "You were a really useful hostage though."

Steve didn't say anything, just nodded as he watched them drive off.

"Aren't you worried he'll follow us, call us in to the cops?" Kara asked.

"He doesn't have enough fuel," Daniel said. "I think we'll be fine."

Daniel had ordered both vans to proceed to a commercial corridor of gas stations, restaurants and cheap motels called Gasoline Alley, a few kilometres south of the city of Red Deer. They linked up at a fast food restaurant parking lot, where they hopped into one van, leaving the other vehicle behind and tossing the licence plate into a dumpster to buy them some extra time in case the van was found sooner than expected. From there, Daniel had plotted the longest possible route from Red Deer to southern BC, to avoid detection, he said. And flying wasn't an option because booking a ticket would give away their identities.

They also needed to maintain as much control over their environment and their three prisoners as possible, and driving was the only method of transportation that afforded them both.

So the van had headed south. During the eighteen-hour trip, they made a few stops for bathroom breaks at isolated public parks or campsites and occasionally grabbed food and drink.

Ryan did the bulk of the driving but got a few breaks to snooze in the back. Billy laid claim to the rear bench seat, where he spent his time hunched over the laptops Kara had retrieved from the Town Cars. Ryan had noticed Daniel and Billy having a brief conversation in Red Deer, one that he didn't think he was supposed to see because they were standing several metres away from both vans. Whatever Billy was up to, Ryan was sure he'd find out in time. He was probably just looking for information to bolster their case against Strongback, Smith and Wright, who all sat on one of the middle bench seats. But every so often Billy would insert his flash drive into one of the laptops, which were plugged into an inverter they had purchased to keep the batteries charged, and Ryan could hear the laptop whir.

When they reached Fort Macleod early on the morning of April 16, the van turned due west. Within a couple of hours they were enveloped in the Rocky Mountains as they approached the British Columbia border. Ryan had grabbed a few hours of sleep as Gary drove, then Kara, but Billy refused to move from his station, still tapping away at all three laptops. When Ryan asked him what he was doing, Billy didn't answer, his gaze fixed unwaveringly on the glowing screens in front of him. When they left the Rockies and entered the BC interior, Billy finally closed the last of the laptops, rolled over on his bench seat and slept.

At Cranbrook, they pulled into a Walmart parking lot and, without comment or explanation, Daniel and Billy disappeared into the store. When they emerged twenty minutes later, Billy was clutching a bag containing several flashlights, batteries, a MacBook Pro laptop, a car charging kit for the laptop, a handheld GPS and a mobile Internet access stick.

For the entire trip, their three captives refused to say anything. Craig and Daniel tried to cajole them into talking, but all three remained steadfastly silent, asking only for the occasional bathroom break, during which they were escorted by at least two people. Their hands were left unbound on the understanding that any attempts at escape would be dealt with harshly.

Daniel told Ryan, Craig and Kara privately that he'd been in touch with his sources in Edmonton, who confirmed that Dana was in custody. The RCMP were investigating her on espionage charges. They had also explained Dana's motive for turning traitor.

"These Tri-State people used some of their cash to have her daughter kidnapped a little more than a year ago, and they told Dana that if she didn't play along, didn't help get me, she'd never see the girl again. They found her through the GIP, Saudi intelligence, which, like any agency, keeps tabs on operatives of other countries." Daniel shrugged. "Dana lost her husband to cancer three years ago. Her daughter is all she has left. So of course she went along with it. She didn't trust that CSIS would help get her daughter back without these three bringing the GIP into the mix and making it worse."

"I wish she'd said something," Craig sighed, despondently. "I can't believe I didn't see she was using me."

"She was way too good looking for you," Billy piped up from the back. "I can't believe you didn't see it either."

"Billy, not now," Daniel chided him. "I know you genuinely cared for her, Craig. Of course you weren't going to clue into it. Looking back now, there were signs over the last few days that something was amiss with her. She seemed nervous and stressed, but I didn't see this coming either. We both trusted her. A lot."

"At least I'm not the only sucker then," Craig said, managing a weak smile.

When they reached Chilliwack, the van merged with traffic on the Trans-Canada Highway, heading to Lindell Beach. By late afternoon, the van had passed the village on the shores of Cultus Lake. They were expected at their drop-off point shortly after 4:00 AM, but that was still many hours away, and the location they were headed to was so small that a strange van packed with people loitering would

undoubtedly be noticed by the locals. So they had alternated weaving along the back roads with extended stops
spent staring out the windows of the van, doing nothing.

By sunset, Ryan felt ready to scream. He had been in
and out, but mostly in, a van for a full twenty-four hours, and
he was growing testy. At eleven o'clock, Daniel told Ryan to
head due south.

Just as Kosikar Road started to bend west, Daniel told
Ryan to kill the headlights and steer the van off the road into
a small valley, walled in on both sides by tree-covered rises.
Daniel and Gary then spent an hour surveying the surrounding area. Craig made a call on his cellphone, exchanging only
a few cryptic words. When Gary and Daniel returned, they
opened the side door to the van and motioned for their three
prisoners to join them. Edward followed.

"If you sense any trouble, get out of here," Daniel had
told Ryan. "We'll be fine on the other end. Make sure you
get somewhere safe. I'll be in touch."

That had been two hours ago. Ryan slapped himself
across the face as he struggled to remain awake.

He so wanted this to be over.

———⟨⟨⟨⟩⟩⟩———

The woods were quiet. The trees weren't as thick as
they might be farther north, but getting through the under-
brush still required a fair bit of work. Wisely or not, Daniel
had decided to stay off the main trail, to avoid being seen.

That meant bushwhacking it and using a handheld GPS and flashlights to find their way.

The group of seven hiked through the darkness, using their flashlights to scour the ground ahead of them. Daniel and Craig led the group, followed by their three prisoners, with Gary and Edward bringing up the rear. Daniel carried a cheap backpack in which was tucked all three of the laptops Kara had seized from the Town Cars.

Being seen by anyone wasn't beyond the realm of possibility. Many trails criss-crossed the border between British Columbia and Washington State. The area hosted scores of smuggling routes, most of which were known by the authorities and patrolled. Anything and everything came across the border on these trails—BC-grown marijuana went into the States while American guns and tobacco were smuggled into Canada. These paths also had a human dimension—so-called child brides from fundamentalist Mormon camps destined to marry older men in plural marriages in Utah and farther south, while refugees from South America who had successfully entered the United States dashed up these trails into Canada in search of freedom.

A sudden shuffling of brush caused Daniel to stop abruptly, holding up his hand for the others to stop. They listened for a few moments but heard nothing else. Daniel squinted into the distance.

"Someone's coming," he whispered.

"Our contacts?" Gary asked.

"They weren't supposed to cross the border," Craig said, suddenly wary.

They heard the sound of feet beating down nature, crushing leaves and twigs. When the shape was about fifty metres away, it stopped, and a bright light flashed into their faces.

"Hold it," Thresher gasped, breathing hard. In his left hand he held a lantern, in his right a gun.

Daniel squinted then scowled.

"Gavin Thresher," Daniel growled, placing his hands in front of him, as if in surrender.

"Nice to finally see you again," Thresher puffed, the gun not moving.

"I could have done without this meeting," Daniel growled. "Having fun ruining people's lives?"

"Shut up!" Thresher said, thrusting his gun towards Daniel.

"I see you brought a little peon, too." Daniel gestured to Young, who was standing behind the older man, also pointing a gun at the group.

"Send them this way. All three. Move it," Thresher ordered, gesturing with his gun hand.

Daniel looked back over his shoulder and nodded. One by one, all three oil execs moved towards Thresher and Young.

"And now, Daniel, or as we've been calling you, Gunsight, what shall we do with you?" Thresher asked.

"Gunsight?" Daniel said. "Sounds too terminal for a bureaucrat such as yourself."

"Well, it's fitting, for the moment at least," Thresher chuckled. "Because I have you in mine."

"This is all really some sort of B-movie to you, isn't it?" Daniel exploded, stepping towards Thresher, but the CSIS man waved his gun insistently.

"Don't," Thresher said. "I do my job. It gets me the things I want. So I'm going to do everything I can to keep it, even if that means getting rid of *you*."

"Another trip to Riyadh?" Daniel said.

"Try the bottom of the nearest lake," Thresher said. "I think you've proven you're more than capable of escaping the tightest bonds, so I think it's in the best interests of all concerned to just terminate you."

"What's stopping you? You've already got the blood of the thousands who died on 9/11 on your hands. What's a few more?" Daniel shot back.

"Don't be a simpleton," Thresher snapped. "So melodramatic. I'm protecting our country's interests. These three people's lives are worth far too much for you to ruin them. Canada will be better off because they lived and you all died."

"You've been behind all this?" Daniel asked.

"Just took over the operation," Thresher said. "I mean, yes, I was trying to get rid of you specifically, but these three only just came to my attention."

"Do you honestly think I'd put myself in a position where I could be silenced and have the story I have to tell die with me?" Daniel asked. "Do you really think by doing this you'll be safe? That no one will know what you and they and even our government has done?"

Thresher shifted his gun hand so that it was on top of the lantern in his left hand, taking full aim at Daniel.

"I don't care," Thresher said, his shaking arms going eerily calm.

And then in that second, Thresher fell straight forward, landing face first in the mud. Behind him stood Young, holding his gun by the barrel and looking down at the man he had just felled.

"How long have you been waiting to do that?" Daniel said to Young.

"Are you kidding me?" Edward thundered. "You put us through that and you knew about Young all along?"

"Is everybody okay?" Young asked, leaning over and extracting a pair of flex-cuffs from his belt.

"We're fine," Daniel said, watching as Young wrapped the cuffs around Thresher's wrists. "Just a little scared, that's all."

"A *little* scared?" Gary asked, incredulous.

"Why didn't you say anything?" Craig asked.

"Because I wanted Thresher to find us," Daniel replied.

"Huh?" Edward asked.

THE PRODIGAL SPY

"I couldn't have him tromping around after us when we thought everything was wrapped up," Daniel managed. "So this gentleman and I," he pointed to Young, "made it easy for Thresher to find us. We were never in any real danger."

Daniel turned towards Young. "And the package?" he asked.

"Uploaded, sir," Young nodded. "I made sure to cover everyone's tracks as well." He shook hands with Daniel then tossed Thresher's limp frame over his shoulder and marched off into the woods.

"What was that about?" Craig asked.

"It's time to rewrite some history, my friends." Daniel said, leading the group back towards the trail.

"You can't do this!" Wright yelled suddenly, digging his heels into the dirt as Gary and Edward pulled him along. "This is illegal! It's unconstitutional!"

"Well, you're right about that," Daniel said. "At least the last two parts. This is technically illegal, and yes, we are depriving you of some fundamental rights. But once you are in the U.S., everything will be above board, that I promise you."

Wright responded by spitting at Daniel, but the seasoned spy had seen it coming and stepped to one side, instantly silencing Wright's protests by grabbing him by the throat.

"Losing everything you value is tough, isn't it," Daniel said, maintaining eye contact with the trembling Wright as he squeezed even harder. "There's an accident, things get

a little out of hand and before you know it, life as you knew
it is over."

"Daniel," Edward said, trying to get his friend's attention and touching his arm.

Daniel ignored him and kept squeezing. "No one in
either of those towers, no one in the Pentagon and no one
on any four of those planes had a chance," Daniel whispered
softly. "So why should you?"

"We didn't know," Strongback spoke up suddenly.
"We didn't know what he would do with the money. We only
found out afterwards."

"I know," Daniel said without looking at her. Wright
was choking now, wriggling to get away from the grip cutting off his air supply. "Trust me, I know all about it. And
because I know all about it, my life got turned upside down.
But in the end, you did know," Daniel said, his grip unwav-
ering as Wright's eyes bulged. "And you said nothing. You
came after me, instead, and then you came after my son."

Daniel pulled Wright even closer. The tip of his nose
touched Wright's.

"I don't really care what they do with you," Daniel
growled. "All that matters to me is, once I get you across this
border, I get my life back."

Daniel released his grip and slapped Wright's face.
The former oil tycoon fell to his knees and dissolved into a fit
of coughing, gasping for breath. Gary gave him a moment
then pulled him up to his feet, guiding him to the trail.

"We can pay you," Strongback said, her voice feeble now in the echoing surrounds of the forest. "You don't have to do this. You get your life back; we never come looking for you again. You have the information that can destroy us if we do."

"We are rich! Very rich!" Smith said suddenly, surprising everyone. The old Texan hadn't uttered so much as a word the entire trip.

Daniel raised his flashlight to his own face and smiled. "I know you are. Oh...I know." And he turned and kept walking.

Another hour passed as the march continued in total silence. Daniel consulted the handheld GPS he had picked up in Cranbrook and turned to the others.

"We're here," he said, indicating they had crossed the border.

Daniel didn't pause to savour the moment; he kept on walking straight ahead. Technically, he was illegally in the U.S., but, in his opinion, the rules no longer applied.

It was tough to estimate distance, but Daniel did his best. The straggling line continued forward for another kilometre. Guessing he was close enough, Daniel stopped and motioned to the others to stop. On cue, the entire party extinguished their flashlights and waited.

A gentle breeze rustled the trees, scattering the sounds everywhere around them. Owls hooted, and other animals chattered to one another as they roamed the dark, foraging for food. The sky they could see above the trees was dotted with brilliant stars.

At first Daniel couldn't tell if his eyes were playing tricks on him, but the darkness ahead and around them seemed to move. He waited, squinting harder. Yes, there they were. Dark shapes materializing from the forest in front of them, hunched over, moving swiftly but silently towards them. Daniel slowly placed his flashlight on the ground then stood and raised his hands over his head. Gary, Edward and Craig followed suit.

As the shapes grew closer, Daniel began to wonder who they were exactly. He knew Craig had arranged for someone to meet them, but he hadn't been expecting something so clandestine...the way they moved smacked of elite Special Forces. The closer they came, the more features Daniel could discern. Each shape was a person, moving forward, hunched over. They wore dark clothing, balaclavas over their heads and night-vision goggles covered their eyes. Each of the ten men that now rushed towards them was hunched over for a reason—they all carried silenced submachine guns.

The lead person held up a clenched fist, and the men behind him froze. "Zulu, Bravo, X-ray," a voice said softly.

Craig cleared his throat then spoke. "Tango, Whisky, Foxtrot."

Craig had been responsible for arranging the rendezvous, so only he knew the correct response to the challenge from the troop. Any other response, and Daniel and his whole party would have been cut down in a hail of silent bullets.

The soldiers relaxed, dropping their guns to their sides and approached. With the night-vision goggles, they had probably seen Daniel and his entourage coming for miles.

The first soldier walked up to Daniel and flipped up his goggles, blinking against the darkness. He held out a hand.

"Special Agent Cory Sarrazin, HRT," the man said, shaking Daniel's hand.

HRT? Daniel thought. *Whoa! Impressive.*

Sarrazin made the rounds, introducing himself to Edward, Gary and Craig. The rest of the FBI's Hostage Rescue Team, among the most elite SWAT teams in the world, stood back and watched through their goggles. They weren't soldiers after all—they were federal agents.

"I wasn't expecting such august company," Daniel said as Sarrazin completed his introductions.

"The president didn't want to take any risks," the agent replied. "We've been watching you for quite a while. Don't worry." Sarrazin held up his hands in mock defence. "We never crossed the Canadian border."

"And I never crossed yours," Daniel said with a chuckle.

"These our guests?" Sarrazin asked, pointing at Strongback, Smith and Wright.

"They are," Craig said, stepping forward. Sarrazin waved a hand over his head and six of his men ran forward, three holding the prisoners in place, the other three frisking them for any weapons. When they were done, Wright, Strongback and Smith were restrained in flex-cuffs.

"Here. Take this," Craig said, stepping forward with his hand extended.

Sarrazin looked at the flash drive in Craig's hand then looked up. "It's all there?"

"It is," Craig affirmed.

"These too," Daniel said, handing over the bag with the laptops.

Sarrazin took the thumb drive and placed it in a pocket on his battle vest. He handed the bag to one of his officers. "I understand you're coming with us, sir?" he asked Craig.

Craig shook his head. "No, sorry. I have some unfinished business back in Canada."

Sarrazin reached up and flipped his goggles down over his eyes. "Too bad, sir. I understand the president was hoping to speak to you."

"Give him my regards. I'll see him soon."

"If he happens to ask, I'll mention it, sir," Sarrazin said. He brought up his submachine gun from his sling and gestured with it. His men pushed their prisoners forward and disappeared into woods and into the United States. Then he turned back to Daniel.

"I don't know much, but I know you did most of the heavy lifting on these guys," Sarrazin said. "I just wanted to say thanks." And he extended his hand again.

"Agent," Daniel said, shaking his hand, "whatever relief you might feel, mine is a hundredfold."

Sarrazin nodded, gave a wave and took off silently after his men. Craig, Daniel, Edward and Gary all waited until the group had disappeared from sight then began the hike back to Canada and their waiting compatriots.

———

It was after five in the morning when Daniel, Edward, Gary and Craig emerged from the trees and returned to the van. Ryan had found his second wind, but Kara had long since succumbed to sleep. Ryan was privately glad—her soft breathing was a much more welcome background than Billy's rumbling snores.

Ryan stepped out of the van as the four approached, obviously weary from their midnight hike. "Success?" he asked. He realized with some surprise that Craig was still with them. Ryan had been under the impression he would follow the detainees back into the United States.

"Success," Daniel replied softly. He told Ryan about the rendezvous in the woods with Gavin Thresher and Adam Young.

"Kara was sending our information to Young the entire time," Daniel said with a faint smile. "He relayed it to Thresher…in a way. Now he's taken care of."

"Why did you have Kara feeding him information?" Ryan asked.

"I knew when I came back to Canada that CSIS would be after me. I'd caught wind overseas that Saudi Arabia specifically was putting all kinds of pressure on CSIS to track me down, and they were working through Thresher's office to find me. So I connected with Adam through a friend about a year ago. We set things up to finally get Thresher off my back."

"Which friend?" Ryan asked.

"No," Daniel shook his head. "There are some secrets I still need to keep for now. I owe a lot of people for their help these past nine years. But you can believe me when I say it's no one you know."

"But Thresher would have killed you?" Ryan asked unbelieving.

"I suppose," Daniel shrugged. "It makes sense from his point of view. I'm Canadian, I'm difficult to track *and* I'm a pain in the ass. He can't just ship me off to another country, and the only guarantee I'd stay quiet is if I was dead."

He looked around him at his friends, all gathered around him.

"I owe you all so much," he said.

And then as if from nowhere, the magnitude of the days' events and the stress of the past nine years came crashing down on him. Daniel covered his face with his hands, and his entire body quaked.

Ryan rushed to his father and wrapped his arms around him. "It's over, Dad," he whispered. "It's over."

Daniel shook his head, shoulders slumped. Ryan led his father into the van.

Gary got behind the wheel and backed the van out of the valley, slowly edging it onto Kosikar Road, and headed north. It wasn't long before Edward and Craig were both leaning against the windows of the van, sleeping deeply.

Ryan continued to hold his trembling father. Then, almost like a child secure in the arms of a parent, Daniel drifted off to sleep on his son's shoulder. Ryan was surprised; it was the first time since this had all started that he had seen his father sleep.

Ryan had no idea where Gary was taking them, but he didn't care. Unable to sleep himself, Ryan simply stared out the side window. The deep black of night was slowly growing indigo with the promise of a new day.

Ryan wondered briefly what the day and future would hold, but decided that, just for a little while, he didn't want to know, nor did he care.

———⧉———

Gavin Thresher raced into his office shortly after sunrise, practically sprinting for the door. He was livid.

He had awoken in his car in the CSIS parking lot with a pounding headache and an ominous feeling. He wasn't absolutely certain what had happened in the woods the previous night, but he had a pretty good idea.

He didn't really expect Adam Young to be seated at his desk when he stormed in, but he kind of hoped for it.

Young's office chair, however, was empty. Thresher pulled out all the desk drawers but found nothing beyond some blank notepads and pens—no pictures or personal items of any kind. Nothing to show that Adam Young had ever worked at this station.

Thresher went into his office and booted up his computer. He didn't know how long he'd been unconscious, but he needed to get back on Davis' trail as soon as possible. Once Gunsight was dealt with, he would turn his attention to tracking down Adam Young.

He signed in to the CSIS network and typed in the name of the file: GUNSIGHT.

ZERO ITEMS FOUND.

Thresher frowned and tried again.

ZERO ITEMS FOUND.

He deleted "GUNSIGHT" and typed in "DANIEL DAVIS." The result was the same.

"What the hell?" Thresher mumbled, a very bad feeling washing over him.

"Looking for something?" a voice called from the doorway. Thresher looked up, annoyed to see two people who were obviously law enforcement.

"Sorry, I didn't see you there," Thresher said. "Just a file I'm trying to find."

Susan Bartlett took a few steps inside followed by Aly Talwar.

She was feeling anxious. A few hours previous she had received an email from an unknown Gmail address predicting the CSIS computer network would experience a major problem. It even predicted the exact nature of the problem and gave the name of the person responsible.

"Lots of people are having that same problem right now," Susan said. "It seems someone uploaded a worm last night that has disrupted most of the CSIS network. It's taken out a lot of files so far."

"How did that happen?" Thresher asked.

"We were hoping you could tell us," Talwar replied. They approached Thresher's desk. "According to the logs, you're the one who uploaded it."

I don't believe it, Thresher thought. "It wasn't me."

"Really?" Susan asked, but she didn't sound as if she believed him.

"It was my assistant, Adam. Adam Young." Thresher felt panic rising in his throat. "Here, let me show you."

Thresher typed Young's name into the database window and pressed Enter.

ZERO ITEMS FOUND.

"I don't believe it," Thresher said, fighting the urge to punch the monitor.

The officers moved in and took Thresher into custody, leading him out of the office. Thresher seethed the entire time. He knew Daniel was to blame for this. And he silently swore he would get Davis if it was the last thing he did.

CHAPTER 49

Erasmus Island, British Colombia

April 20

11:30 AM

Ryan had always wondered who owned these island houses.

As a boy living in Vancouver, Ryan had made more than his fair share of ferry trips between the mainland and Vancouver Island, across the Strait of Georgia, either to camp near Tofino or visit friends on the island. On each of those trips, Ryan had marvelled at some of the real estate that floated out in the strait—not the luxurious, sometimes ostentatious yachts but the actual houses built on the smaller islands. Some of the houses were beautiful, others a little rundown, but it was the isolation that intrigued Ryan the most. How did they get power? Phone? Internet? And what did you do if you ran out of milk late at night?

Now Ryan was actually inside one of those houses on one of the islands, separated, though, from the gawkers like him that crowded the decks of the ferries. He was on Erasmus Island, technically more a part of the actual mainland of BC, but still separated by the waters of Discovery Passage that flowed in between the hundreds of small islands. Sandwiched between the mainland and East Thurlow Island, the place was as private as one could get. Ryan could see nothing but water and other islands no matter which way he turned.

The island was only fifty-four acres in size, but to Ryan and the rest, the island seemed much larger as they approached. After leaving Lindell Beach, the sleepy crew ditched the van and rented two more vehicles. They drove all the way to Vancouver without stopping and hopped on one of the BC ferries to Nanaimo. From there they went north on the east coast of the island to Campbell River where Daniel stopped at a grocery store for supplies, then guided the group to a large boat moored at the local marina. Daniel fired up the boat and coaxed the vessel out into the strait. It was a tad chilly, but they spent the first few hours above deck, relishing the bracing ocean air.

No one in the group asked where they were going. They simply followed Daniel without question. Even Billy, so entrenched in his life at UBC, so disoriented from the separation from his daily routines, hadn't complained. In fact, of all seven of them, Billy seemed the most relaxed.

Ryan was standing at his father's side when Erasmus Island came into view.

His father pointed. "That's where we're going," he said, handing his son a pair of binoculars.

Ryan looked through the binoculars then glanced back at his father, stunned. The house on the island was no quaint wooden cabin. It was a two-storey home with shiny glass windows dominating its ocean-facing exterior. A pier jutted out into the water for docking the boat. Ryan could make out satellite dishes and solar panels on the roof, as well as larger panels stationed across the island. He could see other outbuildings, but the rest of the island was left in its natural state with lush green deep grasses and trees.

"Your grandfather bought the island back in the 1950s. It has been in the family ever since," Daniel explained. "He never did anything with it. Just came out here, pitched a tent and spent his time fishing and boating. When he passed on, I inherited the island, but I didn't start building on it until the 1990s. It took a long time to get the money together. You'd be surprised at how much a contractor charges to build a house out here." Daniel grinned widely, the biggest smile Ryan had seen from his father since they'd been reunited.

"So how come I didn't know about this?" Ryan asked.

"We came here a couple of times when you were little, too young to really remember. After your mother left, I forgot about it for a while. But as I got older, I thought it might be nice to have a secluded place to retire when the time came, so I started work on it. The problem is, it's not exactly convenient to get to—you either drive, take the ferry then sail out or buy a helicopter. And by the time I could afford to buy the helicopter...well...I was dead."

Ryan looked at his father with a raised eyebrow.

"I'm serious!" his father protested.

"So how come I didn't inherit it?"

"Well, I wasn't actually dead," Daniel reminded him playfully. "And I figured that if I needed to maintain the ruse for a long period of time, into my old age, I was going to need an out-of-the-way place to hide. I put the title in Uncle Ed's name just before I disappeared so it would at least stay in the family. Would hate to sell it."

"So why are we going there now?" Ryan asked.

"To rest," Daniel said. "And decide our next course of action."

Ryan was silent for a moment then finally asked. "So what do you do if you run out of milk?"

Daniel laughed. "You go buy a cow. Trust me; it's easier."

When the boat docked, it was near dusk, and everyone helped carry the supplies ashore. Daniel gave them a tour of the home, which had a vast, open, hardwood interior. There were even two small guest cottages out back. On that first night, Daniel simply left the others to their own devices. Kara bathed, Ryan watched hockey via satellite and the men took turns touring the island. Billy, however, locked himself away in an office with the laptop Daniel had bought him in Cranbrook.

Ryan, Daniel, Kara and Billy each chose one of the four bedrooms in the house. Craig, Edward and Gary opted to occupy the guest cottages. As he fell asleep, Ryan listened to the sound of surf slapping the edges of the island, the cries of seabirds sweeping over the waters and, for the first time in almost two weeks, he allowed himself to fully and completely relax.

By the time he awoke the next morning, the coffee was already brewing and the older men were up, watching the morning take shape out over the water.

"Ryan," Daniel said. "Help yourself to whatever you want. But make sure you're here at noon for a meeting."

Daniel had repeated the message to everyone. At noon, they all gathered around a large table made from sanded driftwood. Everyone looked refreshed and relatively recovered. Daniel asked Billy, who was clutching his laptop, to sit next to him. Then Daniel started to speak.

"We've all been through something tremendous, something that has made a substantial difference in the world," Daniel said. "Craig made a few calls this morning and found out that, later today, the Attorney General of the United States will be indicting Strongback, Smith and Wright on numerous terrorism, conspiracy and fraud charges. They plan to make everything public. The American people will finally know the role that some of their own played in the 9/11 attacks.

"I've also been in touch with friends in Vancouver. That office we knocked over—Mansouri Consulting—was a temporary office for the GIP, Saudi intelligence. Everyone employed there, as well as several embassy staff in Ottawa, have been expelled from the country for espionage. That includes those goofs that tried to grab us in Edmonton."

There were smiles all around the table as Daniel paused. Only Billy was quiet, seemingly on edge.

"We're all here right now because we didn't play the game by the rules," Daniel said, suddenly serious. "If Edward, Gary and I had still been CSIS employees, we never could have apprehended the Tri-State execs. Nor would we have had enough solid proof to take direct action. We would have had to sit back and keep watching them, waiting for them to slip up and give us that one piece of evidence we needed to justify making a move. We couldn't go to the RCMP with the circumstantial evidence we had—it's not a judgement against Canada and the way it operates. If the situation had been reversed, I imagine Craig would have faced the same problems in the U.S. That's the nature of being the good guy, I guess. You have to act the way you'd expect the good guys to act."

Craig nodded.

"Espionage is a peculiar business," Daniel continued. "It has rules, believe it or not, that are little different from what you might expect, and a lot of those rules are simply based on respect. For instance, sending a team of foreign agents to try to kidnap Ryan is considered, for lack of a better term, extremely rude in the intelligence world. It's something intelligence agencies just don't do—harming or killing the citizen of a country they're spying on. Or, at least, they try not to. It ratchets up the body count—as they kill one of ours, so we kill one of theirs, and so on. It's strange, but there's a kind of grace and civility in spy work, at least most of the time.

"But following that same protocol of civility often includes the kinds of rules that are prohibitive, so it's hard to take action when you need to," Daniel said sharply. "It might be in your country's best interests to kidnap someone and make them talk, but that's against the rules. Even from a purely bureaucratic perspective, so many rules prevent us from getting to the people we really need to get to. I know everyone looks at CSIS and sees an agency that taps your phones, harasses your neighbours and intrudes on people's lives in what is supposed to be a free country. But the fact of the matter is, even when CSIS gets the information it needs, it has no authority to act on the information. CSIS agents don't have arrest powers and don't carry guns, and that's the case for intelligence agents in most other countries, too."

Craig nodded again.

"We obtain the information we need, and we can prove a point, but all too often, rules, protocol and convention get in our way," Daniel said. "We can line up everything we have on the biggest spy in the nation, let's say, but if there is no political will to act on that information, nothing will happen. That's why secrecy can be such a problem when the agency that keeps or discovers secrets is an arm of government. If the prime minister says, 'Don't do anything,' well, we don't, and we're also under strict orders not to tell anyone else about what we know so that they can act on the information."

Daniel was surprisingly calm as he spoke. The monologue was riveting, insightful even, but Ryan hadn't the slightest clue why his father was giving them a lesson in Intelligence Gathering 101.

"Within any government organization, you can find rot, ego and corruption. It's not only CSIS that suffers from problems and leaks or has people more interested in bolstering their careers than in doing the right thing."

"True story," Kara said softly.

"Take Gavin Thresher, for example. Career bureaucrat. Would rather make other people's lives exponentially worse in return for a paycheque. I don't want to get into a lot of detail, but he and I have been at each other's throats over this very issue. I wanted to do what's right. He just wanted to do what was best for him.

"It extends throughout the entire public service. So organizations such as CSIS, CSE, the CIA or SIS can't act when and the way they'd like to because other people or agencies get in the way. Whether it's in an office at CSIS or in the prime minister's office, obstacles will always be there, rules prescribing what you can and cannot do. And if we had followed those rules over the last two weeks, I would still be 'dead,' and the American people would still not know who was behind 9/11."

Daniel cast both arms wide, as if gathering the group into them. "Some of you knew what was going on, some of you had a rough idea and a few of you didn't have a clue. Yet working together, we were able to bring about the endgame to what I've spent almost a decade pursuing on my own. If it weren't for all of you, it wouldn't have gotten done."

"Hell yeah," Gary said.

"What are you saying, Dad?" Ryan asked quizzically. Everyone else stared at him. He had a feeling Daniel had told them while he was still in bed.

"What if we could work together?" Daniel replied. "I mean, look at all the talent in this room. We've got seven people who've demonstrated in two short weeks how superior they are to some of the world's most highly funded and well-trained intelligence agencies. We went toe-to-toe with some pretty skilled and dangerous people, and in the end, the bad guys got their comeuppance. In my entire career, I have never experienced anything like this. I swear. Believe me, the bad guys don't always get caught." Daniel paused for a moment and looked over the whole group. "So what if *we* caught the bad guys?"

Another pregnant pause followed as Daniel looked each person in the eye individually, but he really wanted to make eye contact with just one person—Ryan. All of the other heads around the table were nodding slowly, even Billy's.

"You're serious? Us? The seven of us? You want us to start our own...spy business?" Ryan asked, floored by his father's suggestion.

"It might get a little bigger than the seven of us in time," Daniel said. "And I have no illusions of stamping out all of the world's hotspots from a tiny island off the BC coast. But we have the beginnings here of something powerful. We could do the world a lot of good. I know what it's like to try to do this kind of work without any support."

"It sounds a bit dicey, Dad," Ryan said. "I mean, isn't that how some of the world's most atrocious acts get committed, by people thinking they know better? I mean, I'm all for making the world a better place, but how will we stop ourselves from going too far?"

"Son," Daniel said, putting a hand on Ryan's shoulder. "I want us to make sure no other child ever has to lose his or her parents. I'm not trying to tug on your heartstrings, Ryan. I honestly mean that. If any number of people had come forward nine years ago, I never would have had to leave you."

Ryan was silent. He wasn't necessarily opposed to his father's proposal. In fact, he liked the idea. But he was thinking out loud, wrestling with the doubts and questions.

"We decide as a group," Daniel said. "We look for the truly wrong, and we decide together. If one person says no, nothing happens."

Ryan nodded. He could live with that.

"And it's not only the bigger world that needs our help," Daniel said. "I owe you all a tremendous debt. I know that some of us in this very room have some pretty big problems that we can't ask the police to solve. I'm hoping you'll let me try to repay the debt I owe you by helping out."

"Meaning?" Ryan asked, but Daniel shook his head.

"We'll leave it at that for now," Daniel said.

Ryan cast a quick glance at Kara as he remembered Daniel's words at the farmhouse, about her having her own story to tell, but she just stared blankly back at him.

"What about your new friend? That Adam Young guy? Is he joining us too?" Billy piped up.

"We're really not recruiting right now, Billy," Daniel said. "Besides, in my experience, it's good to have some people here and there you can go to when you need them. If we need Adam's help, he'll be available."

"And how do you propose to fund this private army?" Ryan asked, zeroing in on the one big flaw in his father's argument. "If it took you twenty-odd years to save up to build this place," he gestured to the house around him, "how are we going to pay for all the stuff we're going to need to do what you're proposing?"

Daniel grinned. "I've already thought of that. Billy?"

Daniel turned in his chair and gestured to Billy, who placed his laptop on the table.

"The easiest and most straight-forward way to hack anything is to know a valuable piece of information," Billy said, as if he was teaching a class. He was in his element. "Information technology is just the exchange of information. You have to give a certain amount of information to get the information you want. You can write all the whizz-bang programs in the world, or try to sneak through as many backdoors as you can find, but at the end of the day, if you have the information you need, you can get the information you want.

"Remember back at the farmhouse, when we finally got into that folder? It was theoretically impossible to obtain the information we wanted because the key to get into the folder was highly encrypted," Billy said. "We needed the exact information to pull those random units together to form something we could read and digest. Once we had the key, we could unlock everything."

Billy hit a few keys, then turned the laptop around for everyone at the table to see. Several browser windows were open, all minimized so it was difficult to make out details on any of them.

"So let's take our three targets, for example." Billy clicked on one of the windows, enlarging it. "This is an offshore account belonging to one of their holding companies, somewhere in the Cayman Islands." Billy opened another window. "This particular account is in Lichtenstein. If you trace this money back from its source, you'll see that our oil execs had been trying very hard to hide it from the Internal Revenue Service. After all, the IRS can't tax what it doesn't know you have, right?"

Billy opened another window, an account also in Lichtenstein. The country had become quite popular with people trying to hide their money since Swiss authorities had relaxed some of their rules. "So, this is our account…"

"Wait a minute!" Ryan said. "We have an account?"

"Just listen, Ryan," Daniel whispered.

"At Daniel's suggestion, I searched our targets' laptops, looking for nuggets of information. Now for bank accounts like this, they're not going to have some measly four- or six-letter PIN. If an account is truly secure, especially when the nearest branch is thousands of kilometres away, banks have to give their customers something more robust, like a longer key, to access their account. It won't be something you can easily memorize. You have to write it down and hide it somewhere."

Billy opened up a text document containing line after line of random code, like the key the CSE had given them. "This isn't just one code; these belong to dozens of accounts I traced to our three targets. Now, banks like this can, if they so choose, ask for extra information to verify your identity before you make an electronic transaction. For example, questions like 'What's the name of your dog?' 'What hospital were you born in?' and so on. Well, thanks to Craig, we were able to get a lot of personal information about our three oil execs. But it turns out we really didn't need it."

Ryan knew what was coming, and he could scarcely believe it.

"So, at Daniel's suggestion, I took a broader look and found twenty-seven different offshore accounts in the names of our three targets totalling more than five billion dollars. I got into fourteen of those accounts without being asked for extra information, and I had the personal information for six others. I also received some offshore account information from Daniel," Billy said as he opened up another screen, "and simply executed a series of transfers to that account. Now we've set up other accounts over the last few days to keep the money moved around, so it can't be easily traced." Billy opened another window. "But this is a screen shot of the total amount we were able to transfer."

Ryan looked, and his jaw dropped. What Billy was really saying was that he'd helped steal approximately 300 million dollars.

"But...but...won't the money be traced?" Ryan asked, stammering.

"Unlikely," Billy said. "I tossed the Internet stick overboard on the way here, and the police, if they learn of the theft, would have to trace it back to its last known location in order to find us, and that's even if they bother. On its face, it looks like someone with proper access to the accounts transferred money to some other accounts. Remember, these accounts are numbered; there aren't necessarily names or faces associated with them. So no one can really prove who did this."

Ryan was still amazed. "We can get away with this?"

"Absolutely," Daniel said.

"And that's going to be enough?"

"We can't just put it in a savings account. We will lose some as we launder it, but we'll have enough that we can take care of one another and still do some good. Plus there will be plenty of opportunities to make more, Ryan. Don't worry."

"So this island will be our base?" Ryan asked.

Daniel smiled and embraced his son. "For a little while. If we hole up in the same place all the time, we'll become conspicuous, plus we're going to get really tired of each other. It's best if we put on the appearance of living something resembling a normal life, but…"

Ryan waited, but his father wouldn't finish. "But what?"

"Well," Daniel said, "I'm afraid you and Billy are going to have to die first."

JASON CONNOR

Jason Connor is a writer and filmmaker who has shot adventure documentaries and current affairs shows for broadcast television for many of the major networks. His passion for journalism is evident in the dense yet engaging style of research and facts imbedded in his works of fiction.

He has spent many years travelling the world in search of challenges that appeal to his deep interest in languages and cultures, which have led him deeper into collaborating with indigenous peoples in many regions of the globe.